About the Author

Lynne Graham lives in Northern Ireland and has been a keen romance reader since her teens. Happily married, Lynne has five children. Her eldest is her only natural child. Her other children, who are every bit as dear to her heart, are adopted. The family has a variety of pets, and Lynne loves gardening, cooking, collecting all sorts and is crazy about every aspect of Christmas.

The Tycoon's Affair

July 2025
Tempted by Desire

January 2026
Stealing his Heart

August 2025
Craving his Love

February 2026
Playing with Power

September 2025
Business with Pleasure

March 2026
After Hours Passion

The Tycoon's Affair:
After Hours Passion

LYNNE GRAHAM

MILLS & BOON

All rights reserved including the right of reproduction in whole or in part in any form. This edition is published by arrangement with Harlequin Enterprises ULC.

This is a work of fiction. Names, characters, places, locations and incidents are purely fictional and bear no relationship to any real life individuals, living or dead, or to any actual places, business establishments, locations, events or incidents. Any resemblance is entirely coincidental.

Without limiting the author's and publisher's exclusive rights, any unauthorised use of this publication to train generative artificial intelligence (AI) technologies is expressly prohibited. HarperCollins also exercise their rights under Article 4(3) of the Digital Single Market Directive 2019/790 and expressly reserve this publication from the text and data mining exception.

® and ™ are trademarks owned and used by the trademark owner and/or its licensee. Trademarks marked with ® are registered with the United Kingdom Patent Office and/or the Office for Harmonisation in the Internal Market and in other countries.

First Published in Great Britain 2026
by Mills & Boon, an imprint of HarperCollins*Publishers* Ltd
1 London Bridge Street, London, SE1 9GF

www.harpercollins.co.uk

HarperCollins*Publishers*
Macken House, 39/40 Mayor Street Upper,
Dublin 1, D01 C9W8, Ireland

The Tycoon's Affair: After Hours Passion © 2026 Harlequin Enterprises ULC.

Sold for the Greek's Heir © 2017 Lynne Graham
Promoted to the Greek's Wife © 2022 Lynne Graham
The Sicilian's Stolen Son © 2016 Lynne Graham

ISBN: 978-0-263-42115-6

Printed and Bound in the UK using 100% Renewable Electricity
at CPI Group (UK) Ltd, Croydon, CR0 4YY

SOLD FOR THE GREEK'S HEIR

For Rachel and Michael for their unswerving support and their ability to consider my characters as seriously as I do.

CHAPTER ONE

IN THE PIT, Jax Antonakos climbed out of the low-slung car, adrenalin still pumping fiercely from the excitement of the race. Only a show race for charity, though, he reminded himself wryly, bracing himself as he was engulfed by a large, noisy crowd of people.

He yanked off his helmet, revealing tousled black hair and eyes as strikingly green as emeralds, and the usual collective female gasp of appreciation sounded. While he stripped off his track regalia, photographers flashed cameras, journalists demanded quotes and shot questions at him and beautiful women tried to sidle closer to him, but then all of that was the norm in Jax's goldfish bowl of a world.

Jax, however, ignored all of them to stride over and congratulate the winner of the race and the reigning world champion.

'You gave me a good run for a man who hasn't been behind a wheel in years!' Dirk conceded cheerfully. 'Maybe you shouldn't be pushing numbers behind a desk, maybe you should still be racing.'

'No, Jax is a business genius,' a female voice crowed from Jax's other side, and before he could react the bubbly brunette wrapped her arms round him with enthusiasm. 'Thank you so much for stepping in last minute to do this when Stefan had to let me down. You know how grateful I am.'

'Kat,' Jax acknowledged, frowning as the photographers predictably went for a shot of them as a couple. But he and Kat Valtinos weren't a couple, no matter how much the media and their families wanted them to be, both of them being conveniently young, single and very rich.

Jax stepped back from Kat with a guarded smile. He liked Kat, he had *always* liked her but his father was in for a disappointment if he was still hoping for a dynastic marriage that would unite their parents' massive business empires. Unfortunately the photos would only encourage him in that delusion.

'Let's get you a drink,' Kat urged, closing a possessive arm round his spine. 'I really appreciate you flying out here and doing this for me today at such short notice—'

'It was for a good cause,' Jax pointed out. 'And you're a friend—'

'A friend who could be *so* much more,' Kat whispered with laden intent in his ear.

'I enjoyed the race,' Jax admitted, choosing to be tactful and sidestep her leading comment. After all, there was no kind way of telling her *why* she was wasting her time chasing him and, with his reputation for womanising, it would be sheer hypocrisy for him to do so. Even now he retained fond memories of Kat's raunchy wildness when they were teenagers and he had been on the outskirts of the same social set but he still wasn't willing to marry a woman who had slept with every one of his friends. If that was a double standard, so be it, he acknowledged grimly.

In any case, he didn't want a wife, *any* kind of wife. Nor was he prepared to deliver the grandchildren his father, Heracles Antonakos, was so eager to have. Parenting was a minefield: Jax knew that better than anyone because he had stumbled through his own very unhappy childhood, filled as it had been with constant change and even more constant emotional drama.

His parents had gone through a bitter divorce when he was only a toddler and for the following twenty-five years his father had pretty much ignored his younger son's existence. Heracles's elder son, Argo, had been born from his first marriage. Widowed, Heracles had plunged into his second marriage far too quickly and he had never forgiven his second wife, Jax's mother, for her subsequent infidelity. Jax had paid the price for his mother's extra-marital affair in more ways than one. He had had no safe harbour from which to escape the fallout of his mother's broken relationships, nor any paternal support. He had struggled alone through Mariana's divorces, suicide attempts and regular stays in rehabilitation facilities.

And one of his earliest memories was of hiding in terror in a cupboard from one of his mother's druggie meltdowns. He must have been about three years old, he mused, old enough and wise enough to know that he would be kicked and punched if she found him before the rage wore off. His mother, a gorgeous, much-adored film star on the public stage and a drug-addled monster behind closed doors. That was the woman whose tender mercies his father had left him to rely on as a defenceless child.

And then, when he was twenty-six years old, everything had suddenly and quite miraculously changed. His half-brother, Argo, had died in a bungled mugging in a city street and without the smallest warning Heracles Antonakos had moved on surprisingly fast from his grief and had begun to take a passionate interest in the younger son he had snubbed for years. Of course, Jax's mother had been gone by then, Jax reminded himself ruefully, but he still could not adequately explain or understand the very abruptness of his father's change in attitude. Even so, the paternal recognition and support he had craved from his earliest years had unexpectedly and finally become his. Naturally he still wondered if his father's change of heart would last and life being what it was, of course, he had discovered a whole new set of challenges because life as the Antonakos heir was not all peaches and cream.

As the only son of one of the richest men in the world Jax had more money than he knew what to do with. Everywhere he went in Europe he was photographed and treated like a celebrity. Bands of adoring, manipulative and rapacious women tracked and hunted him much as if he were big game. But in the business field, he reminded himself with determined positivity, he had countless stimulating projects to command his interest and engage his brilliant mind.

One of Jax's bodyguards brought a phone to him, his expression dour and apologetic. Jax compressed his lips and accepted the predictable call from his father. Heracles ranted and raved in a rage about the risk Jax had taken by going on the race track and driving at breakneck speeds. Jax said nothing because over the past two years he had learned that arguing or trying to soothe only extended such frenzied sermons. Since Argo's shocking death, Heracles had developed a morbid and excessive fear of Jax participating in any activity that could possibly harm him and if he could have got away with wrapping his only surviving son in cotton wool and packing him away safely in a box he would have done so. While Jax valued his father's new apparent attachment to him even if he didn't quite trust it, he loathed the restrictive and interfering trappings of expectation that came with it.

Only for the sake of peace had Jax accepted the five heavily armed bodyguards he didn't need and who accompanied him everywhere he went. But he remained every bit as stubborn and fiercely independent as he had always been and when he felt the need to relieve stress he still went deep-sea diving, mountain climbing and flying. He still slept with unsuitable women as well…the sort of women even his father couldn't expect him to marry.

And why not? He loved being single and free as the air because he hated anyone trying to tell him what to do. On the only occasions he had strayed from that practical stance he had ended up in disastrous relationships, so now he didn't *ever* do relationships, he only did sex and uncomplicated sex at that. Once he had run off with another man's fiancée and barely lived to tell the tale, he recalled darkly.

Franca had crept into his bed one night when he was drunk and the deed of betrayal had been done before he'd even recognised *who* he was doing it with. Franca, of course, had simply used him to escape a life that had no longer suited her but he hadn't grasped that little fact. He had fallen hook, line and sinker for her 'damsel in distress' vibe long before he'd appreciated that he was dealing with a highly manipulative and destructive alcoholic. He had betrayed his friendship with his former business partner, Rio, but in the end he had more than paid his dues sorting Franca out. But had he learned? Had he hell. After Franca had come his second biggest mistake...

Yet another female-shaped mistake. So, he didn't want a wife and he didn't want children either and *nothing*, certainly not any dormant desire to please his long-absent father, was going to change that, he reflected cynically as Kat Valtinos approached him bearing drinks and a winning smile...

'I hate you doing work like this,' Kreon Thiarkis hissed under his breath as his daughter brought him a drink. 'It's demeaning—'

'Hard work is never demeaning, Dad,' Lucy declared, her dimples flashing as she smiled down soothingly at him. 'Don't be a snob. I'm not half as posh as you are and I never will be.'

Kreon bit back tart words of disagreement because he didn't want to hurt his daughter's feelings, most particularly because she had only been in his life for the last six months and he was afraid of driving her away by acting like a heavy-handed parent. After all, Lucy had never had a proper parent to look out for her, he acknowledged guiltily. But fiercely independent and proud as she was at twenty-one years old, she had been very much down on her luck when she'd finally approached Kreon, toting his baby granddaughter in her arms, both of them shabbily dressed and half starved. The older man's heart softened at the thought of little Bella, who was the most adorable toddler and the light of his life and his wife, Iola's, for he and Iola had met and married too late in life to have a family. He loved having the two of them in his home but he was firmly convinced that his daughter and her child still very much needed a husband to look after them when he himself was no longer around.

And that would have been *so* easy to achieve if only Lucy weren't so defensive and insecure, Kreon reflected in frustration, because his daughter was an extraordinarily beautiful girl. In the bar where she worked men stopped in their tracks simply to stare at her. With a mane of strawberry-blonde curls reaching halfway down her back, creamy skin and big blue eyes, she was a classic beauty and dainty as a doll. She made more on tips than any other waitress in the hotel and was, he had been reliably assured by the owner, who was a friend, a terrific asset to business.

Lucy went about her work, ruefully aware that the job she had insisted on taking only annoyed her father. Unfortunately, being a single parent was an expensive challenge even with the wonderful support her father and stepmother had given her in recent months. She was very grateful that she had come to Greece to finally meet her long-lost father for he and his wife had freely given both her and her daughter love, kindness and acceptance. Her father was the son of a Greek who had married an Englishwoman and he had grown up in London. Kreon was a wonderfully supportive parent and grandparent. Without a word of protest or reproach he had taken in Lucy and her child even though she hadn't warned him about Bella when he'd first invited her out to Greece.

But while Lucy was willing to accept free accommodation as well as her stepmother Iola's help as a sitter with Bella, she was determined not to become a permanent burden or to take too much advantage of the older couple's generosity. She was willing to admit that she had desperately needed help when she'd first arrived in Athens but she was trying very hard now to stand on her own two feet. Her earnings might be small but that salary meant she could pay for the necessities like clothing for herself and her child and for the moment that was enough to ease her pride.

As she stepped away from a customer, her boss and the hotel owner, Andreus, signalled to her. 'We're hosting an important business meeting here in the rear conference room tomorrow morning at eleven,' he informed her. 'I'd like you to serve the drinks and snacks. I only need you for a couple of hours but I'll pay you for a full shift.'

'I'll check with Iola but that should be fine because she doesn't usually go out in the morning,' Lucy said, before taking off to serve a customer waving his hand in the air to get her attention.

The customer tried to chat her up and get her phone number but Lucy simply smiled politely and ignored his efforts because she wasn't even slightly interested in dating, or indeed in anything more physical, being well aware that the very fact she already had a child encouraged most men to assume that she would be a good bet for a casual encounter. She had been there, done that, lost the tee shirt and got a baby for her pains. Unhappily, as a green-as-grass nineteen-year-old virgin she hadn't grasped that she was involved in a casual fling until it was far too late to protect herself and she had been ditched. In fact, having been treated with such devastating contempt and dismissal by Bella's father, that final humiliation was still etched into her soul like a burn of shame that refused to heal whenever she thought about it...which was why she didn't allow herself to think about it *or* him very often.

In any case, what was the point in agonising over past mistakes and misjudgements, not to mention the most painful and cruel rejections she had suffered? Agonising never did change anything. Lucy had learned that the hard way time and time again when she was a vulnerable child growing up in care, subject to the whims of others and unable to control where she lived or even *who* she lived with. Now it meant that she found it hard to trust people and if she didn't have a certain amount of independence and choice she tended to feel horribly trapped and powerless.

But life, she reminded herself with dogged positivity, *was* getting better because for the first time in years she was daring to start putting down roots. She was happier than she had been in years and hoping to come up with a plan to improve her career prospects for Bella's sake. Very probably she would accept her father's offer to pay for some sort of job training or further education that would enable her to move out of low-paid employment. Perhaps it was finally time to start making some long-term decisions and think like a responsible adult, she told herself firmly.

'You're worth so much more than this kind of grunt work...' Bella's father had told Lucy two years earlier in Spain.

Well, look just how badly daring to have dreams and believe in them had turned out for her then, Lucy reflected, rigid with regret and pain as she stood at the bar to collect an order. Her friend at the time, another waitress called Tara, had been far more realistic about that relationship.

'He'll sleep with you and dump you and move on the minute he gets bored,' Tara had forecast, although the words she had used had been much earthier. 'Guys like that don't stick with girls like us. We're only good enough to party with for a few nights.'

Perspiration broke on Lucy's short upper lip and she wanted to punch herself hard for letting herself drift even momentarily down that bad memory lane, because hindsight only made her more ashamed of how stupid and naïve she had been. It was not as if she hadn't known what men were like, not as if she had grown up in some little princess castle, always protected and loved. She should have known better and she had yet to forgive herself for her rashness.

But at the end of her shift, when she got home to her father's very comfortable small town house and crept into the bedroom she shared with her daughter, she realised that nothing was quite that cut and dried. Bella slept nestled in her cot, curly black hair dark against the bedding, her olive skin flushed by sleep, long lashes screening her bright green eyes. Bella was gorgeous, like a little angel, Lucy thought with her eyes stinging and, although she could be sorry for everything else, she could not find it in her heart to regret Bella's existence in *any* way.

'Come with us to this dinner on Saturday night,' Iola urged over breakfast the next morning. She was a curvy brunette in her late forties with smiling dark eyes. 'It would please your father so much.'

Lucy went pink as she washed her daughter's face clean of breakfast debris. She knew that her dining out with them would please Kreon, but she also knew it would entail fending off the advances of at least two handpicked young men because her father's current main aim in life seemed to centre on finding her an eligible boyfriend. In that line Kreon was old-fashioned because he refused to credit that Lucy choosing to remain a single parent could be a viable plan for the future.

'Mum… Mum,' Bella carolled cheerfully as she was released from the high chair and set down to toddle somewhat clumsily round the room.

Lucy steadied her daughter as she almost fell over the toy box and ruffled her untidy curls. Curls, aside of the colour, just like her own, frizzy and ungovernable in humid weather, explosive when washed. Lucy looked back at her stepmother uncomfortably. She felt like an ungrateful brat for her reluctance to do what her father wanted her to do. 'I'm just not interested in meeting anyone at present…maybe in a few months I'll feel differently,' she added without much conviction.

'You had a bad breakup and you went through a lot alone afterwards,' Iola acknowledged gently. 'But your father's a man and he doesn't get it. I did try to explain to him that this is more of a healing time for you—'

'Yes, that's it, that's *exactly* it!' Lucy exclaimed, giving the older woman a sudden impulsive and appreciative hug. 'I'm not ready right now, not sure if I'll ever be though…'

'Not all men are like Bella's father. There *are* decent caring men out there,' Iola reminded her quietly.

'Nobody knows that better than me. I kissed a lot of frogs before I met Kreon.'

Lucy grinned and then laughed because her stepmother really did understand her viewpoint. A few minutes later, she left the town house and set out to walk to the small select Hotel Palati where she worked. Sited in an exclusive district in Athens, the hotel catered mainly to a business clientele.

Her father had met Iola when he'd engaged her as a PA in a property rental business that had eventually gone bust. But then Kreon had led a chequered 'boom to bust and back again' life and had been divorced once for infidelity. Lucy had respected his honesty with her. Even on the subject of her late mother, Kreon had proved to be painfully frank. Kreon hadn't once whitewashed his own failings or hidden the fact that he had gained a criminal record over some pyramid selling scheme he had got involved with as a younger man. Yet in spite of that honesty, Lucy still wasn't quite sure what actually funded her father's comfortable lifestyle.

She knew that Kreon gambled and took bets on a near professional basis and that he was always enthusiastically involved in some hopefully lucrative business scheme of one kind or another. Whatever he did, he seemed to be successful at it. Even so, she would not have been entirely surprised to learn that some of his ventures skated a little too close to the edge of breaking the law. But basically because he and Iola had given Lucy and her daughter both the home and the love Lucy had never known before, she closed her eyes to that suspicion and minded her own business the best she could.

After all, there truly *were* shades of grey between the black and white of absolute right and absolute wrong, she ruminated ruefully. Nothing and nobody was perfect. Even at the height of her passionate infatuation with Jax, she had recognised that he was flawed and all too human. He had been moody, controlling, domineering and arrogant and they had fought like cat and dog on a regular basis because, while Lucy might be only five feet tall and undersized, she was no pushover. At heart, she was stubborn and gutsy and quick-tempered. Even if Jax hadn't let her down so horribly, it would never have worked between them, she reasoned, feeling pleasantly philosophical on that score and firmly stifling the painful little push of heartache that still hollowed out her tummy. So, she'd had her heart broken just as Iola and thousands of other women *and* men had. It had only made her more resilient and less foolish and naïve, she told herself squarely.

The hotel manager showed her into the lofty-ceilinged back room, which had been comprehensively redecorated only weeks earlier with an opulence that was calculated to appeal to the more discerning customers.

Sometimes when Lucy daydreamed she wondered, if she had come from a more fortunate background, would she have become one of the elegant well-educated young businesswomen she saw round the hotel. Unfortunately she had been handicapped at the outset of life by her birth. Her parents' marriage had broken down after her mother had had an affair.

'Annabel always thought some better man was waiting for her round the next corner,' Kreon had said wryly of Lucy's mother. 'I wasn't rich and I lived by my wits and she had big ideas. We were living in London then where she was struggling to get the finance to set up her nursery business. But my father had returned to Greece after my mother died and he fell ill out here. I *had* to go to him. When I left London I had no idea Annabel was pregnant and when I contacted her to tell her that I was coming back she told me we were finished because she had met someone else. Now from what you're telling me, it seems she may have learned that she had this dreadful disease and she didn't want me around even though she had my child. I can't understand that, I will *never* understand that…'

And Lucy couldn't understand it either because, just listening to Kreon talking, she had recognised that he *had* loved her mother and had planned to return to London to be with her. But the more Kreon had spoken of her mother's beauty and her feverish love and need for fresh male attention, the more Lucy had suspected that there definitely *had* been another man and Annabel had burnt her boats for ever with Kreon shortly before illness had cruelly claimed her future.

Lucy had been two years old when Annabel was hospitalised and her daughter put into care. Her only memory of her mother was of a beautiful redhead lying in bed and shouting at her, so she wasn't sure that the mother who had surrendered her to the authorities had been that much of a loss in the parent stakes. Kreon had described a flighty, selfish personality, ill-suited to the kind of personal sacrifices a mother was often forced to make. And when, to Lucy's very great astonishment, Kreon had revealed that Annabel had actually had two other daughters being raised by her own mother somewhere in northern England, Lucy had been silenced by that shattering news.

Apparently she had two half-sisters somewhere, born from her mother's previous liaisons. Some day Lucy planned to look into that startling discovery but she didn't even know where you started in such a search because, not only had she no money to pursue enquiries, but also no names even to begin with. Naturally all these years on Kreon didn't recall such details about Annabel's background and history. After all, he had never met Annabel's mother and had been stonewalled by Annabel when he'd asked to do so. All he had remembered was that Annabel never went to visit the two little girls she had left behind her and he had said that even then he had recognised that as a warning sign that Annabel's attachments were of the shallow sort.

Lucy had counted herself lucky that she was not equally superficial because she adored Bella and would have laid down her life for her child, counting Bella as one of the few good developments in a life that had been far from easy or happy. On the other hand, had she cared less about Jax she would have been less devastated when he disappeared. My goodness, she had fallen apart at the seams and done stupid stuff, she recalled ruefully. She had been thrown off his father's yacht and warned never to show her face at the marina again while being marched off by security guards. She had been shouted at, called nasty names and utterly humiliated in her fruitless pursuit of Jax. All because she was fundamentally stupid, she conceded with regret.

After all, it had been crazy of her to believe that she meant anything more to Jax than an easily forgettable sexual fling, and when he was done with a woman, he was definitely *done*. The crewman on the yacht had called her a cheap whore as he'd bodily manhandled her off the polished deck and forced her down the gangway. She had fallen, been hurt and bruised by that brutality and she had been pregnant at the time. That was one reason she had never told her father the whole truth about Bella's parentage, preferring him to assume that Bella was the result of some one-night stand with a man in Spain. She knew Kreon would seek revenge and restitution if she ever told him the whole story.

So, in a way, staying silent was protecting her father from doing anything rash, she reasoned uneasily. Kreon was extremely protective. He would hit the roof if he realised that Lucy had been homeless even though Bella's father was a rich man, who could so easily have helped her and their child. A rich man, who was also Greek. That information wouldn't help either when Kreon was so immensely proud of his heritage.

But then Lucy had long since decided that rich people were pretty much untouchable, unlike the rest of humanity. The very rich had the power and the money to hold the rest of the world at bay and she saw the evidence of that galling fact every time she saw Jax in the media. Jax surrounded by bodyguards and beautiful women, never alone, never approachable, as protected and distanced from ordinary people as an exhibit in a locked museum case. Jax Antonakos, renowned entrepreneur and billionaire in his own right with a daddy who had billions also.

Her hands trembled as she set out china on the trolley awaiting her. She hated Jax now with the same passion she had once put into loving him. He had strung her along, faked so many things and she could never,

ever forgive the fact that he had quite deliberately left her stranded in Spain without a home or a job or any means of support. That she had been pregnant into the bargain was just her bad luck, but then Lucy had little experience of good luck.

A cluster of chattering businessmen entered and she served the coffee, standing back by the wall to dutifully await any further requests. Beyond the ajar door there was a burst of comment and then a sudden hush and the sound of many footsteps crossing the tiled hallway outside. The door whipped back noisily on its hinges and two men strode in, talking into ear pieces while checking the exit doors and all the windows, and that level of security warned Lucy that someone tremendously important was evidently about to arrive. The security men backed against the wall in silence and two more arrived to take up stances on the other side of the room. The almost militaristic security detail seemed so over the top for a small business meeting that Lucy almost laughed out loud.

And then Jax walked in and she stopped breathing and any desire to laugh died in her suddenly constricted lungs…

CHAPTER TWO

THE INSTANT LUCY saw that untidy black hair and the gorgeous green eyes so arrestingly bright against his bronzed skin, she wanted to run and keep on running and only innate discipline kept her where she was while she questioned her reaction. Why should *she* want to run? What had she done to be ashamed of? She was not a coward, she had never been a coward, she reminded herself doggedly, unnerved by that craven desire to flee. Indeed if anyone should be embarrassed it should be Jax for the cruel way he had treated her.

Couples broke up all the time but the process didn't have to be downright nasty. She hadn't been a stalker. There had been no excuse for threats and no need whatsoever to run her out of the neighbourhood.

Recollecting that vicious goodbye, Lucy lifted her chin high. Seated centre stage at the circular table, the cynosure of all attention and conversation, Jax mercifully wasn't looking round the room enough to notice her. Lucy might have overcome the urge to run but it did annoy her to find herself in a subservient role in Jax's radius again. In a mad moment she had once fantasised about swanning through some swanky club some day looking like a million dollars and seeing Jax and totally ignoring him to demonstrate her disdain and overall superiority as a decent human being. But now that she was actually on the spot she discovered that she was indefensibly and horribly curious and could only stare at him.

He had kept his black hair short. Once he had worn it long but he had had it cropped not long after she'd first met him, hitting the more conventional note she had suspected his father preferred. In retrospect she found it hard to credit that they had once bonded over their absent fathers. Jax had admitted how recently his father had come back into his life and had shared his grief over the death of the half-brother he had loved, not to mention his mother's abuse and infidelities. None of those deep conversations had fitted into what she assumed could be described as a typical short-term fling. But then that was Jax, a tough individualist, unpredictable, fiery and mysterious…the archetypal brooding hero beloved of teenaged girls with an overly romantic disposition, she concluded sourly.

That he *was* startlingly handsome had undoubtedly influenced the fantasies she had woven, she acknowledged, chewing at her lower lip, fingernails biting painfully into her palms. High cheekbones, strong clean jaw line, stunning eyes set beneath well-shaped ebony brows. Of course his mother had been a very famous and stunningly beautiful Spanish movie star and he had inherited her looks. In a big magazine article she had once read about him, which had been accompanied by a close-up photo, the journalist had raved about those dazzling wild green eyes and the spiky length of his sooty lashes.

Bella had *his* eyes. Lucy swallowed hard, recalling her feelings as her daughter's blue eyes at birth had slowly transformed to an eerily familiar emerald in her innocent little face. Innocent, something Jax was not and had never been. And reading about his sexual exploits over the past two years had helped Lucy to understand that he had always been a selfish, ruthless womaniser but she had been too trusting and inexperienced to recognise his true nature. Her heart was fluttering a beat so fast behind her breastbone that she wanted to press a hand against it to slow it down.

And then the truth of her response hit her and she was aghast that in spite of everything her body could still react to the presence of his. He glanced up from the file he had been perusing and for a split second, a literal *single* heartbeat, she clashed in dismay with his fierce gaze. It was like an electric shock pulsing low in her pelvis, tightening bone and sinew, awakening sensations she had almost forgotten and had never felt since. Every pulse she possessed went crazy, her breath catching in her throat, her very skin as achingly sensitive as if he had actually *touched* her. And then that tiny moment was over and past as Jax blanked her and passed the file back to someone at the table while making some comment about profit margins.

Her Greek vocabulary was slowly growing but in unfamiliar scenarios she still got as lost as any non-Greek-speaking foreigner. And *of course* Jax was going to blank her, she told herself shakily. Had she really thought he would greet a worker bee as low on the proverbial food chain as a waitress? Her mouth compressed as she wondered anxiously how he would react to the news that he was a father were she to tell him. With furious hostility and denial, she reckoned, her skin turning clammy at the prospect. Jax had once been very upfront about the fact that he didn't ever want children. Bearing that in mind, Lucy ruminated grimly, he should have been more careful to ensure that he didn't get her pregnant.

Jax's lean, chiselled features were rigid. He refused to look back in Lucy's direction. He didn't need to. That momentary image was stamped into his brain like a punch. What the hell was she doing in Athens? And her sudden appearance in his presence? Some sort of a set-up? And if so, why? Jax never took anything at face value any more. After all, he had once accepted Lucy for what she appeared to be and learned his very great error.

Bile tinged his mouth as he briefly recalled what he had read in that investigation file on her background: a string of drug offences stretching back years and convictions for soliciting sex. He had felt like a complete idiot. He had rushed off to see her, *confront* her even though it was late at night and then he had seen who she really was for himself…down an alley with a man enthusiastically giving up what she had made him wait weeks to enjoy.

Disgust and distaste flooded Jax, bringing back even less welcome memories of his mother's rampant promiscuity and empty promises of fidelity. He had seen her cheating break more than one man who had adored her. His father didn't know it because he had never dared to ask what his son's life had been like with his mother but Heracles had not been the only man to be chewed up and spat out in pieces by Mariana, who had wilfully followed every stray sexual impulse. As for Lucy, she was a liar and a cheat and he did not forgive betrayal. The entire episode had been sordid in the extreme. So why was he remembering that she had given him the wildest, hottest sex he had ever had?

A stubborn push of raunchily sexual images infiltrated Jax's hind brain even while he fought to hold them at bay and kept on talking about the project on the table. Hard as a rock behind his zip, Jax went rigid with angry aggression. How dared Lucy even walk into a room that contained him? He had always told himself that he had not inherited his father's notorious temper and equally notorious ability to hold a grudge but just then he recognised that he had lied to himself. Had it been possible to bodily throw Lucy out, he would have done so!

One of the bodyguards nudged Lucy's elbow and she glanced up, dragged from her own bemused thoughts with a vengeance. The older man indicated the coffee on the trolley and angled his head in his employer's direction, clearly urging her to get on with her job.

Reddening all the way up to her hairline, Lucy unfroze in an effort to behave normally. Even so she had to fight a huge inner battle to force her legs over to the trolley and pour Jax a coffee when all she really wanted to do was empty the entire contents of the pot over his hateful, arrogant head. Without him looking once at her or indeed acknowledging her in any way, she settled the coffee at his elbow with a hand that trembled slightly. Next she laid out the snacks and topped up the cups, signalling the bar waiter at the door when one of the men requested a shot of ouzo to wash down his coffee.

From below screening lashes and the almost infinitesimal movements of his proud dark head, Jax tracked Lucy's every move like a predator planning an attack. A blinding flash of memory assailed him: skin as translucent as fine porcelain in the dawn light, his fingers knotted into tumbling golden ringlets spread across a pillow, glorious bright blue eyes holding his, a tiny slender body with surprisingly sexy little curves reaching up to his. A little curvier than she used to be, he estimated abstractedly, remembering for a few seconds and then suddenly emerging again from that uncharacteristic reverie to answer a question, angrier and hotter than he had been in years.

The louse could at least have thanked her for the coffee, Lucy reflected with growing annoyance. Even a nod would have been acceptable but then Jax had always been a law unto himself, ferociously uncompromising and challenging, driven to succeed, survive and flourish as if it was in his genes. And perhaps it was. Only in a fantasy could there ever have been a scenario in which she believed that Jax Antonakos would settle down with a humble waitress... Bitterness gripped her and resentment shot through her like a sheet of lightning flashing off all her exposed nerve endings with painful effect.

Who the hell did Jax Antonakos think he was to treat her with such derisive dismissal?

Jax summoned Zenas, his head security guard, with an almost imperceptible flicker of his gaze and passed him a note. Zenas stood back to read it and confusion gripped his features for an instant before discipline kicked in and he left the room to do his employer's bidding. Lucy paid little heed to the byplay and only tensed when her own boss appeared in the doorway and silently summoned her out into the hallway.

A frown line bisected the older man's brow as he studied her. 'Mr Antonakos wants to speak to you in private when he's finished. I'm not sure how your father would feel about that request—'

Comprehension gripped Lucy fast. Andreus had no idea that she already knew Jax. He simply thought that Jax was trying to get off with her.

'Please don't mention this to Dad,' she muttered unevenly, for that was not a connection she wanted made. Once a link of any kind was established, secrets could spill out.

Andreus cast open the door of a smaller room across the corridor. 'Wait in there…but only if you *want* to,' he added with deliberate meaning. 'This is nothing to do with your employment here or with me. I have only passed on his request because I am very reluctant to offend so powerful a man.'

Lucy turned a slow, painful red, rage mushrooming inside her again as she imagined what her employer must be thinking. Jax wouldn't care about appearances. Jax had never *had* to care about appearances. For an instant she almost walked away from the opportunity to tell Jax what she thought of him. But she was too nervous, too aware of what had happened the last time her very existence nearby had become objectionable to Jax Antonakos. He had paid her then boss in Spain to sack her and she had lost her job and the accommodation that went with it. That was the kind of power the super wealthy had. Her boss in those days had been outrageously frank with her, admitting that he couldn't afford to keep her on when so much money to do otherwise was on offer and that he had had a poor summer season.

She paced the floor in the small room that was normally used as an office by the hotel housekeeper, thinking herself lucky that Jax hadn't had a room in the hotel and called her there, which would have looked even worse. Why on earth after ignoring her would he have demanded a meeting? From his point of view that made no sense, she reasoned with a frown. After all, he had ditched her two years earlier without an explanation or even a text. He hadn't turned up for their last date, hadn't phoned, hadn't done anything and when she had tried to contact him he had blocked her calls. Either he had simply tired of her or she had done or said something that had offended.

It hurt to look back and recall how many weeks she had tormented herself by pathetically wondering what she had done to annoy Jax. But nothing could have justified his subsequent behaviour in having her sacked and forced to leave the area like some vagrant whose very presence was offensive. That more than anything was what she could not forgive.

'You literally have three minutes or you'll miss your flight,' Zenas warned Jax outside the door.

Jax strode into the room, absently wondering if there was actual truth in the idea that human beings needed closure following certain experiences because he could not imagine any other reason why he should still feel driven to confront Lucy. Two years ago, he had never wanted to see or speak to her again. But possibly curiosity provided more motivation than he was willing to admit, he reasoned impatiently, angry tension tightening his lean, darkly handsome features.

'What the hell are you doing in Athens?' Jax demanded.

Lucy spun round from the window to face him, inwardly reeling from the shock of Jax in the flesh standing close enough to touch. He was so tall and he radiated restive energy and dominant vibes in waves. Tensing, she lifted her head up but she still had to tip it back to actually see any part of him above chest level. Not for the first time her diminutive height struck her as an embarrassing flaw. Being almost child-sized often meant that people didn't take her seriously or treat her like an adult. 'What's that got to do with you?' she slung back sharply, her tone similar to his own.

Jax drew himself up to his full six-foot-three-inch height and glowered down at her, green eyes luminescent with rage because it had been two years since anyone but his father had challenged him. 'Answer me,' he ground out impatiently.

'I don't owe you any answers...I don't owe you the time of day,' Lucy traded with the kind of provocation that struck a deep and unwelcome note of familiarity with Jax.

'You *will* answer me,' Jax raked back at her in a raw undertone, watching as she angled her head back and struck an attitude, hand on hip. Strawberry golden curls slid round her shoulders, her hair falling round her heart-shaped face, accentuating the defiant blue of her eyes and the lush fullness of her rosy lips.

And that fast, that urgently, Jax wanted to throw her down on the desk and control her the only way he had ever really controlled her, with the seething passion that was the mainstay of his character. For the briefest of moments he allowed himself to imagine the hot, wet tightness of her and the pulse at his groin reacted with unbridled enthusiasm. He reminded himself that it had been a toxic relationship and that she had played him like a con artist with her stories, her fake innocence and her lies. A dizzy surge of rage ignited inside him like a threatening fireball.

'If you don't answer me you will live to regret it,' Jax threatened in a wrathful undertone, every drop of his merciless Antonakos blood burning through him and hungry for a fight.

An angry spurt of fear made Lucy's stomach turn over sickly. He was too influential to challenge as even her boss had reminded her. She knew Jax could cause trouble for her, maybe even for her father as well if she wasn't careful. She might hate Jax but it would be insane to risk such penalties. 'What am I doing in Athens?' she repeated flatly. 'I finally looked up my birth father and he lives here—'

'But that was all lies,' Jax breathed in momentary bewilderment. 'You don't *have* a Greek father.'

Her smooth brow furrowed with genuine confusion. 'Lies? I don't know what you're talking about. I believe my birth certificate is as accurate as anyone else's. At the moment I'm living with my father and his wife.'

'That's not possible,' Jax told her, stiffening as a light knock on the door warned him that their time was up if he planned to make it to the airport. His long, lean frame swivelled as he half turned towards the door to leave, common sense and practicality powering him.

'I just want you to know that I hate you and I'll never forgive you for what you did to me,' Lucy confided in a belated rush of angry frustration that she could not tell him what she really thought of him any more bluntly than that. In truth she wanted to scream at him, she wanted to throw herself at him and hammer him with angry fists for hurting her.

'I didn't *do* anything to you,' Jax parried with complete cool.

'It was vicious...what you did, unnecessary!' Lucy condemned chokily, bitterness almost overpowering her along with a very human need to hit back. 'Having me sacked? Leaving me penniless and homeless and forced to go back to the UK when I had nothing there!'

An ebony brow elevated at that improbable accusation of bullying behaviour on his part, Jax swung back to her just as another knock sounded on the door. Whatever else he might be, Jax prided himself on never having treated a woman badly. 'I don't have time for this and I shouldn't make time for it either,' he acknowledged grimly. 'You're a liar and a cheat—'

'Of course you're going to say stuff like that, rewrite history, because you're so up yourself now,' Lucy shot back at him in disgust as she thought about her innocent, trusting little daughter. 'But I never lied to you or cheated on you and you never once thought about consequences, did you?'

He wanted her phone number but he wouldn't ask for it, wouldn't allow himself to ask for it. He knew what she was. He didn't want anything to do with her. So, having reached that decision and feeling invigorated by it, he could not explain why he then turned back like a man with a split personality and told her to meet him for a drink the following evening at a little bar he patronised on the marina, a haunt of his for quiet moments, which the paparazzi had yet to discover. Even as he walked back out again, he was questioning the decision and regretting it, lean brown hands clenching into impatient fists. What the hell had he done that for?

But what had she meant by 'consequences'? And how come she *did* have a Greek father when according to that file she did not?

He was simply curious, nothing wrong or surprising about that. His libido was not in the driver's seat, he assured himself with solid conviction. Stray memories had briefly aroused him when he saw her again, nothing more meaningful. All men remembered incredibly good sex. Furthermore, he had a little black book of phonebook proportions to turn to when he felt like sex, hot and cold running women on tap wherever he travelled. *That* was the world he lived in. There was no way he could ever be tempted to revisit a manipulative little cheat like Lucy Dixon, he reflected with satisfaction.

Naturally, becoming the Antonakos heir had ensured that Jax became significantly more cynical about women. He didn't listen to sob stories any more, he didn't let his inherently dangerous streak of chivalry rule him. Indeed the sight of a woman in need of rescue was more like aversion therapy to him now. He knew from experience that that kind of woman was likely to be far more trouble than she was worth.

After all, how many times had he felt he had no choice but to race to his mother's rescue? When the men she betrayed became violent as her lies were exposed? When she needed another spell in some discreet rehabilitation facility before she could be seen in public again? When he was forced to lie to protect *her*?

And yet at heart he had always known that his

mother was a deeply disturbed and egocentric human being, undeserving of his care and respect. That was why his little sister, Tina, had died, he reminded himself bitterly. Mariana's self-centred neglect of her younger child had directly led to the incident in which the toddler had drowned. But he had only been fourteen, so what could he possibly have done when so many adults had witnessed the insanity of his mother's lifestyle and yet failed to act to protect either of her children?

Lucy walked home in a pensive mood. Of course she wouldn't meet him, she told herself firmly. What would be the point? *Bella!* Jax was a father whether he liked it or not but she knew he wouldn't like that news any more than he liked her. And why was her being in Greece such a big deal? What was it to him? It was not as though they were likely to bump into each other again in normal life. Jax lived against a backdrop of massive yachts, private jets and private islands. He didn't rub shoulders with ordinary working people.

Yet a giant ball of despair was threatening to swallow Lucy up and she didn't know why. Seeing Jax again, she recognised, had *hurt* and hurt much more than she had expected. It had brought back memories she didn't want. She had loved him and had given her trust to a man for the first time ever. His sudden volte-face had almost destroyed her because she had given him so much she had felt bare to the world without him.

And yet he *still* wasn't married. She had thought for sure that he would marry the wealthy heiress his father kept pushing in his direction, the very lovely but very bitchy Kat Valtinos. But then Jax was bone-deep stubborn. You could take a horse to water but you couldn't make it drink and getting Jax to do anything he didn't want to do was like trying to push a boulder up a steep hill.

Kat Valtinos had organised the party the night Lucy had met Jax on his father's enormous yacht. Lucy's memory wafted her back two years into the past. Back then, Jax had been in Spain setting up a new resort on the coast. When the caterers had mucked up with a double booking, Kat had personally trawled through the local bars seeking waitresses for the event.

'You two will do,' she had said to Lucy and Tara, looking them up and down as though they were auditioning as strippers. 'You're young and pretty and sexy. Just what men like. You put your make-up on with a trowel,' she had told Tara critically and to Lucy she had said, 'You need to show more leg and cleavage.'

If the money hadn't been so good, Lucy wouldn't have done it but back then she had lived on a budget where no tips meant stale bread and going hungry. Their boss didn't feed them for free and they had no cooking facilities in their mean little attic room, which had been hot as hell up under the eaves above the restaurant kitchen. Any extra cash was deeply welcome in those days.

The party had been full of blowhard bellicose men talking themselves up in Antonakos's company and drinking too much. One of them had cornered Lucy when she was sent to a lower deck to restock the bar from the supplies stored there. She had been trying to fight him off when Jax had intervened. Jax, blue-black glossy hair brushing his shoulders, green eyes glittering like shards of glass, who had dragged the guy off her with punishing hands and hit him hard without hesitation.

'Are you OK?' the most gorgeous guy she had ever seen had asked, pulling her off the wall she had slumped against, smoothing down the skirt the creep had been trying to wrench up. '*Diavolos*, you're so tiny. Did he hurt you?'

'Only a little,' she had said shakily, trembling like a leaf and in absolutely no doubt that Jax had saved her from a serious assault because, with the noisy party taking place on the deck above, the lower deck had been deserted and nobody would have heard her crying out.

'Take a moment to recover,' Jax had urged, guiding her into an opulent saloon to push her down into a seat where her cotton-wool legs had collapsed under her as if he had flipped a switch. 'What were you doing down here on this deck?'

He had issued instructions on the phone to a crew member to have the bar supplies refreshed. And the whole time she had just been staring at him like a brainless idiot, utterly intimidated by everything about him from the expensive quality of his lightweight grey suit and hand-stitched shoes to the sheer beauty of his perfect features from his edgy cheekbones to his sculpted mouth. It was the eyes that had got to her the most, the tender concern she'd seen there and then the budding all-male appreciation. He had the most stunning eyes and his rare smile had been like the sun coming out on a dark day.

'Are you OK?' he repeated.

Well, no, in fact from that moment she had never

been OK again. Something she'd needed to survive had lurched into strange territory and softened to let him in, no matter that it had gone against sense and practicality and her life experience. She had truly never been the same since.

CHAPTER THREE

LUCY WAS RIVEN with extreme guilt by the time she finally climbed on the bus that would take her down to the marina.

She had had to lie to Iola simply to get out. She had pretended that she was joining a couple of the other waitresses for a few drinks. To weigh down her conscience even more, Iola had been delighted to believe that her stepdaughter was finally going out and about. Her stepmother had hovered helpfully, urging her to put on make-up and wear the pretty white sundress that Iola had bought for her a few weeks earlier. But how *could* Lucy have admitted that she was heading out to meet Bella's father? After all, she had already lied on that subject by declaring that she had no way of getting in touch with the man who had fathered her daughter. Kreon and Iola had averted their eyes in dismay and embarrassment at that claim, clearly assuming that she did not know the man's name.

Indeed, one lie only led to more lies, Lucy conceded shamefacedly, annoyed that she had found it impossible to be more honest. But Kreon would raise the roof if he discovered that Jax was Bella's father and she didn't want to put Kreon in the potential firing line of Antonakos displeasure.

And why was she off to meet Jax when she had sworn she would not do so?

Obviously she was thinking about her daughter's needs, wondering if there was any chance that Jax could have changed his outlook on children and could possibly be willing to embrace the news that he was a parent. It was definitely her duty to check out that possibility and finally tell him that he had a child, she told herself staunchly even while her heart hammered and her breath caught in her throat at the prospect of seeing Jax again.

You're pathetic, she scolded herself angrily as she marched past crowded bars, ignoring the men who called out to her. He's a very good-looking guy and of course you still notice that but that's all, leave it there. You are *not* a silly impulsive teenager any more, she coached herself, you know what he is and what he's like and *you know better*.

Jax lounged outside the bar with Zenas close by, the rest of his security detail settled within hailing distance. He didn't know why he had come until he saw Lucy, her dress flowing and dancing round her slender knees, the pristine white lighting up below the street lights, her strawberry-blonde ringlets a vivid fall round her narrow shoulders. And then he knew why he had come and he hated that surge of absolute primal lust, raw distaste flaming through him even as his jeans became uncomfortably tight. A wave of male heads slowly turned to check her out as she passed by. Jax gritted his even white teeth at that familiar display.

'The waitress...*really*?' Zenas teased from the shadows.

'I need to have this conversation in private,' Jax warned his old school friend quietly, relieved that Zenas had only joined the team the year before and had no idea of his prior acquaintance with Lucy.

Zenas strolled obediently across the street and plonked himself down on a bench. Jax lifted his newspaper, refusing to continue watching Lucy walk towards him, perturbed by the level of his own interest. He would get answers from her, satisfy his curiosity and leave. There would be nothing more personal and absolutely *no* sex.

Lucy saw Jax outside the bar, arrogant dark head bent, the bold cut of his chiselled profile golden beneath the lights, his black hair still long enough to tousle in the light breeze. And her heart bounced inside her like a rubber ball because she was helplessly reliving the excitement he had always induced in her. There were flutters in her tummy, crazy tingles pinching the tips of her breasts taut and a dangerous hot, liquid awareness pulsing into being between her legs. Just as quickly her entire body felt overheated and she was seriously embarrassed for herself.

As she took a seat Jax glanced up at her from below his ridiculously long lashes, crescents of uncompromising green running assessingly across her flushed face. 'At least you're on time for once...I assume you hurried.'

Lucy blinked and bit down on her tongue hard. Her poor timekeeping had always infuriated Jax because he hated being kept waiting and never, ever understood how time could sometimes run away from her.

He had always contended that being late was rude and indefensible. But then Jax, who was relentlessly practical and full of ferocious initiative in tough scenarios, had probably never had a weakness for daydreaming.

Daydreaming, however, had always been Lucy's escape from challenging experiences. When she didn't fit in at the many different schools she had attended she had floated away on a fluffy cloud inside her own mind. When life was especially difficult, fantasies had become her consolation and she would dream of a world in which she had love and security and happiness.

In the smouldering silence that had now fallen, Lucy forced herself out of her abstraction and registered that Jax was watching her with impatient green eyes as if he had guessed that she had momentarily drifted away with the fairies. In receipt of that aggravated look, she felt her mouth run dry as a bone. In desperation she spun his newspaper round, her attention falling on a recent custody case that had attracted a lot of media coverage. 'Oh, my goodness...' she muttered as she slowly traced the headline with a fingertip while she carefully translated it. 'The *father* got the kid? How could they take a child away from his mother?'

Jax shrugged an uninterested shoulder as he signalled the waiter. 'Why not? Life has moved on. Fathers are now equal to mothers—'

'Yes, but—'

'Read it and you'll see why the family court reached that decision,' Jax said drily.

'I can't read Greek well enough yet,' she admitted grudgingly.

'The father is willing to work at home to be with the child while the mother would be leaving him in a nursery all day. Why are we talking about this anyway?' Jax demanded impatiently.

'It's an interesting case,' Lucy proffered stiffly. 'The mother's a paramedic who doesn't have the option of working at home.'

'While the father wants his child and what's best for his child, which is as it should be,' Jax interposed as a bottle of wine and glasses arrived at the table.

A cold skitter of fear pierced Lucy's tense body as a glass of wine appeared in front of her. 'Is that how you would feel?'

'We're not talking about me. I won't be fathering any children,' Jax declared with a cynical twist of his expressive mouth. 'Don't need the hassle or the responsibility. But if I *did* have a child I certainly wouldn't sit back and allow a woman to take my child away from me...in fact that is the very last thing I would do.'

A quiver of sheer fright rippled down Lucy's taut spine as she reached for her wine. That risk, that particular fear of losing her child, had never once crossed her mind as a possibility. And why hadn't it? Jax might not want children but he *was* a very possessive guy. What was his was very much his, not to be shared or touched or even looked at by anyone else. Once he had treated Lucy like that, enraging her with his determination to own her body and soul and control her every move. Suppose she told him about Bella and he felt the same way about his daughter?

Sobered by that fear, Lucy decided there and then to continue keeping Bella a secret until she had, at least, taken legal advice. In fact maybe the legal route would be the best way to go when it came to breaking that news, she thought cravenly. It would be more impersonal and less likely to lead to confrontation and bad feeling. Just at that moment Lucy could not face telling Jax that he was the father of her child and that because of his behaviour after their breakup she had had no way of telling him that she was pregnant. That was not her fault, she reminded herself. That was unquestionably *his* fault.

'When did you move to Athens?' Jax prompted.

'Six months ago...I was struggling to make ends meet in London,' she confided, almost rolling her eyes at that severe understatement before taking several fortifying swallows of wine.

'When we talked in Spain, you had no plans to track your father down,' he reminded her with a frown. 'You thought he had deserted your mother and you *said*—'

'I was wrong. When I needed help, my father came through for me,' Lucy admitted. 'Why did you ask me to meet you?'

Jax watched her sip at the wine, one little finger rubbing back and forth over the stem of the glass, her lush mouth rosy and moist. Like a sex-starved adolescent, he remembered the feel of her mouth, the flick of her teasing little tongue and he went rigid.

'*Jax?*' she pressed, setting down the glass.

Lean, dark features taut, Jax topped up the wine. He had tried to teach her about wine once: how to select it, savour it, how to truly *taste* it, and she was still knocking it back as if it were cheap plonk. That had been another lesson that had inexplicably ended up between the sheets. But then nothing had ever gone to plan with Lucy. His self-discipline had vanished.

When he had taken her shopping he had taken her in the changing cubicle up against the wall, stifling her frantic cries with his hand. Yes, she had definitely *earned* that red dress he had later seen her wearing while she gave her body to another man.

'Why?' Lucy prompted in growing frustration at his brooding silence.

Jax inclined his head to Zenas and spoke to him soft and low when he approached. 'We'll go somewhere more private—'

Lucy collided with smouldering green eyes like highly polished emeralds and stiffened in instant rejection of that idea. 'No.'

'I don't know what I was thinking of. This is not the place to talk.' Or fight, Jax reflected, in no doubt that angry words were likely to be exchanged when he challenged her.

Lucy gulped down more wine in an effort to steady herself and think carefully before she spoke. 'I don't want to go anywhere else with you,' she argued.

'Don't lie,' Jax advised in the driest of tones. 'I could have you on your back in five minutes if that's what I wanted…but it's *not*.'

A tide of outraged colour slowly dappled Lucy's creamy skin as she gazed back at him, aghast at his crudity. 'I can't believe you said that.'

Jax shrugged again, a knowing look in his stunning eyes. 'It's only what we're both thinking about.'

Lucy bristled like a cat stroked the wrong way and threw her shoulders back. 'No, it's not. Speak for yourself.'

'I fell for the virgin ploy once. Don't push your luck, *koukla mou*,' Jax advised as he thrust back his chair and began to rise. 'Born-again virgins push the wrong buttons with me.'

'Don't call me that...I'm *not* anyone's doll!' Lucy protested, aware of the meaning of those words because her father used them around Bella.

'Don't push your luck, Tinker Bell,' Jax stabbed instead.

And the sound of that once familiar pet name hurt like the unexpected swipe of a knife across tender skin. It turned her pale because it took her back to a place she didn't want to go, to a period when she had fondly believed herself to be loved and safe and cherished. But it had all been a lie and a seriously cruel lie at that. It hurt even more that she had adored that lie and longed for it to last for ever and ever, just like in the fairy tales.

'You still haven't told me what this is about,' Lucy argued as she drank down her wine with desperate little swallows that pained her throat. 'I'm staying here.'

A long silver limousine purred along the kerb. They were in a pedestrian zone and the car shouldn't have been there but the two police officers lounging across the street did nothing to interfere with its progress.

'Get in the car or I'll throw you in it!' Jax bit out in a driven undertone, what little patience he had taxed by her obstinacy.

He had made a mistake, he thought furiously, turning his head and unexpectedly encountering Zenas's shocked appraisal, registering that the other man had heard that threat.

Incredulous, Lucy giggled. 'You wouldn't dare,' she told him.

And he *did*. He picked her up off the chair and

shoved her into the back seat of the limo as if she were a lost parcel he was retrieving, aware throughout that his bodyguards were watching him as if he had gone insane. But it was entirely Lucy's fault. She would never ever do as she was told. She would never ever accept that he knew best. And the whole situation was going to hell in a hand basket fast and he could blame himself for that because he should never have arranged to meet her in the first place. Why the hell did what had happened two years ago even *matter* to him?

So, she had lied to engage his sympathy and ensnare him, pretending to be younger and more innocent than she actually was. He already knew why she had done it. She had lied to impress him because he was rich and there was nothing more complex behind her behaviour back then than greed and a desire to rise in the world. He had been cunningly targeted and chased by hundreds of other women for the same reasons. Why was *her* deception still raw?

As he swung into the car, radiating blazing tension, his dazzling eyes splintered like green lightning with anger and Lucy stared at him.

'You still have a terrible temper,' she complained. 'And you just kidnapped me and the police did nothing—'

'Maybe you should've tried a little screaming and struggling to demonstrate fear,' Jax mocked, convinced that she was secretly delighted to be in his limo again and probably already planning a lucrative rehash of their Spanish fling.

No way, he swore to himself, black lashes almost hitting his cheekbones as he glanced studiously away from her, sitting there as she was watching him like a little spider planning an intricate web in which to capture him. On the other hand, *he* could play her the way she had once played him, he conceded grimly. And while he was doing that he could do whatever he wanted to do with her. That thought, that very idea took him aback because he didn't usually play games with women. But there was no denying that the concept of playing games with Lucy hugely turned him on.

Lucy breathed in slow and deep to calm herself. She focussed on the strong male thigh next to her own, the fine fabric of his trousers pulled taut across his powerful muscles and across his crotch. Her attention lingered there a split second longer and then hurriedly shifted because it was obvious that he was aroused. Why? Did he *ever* think of anything but sex? Colour warmed her cheeks because once they had had a very physical relationship. It had lasted six weeks, with them only becoming intimate in the last two, but during it she had realised that sex was unbelievably important to Jax and an unapologetic drive he made no attempt to restrain. Bella, after all, had been conceived in a brazen episode in a changing-room cubicle, she recalled in serious mortification. She had *tried* to say no but she had never been very good at denying Jax when her own body burned for his like a fire that couldn't be doused.

'I hate you,' she told him truthfully, still thinking about that changing-room cubicle in which the use of precautions hadn't figured.

'Because I found you out?' Jax drawled in a tone of boredom. 'Or because I dumped you?'

Lucy's nails bit crescents into the soft skin of her

palms. She had told him the truth: she *did* hate him. In fact the idea of wreaking revenge on Jax energised her. He was so unbearably confident, sure of his every move in a way she had never been. He was clever, successful and rich. He was also worshipped like the Greek god he resembled by women more akin to groupies than anything else.

'Where are you taking me?' she demanded curtly. 'Why do you even want to talk to me? It's a bit late in the day, isn't it?'

'Is it?' Jax traded unfathomably, leaning forward to press a button that opened a gleaming bar.

'I don't understand you!' Lucy bit out in frustration.

'Why would you?'

Jax thrust a foaming glass of champagne into her hand, thoroughly disconcerting her. Big blue eyes skimmed up to his in confusion and she looked so lost and bewildered that a momentary pang of conscience pierced his tough hide. Of course it wasn't real, he recognised angrily.

Fool me once, shame on you, fool me twice, shame on me.

He knew he could trust Lucy to put in an award-winning performance. He would get what he wanted. He would get answers and doubtless tears, self-justification and grovelling into the bargain. He positively warmed to an image of Lucy grovelling and a smile flashed across his forbidding mouth. Lucy on her knees poised to please...just what the doctor would order for a bored billionaire.

That was what lay at the root of his bizarre behaviour, he reasoned broodingly. He was bored. Bored with the flattery of too many far too eager to please women. Well, Lucy had never been into the art of hanging off his every word and complimenting him on his brilliance. Lucy had fought him and criticised him and driven him crazy on many occasions. Yet he had only been with her six short weeks interspersed with the business trips that had parted them. Six weeks. That was a sobering acknowledgement. Why did he remember so much about her when generally he was challenged to recall the name of a woman he had shared a bed with only a week ago?

She had hurt his pride. That was why. That was the only reason he still remembered her, Jax decided. Well, that and the supercharged, highly satisfying sex...

Lucy sipped the champagne, bubbles bursting under her nose and tickling, tiny beads of moisture cooling her too hot face. She felt out of control and she didn't like it. She was in Jax's car and she didn't know where he was taking her or why he would want to talk to her after so long. She crossed her legs, then re-crossed them, looking everywhere but at him.

'I want to go home,' she said abruptly.

'No, you don't.'

'I don't trust you. I don't want to be anywhere alone with you,' she told him sharply.

'My housekeeper lives in,' Jax murmured flatly.

'Like that's going to change my mind!' Lucy scoffed. 'Nobody you employ will go up against you. Do you think I'm stupid?'

'A little hysterical,' Jax confided. 'And it's undeserved. I've never harmed you in any way.'

'But your employees will if you tell them to. I was dragged off of *Sea Queen* two years ago and I got hurt,' Lucy told him reluctantly.

Jax turned his head to frown at her as the limousine coasted to a halt. 'What on earth are you talking about?' he demanded.

The door beside him clicked open and then the one beside her. She climbed out onto a well-lit driveway fronting an ultra-modern villa of quite astonishing size. The cool night air hit her hard and she felt slightly dizzy. A large glass of wine topped up by champagne had been too much for her system, she acknowledged heavily. Alcohol always hit her hard.

'We'll discuss this indoors,' Jax ground out impatiently. 'Come on...'

How had she got herself into this situation? Lucy asked herself with angry self-loathing. She didn't know where she was and had no idea how to get home again. She *should* have kicked up a major fuss when Jax had lifted her out of her chair at the bar but she had let him get away with it sooner than cause a public scene. In certain moods, Jax was as unstoppable as a juggernaut. He didn't care what anybody thought. The only opinion he cared for was his own.

'I want a taxi home,' she informed him. 'Right now...'

'I thought you were dying to tell me about the assault on the yacht,' Jax murmured, shooting her a politely enquiring appraisal that she immediately distrusted.

Lucy hovered uncertainly, noting the security team standing around and the older woman waiting to greet them at the front door. Compressing her lips, she forced herself to follow Jax, carefully picking her path up the steps into the contemporary hall. The preponderance of mirrors and multiple reflections confused her and she didn't object when Jax rested a light hand on her back to guide her into a huge reception room furnished with sofas and monochromatic modern art works.

'Assault…yacht,' Jax prodded expectantly. 'When did this happen?'

'About two weeks after I last saw you in Spain—'

'I had already left the country by then. Tell me what happened.'

'I went looking for you and I was told you weren't on board the *Sea Queen*—'

'Which was true.'

'The crew member that dealt with me was horrible. He called me names and manhandled me—'

Jax had fallen very still. 'In what way were you "manhandled"?'

'I said that I wasn't willing to leave until I was given a phone number or an address where I could contact you. Maybe that was foolish,' Lucy muttered ruefully. 'Anyway, this big bald guy got really aggressive and called me a whore and just dragged me across the deck and pushed me down the gangway. I fell at the foot, bloodied my knees and my elbows and nobody helped me. And someone had called the marina security to escort me away and they accused me of trespassing in a restricted area. It was hideous.'

A frown line had drawn his fine ebony brows together. 'I refuse to credit that any member of the crew would be so rough with a woman—'

Lucy bridled. 'Well, believe it…it happened!'

'Nor can I accept that there was verbal abuse. But I can confirm that you would not have been given my phone number or address because I left that instruction,' he admitted grimly.

'Why was that necessary? What did you think I was going to do?' Lucy framed in an angry rush. 'Spring a terrorist attack on you? Turn into a stalker?'

'I didn't want you making a nuisance of yourself,' Jax advanced flatly, turning away from her for an instant, memories interfering with his thoughts.

What she had made him feel had been too intense. In the aftermath of his discovery of her true nature, he had overreacted, he acknowledged with hindsight, stepping back and instinctively protecting himself from further exposure to her. It had seemed imperative that he neither speak to her nor see her again.

'I can't understand why you went to the yacht or why you tried to contact me again,' he said drily, swinging back to her with his brain fixed firmly in the present.

Bitter recriminations bubbled on Lucy's lips and she swallowed them back because she didn't want to make an announcement about Bella in the midst of a heated dispute. And Jax might be poised in front of her as ice cool and expressionless as a glacier but the atmosphere felt combustible and the tension was horrendous.

'Obviously I tried to contact you…but you simply vanished. I didn't hear from you again. Most people would seek an explanation—'

'There was a *very* obvious explanation. I'd grown bored,' Jax murmured with derision.

'Sometimes you are a very nasty piece of work,' Lucy mumbled shakily, appalled that he could throw that humiliating statement in her face.

'Put your cards on the table, *koukla mou*. And maybe I will too.'

'I don't know what you're getting at—'

'Stop acting like a poor little victim—stop faking it,' Jax urged with stark impatience. 'You told me a lot of lies back then—'

'No, I didn't!' Lucy broke in furiously.

Exasperation gripped Jax. She was moving agitatedly round the room, luminous blue eyes fixed intently to him. The floor lamp behind her turned that pale dress almost transparent, clearly delineating the rounded swell of her small, succulent breasts and the shadowy outline of her pink areolae. He went hard, his reaction instantaneous.

'*What* lies?' Lucy demanded hotly, watching the fluid movement of his long, lithe body as he paced the tiled floor in front of her.

He was so beautiful he still took her breath away. It wasn't merely his lean, strong face and stunning green eyes. Jax simply radiated masculine power from the aggressive angle of his arrogant head to the square swing of his wide shoulders and the decisive gait of his long, muscular legs. She was so busy staring, so busy drinking him in with greedy eyes that she couldn't concentrate. A prickling sensation assailed her nipples and tightened them into hard little nubs while a sliding, pulsing warmth began low in her pelvis.

'What lies?' she mumbled afresh, her brain in a fog.

Throbbing with arousal, Jax compressed his sculpted lips. He was done with conversation. Lucy would verbally twist and turn and prevaricate and embellish and evade until he was ready to strangle her. And why was he even bothering? He didn't ever travel an emotional road with women these days. He wasn't interested in their motivations and their deepest secrets. He kept it simple, straight. So, why wasn't he being straight with himself? He hadn't brought Lucy home to *talk* to her, had he? His mouth quirked into a flashing sardonic smile as he studied her.

It was the bad-boy smile Lucy had seen Jax wear a dozen times in glossy photos. It wasn't the smile that had once made her heart jump and fill to overflowing with love. It was a dark edgy smile with a sensual hint of threat in it.

A forbidden tingle of anticipation infiltrated what remained of her defences. She took a sudden step back, struggling to keep her distance and stay in control. But Jax reached out a hand and closed it round hers in a sudden movement, pulling her to him before she could back off. He wrapped both arms round her, lifting her easily off her feet to hoist her high against him.

It was a decisive moment and she knew it, knew she should push her hands down on his shoulders to force him to put her down and release her. But nothing was ever that simple for Lucy when it came to Jax. As he brought her down he nuzzled against her neck, dark stubble scratching her tender skin, and a shudder of awareness powerful enough to leave her dizzy enveloped her. The scent of his cologne laced with clean, husky male flared her nostrils; he smelled so unbelievably good she wanted to bury her nose in his hair. Her hands went round his neck and for a split second as he worked his erotic path towards her parted lips she clung like a limpet.

Just one kiss, she bargained with herself, just *one*, but the man who had once seduced her with kisses had no intention of breaking his perfect track record. He always knew what she wanted and he gave it to her, all the seething passion he had taught her to crave. He kissed her and she went up in flames. Her body flared into shocking awareness and suddenly burned back to almost painful life with every plunging thrust of his tongue. She gasped and quivered, filled with all the hunger she had suppressed.

He brought her down on a firm but yielding surface and her head fell back as he wrenched down her dress to squeeze a straining pink nipple between his fingertips, swiftly following it up as she arched up to him in response with the warm sucking pull of his mouth. It was as if a river of liquid fire ran down through her to engulf her feminine core. A strangled moan of excitement was torn from her as his mouth traced a fiery path down over her twisting body, long, lean fingers clenching on a slender thigh.

And just then she wondered how he had contrived that skin-to-skin contact and the answer shook her so much that she yanked herself violently free and rolled off the sofa, hitting her hip painfully hard in the fall. Her dress fell round her knees. Tears of pain and mortification in her eyes, she got onto her knees and, with great difficulty, clumsily and awkwardly hauled her dress back up over her exposed body, shame roaring through her in long agonising waves.

'*Thee mou...*' Jax began rawly.

'I want a taxi home. This is not going any further,' Lucy swore breathlessly, unable to even make herself look at him.

Jax wanted to break something. Instead he breathed in very deep. Lucy hadn't changed. She had to have all the ducks in line before she would fire. Two years ago, that simple process of withholding sex had worked on him but he was no longer that suggestible, Jax told himself with fierce conviction. Yet when he touched her, she *owned* him, he recognised, unnerved by that realisation.

As she struggled with a singular lack of dignity or cool to refasten the difficult ties on her slender shoulders, Lucy's hatred of Jax rose like a tide of poison inside her. Ten seconds and he had had her half naked, nothing but a pair of knickers standing between her and total nudity. She had been a pushover. Maybe she was so starved of sex she *did* need a man in her life, she decided, her eyes stinging with hot, angry tears. But that man would not be Jax Antonakos.

'The limo will take you back home,' Jax told her flatly. 'That is if you *really* want to leave.'

'It's my turn to do the walking away,' Lucy framed gruffly, loathing coursing through her slight body in such powerful waves that she trembled with it. 'I wish I'd done it two years ago. What were you planning on happening? Another session of unprotected sex? Haven't you ever had consequences from that?'

'What the hell are you trying to imply?' Jax demanded in a raw undertone.

Lucy flung her head back, all fired up on adrenalin and resentment and bitterness. 'When you got bored and dumped me,' she told him shakily, 'you left me pregnant—'

CHAPTER FOUR

JAX HAD FALLEN very still. 'That's not possible—'

'Why? Are you infertile?' Lucy shot back at him, unimpressed. 'I don't think so because we have a *child*, Jax. A little girl, who's fifteen months old.'

Jax stared back at her in rampant disbelief, hard lines settling between his nose and mouth, his handsome bone structure drawn stark and taut. 'Impossible,' he said again, green eyes brilliant with outraged denial.

'That last week we were together you had sex with me in a changing-room cubicle and you didn't take precautions,' Lucy reminded him angrily. 'Why do you think I tried so hard to get in touch with you that I got thrown off the yacht? I needed help.'

Shock ensured that Jax's brain continued to rebel and tell him that what she was saying was totally and absolutely impossible but his memory was infinitely more accurate. He knew he had taken that risk and had thought nothing of it at the time, indeed revelling in the reality that not even the thin layer of a condom separated him from her. He also realised in that moment that if she was telling him the truth, he had very probably made the biggest, messiest mistake of his life.

Panic hurtled through Lucy when she saw the shrewd dawning of genuine concern in his glittering green eyes. What had she done? Throwing it at him like that? Oh, my goodness, what had she done? Dully she recognised that she had been hitting back at him the only way she knew how. Needing to shock and hurt him as he had once shocked and hurt her with his rejection. But she knew instantly that she should not have used Bella like a weapon against him.

'This has to be discussed,' Jax intoned in a driven undertone.

'Not tonight. I want to go home,' Lucy breathed tightly. 'Right now.'

'You can't tell me I could be a father and then—'

'Yes, I can,' Lucy incised fiercely. 'I can do whatever I like just as you do whatever you like. And it's not a question of "*could* be a father". Bella is yours because I've never been with anyone else!'

Jax knew that was a lie for he had seen her cheat on him with his own eyes but DNA testing would provide proof neither of them could refute. He was appalled by the idea that he could have unwittingly had a child with a woman who not only lied and cheated but also had a criminal record. Even his parents' numerous unsuccessful marriages and affairs paled beside such a development. And the existence of an illegitimate Antonakos heir would send his father through the roof.

'I want to see the child,' Jax told her doggedly.

Lucy lost all her hectic colour. 'No.'

'If that child is half mine, you don't get to say no. I'll call in the family legal team,' Jax warned her without skipping a beat. 'Who looks after her when you're at work?'

That reference to lawyers and the reality that she was a working mum made a cold, hollow sensation of fear spread inside Lucy's tummy. 'My stepmother,' she told him, struggling to suppress the defiance rising inside her because a mood of conciliation struck her as being far more sensible in the circumstances.

'I'll call in with you tomorrow and we'll take care of the necessities,' Jax breathed coldly as he strode out to the hall. 'I need your address—'

'No.' The sense of being trapped built up inside Lucy until she felt almost suffocated by it. She had told him about Bella. She had done it in a recklessly provocative way too, absolutely the worst way to give Jax bad news. As volatile as he was, he didn't need the encouragement. And she had no doubt at all that learning that he was a father was very bad news on his terms because from the instant the concept had set in, Jax had turned icy-cold and businesslike. Now, however, Lucy recognised that she had to deal with the fallout from her impulsive decision and that would entail finally telling Kreon and Iola the truth.

'If you come in the morning I'll be there,' Lucy conceded abruptly. 'I usually only work evenings. My father and stepmother have a funeral to attend, so they won't be at home.'

Jax demanded the address and then stood poised in the doorway of his home watching her clamber into the limousine outside. Lucy tore her gaze from his forbidding stance and told herself that she had only done what had had to be done. He had the right to know about Bella. It was his own fault that he hadn't found out about his daughter sooner. Maybe he wouldn't want anything to do with their child, Lucy reasoned with sudden hope that that might be the case. And then she felt horribly guilty because she knew how much it hurt not to have a father and she didn't want her daughter to suffer the same way.

Yet when she looked back to her affair with Jax she could never have believed that they would have ended up so bitterly opposed. That night after the yacht party, Jax had sought her out and insisted on seeing her back to her room at the bar.

'You *are* over twenty-one?' he had checked. 'I don't get involved with anyone younger than that.'

'I'm twenty-three,' Lucy had lied instantly, adding on four years to her age, determined to make that all important grade for him.

He had told her he would pick her up for dinner the following evening. She had told him she was working.

'Take a night off,' Jax had urged.

'I can't afford to,' she had argued.

'I'll cover the cost of it,' Jax had declared.

'But then you'd be paying for my time and I couldn't agree to that—'

'You're very difficult,' Jax had condemned.

'And you don't understand how to take no for an answer.'

'I want to see you again,' Jax had proclaimed impatiently.

'I'm free Thursday night.'

'I don't want to wait that long.'

'All right. You can see me at midnight tomorrow when I finish my shift...unless that's too late for you?'

'No, that will do.'

'But know upfront I'm not spending the night with

you, so if that's what you're expecting, just forget about me,' she had warned him staunchly.

Lucy had learned to be blunt with men. She thought of it as managing their expectations. She had gone out with so many men who had simply assumed that she would sleep with them at the end of the night and who had reacted badly to a refusal. But her body was the one element in her world that Lucy had always felt was truly hers and until she finally met someone who could make her want him enough to move beyond that she had no intention of sharing her body with anyone. She genuinely hadn't expected Jax to be any different and she had slowly learned her mistake until saying no to Jax had become painful because she hadn't been able to control her own hunger.

'You're too defensive. Not every guy is out to nail you—'

'You mean you're *not*?' Lucy had exclaimed in surprise.

'I can see that trying to be smooth and seductive with you will be a huge challenge,' Jax had laughed, flashing her a highly amused smile.

And she had started falling for him that very night because that glorious charismatic smile of his had stopped her in her tracks and left her short of breath. She had met him the following night, sharing tapas and a couple of drinks with him in an upmarket bar. But sadly, she had dropped off to sleep in the middle of the conversation, bone tired from being on her feet serving all day. He had shaken her awake and taken her home without even attempting to kiss her, confiding that yawns weren't sexy. He had put his phone number in her phone while she slept and the next day he began texting her, first letting her know that he would be out of the country for a couple of days, then arranging to see her on her next free night.

A day later Kat Valtinos had shown up at the bar and cornered her. 'Jax is the ultimate playboy and you're the British equivalent of trailer trash—'

'Probably,' Lucy had conceded, looking back on her troubled poverty-stricken past.

'Obviously Jax will get bored fast and you look like the clingy sort.'

'I haven't had a chance to cling yet but I'm a quick learner. Does he like clingy women?' Lucy had asked, wide-eyed. 'Is he your boyfriend?'

'No, a very good friend,' Kat had declared. 'But you're wasting your time. I intend to marry him.'

'Tell that to him, not to me,' Lucy had advised and got back to work, ignoring the bitchy brunette until she'd finally stalked out in a snit at not being taken seriously.

The following morning, Lucy rose early after a sleepless night of wandering painfully through her mortifyingly fresh memories of being with Jax two years earlier. She watched her father and stepmother leave to attend the funeral. Over breakfast they had been too preoccupied with a sad and affectionate exchange of stories about their now deceased friend to notice how heavy-eyed and silent Lucy was.

But Lucy was also restless with anxiety and operating on pure adrenalin. Now that Jax knew about Bella she had to worry about how he would act on that information. She winced at the knowledge that Jax had power over her again. Certainly he had rights as a father that she could not deny. But would he choose to exercise those rights and seek an active parenting role?

Barely an hour later, Lucy received her first taste of Jax choosing to exercise his rights. A smartly dressed, fast-speaking lawyer arrived and asked her to agree to DNA testing and no sooner had she given consent, her face burning at the humiliating suspicion that Jax could doubt that he had fathered her child, than a lab technician arrived and took samples. That matter dealt with, the lawyer then settled a confidentiality agreement down in front of her. It seemed to be what Lucy had seen referred to as a 'gagging order' in the media and she refused to sign it, sticking to her guns when the older man persisted in his persuasions.

'Mr Antonakos does not like what I shall describe as private matters broadcast in the public domain. If you sign this document, it will form a secure basis for good relations between you in the future.'

'I can assure you that I have no intention of speaking to the press but I'm not prepared to sign anything that says I cannot talk about my own daughter,' she told him quietly.

By the time the older man departed, Lucy fully understood that he had been engaged in a potential damage-limitation plan. And Lucy was utterly unnerved by Jax acting to protect himself and the reputation of the Antonakos family even before he had definitive proof that her child was his. She was appalled that he could distrust her so much that he suspected that she might sell nasty stories about him to the newspapers.

In truth she did have a very low opinion of Jax but she had every intention of keeping that low opinion to herself for her daughter's sake. Whatever else Jax was, he was and always would be her daughter's father and she didn't want to do anything to damage that relationship. That meant, she registered with a sinking heart, that she would have to keep her personal feelings very much to herself. Airing her anger, resentment and bitterness would be destructive and the situation they were in where they shared a child but nothing else would be difficult enough to deal with.

An hour after the lawyer departed, Jax arrived and, for once, not in a limousine. He roared up outside on a motorbike and it was only as he doffed his helmet on the way to the front door that she realised it was him and not someone making a delivery. He was trying to be discreet, endeavouring to ensure that he wasn't recognised, she realised. When she had first met Jax in Spain he had only recently stepped into his late brother's role and as he had been relatively unknown there had been no paparazzi following him around then. Now that a kind of celebrity madness erupted around Jax's every public appearance she was grateful that he was being careful because she did not want to see her face or her daughter's appearing in articles full of embarrassing speculations.

Lucy opened the front door and stepped back. Jax strode in, bringing with him the scent of fresh air, leather and masculinity. In the narrow hall, he towered over her and she thrust the door quickly shut to walk into the spacious front room, which was sprinkled with colourful toys and baby equipment.

Jax slung his motorbike helmet down on a chair and raked impatient fingers through his black hair. 'Where is she?' he demanded.

'Bella's having a nap. I'll get her up in ten minutes. She wakes very early in the morning and then she gets tired again...' Realising that she was gabbling, Lucy flushed, insanely conscious of Jax's stare.

Lucy sported cropped jeans, a pink tee shirt and bare feet. She looked very young and cute and definitely hadn't dressed up for his benefit. Jax was irritated that she had not made the effort. He hadn't slept much the night before. The cold shower hadn't worked any miracle and that sexual tension piled on top of the shocking announcement Lucy had made had done nothing to help. When he had a problem Jax liked a plan to work towards, a plan with firm boundaries. Unhappily there was no convenient plan available to tell him how a man behaved when he discovered he was a father even though he had never wanted that particular joy. But he *had* been reckless with Lucy in the birth-control department and in retrospect he could not forgive or excuse himself for that lack of responsibility. Of course, he reminded himself wryly, the kid might not be his, in which case he was dealing with nothing more than a storm in a teacup.

'Stop staring at me,' Lucy told him, cheeks burning from the intensity of his scrutiny.

'Of course I'm staring. You dropped a bomb on me last night. I'm still reeling,' Jax breathed in a raw undertone, green eyes glittering warily below curling ebony lashes.

'Well, I've been mentally reeling from the minute I discovered I was pregnant,' Lucy confided truthfully. 'With time you get used to the idea. I couldn't bear to imagine life without Bella now.'

Jax scanned the youthful glow of her unblemished

skin and the luxuriant tumble of strawberry-blonde ringlets that merely highlighted her bright blue eyes. He acknowledged her beauty for there was no denying what was right in front of him. As his body began to react he clenched his teeth together hard and wandered back towards the front door, determined not to let his libido take over when there would soon be a child in the room.

'Coffee?' Lucy pressed as the awkward silence stretched when he reappeared in the doorway.

'This is not a social visit,' Jax answered.

A cry sounded out somewhere above them and Lucy scurried upstairs, her face flushed by his deflating statement.

Jax plonked himself down on a sofa and struggled to relax but it had been more years than he cared to recall since he had been around a baby. He was godfather to several but his role had never been hands-on, nor would it ever have been more because nobody expected a single man, who was also erroneously known as his actress mother's only child, to be comfortable dealing with young children. Ironically Jax had learned the daily routine of how to look after a baby when he was only twelve years old. It had been the end of the summer before his mother had finally engaged a nanny because Jax was returning to boarding school.

He heard the creak of the stairs and vaulted upright. As he straightened his shoulders Lucy walked into the lounge and he immediately saw the child in her arms. He froze into a statue in the same moment that he saw the little girl's black curly hair and the green eyes. That fast, that dramatically, Jax knew he didn't need a DNA test to prove to anyone that the little girl was his. Lucy's child was the living image of his kid sister, Tina, and that uncanny resemblance hit him like an avalanche. His mother had had very strong genes, he reckoned ruefully, for both he and the little sister who had died as a toddler had looked far more like Mariana than the men who had fathered her two children. He knew too that his striking likeness to his mother had only been another nail in his coffin as far as his oversensitive father was concerned.

'This is Bella…' Lucy framed, kneeling down to settle the little girl gently on the floor.

A thumb planted in her rosebud mouth, Bella studied Jax fixedly, her green eyes full of curiosity.

Jax bent down and lifted a toy that broke straight into a catchy tune as soon as he pressed the right button. Bella grinned and came closer, steadying herself on one powerful thigh with a clutching little hand.

'She's not scared,' Jax remarked, marvelling that he could still speak normally after being plunged without warning into some of his darkest memories. The remnants of that guilt, anger and pain still resonated powerfully with him.

'No, she's quite confident and she likes men. My father makes a fuss of her and spoils her. I suppose we all spoil her a bit,' Lucy conceded, staring at the little tableau of Jax and his daughter as they each assessed the other. 'She looks very like you—'

Jax skated a teasing forefinger off Bella's determined little chin and swallowed thickly, struggling to master his almost overwhelming emotions. He should not cloud his first meeting with his daughter with such tragic memories, he censured himself fiercely. The past was the past and it would be wiser to leave the sad little ghost of Tina safely buried there.

'What is it?' Lucy prompted, troubled by the feverish glitter of Jax's stunning eyes, their brilliance enhanced by the surround of spiky black lashes. 'What's wrong?'

'Nothing,' Jax insisted, his wide sensual mouth slashing into a sudden forced smile, for he had shared far too much private stuff with Lucy in the past and he had no plans to make himself vulnerable in that way again 'But when she was born you should have moved heaven and earth to ensure that I knew I was a father.'

Unprepared for that criticism when she had tried every way she knew how to contact him, Lucy stiffened. 'That's not fair—'

'What isn't fair,' Jax fielded as he accepted the little plastic doll that Bella brought him, 'is that this little girl and I weren't able to be in each other's lives from the start.'

Lucy's bright blue eyes hardened. 'As you said though, when you dumped me, you didn't want me making a *nuisance* of myself,' she reminded him thinly. 'If you didn't want to hear from me ever again, how was I supposed to tell you?'

Not trusting himself to speak in the mood he was in, Jax shrugged a muscular shoulder in brooding silence.

'Didn't think you'd have an answer for that,' Lucy sniped, leaning down to clasp Bella's hand and guide her into the kitchen where she set about filling a toddler cup with milk.

Bella pushed against the back door, keen to get out onto the patio and play. Lucy opened it and watched her daughter toddle out into the sunlight to retrieve the little plastic pram she loved.

His child, *his* daughter, a new generation in the Antonakos family, Jax acknowledged, watching Bella swig her milk and then set down the cup with exaggerated care before pushing the little pram out onto the small lawn. Somehow, he didn't know how, he didn't care, Lucy *should* have contacted him, he thought angrily.

'I have missed out on over a year of my daughter's life,' Jax intoned grimly. 'That is not acceptable—'

Under sudden attack, Lucy spun. 'No, what was unacceptable back then was the way you treated me!' she condemned with spirit.

Jax thought about the contents of the investigative file he had been given. He saw no point in throwing the contents of that file in Lucy's face now. Likewise her little session in that alleyway. His reaction had been all too human. He had let his anger and aggression take over and dictate his moves. 'I'm afraid it never occurred to me that you could be pregnant,' he admitted in a harsh undertone. 'I should've acknowledged that possibility and made provision for it but I didn't. That was a serious oversight on my part.'

A little of the tension in Lucy's slender shoulders eased. 'Yes, it was.'

'Then let us not waste time stating the obvious and rehashing a past we both prefer to forget,' Jax countered impatiently.

'We can't forget it when Bella was born from it,' Lucy argued helplessly. 'We may not like each other but we'll just have to live with that. I'll make coffee, and not because this is a social occasion but because we need to learn how to act civilised.'

As Lucy left the doorway to switch on the kettle Jax strode out onto the patio, unable to let his newly discovered daughter out of his sight and reach. It crossed his mind that he had no intention of living with his distaste of Lucy and forging a civilised alliance with her as a co-parent. With what he knew about her past, he didn't, *couldn't* possibly trust her to be a caring decent mother. Bella's well-being came first and nobody would ever persuade him that his child could be safe with a mother who had once dealt in drugs and sold her body. It didn't matter that to all intents and purposes Lucy appeared to have turned over a new leaf.

Jax, after all, was the son of a drug addict. He had heard too many promises, seen all too many fresh starts *and* witnessed the subsequent falls from grace. Bella would always be at risk of harm if she remained with her mother, he decided cynically. He would have to fight Lucy through the courts for custody of their daughter. He was sure that she loved Bella to the best of her ability but with her fatal weakness for substance abuse he couldn't trust her to always put their daughter's needs first.

'Are we capable of behaving like friends?' Lucy asked Jax hopefully as she hovered in the doorway.

Jax glanced at her in astonishment, questioning how she contrived to still look so young and innocent in spite of her misspent past. Friends? Never, he conceded wryly. And once Lucy received the first official communication from the Antonakos legal team and realised what he planned to do friendship would be the last thing on her mind. But what other choice did he have?

'You have to stop blaming me for everything that's gone wrong,' Lucy told him squarely. 'In any relationship it takes two people to screw up. Remember that...'

As she spoke Bella fell flat on her face on the lawn and let out a yell, followed by frantic sobbing. Jax strode across a flower bed and snatched the little girl up into his arms, speaking softly to her, smoothing a lean brown hand gently over her shaking back to soothe her before getting down on his knees to show her something on the ground in the clear hope of distracting her from the fright she had sustained. Lucy stared at that seemingly effortless display of child management in sheer amazement, involuntarily impressed.

'Jax...' she muttered in a daze.

Once Bella was restored to calm again, Jax set her down. His lean, strong face taut, he glanced at Lucy, noting how the sunshine lit up the shades of red in her hair and illuminated her perfect skin. Lucy bent to pick up the pram and the shapely curve of her heart-shaped derriere pulled tight below the cropped jeans she wore. Jax remembered ripping her jeans off her, desperate to sink into the damp, welcoming heat of her, and fierce tension gripped him as he suppressed the hunger flaring through him like a dangerous burning brand. 'In a couple of days I'd like to take Bella out. I'll bring a nanny with me if that keeps you happy.'

'I assumed you would be waiting for the DNA results before you did anything official,' Lucy parried, thoroughly disconcerted by his request as she walked back to him.

'The DNA tests will only confirm what I already know,' Jax murmured. 'Are you going to make me fight for access to her?'

Lucy winced and set her teeth together. If in doubt, weigh in with the threats. That was Jax. He could afford the very best lawyers. Ultimately he would be entitled to time with his daughter whatever she did or said and trying to ignore that reality would be foolish. In any case, didn't she want Bella to have a father? Yes, she did, but she hadn't expected to have to share her time with her daughter quite so immediately.

'No, but I wouldn't want her away from me for more than a couple of hours at a time,' she admitted. 'She's still very young.'

'I can agree to that,' Jax traded. 'Give me your phone number and I'll be in touch.'

Bella cuddled to her, Lucy watched Jax swing back onto the motorbike, the lithe powerful lines of his big muscular body moulded by his designer jeans and leather jacket. Across the road a car started up and pulled out to follow him, his security team, she assumed.

When her father and stepmother returned from the funeral, Lucy sat them down and finally told them the truth.

Straight away her father erupted like a raging volcano. '*Jax Antonakos?* Are you serious?'

'Please don't get mad,' Lucy pleaded. 'It will only make this situation worse.'

'You were only nineteen, Lucy,' her father protested with pained condemnation. 'He must be nearly ten years older than you!'

'Well, he can't be blamed for that. When he said I had

to be over twenty-one to spend time with him I lied,' she admitted ruefully. 'I said I was twenty-three—'

'You *lied* to him?' Kreon repeated censoriously.

'Calm down, Kreon,' Iola interposed gently. 'She was a typical teenager and when a handsome young man approached her, she pretended to be older and more sophisticated than she was. A lot of girls that age would have done the same thing.'

'Yes,' Lucy admitted, her cheeks burning.

Iola dragged the rest of the story of those six weeks in Spain from Lucy while Kreon sat fuming, his anger unhidden. 'I knew his father, you know,' he told them abruptly. 'And he was a selfish, arrogant thug of a man too.'

'Jax's father? You *knew* him? *How?*' Lucy asked, astonished by that admission.

'My parents worked for the family of Heracles Antonakos's first wife, Sofia, in London. Sofia and I grew up together and we never lost that friendship even though she lived in a very different world. She was only thirty when she died,' Kreon revealed gruffly.

'I'm really sorry I didn't tell you the truth from the start,' Lucy confessed. 'I didn't want to upset you—'

'Never you mind about me being upset,' Kreon told her through compressed lips. 'Be grateful I'm here to support you. Antonakos sending in the lawyers straight off is your first warning of his plans—'

'What do you mean?' Iola interjected worriedly.

'Well, was what happened this morning a nice or considerate thing to do to the mother of your child? Demanding DNA testing? Trying to browbeat Lucy into signing a confidentiality agreement? As a first warning shot, it tells us all we need to know...'

'Jax is trying to protect himself. I can't blame him for that,' Lucy muttered ruefully, troubled by her father's angry gravity and all too conscious that she was the cause of the lines of stress that had appeared on his weathered face.

'He can protect himself all he likes but not at your expense or Bella's,' Kreon replied.

Lucy was anxious and preoccupied when she went into work that evening and she struggled to remember the drinks orders and deliver them back to the correct tables. Her father's genuine fear of what Jax might be planning had seriously scared her. Not for the first time she wished she had the ability to get inside Jax's head.

Earlier that day he had been strangely distant with her but very different in his wholehearted response to Bella. In retrospect it was hard to credit that he had been kissing her, *touching* her only the night before. Of course, that made sense, she told herself squarely. Everything had changed the minute she'd told Jax about their daughter. She recalled his glacier cool when she had first told him at his house and barely restrained a shiver of apprehension. Her father's concern had set off all her internal alarms and had left her on the edge of panic and thinking thoughts she had believed she would never think again...

What if she simply upped sticks and vanished? She had done it before and she could do it again. But it would be wrong, her inner voice warned her sternly. It would be wrong not to give Jax the opportunity to form a relationship with his daughter. It would be equally wrong for Lucy to run away from the life her father and stepmother had generously offered her. Running away from her problems would be the childish thing to do and she wasn't a child any more...

CHAPTER FIVE

'So, you are Lucy's father,' Jax commented, lounging back against his office desk with lethal cool, not a shade of what he was thinking revealed by his lean, darkly handsome features. 'Where were you all the years Lucy was growing up in the care system?'

Kreon straightened his shoulders. 'That's my business and Lucy's. She's welcome to tell you if she wants. But I'm here now to protect the welfare of my daughter and my granddaughter.'

'I don't understand how you plan to do that,' Jax remarked.

'Oh, that's very simple,' Kreon told him almost cheerfully. 'I have access to secrets that your father would kill to keep out of the newspapers—'

Taken aback, Jax laughed. 'My father fears nothing. Is this some sort of clumsy blackmail attempt? I advise you to back off now before I call the police.'

'That will be your decision but it won't stop me sharing your family secrets with the press. In fact having me arrested will only add legitimacy to my claims,' Kreon pointed out calmly. 'Your father hates me. I will tell you that for free. But why do you think he leaves me alone? He is afraid of what I might know.'

'You're talking a lot of nonsense and I don't intend to listen to it,' Jax told him, crossing the room to open the door and hasten the older man's departure.

'Your brother, Argo, wasn't your brother because he wasn't your father's child,' Kreon delivered very softly. 'I think Heracles only found that out *after* your brother died and, believe me, he does not want that humiliating truth spread across the newspapers.'

Jax froze, shock washing over him in an almost physical attack that pulled his every muscle taut to breaking point. In a driven movement he thrust the door shut again and swung violently round.

'What do you want?' he demanded of the smaller man, refusing to think of what he had just been told, refusing to join the dots and acknowledge how well that revelation would dovetail with his own quite recent miraculous change of status within the Antonakos family.

'In return for my continuing silence, I want you to marry Lucy.'

Jax stared back at him in savage disbelief. '*Marry...* her?'

'She was a teenager when you wrecked her life. You owe her the security of a wedding ring. It doesn't have to be a life sentence for either of you. But it would give her and Bella the safe harbour and the recognition they need to have a better life—'

'She *wasn't* a teenager!' Jax raked back at him in furious rebuttal.

'Lucy was twenty-one last month. We celebrated with dinner at that hotel where she works.' Kreon shot him a sourly amused appraisal. 'My wife tells me that teenaged girls do lie about their age occasionally.'

'Twenty-one,' Jax repeated thickly, fighting to master the violent anger lashing through him and a powerful urge to strangle Lucy for having dared to lie to him. 'I would require proof of those allegations about my brother, Argo.'

And from an inside pocket Kreon produced a handwritten letter which he handed to Jax. It had been written and sent to Kreon when his father's first wife, Sofia, was terminally ill. Unable to face death with such a weight on her conscience, Sofia had admitted the affair that had led to Argo's conception, although she had not named her lover.

'Why didn't you come forward with this at the time of her death?' Jax demanded harshly a few minutes later. 'With this letter, you were in possession of facts that were unknown to everyone else involved.'

'Sofia couldn't have thought through what she was doing. Your father had just lost his wife and Argo had lost his mother and her letter would have destroyed them both. Back then Heracles had no idea that Argo wasn't his son. What do you think he would have done?' Kreon grimaced. 'He would've disinherited the boy and cast him off.'

Jax stared at the wall, knowing that there was a fair chance his father would have reacted like that in the first heat of his fury. Once Sofia had let that genie out of the bottle there would have been no putting it back.

'I didn't want that responsibility. I'm not a cruel man. It was a secret that shouldn't have been told. I never liked your father and he was a lousy absentee husband but, fond as I was of Sofia, once she was gone I preferred to mind my own business...that is, until an Antonakos threatened the security of my own flesh and blood.'

Long after Kreon had gone, Jax studied the copy of the letter the older man had allowed him to keep. He was still shaken even though the woman had died long before he was born. The contents of that letter would distress his father, although, like Kreon, Jax was inclined to believe that somewhere around the time of Argo's death his father had found out that his eldest son was not actually his son. That would better explain why Heracles had found it possible to move on so fast from that loss and adjust his attitude to Jax almost overnight.

That new knowledge and understanding just about ripped Jax apart, not to mention his view of his family. He had looked up to the big brother he had never really got to know very well and he loved his father. And why *did* he love Heracles, who had proved to be a useless parent when Jax was young and in need of a father? Ultimately, he had recognised that the older man deeply regretted allowing his dented ego and workaholic ways to triumph over the ties of blood. Heracles was hopeless when it came to expressing emotion though and Jax had realised that he suffered from the same flaw. His father had stumbled on blindly after Mariana's infidelity had made him a laughing stock in the media, protecting himself as best he could by avoiding his ex-wife…and unhappily that avoidance had included Jax.

Jax hadn't really thought about how he actually felt about Heracles until that moment, but when he thought of his father being forced to see the tragedy of his first marriage spread across the newspapers he knew he couldn't allow that to happen. Sofia had died after a long drawn-out fight against breast cancer. Heracles was domineering and manipulative and interfering but he had once adored his first wife and the son he had believed to be his.

Jax's first act was to summon Zenas and tell his security chief that he wanted an in-depth private investigation carried out on Kreon Thiarkis and his daughter, Lucy. How the hell had something as basic as Lucy's age been wrong in that file? Her parentage had been incorrectly recorded as well. Lucy *did* have a Greek father. What else could also be wrong? He needed the background and facts he could rely on. He also needed to check out Kreon's ties to his father's first wife, Sofia. And to his father. After all, it was *his* father who had sent that file to him.

Jax began to mull over the other things he had learned. Lucy was still only twenty-one years old? And had been only nineteen when they had first met? Memories swirled in a colourful haze in Jax's head and he marvelled that he had not recognised Lucy's immaturity for what it was. She had been impulsive, outspoken, naïve and unnervingly ignorant about facts he took for granted and a sneaky little unrepentant liar...*obviously*.

And no way was he prepared to marry her! Kreon could not blackmail him into doing what he had never wanted to do, he assured himself stubbornly. On the other hand, Jax also knew he could not stand back and watch his father endure the scandal that would blow up if Kreon went to the press to sell his story. People would enjoy reading about the skeletons hidden in the Antonakos cupboard and his father would lose his dignity. At the age of seventy, Heracles deserved to keep his dignity, Jax decided heavily. He might have been a lousy husband in Kreon's eyes but he had surely not deserved the tragic conclusion to his first marriage. Knowing how badly Heracles had reacted to his own mother's infidelity, Jax could hardly begin to imagine what his father must have felt once he realised that Argo was not his child. Surely Heracles had suffered enough for being a less than stellar husband? How dared Kreon Thiarkis threaten him?

Yet even in the grip of that seething Antonakos rage, Jax could still not stop planning. He knew that it was up to him to control the situation. He reached the stage of listing pros and cons. Were he to marry Lucy, he would get her back into his bed. A sliver of raw anticipation raked through Jax's tense, angry body and he recognised that that was a fringe benefit that he would very much enjoy. At the same time he would also gain a stronger legal right to his daughter and he would not have to fight to gain access to her.

Nevertheless, Jax hated being told what to do and Kreon Thiarkis had just thrown a double whammy at him that came attached to a very high price tag. Primarily he was in a rage because he knew that Kreon had given him a choice but it was the hateful choice of picking between the lesser of two evils: marriage or his aging father's public humiliation. He could tell Kreon to do his worst and then stand by and watch his father get hurt. Unfortunately, family loyalty and a very real affection for his inadequate father warred against that option. But the alternative was to surrender his freedom.

No more hot and cold running women, no more

sexually self-indulgent variety in the bedroom. But then that wasn't quite true, Jax allowed with a sudden strong sense of relief. Even Kreon didn't expect him to stay married to Lucy for ever. Kreon was expecting an eventual divorce, which would still leave Lucy and Bella respectfully acknowledged as members of the Antonakos family and financially secure. *Thee mou*...he could do marriage on a short-term, strictly temporary basis, particularly with Lucy playing the starring role in his bed every night. Furthermore, Bella would have his name and the safeguard of his presence in her daily life. But just how was he expected to cope with a father-in-law he wanted to strike down and kill in cold blood?

As an Antonakos, Jax had little experience of being threatened. He was too rich, too powerful to cross and his father had long enjoyed the same protection. But Kreon was in legal possession of very private and personal information that went right to the heart of Jax's family, the kind of secret nobody wanted exposed and picked over in public. Even worse, one revelation would almost inevitably lead to others. What might be dug up about his own mother? Jax shuddered at the prospect of Mariana's drug-addicted frailties and Tina's death being dragged out into the punishing light of day. At that point it struck him that a wedding ring was a worthwhile sacrifice if it bought peace and left the family's dirty laundry untouched.

Lucy studied the text from Jax with wide incredulous eyes. He had asked her when she finished work.

I'll pick you up when you finish and we'll talk.

Jax? *Talk?* Jax had been known to leave the room or remember a pressing engagement when any form of serious discussion was threatened. Jax didn't believe in talking about stuff. He thought in private and then he acted to fix a problem. He didn't share the reasoning that led to the decision. He believed that talking only heightened the wrong emotions, encouraged divisive stances and made issues seem worse than they were. When she had once tried to talk to him about where their affair was heading he had become angry and he had walked away. Naturally he had, she conceded, because he had known their affair was going nowhere.

But obviously he had to talk to her about Bella, she reasoned ruefully. Even he couldn't make unilateral decisions about the daughter they now had to share. He would want to make arrangements to see Bella again, he would want to ask questions about what the little girl liked and didn't like. That he was prepared to talk was a healthy sign, Lucy told herself heavily, striving to muster some enthusiasm about the idea of sharing her daughter with her father.

Before she even went into work, her own father had lectured her, urging her not to do to Bella what had been done to her. She had grown up without a father because her mother had selfishly chosen not to tell Kreon he had a daughter. Now, quite unnecessarily, Kreon was advising Lucy to take a long-term view and keep her anger and resentment out of the situation.

'I know it's a big ask,' Kreon had conceded, 'but you have to deal with what's happening now and handle it sensibly. Try to concentrate on what's best for Bella.'

Her father's outlook had surprised Lucy because he

seemed to have come to terms with what she had told him about Jax very quickly and had now taken a more detached view of events. Unfortunately everything still felt painfully personal to Lucy. Jax had rejected her but he had *not* rejected their daughter. She knew she shouldn't be thinking that way but she couldn't help it because she was only human.

A car picked her up from the hotel. It wasn't a limo and Jax wasn't in it but she recognised Jax's security guards. She climbed in, smoothed down her denim skirt and worried at her lower lip with the edge of her teeth. She was wondering what Jax wanted while telling herself to keep her temper and her daughter's emotional and physical well-being at the forefront of her mind regardless of what he might say.

Jax had plans as well. He would not confront Lucy about anything until they were safely married. Hopefully by then he would also know how accurate that file he had actually was. But he was also well aware of how deceptive Lucy could be, he reminded himself grimly, thinking of the familiar flash of that red dress below the street lights as she'd walked down that alleyway to have sex with another man. Lucy wasn't the faithful type. Two of his father's three wives had betrayed him with other men and Jax's own mother had never been faithful to anyone. Surrounded from childhood by broken, dishonest relationships, Jax had always tried to avoid emotional involvement and commitment. But when his daughter came into the equation he discovered that he badly wanted to give Bella the storybook family he had never had. Something better, something happier, something lasting...

Lucy walked dry-mouthed and nervous into the

house with the confusing mirrored hall. The elegant drawing room looked more welcoming than it had on her last visit with only a couple of lamps lit to leave the rest of the very large room shrouded in shadow. When Jax stepped out of the shadows, she flinched and stilled on the threshold.

'I ordered supper for you.' Jax indicated the table spread with a selection of snacks.

Jax wore jeans and an open-necked shirt. He shouldn't have taken her breath away in such ordinary garments but he did. The jeans clung to his narrow hips and outlined his long, powerful thighs. The pale shirt accentuated his bronzed skin tone and the blue black of his hair. She sucked in a breath in the tense silence and clashed with shimmering green eyes fringed by black and her heart hammered out a drumbeat inside her.

'Supper,' she repeated, that being the last thing she had expected from him, but she stepped fully into the room to head for the table, grateful to have something other than Jax to focus on.

'Help yourself,' he advised.

Settling down on a sofa, Lucy needed no further encouragement because she was always hungry after work and she was involuntarily impressed that he had remembered that little fact. She filled a plate and poured a cup of tea. 'This is what I call civilised,' she admitted with a wry smile.

'I thought it would be,' Jax said. 'Were you working in that outfit?'

Lucy smoothed a self-conscious hand over her comfy skirt with which she had teamed a black tee shirt. 'Yes…'

Jax gritted his teeth. A tripwire stood in front of

him but he neatly avoided it by refusing to give way to his inner caveman. The short skirt showed off her surprisingly long and very shapely legs and the tee shirt shaped her pert breasts to perfection. Once upon a time he had objected to her wearing the sort of clothing that revealed her body and that had set off heated arguments. Now he was respecting boundaries to preserve the peace. He sank down onto the sofa opposite her while mentally trying to come up with garments that would still be fashionable but which would miraculously shield that glorious body from the visual attention of other men. And he finally registered that there were no such garments on the market. Lucy had always outshone her clothing. From her bright tumbling hair to her luminous skin and radiant blue eyes, Lucy glowed with sheer energy, attracting attention even in a crowded room.

'It's not a short skirt,' Lucy remarked, knowing his flaws.

'No, it's not,' Jax agreed, wishing she hadn't directed his attention to her pale slender thighs and knees because it only made him think about the sheer glory of parting them. Furiously conscious of his growing desire, Jax rocked forward, his lean, strong face taut, green eyes semi screened by his lashes.

'You said you wanted to talk.' Lucy widened her eyes suspiciously. 'Was that a joke?'

'No...' Silence fell while Lucy munched through her third sandwich. 'We have a dilemma and I have come up with a solution,' he spelled out in a roughened undertone as the tip of her tongue chased a crumb from the corner of her mouth.

'Bella isn't a dilemma. She isn't and never will be a

problem,' Lucy assured him quietly. 'I'm not going to be difficult about you seeing her or anything like that.'

Jax breathed in deep, striving to make himself get to the point and bite the bullet. 'If we married, we would be in a position to give Bella far more.'

Lucy put down her sandwich unfinished. *'Married?'* she repeated in consternation. 'But you don't ever want to get married.'

'I didn't plan to have a child either,' Jax reminded her. 'But Bella is here now and that changes the whole picture. I want to give her what I didn't have. A mother, a father and a settled home, all the security that only a traditional family structure can give her.'

Lucy was stunned because she had never dreamt that she would live to hear Jax admit a desire to embrace such conventional ideas. 'Neither of us had that,' she conceded unevenly. 'But life isn't perfect and that's the way it is—'

'But we *can* change that,' Jax sliced in forcefully. 'We don't have to live apart when we could raise Bella together, as a married couple.'

Lucy blinked rapidly, her heart in her mouth, her feet flexing because nervous tension made her want to get up and walk round the room. 'Together?' she repeated in bewilderment.

'We can get married and make a home for our daughter, the kind of home neither of us had the advantage of growing up in,' Jax extended with unearthly calm.

'I don't know much about your background. Well, I know your parents divorced when you were young but—'

Jax stiffened. 'You already know that my mother

was unstable and not a reliable parent. Men came and went in her life. None of them ever stayed. She was too high maintenance. I don't want our daughter to have to adapt to that kind of lifestyle.'

'With respect,' Lucy said uncomfortably, 'I'm not a world-famous, gorgeous actress and I don't think my lifestyle and your mother's would have anything in common.'

Jax released his breath in a small hiss of frustration. 'Do you really believe that your life is going to stay the same now that I know you are raising my daughter?' he pressed in disbelief. 'Do you honestly believe that you can go on working as a waitress and living with your father? Obviously I will take care of all your expenses now—'

'No,' Lucy broke in with a frown. 'I don't want that.'

'But that's what will happen whether you like it or not. Naturally I want my daughter to enjoy the same lifestyle that I enjoy myself and I can't believe that you would deny her what she is entitled to receive. Bella is an Antonakos,' Jax reminded her with pride.

'Yes but...' Lucy's voice ran out of steam as she began to think about everything he had said.

He was asking her to marry him. Jax Antonakos was asking *her* to marry him, offering her the dream conclusion she had once secretly cherished and then buried deep two years earlier. For the space of several frantic minutes Lucy could only stare down into her tea and struggle to come to terms with a proposal she had never expected to receive. A home, two parents and a real family for Bella. That truly was the ultimate ideal for Lucy when it came to her daughter. Her mother had ended up alone raising Lucy and Lucy had ended up alone in the care system because the authorities had failed to trace Kreon. Sometimes she hated herself for making the same mistake with Bella and having to bring her up without a father.

'Are you serious about this?' Lucy asked breathlessly.

'Of course,' Jax asserted levelly.

'But you *never* wanted to get married,' Lucy reminded him helplessly.

'And then Bella came along and turned everything upside down,' Jax confessed with complete honesty. 'This is no longer only about you and me. We have to think about our daughter and about what would make *her* happy.'

'Unhappily married parents wouldn't help,' Lucy pointed out apologetically.

'I see no reason why we shouldn't make a go of it. Even sitting here having a serious conversation I can barely keep my hands off you,' Jax admitted bluntly, his stunning green gaze glittering across her heart-shaped face and watching the flush of awareness slowly build there. 'And if you're honest, it's the same for you.'

Lucy dragged her attention from his sleek, darkly beautiful features with the greatest difficulty. But trying to blank her mind, trying not to look at him was no use when the hunger inside her felt like an insidious virus that refused to die. And she knew what the cure was and that unnerved her. The only cure she knew was the wild, pounding plunge of his body into hers and the explosive release he would give her. And even that wasn't a permanent fix, she thought shamefacedly. She had once craved him as she craved air to breathe. She set her tea down with a jarring crack on the coffee table, her hand trembling.

'Look at me,' Jax urged, breaking the smouldering silence.

And Lucy looked even though she knew she shouldn't, desire clawing at her insides, awakening the yearning buried deep within her body. A ragged breath escaped her, her pulses racing. Her breasts ached but the biggest ache of all was between her legs, at the very heart of her where she was burning with need. That voracious need that hungered for his touch terrified her because it was so ready to rage out of control and sweep all restraint and all common sense before it.

'We're getting married as soon as it can be arranged,' Jax decreed.

Her head flew up. 'You can't just—'

'One of us needs to be decisive. You want to bury your head in the sand and run away from the responsibility.'

'No, I don't.'

'We do it for Bella. Together we make a family,' Jax intoned.

'It's not that simple.'

'Nothing worth having is ever easily acquired,' Jax said drily. 'Everything worthwhile I have ever achieved has come at a cost and there have always been sacrifices involved. Are you willing to make sacrifices for Bella's benefit?'

Lucy leapt upright in frustration. 'Jax! Stop trying to railroad me!'

'In a couple of days the paparazzi will be on to us. I want to pre-empt them with a wedding, a big splashy wedding, which they won't be expecting,' he told her grimly. 'They'll be happy enough to settle for wedding photos.'

'Do you really *want* to do this?' Lucy whispered shakily.

'I want you. I want my daughter. To give her what we both want, to give her what she *deserves*, we have to get married,' Jax countered with measured cool. 'I can handle that. Can you?'

And Lucy thought about that, really seriously thought about that even though her brain did not feel up to that challenge. Even when she had dreamt about marrying Jax two years earlier she had known it was only a dream because Jax had seen too many relationships break down to have any faith in the marriage bond. He had admitted that to her in Spain and afterwards he had seemed unnerved by what he had told her and he had cut their evening short.

'We will fight,' Jax forecast. 'But we're good at making up again.'

Lucy flushed and nodded jerkily and he laughed huskily for they had always ended up in bed after arguments, taking refuge in the sexual unity that bridged their differences.

'And if you don't want to give up work after we're married I'll make a special arrangement for you,' Jax murmured lazily. 'I'll buy a bar and I will be the *only* customer and you can serve me to your heart's content.'

'You say the craziest things,' Lucy muttered, shaking her head while locked to the stunning green eyes gleaming below his black lashes.

'I will say whatever I have to say to get that ring

on your finger,' Jax admitted truthfully. 'The world's your oyster tonight, *koukla mou*.'

But Jax was no perfect pearl for her to acquire, she thought helplessly. Jax was complicated and reserved and unpredictable. Living with Jax would not be easy; it would be a roller coaster of highs and lows. Yet didn't she want to take the chance? It was a chance she had never thought she would have. Yes, Jax had treated her badly in the past but marriage was an equal partnership and this time around she wouldn't have to surrender her independence or her self-respect because money wouldn't be an issue. Giving her daughter the secure and loving childhood she had not had herself would mean so much to her. How could she refuse that offer?

'I'll marry you,' Lucy breathed tautly. 'But you'd better not make me regret it.'

Thinking of the secrets he had withheld and the complete honesty that he would eventually have to practise, Jax breathed in deep. He had given way to blackmail to protect his family but in marrying, he acknowledged grimly, he would be protecting his new family from potential harm as well.

'I should be honest,' Lucy murmured, her blue eyes awash with regret and apology. 'I don't trust you.'

Jax, who had learned never to trust anyone, particularly one's nearest and dearest, almost laughed out loud. Lucy would flourish like a tropical flower in the Antonakos family.

CHAPTER SIX

EVEN A FEW days before the wedding Lucy still couldn't quite accept that she was getting married. She was very tense and stressed. Jax had insisted on picking up the bill for the hundreds of guests invited and her father had been dismayed to discover that he was only allowed to cover his daughter's more personal expenses. In the same way Jax had organised the church and the venue for the reception.

And he had done all of that from a safe distance, leaving Lucy to handle her father's hurt pride and angry complaints. Jax, after all, was the man who had never planned to marry and since the moment Lucy had agreed to marry him Jax had come no closer to the centre of bridal activity than a phone call because he had hired a wedding planner to take care of everything. Lucy had had the freedom to make her own choices but had relied heavily on the planner's advice because she knew nothing about high-society weddings. Her brain was still stuffed, however, with the turmoil of selecting flowers, colour schemes and table arrangements from frighteningly long lists of options and having to discuss every possibility.

Iola had gone shopping with Lucy for a dress and

Jax had been allowed no input there. Lucy had gone for lace and a fancy pleated train that would be removable if she was dancing and she had picked the sweetest little outfit for Bella.

It was ironic that Jax had pretty much vanished as soon as she'd accepted his proposal and that had really annoyed Lucy. He had said that he had too much work to get through and he had only visited the house once when she had insisted he come and meet her father and her stepmother. That had been a very awkward hour of stilted conversation, she recalled ruefully. Jax had been very cool and polite and her father had been stiff and formal. Iola and Lucy's efforts to lighten the atmosphere had made little difference. It had been painfully obvious to Lucy that her father and her bridegroom didn't much like the look of each other.

And then there was the troubling question of her future father-in-law, Heracles Antonakos.

Lucy had assumed that Jax's father would want to meet her in advance but apparently not, and Jax did not seem to know whether or not his father would attend their wedding, an admission that had made her wince. Obviously, Heracles Antonakos was not impressed by his son's decision to marry a waitress and he wanted nothing to do with the event. But Jax refused to be drawn on the sensitive subject and had urged her to be patient.

'It's a delivery…for you,' Iola called up the stairs to Lucy.

Lucy clattered downstairs and signed for the package she was given, turning it over and back before walking into the kitchen to open it. She extracted a letter and a small jewellery box and frowned.

'Is it a wedding present?' Iola asked.

'No...it's from some woman called Polly, who *says* she's one of my sisters,' Lucy whispered in deep shock, reading the closely typed lines to learn that her mother had only passed away a few years before at a hospice and commenting on the fact to Iola.

'I always assumed that Mum had died when I was a child...possibly during the three years I was adopted because of course I wouldn't have been told about it then,' Lucy confided. 'But according to my sisters they too only found out about her death afterwards because she didn't want to see any of us while she was so ill. But she left us all rings given to her by our fathers...and it was only then that my sisters found out that I existed.'

'Strange,' Iola commented. 'But if she was very ill, possibly she wasn't thinking very clearly. Is there a ring in that box?'

Lucy opened the box and extracted a small ruby ring with a smile. 'It's very pretty. I'll wear it when I get married. It's wonderful to have something that my mother actually wore,' she murmured with a sad look in her eyes.

'Read the rest of the letter,' her stepmother urged. 'Tell me about your sisters.'

Unfortunately Polly didn't offer much information beyond the fact that she was married and had children just like Lucy's other sister, Ellie, who was a doctor. What she did say was that she and Ellie very much wanted to meet Lucy and get to know her.

'She couldn't have chosen a worse time to contact me,' Lucy mumbled, settling down to read the letter again. 'She hasn't given me an address or anything but she has given me a phone number, which I could use to talk to her.'

'You could invite your sisters to your wedding,' Iola suggested.

Lucy grimaced. 'No. I don't know them and I don't think Polly knows I'm a mother as well either. It would all be too awkward for a first meeting and in any case they would need more warning than a few days to attend. I'll call her as soon as we get back from our honeymoon. But my goodness, this is exciting,' she muttered abstractedly. 'I wonder what Polly and Ellie are like. Do I look like them? Do you think they have the same father?'

Kreon walked in and Lucy handed him the letter straight away to read. He stared down at the ring on the table and then he lifted it. 'I gave this to Annabel as an engagement ring. It's not a real ruby, you know, but it looks well. It was all I could afford at the time—'

Lucy laughed and removed it from his hand. 'I will still wear it with pride, Dad.'

'You have your mother's bright and beautiful smile,' Kreon told her fondly. 'But you have a kindness as well, which she never had.'

'Maybe I inherited that from you,' Lucy replied, watching her daughter hug her grandfather's knees and raise her arms to be lifted with all the confidence of a child who knew she could always expect a welcome.

Lucy couldn't sleep that night. Jax phoned and she told him about Polly's letter. It shook her that her most driving instinct was to share that very private news with Jax even when he wasn't around. But then Jax knew better than most about complex family divisions, she reasoned, shying away from the inner awareness that she trusted Jax more and wanted to share everything with him more than she was willing to admit.

Jax urged her to do nothing until he had checked out her sisters and she got cross with him then and told him to mind his own business. Not that he could do anything else, she conceded, when there wasn't enough personal information in that letter to allow Lucy or indeed Jax to identify either of her sisters or even work out where they lived. Polly had kept the letter short and sweet as a first approach and Lucy's mind buzzed with conjecture about the siblings she had never met.

Some of her excitement gradually subsided, however, when she thought about Ellie being an actual *doctor*. Ellie was obviously very well-educated and clever and possibly Polly was as well. Lucy could well be the odd one out, the lesser sister, the oddball who didn't fit in. That idea troubled Lucy because it seemed to her that that was the story of her entire life: never quite fitting in anywhere. Not with her mother, not in the foster homes, not even in the short-lived adoption she had enjoyed until her adoptive parents died in a car crash and she was sent back into care. And she hadn't fitted in with Jax either, had she? He had dumped her and walked away without a backward glance. Yet now, he was marrying her. How did that make sense?

He was only marrying her for Bella's benefit, she reminded herself, feeling her pride sting and her heart sink at that awareness. Could their desire to do well by their daughter be enough to sustain a marriage? Lucy didn't want make-believe and she didn't believe in perfect. She believed that she had realistic expectations. But she did desperately *want* to have a real marriage and be part of a proper family. It was what she had dreamt of all her life and never managed to achieve. Now that Jax was offering her that opportunity she planned to make the most of it.

The morning of the wedding dawned bright and sunny and, having done her hair and her make-up for herself, Lucy donned her gown. It was a perfect fit, swirling round her in delicate shimmering white lace. As a mother she had felt self-conscious about wearing white but she hadn't felt the need to make a statement either by choosing another colour. In any case she was marrying the man who had become her first lover and the father of her daughter and she wasn't ashamed of either fact.

A heaving bunch of paparazzi waited behind crash barriers outside the vast Metropolitan Cathedral in the city where the Greek Orthodox ceremony was being held. Lucy was unnerved by the questions shouted and the flash of cameras and she gripped her father's arm tightly as they negotiated the shallow steps and moved below the arches into the church.

'Royalty once got married here,' Kreon murmured with satisfaction. 'I never dreamt that one day I would see my own child taking her vows below this roof.'

The comment lightened Lucy's tension as nothing else could have done. 'Glad I've finally done something to make you proud but why are the paparazzi so interested?'

'You are about to become a member of one of the foremost families in Greece. Naturally, the public want to know who has captured the notorious playboy, Jax Antonakos—'

'I wouldn't say captured is the right word,' Lucy muttered uncomfortably as they paused at the end of the aisle and her father shook out her small train for her and offered his arm to her again with a proud smile.

'He's a very fortunate man. I hope he appreciates that. You look really beautiful,' the older man declared with satisfaction.

Tears stung the backs of Lucy's eyes because she was touched by her father's faith in her. She watched Jax turn his handsome dark head and look at her and the ability to breathe died in her throat. The closer she drew to him on their slow walk down the aisle, the more gorgeous he appeared, his dramatic green eyes welded to her approach. Colour warmed her cheeks and tingling heat surged low in her pelvis. She felt as if all her dreams were coming true in that moment and she scolded herself for being too emotional and sentimental. Jax was neither sentimental nor romantic. He didn't love her and she didn't love him, she reminded herself firmly, but they had Bella to bind them and, in time, maybe they would find that more than their daughter kept them together.

Jax studied Lucy with heavily lidded eyes, his attention roaming over every exquisite shapely inch of her petite body. The gown was a triumph, a delicate lace affair of simple design that enhanced her slight stature and gave her elegance. He didn't look to see how his father was reacting. Only minutes earlier he had noticed his father's absorption in Bella where she sat on Iola's knee across the aisle. Heracles longed for grandchildren, and the knowledge that he had a little granddaughter he had yet to meet had at the very last minute made him decide to attend the wedding. True, Jax wasn't expecting his father to be in a party mood because Heracles hated Kreon Thiarkis and hated that his son was marrying Kreon's daughter, but Jax was relieved that Heracles had put family first and shelved his reservations to share their day.

Some of the ceremony went over Lucy's head, for which she blamed Jax, who had said he was too busy to attend a rehearsal at the cathedral when the services of an interpreter had been available. She concentrated on the simple Greek words that she knew and smiled nervously up at Jax when he slid the ring onto her finger. Their eyes met and the burn inside her spread like wild fire. It was utterly inappropriate but she had never wanted so badly to be kissed. Jax angled his arrogant dark head back and gave her a teasing smile of naked challenge and she went for it as she had always gone for it when he egged her on. She stretched up awkwardly in her very high heels, her hands clutching at his arms to steady herself, and *still* she wasn't tall enough.

With a husky sound of sensual amusement, Jax gathered her up and raised her to his level to taste her lush parted lips for himself. And for a split second, Lucy forgot everything. She forgot that she was in public, she forgot the guests shifting in their seats and the imposing robed Archbishop who had conducted the service. The taste of Jax's mouth was like a shaft of sunlight bursting inside her after a long winter. It charged her up, rendered her helpless with longing, and the plunge of his tongue into the moist interior of her mouth only multiplied the explosive effect of that kiss on her body. Her heart hammered, her pulses raced as

Jax slowly slid her down his lean, powerful frame to stand on her own feet again.

She caught a glimpse of Iola's grin and just as suddenly appreciated that she was still in public view. A swoosh of mortified pink lit up her heart-shaped face as Jax closed his hand over hers and walked her back down the aisle.

Jax was amazed that he felt so relaxed. He had expected to loathe every minute of the wedding. Knowing he was protecting his father was one thing, doing what had to be done when it went against his own instincts was another. But that hot little taste of Lucy's passion assuaged those feelings. She wanted him, she wanted him just as much as he wanted her, and for the moment that was as much consolation for his sacrifice of freedom as he needed.

He had struggled against anger, resentment and bitterness throughout the two weeks it had taken to set up the wedding. He had kept his distance from Lucy because he was afraid that she would guess that he was not the enthusiastic bridegroom he was purporting to be. Deception of any kind had always been a challenge for Jax. He was very talented at keeping his feelings to himself but he was very bad at *faking* anything. He had found the drinks engagement with Kreon and Iola extremely uncomfortable and Lucy's demands for his opinion on the colour of the bridal flowers and such nonsense had simply exasperated him. For two solid weeks, Jax had rigorously reminded himself that he was acquiring Lucy and his daughter and protecting his father by getting married. But even that couldn't disperse the sour flavour of having to do what he had always sworn he would not do and take a wife.

Outside the cathedral the paparazzi went into a frenzy of excitement when the bride and groom appeared. Jax's father stalked silently from cathedral to limousine without pause. It was ironic that Heracles was furious with his son for marrying Lucy. Only after Jax had pointed out that he had had a daughter with Lucy had Heracles gone from raging to dark muttering, finally accepting that a waitress, who was also the daughter of an obnoxious criminal, was entering the Antonakos family. And having learned about that criminal record, Jax had not argued in his father-in-law's favour. Agreeing that Kreon was obnoxious had somewhat soothed his father's ire.

Jax had been tempted to bring up the file he had been given on Lucy two years earlier but he had decided to take a rain check on that line of enquiry until after the wedding. Getting information about Kreon Thiarkis had been surprisingly easy but getting information on Lucy was proving deeply problematic. She had lived in so many different places and had even been adopted at one stage when her name had been changed. Indeed the discovery of just how grim Lucy's growing years had been had saddened Jax. Some years after the adoption she had gone back to using the name she had been given at birth. But Lucy's frequent childhood moves read like a depressing indictment of social services care and the investigator striving to trace her movements during her adolescence was currently at an admitted standstill.

Of course, you could simply ask her for the details, Jax reminded himself wryly. Could he trust her answers? Or would she lie to mislead him, hoping to cover up conduct she might now be ashamed of? Jax needed the confidence of knowing that he had the *whole* truth. Naturally he expected her to deny the drugs offences but, so far, no official record of any such offences had been found. Was it possible that the detective agency his father had used had confused Lucy's identity with someone else's? Was it even remotely possible that she was innocent of the charges in that file? But then hadn't he been equally shocked when he'd seen her with that man in the alleyway? Lucy didn't wear her sins or her flaws on her lovely face.

With the ease of long practice Jax buried the memory of Lucy's betrayal deep where he didn't have to think about it. If he thought about it, he mused grimly, it would drive him off the edge, the way it had two years ago when he had tried to find solace in the bottom of a bottle: the aftershocks of giving up Lucy had been little short of terrifying for a male who needed to stay in emotional control. For a short while he had been overpowered by his conflicting feelings, not something he was willing to recall or relive. In fact even remembering that made him flinch.

They arrived at the hotel and settled down with Bella in a private room set aside for their use to drink champagne and await the arrival of their guests. Poised by the window, Jax tensed. 'That's my father's car arriving. Come on. I want to introduce you and Bella.'

By the time Jax and Lucy reached the grand foyer, however, Iola and Kreon were already greeting Heracles. And then there was one of those strange little moments of absolute stillness as Kreon said something and Heracles backed up and then suddenly lurched forward and punched the younger man with angry ferocity. Lucy was aghast when the fight broke out. Her father responded, lurching clumsily after Heracles to return that punch and then receiving yet another for his pains, for Heracles was very fit and fast on his feet for his age. Further violence was only forestalled by the Antonakos bodyguards who stood between the two men to keep them apart. Heracles let out an angry roar of frustration.

'Stay back,' Jax warned Lucy, striding in to intervene and grip his father by both his arms to restrain him, since it was obvious that none of their staff had the nerve to lay actual hands on their irate employer.

All red in the face and still patently desperate for a fight, Heracles roared something angry in Greek. Jax stole a glimpse at the guests piling through the entrance doors and then stopping dead to stare at the spectacle and he suppressed a groan. He said something to his father and shepherded him over to a door of the private room. Pushing open the door, he gestured to Lucy's father to follow him. Looking reluctant but red-faced and more than a little embarrassed, Kreon finally did so. Jax was trying to sort the argument out, Lucy recognised ruefully while wondering what Heracles Antonakos had against her father that had so overpowered his manners.

'Men!' Iola proclaimed dramatically at her elbow, making Lucy emit a startled laugh. 'Thank heaven, Jax got them out of sight.'

'What sparked off that punch?' Lucy demanded in bewilderment.

'Apparently Kreon and Jax's father have some past history. Kreon didn't go into detail but it's obvious that Jax's father hates him and almost didn't come to his son's wedding because he knew Kreon would be here.' Iola rolled her eyes. 'Don't let it spoil your day.'

'I shan't,' Lucy responded, stroking Bella's curls distractedly while thinking that family relations promised to be taxing with their fathers at odds.

With Iola by her side, Lucy welcomed guests and chatted until she saw Heracles and Kreon emerge again together with drinks in their hands and actually speaking to each other. But when Jax strode back to join her, raw tension was still stamped on his lean, darkly handsome features.

'Evidently you're quite successful in the peacemaker stakes,' Lucy remarked as he steered her into the function room to take their seats, mercifully moving her right before she had to greet Kat Valtinos, who looked ravishing in a cutaway emerald dress teamed with feathers in her hair.

'No, they achieved that without any help from me. I only stayed to ensure that hostilities didn't break out again,' Jax admitted. 'You still haven't met my father and I need to explain what happened out there.'

'Don't break the habit of a lifetime and tell me something,' Lucy urged with helpless sarcasm.

'It's not something I want to talk about but I must,' Jax breathed stiffly. 'However, it's old history and nothing to do with us. No doubt you're wondering why my father went for yours…'

'Kreon does seem to be an acquired taste with some people.'

'This is not a teasing matter,' Jax censured.

As she settled down beside him at the top table Lucy was watching Heracles Antonakos make their daughter's acquaintance. Bella was fearless and she stared up at the older man and handed him her stuffed rabbit. Heracles's craggy face broke into a sudden unexpected smile and he sat down with Iola by his side and accepted the rabbit to make it walk across the seat beside him. Bella started to giggle and clutched at the leg of his trousers to stay upright.

'He likes Bella,' Lucy noted with satisfaction, willing to overlook and forgive a great deal if her daughter was accepted and appreciated.

'He loves children.' Jax fell broodingly silent and she glanced curiously at his lean, taut profile, helplessly admiring the classic perfection of it. 'My father discovered after my brother, Argo, died that he could not have been his child. Argo needed a transfusion after the attack and I suspect it was discovered in the minutes before he died that he did not share my father's or my rare blood group.'

Lucy's eyes widened because she was completely disconcerted by that bombshell. 'My goodness, Heracles must have been devastated to find that out—'

'Particularly as he idolised his first wife and despised my mother...and me...for my mother's infidelity. When he found out that he hadn't fathered Argo he immediately suspected your father because of the close friendship Kreon had had with Sofia.'

Lucy winced. 'I honestly don't think it was that sort of friendship.'

'It wasn't. Kreon saw Sofia as a little sister. His mother, your grandmother on Kreon's side, was Sofia's nanny and as children Kreon and Sofia spent a lot of time together,' Jax told her. 'Unfortunately having married Sofia my father distrusted their friendship and became jealous.'

'In other words, your father is an old dinosaur who can't credit that a man and a woman can have a platonic friendship,' Lucy commented, still watching Heracles as he lifted Bella onto his knee with careful hands.

'I wouldn't appreciate my wife being that friendly with another man either,' Jax admitted.

'Sadly I don't currently have any close male friends to torment you with.' Lucy sighed with unhidden regret on that score.

'You're a little witch,' Jax growled, running his forefinger along the lush line of her full lower lip. 'Why does that make me want to kiss you again?'

'You love a challenge?' Lucy whispered unevenly, meeting those stunning green eyes in a head-on clash and feeling more than a little dizzy with excitement, her lips parting.

'But I don't enjoy an audience,' Jax countered, running a finger back and forth across the delicate bones of her wrist below the level of the table.

Lucy was breathing in rapid shallow little gusts, insanely conscious of her body responding to him on every level. She could feel her breasts full and constricted within the bodice of her dress, her distended nipples pushing hard against the scratchy lace of her bra and then there was the tight locked-down tension and heat between her thighs, not to mention the dulled little throb there that made her ache and stiffen her posture.

'It's showtime—but not for what we want,' Jax murmured drily as Iola took a seat beside him and Heracles settled down beside Lucy with Bella still on his knee.

'She's very cute,' Heracles said of her daughter. 'She knows what she wants.'

'Mum... Mum,' Bella framed, lurching straight off Jax's father into her mother's arms and flopping down sleepily.

'She needs a nap,' Lucy sighed.

'Where's the nanny I hired for the day?' Jax asked.

The older woman was already approaching Lucy, ready to take the tired toddler off her hands, but Lucy stood up. 'I'll come upstairs with you and get her settled.'

'Your bride doesn't take hints, does she?' Heracles remarked with some amusement to his son. 'You'll have your hands full with the two of them.'

Jax, who very much wanted to follow his bride upstairs and have her settle *him* down, grimaced. 'I know it.'

'Well, you can't make worse choices than I did. I won't say anything more,' his father declared piously. 'With my track record, I can't afford to preach, can I?'

'No, you can't.'

'Three marriages ending in one death and two divorces and your mother was almost as bad. We didn't set you much of an example, did we?' Heracles sighed heavily. 'By the way, I've set up the island for your honeymoon—'

Thoroughly taken aback, Jax frowned. 'But you live on Tifnos,' Jax objected, because he had been planning to take Lucy cruising round the Mediterranean on the yacht.

'Tifnos is yours now that you're a father. It was built to be a family home and I'm tired of living there alone in that great barn of a house. I've signed it over to you and I'm in the process of buying an estate outside Athens,' the older man told him in a tone of finality. 'It's time for me to step back and make room for the next generation.'

CHAPTER SEVEN

Lucy came out of the room where she had left the nanny watching over Bella and smiled at the sight of Kreon waiting for her. 'Dad? What are you doing up here?' she asked with a grin. 'Are you trying to escape all the polite chit-chat? Or have you heard a rumour that the food's going to be bad?'

Kreon shifted uneasily on his feet, his face grave and troubled. 'I have done something wrong and it concerns you.'

'What on earth are you talking about?' Lucy laughed as he urged her into an alcove with seats.

'Talking to Heracles made me see stuff…differently.' Her father selected his words with an air of discomfiture as he sat down. 'It made me appreciate that we've all had our tragedies and our triumphs but it's how we deal with them that makes us who we are. I'd like to be proud of who I am but right now I'm *not*.'

Lucy narrowed her eyes in confusion. 'You don't sound like yourself.'

'Jax's father neglected Jax because he despised Jax's mother, whom he divorced. He knows he can never make it up to Jax and he has to live with it every day, knowing that all those years he left his boy to deal alone with a very difficult woman,' Kreon told her.

'But you and I have a different history,' Lucy reasoned, tucking that fresh information about Jax into her memory to take out and ponder at a more suitable time. 'You didn't even know that my mother was pregnant when you left London and she didn't tell you later when she could have done—'

'That's not what I'm talking about,' Kreon told her heavily. 'For many years I hated Heracles Antonakos because he put me down over my friendship with his wife. I'm ashamed to admit that I took my resentment out on his son.'

Lucy's smooth brow had furrowed. 'In what way?'

'When Sofia was dying, she had a letter sent to me in which she confessed her darkest secret. She didn't have the nerve to tell her husband so she told me instead.' Kreon drew a crumpled envelope from his pocket and passed it to her. 'Give it to Jax, let him decide what to do with it now. In it Sofia confesses to having an affair and she admits that Jax's brother wasn't fathered by Heracles. I went to see Jax a couple of weeks ago and I threatened to take that letter to the newspapers.'

'Good grief...why would you threaten to do something so horrible?' Lucy demanded in total disbelief.

'I wanted Jax to marry you and take care of you and Bella. I thought he owed you that security and I *still* believe that he does but coercing him into doing it was wrong and unjust. He was protecting his father from more heartache and I shouldn't have put him in that position. He is not responsible for his father's mistakes.'

Lucy had turned very pale and her stomach was

curdling as if she had eaten something that disagreed with her. She studied her father in slowly dawning horror and comprehension. 'Are you telling me that you blackmailed Jax into proposing to me?'

As Kreon gave a guilty nod of silent confirmation, Lucy felt as though the bottom had just dropped out of her world. She stared at the brand-new wedding ring on her finger and felt sick. Jax hadn't wanted to marry her. No, he had been *forced* to marry her. It was ghastly. She looked at her father in stricken condemnation. 'Were you insane? I mean, what on earth could persuade you that *that* was an acceptable way to behave towards Bella's father?'

'I was angry with him. I wanted to punish Jax for seducing and abandoning you. It's not an excuse but at the time I honestly believed I was doing what was best for you and my granddaughter.'

'Because Jax is rich and powerful,' Lucy slotted in sickly. 'And now you feel bad about it because you've realised that rich and powerful people like Heracles Antonakos make mistakes and suffer just like everyone else.'

Kreon sighed. 'That's probably it in a nutshell. When I listened to Heracles talking I felt my anger draining away. He was a workaholic who neglected all his wives. But he came to the wedding today even though he didn't approve of you because he was making an effort to be supportive of Jax as a father should. That was the *right* kind of effort to make for a child, mine was wrong. What did I do today? I made a sarcastic comment and provoked that punch.'

'I'm really upset,' Lucy admitted, breathing in deep and slow to calm herself down. 'You'd better go back down and join the guests before Iola starts wondering where you are.'

'I'm sorry, Lucy. I've just felt so powerless since you came into my life. You had had such a rough time and I genuinely *did* want to make your life better,' Kreon confessed before he walked away.

And she understood exactly where her father was coming from *but* he had blackmailed Jax. Nausea stirred in Lucy's tummy. Jax, who would hold a grudge beyond the grave. Jax, who idolised the father who had ignored him for so many years, had been vulnerable. A deep sense of anguish flooded Lucy and an even deeper sense of shame. The father she had so easily come to love had let her down badly and shown her his feet of clay. That hurt as well. Was she always going to be a rotten judge of character?

But what did she do now? Well, the middle of a wedding didn't seem the ideal venue in which to open a very difficult conversation with Jax. Oh, by the way, my father mentioned that he blackmailed you... Lucy cringed and winced and hurt all over again. She hurt for her father and for Jax and for Bella, for surely the chances of such a marriage working out looked very poor. But most of all, she was discovering that she hurt for herself. Jax's apparent desire to marry her had filled her with hope and even unleashed a few dreams.

Only now it was obvious that Jax hadn't actually experienced *any* desire to put a ring on her finger. Her father had used the nastiest form of persuasion available to get that wedding ring on her hand. Hadn't it ever occurred to Kreon that it would be his daughter who had to deal with the aftermath of what he had done? Hadn't he appreciated how angry and aggrieved

Jax would feel? Lucy shivered, suddenly feeling very alone and without support. She couldn't depend on her father and now it was equally obvious that she could not depend on her new husband either.

For the first time she badly wanted to speak to the sisters she had never met. It was crazy but she wanted to reach out and see if she could connect with a sister as she so obviously had failed to connect with Jax or her father. Kreon had lied when he said that she could trust him. And Jax hadn't meant all those fine things he had said about how they could be a couple creating a secure family in which to raise a child. He had been forced to talk like that to convince Lucy to agree to marry him and she groaned out loud, remembering how unusually understated Jax had been that evening. She had already put her sister's phone number into her mobile for fear that she might mislay Polly's letter and she dug her phone out of her small ornamental bag.

She got a bad case of cold feet while the phone was ringing and almost stopped the call before it connected. And then it was answered by this sunny, confidence-inducing female voice and Lucy froze.

'It's Lucy...er...your sister...if that's you, Polly,' she gabbled in an uneasy rush.

'Lucy!' Polly proclaimed warmly. 'I'm so very happy to hear from you. Do you have any idea how long Ellie and I have been trying to trace you?'

'Why were you trying?' Lucy asked in genuine puzzlement.

'Because you're our sister and part of our family. Ellie and I always had each other but until recently I know you had no one. Of course, I appreciate that you have your father now—'

'That hasn't worked out so well,' Lucy mumbled in some embarrassment.

'I'm really sorry to hear that. Are you all right, Lucy?' Polly prompted anxiously.

Lucy stared stonily at the wall, hot prickly tears stinging the backs of her aching eyes. 'Well, not so great today...to be brutally honest,' she framed chokily.

'You sound upset,' Polly remarked with care. 'Naturally I don't want to pry but—'

'I'm not upset,' Lucy insisted chokingly. 'It's my wedding day—'

'My wedding day wasn't great either,' Polly told her ruefully. 'I assume the ceremony has already taken place? Do you love the man you married?'

It was a simple question but it froze Lucy from head to toe. She started to shiver, feeling cold and clammy. 'No, we're not in love. We got married because we have a daughter...at least I *thought* that's why we got married but seems I was wrong about that too,' she mumbled shakily.

'I can't believe you're already a mother at only twenty-one,' Polly exclaimed. 'Somehow our detective didn't pick up on that. You sound so unhappy though. Please tell me what's wrong...'

And Lucy compressed her lips, fighting the tears positively attracted by that soft, understanding sibling voice. 'I *can't* tell you—'

'You can tell me anything,' Polly assured her. 'Ellie and I are here and ready and willing to help you if you need us.'

'That's good to know but I still can't tell you,' Lucy repeated doggedly.

'Is your child's father abusive?' Polly demanded worriedly. 'Are you at risk in any way?'

'No...*no*!' Lucy insisted, hastening to shut down that suspicion. 'Look, I've just found out that my father blackmailed my bridegroom into marrying me! That's why I'm upset.'

'Right...' Polly's momentary hesitation spoke volumes and Lucy winced. 'But you're not responsible for what your father does. Lucy, you only have to say the word and, wherever you are and no matter what time of day it is, we'll have you picked up.'

'That's a very generous offer,' Lucy framed, deeply touched.

'Please think about coming to stay with us for a while...you'd be very welcome and it would give you a breathing space in which to decide what you want to do next,' her sister pointed out.

'I'll certainly think about it but I have to go now. I'm sorry. I'll phone you again when I have more time to talk.'

Lucy thrust her phone guiltily back into her bag, wondering what had possessed her to say so much to a woman she had never met. Now Polly probably thought she was more than a little weird. She headed down to the powder room on the ground floor to repair her make-up. Her mascara had run and she asked herself why she had been reduced to tears. The shock of Kreon's confession? The knowledge that Jax had only proposed to protect his cantankerous old father from the humiliation of having it known that his elder son had not been his? Whatever, it was her wedding day and she was on show and she had to get over her emotional reactions and behave normally.

'Where the hell have you been?' Jax demanded as he strode out of the function room to intercept her and closed his hands round her arms to hold her still. 'Is Bella OK?'

'She's fine. I was talking to someone,' Lucy told him, colliding with his stunning black-fringed green eyes and experiencing a jolt not unlike an electric shock.

Jax stared down at her. 'Have you been crying?' he asked, noticing the very faint hint of pink round her eyelids, which he was certain hadn't been visible earlier.

'No, for goodness' sake,' Lucy parried with an uneasy laugh. 'Why would I have been crying?'

Jax had no idea but he could see that Lucy's naturally sunny aura had dimmed. Perhaps Bella was playing up, he reasoned. Weddings were stressful and a strange place and a strange nanny could well have upset his daughter. He dropped a hand to Lucy's spine and guided her back into the function room and towards the top table.

The meal was served. It melted in Lucy's mouth but she might as well have been eating sawdust for all the pleasure it gave her. Her father-in-law asked her some very awkward questions about her past life and she answered as best she could, struggling to breeze lightly past her years in care and becoming much more animated when he asked about Bella.

A professional singer entertained them and then the dancing began. Jax had to almost drag Lucy onto the floor because she couldn't dance very well and was covered in blushes at the thought of having to perform in front of people.

'I just wish this day was over,' she confided, pushing her face against his chest, realising that he was so tall that, from one angle at least, she could literally hide herself.

'You and me both,' Jax admitted, wondering if his father had said something cutting to make her appear so subdued and feeling surprisingly angry at that suspicion.

Of course, the wedding he had been blackmailed into agreeing to could hardly be a source of pleasure for him, Lucy reckoned wretchedly. And what must he think of her father now? He probably knew Kreon had already spent a couple of years of his youth in a cell and now he would believe that Kreon belonged in prison and would think less of her because of it. People did judge you on your background and relatives. Not that he had ever thought that much of her to begin with, Lucy reminded herself unhappily, recalling how she had been cast off like an old shoe in Spain.

'In another few hours we'll be on our way,' Jax remarked, long brown fingers sliding down her back to gather her closer.

Heat curled between her thighs as she felt the evidence of his arousal. Her mouth ran dry. Evidently blackmail didn't douse Jax's libido. He still wanted her. Was that something to celebrate? Or something more to beat herself up about? Was she supposed to settle gratefully for being his sexual outlet? Was that all she was worth? All she deserved? She didn't know any longer. Her brain in turmoil, she forced herself to relax into the hard, muscular warmth of his hold and allowed him to slow-dance her round the floor. Other people were dancing now as well and she no longer felt like the centre of attention.

'Where will we be on our way to?' she asked belatedly.

'That's a surprise,' Jax admitted, still taken aback by what his father had done.

The little island of Tifnos was the Antonakos home but Jax had yet to even spend a night there. As a boy he had been ferried out there but only on day trips to attend several big family social occasions and as an adult he had flown to the island regularly to consult with Heracles about business. But it had never been *his* home because when he had been young he had been lucky if his father even acknowledged his presence among so many other guests. In truth he had always felt like an intruder and an outsider in his father's house and the startling concept of making Tifnos his base raised all sorts of conflicting feelings.

'Oh...' Lucy framed, drinking in the scent of him with flared nostrils. There was definitely something scientific in the effect of pheromones on attraction, she conceded ruefully. She loved Jax's smell; that indefinable combination of designer cologne and husky male had called to her from his first kiss.

Her eyes prickled again and she wrinkled her nose to hold the stupid tears back. Her husband, *blackmailed* into marrying her. Knowing that, she found it a challenge to believe that she could be a true bride and wife. In fact, Kreon's intervention and use of pressure made a nonsense of the entire day. She felt utterly humiliated. She wondered when she would work up the nerve to discuss what Kreon had done with Jax and how he would react when she did. He could well be furious that she had found out. His ferocious pride would rebel against her knowing that he could be forced into doing anything.

She was heading for the bridal suite to get changed for their departure when she saw Kat Valtinos walking towards her and suppressed a sigh because she wasn't in the mood to be patronised or bitched at over the head of Jax.

'Lucy...' Kat murmured with a bright artificial smile. 'Your big day's almost over.'

'Yes. We're leaving soon.' Lucy busied herself fishing out the card to open the door. Kreon and Iola had already taken Bella home for the night and her daughter would be staying with them for the first week Jax and Lucy were away.

'Well, enjoy it while you can,' Kat advised with saccharine sweetness. 'It's not as if your marriage will last long.'

As Lucy thrust the door open she simply ignored the brunette, refusing to be drawn into an exchange with her. Kat had hated her two years ago in Spain for attracting Jax and, from what she had seen of Jax and Kat in the newspapers, Kat must still have cherished hopes of something more coming from their long friendship.

'Jax will take the kid and dump you again,' Kat murmured lethally. 'Don't say you weren't warned.'

Lucy closed the door firmly behind her. Pale and shaky after that nasty little threat of what could be, she concentrated on removing her gown and freshening up. She pulled on a light dress and thrust her sore feet into sandals, touching up her make-up with a light hand. Kat was such a shrew, she reflected ruefully. Jax would *never* try to take Bella from her. Why would he do such a cruel thing? Or even think about separating a mother from her child? It wasn't as though she was an unfit mother. All right, she wasn't perfect. She had been known to snarl a little when Bella tried to get her out of bed at dawn but she *loved* her daughter. Nothing pleased Lucy more than the ability to give Bella all the little things she had never had herself, the small stuff like bedtime stories, favourite foods and lots of hugs.

Her luggage packed and then collected, Lucy went to meet Jax. A limo ferried them to the airport, where they boarded a helicopter.

'Are we going on the yacht?' she asked before the noise of the engine made any conversation impossible.

'No. Tifnos,' Jax told her simply.

And Lucy nodded, secretly intimidated by the prospect. She had read about the fabled private island Heracles had bought as a base in the eighties. Her father-in-law was reputed to live in feudal splendour there in a house that had never been photographed or shown in any publication. But it was supposed to have gardens that could rival the Garden of Eden, a private zoo and literally hundreds of staff.

Lucy felt inadequate. She was far too ordinary for such a backdrop. She had always been ordinary and had once thought that that was what attracted Jax to her. She didn't put on airs, she didn't say things she didn't believe to impress and when she didn't know something she admitted it. Unexpectedly, Jax closed a large hand over hers and then slowly laced his fingers with her own. His thumb massaged her inner wrist soothingly. It was as if she had hoisted a flag telegraphing panic and he had picked up on it. Or as if he was a little apprehensive too...

An idea she swiftly dismissed, for Tifnos was the Antonakos home and he had to be well accustomed to it.

It was fully dark by the time helicopter landed and Jax scooped her out onto the helipad. Momentarily she was thrilled by the dark heavens filled with thousands of the stars that were never visible in the city. Their luggage was piled into a beach buggy and Zenas took the wheel to drive them up a steep hill road hedged in by a forest of pine trees.

And then at the top the Antonakos house stretched like a giant illuminated cruise ship.

'It's big,' she said abruptly.

'Yep, for a man who doesn't like to entertain, Heracles built a very large house,' Jax conceded wryly.

They stepped into a foyer glossy and glittering with pristine marble and chandeliers. It looked exactly like a plush hotel reception without the desk. A double staircase swanned up to the next floor, each tread wide enough to march an army.

'Think movie set,' Jax urged. 'My mother redesigned the entrance, so there are some very theatrical touches.'

A small middle-aged Greek man approached them with a tray of welcoming drinks. Jax passed her a champagne flute but demurred on his account. 'I don't like champagne,' he admitted.

Lucy drank down hers to be polite while she peered into rooms furnished with the kind of opulence that just screamed old money to her. There were statues and collections and cabinets and elaborate artwork everywhere she looked. Suddenly she understood why there were supposedly hundreds of staff. It would take a fair number to look after so many possessions.

Jax set down her glass for her and closed his hand over hers and told the hovering manservant whom he addressed as Theo that they were going to bed.

'Wasn't that a little...offhand?' she pressed self-consciously as they climbed the stairs.

'It's one in the morning and it's our wedding night,' Jax intoned, his hand tightening on hers. 'We can get chatty tomorrow.'

She thought about what she had been avoiding thinking about and colour mantled her cheeks as Jax walked her into a vast room overflowing with urns of white roses and lilies, ornamented with trailing ivy. It was magnificent but not as magnificent as the vast divan bed on the dais scattered with rose petals.

'Heracles wasn't joking when he said he'd set the house up for the bridal couple,' Jax conceded with forbidding cool.

'It's beautiful,' Lucy muttered, because it was and she was grateful that her father-in-law had been prepared to make the effort on their behalf. 'But maybe a little too grand for the likes of me.'

'The "likes of me" now happens to be my wife,' Jax reminded her in reproof. 'And nothing is *too* grand or *too* good for my wife.'

'I'll get used to it...it's just a little overwhelming coming to a house like this,' Lucy confided.

'It's ours now,' Jax revealed, sharing his father's plans with her. 'I think he's hoping we'll go forth and multiply now for him.'

Lucy shrugged a slim shoulder, making no comment on that possibility.

'I think Bella's enough for us at present. I still have to learn how to be a father,' Jax completed, making his opinion clear. 'Do you want a drink or anything to eat? There're snacks waiting on the trolley.'

'No. I only want to get my shoes off,' Lucy admitted, dropping down into a luxurious armchair with a sigh. 'My feet are hurting.'

'Let me...' In the most disconcerting way, Jax crouched down lithely at her feet and unfastened her shoes to slip them off. 'You have such tiny feet. They used to fascinate me.'

Long brown fingers gently stroked the back of a delicate ankle and Lucy snatched in a sudden startled breath because her skin felt super sensitive, as though he had touched her somewhere much more intimate.

'All that got me through the day was the glorious thought of sating myself inside you again, *koukla mou*,' Jax said huskily, rising to lift her bodily out of the chair and settle her down on the huge bed.

Eyes flying wide, cheeks flushing, Lucy stared up at him with bright blue eyes.

'So, why do you look like a cornered rabbit?' Jax asked pleasantly. 'You've been acting strangely all day.'

CHAPTER EIGHT

'I...I FELT OVERWHELMED,' Lucy told him and it was true.

The cathedral wedding, the sleek bejewelled Antonakos relatives and guests and the absence of any actual friends aside of her father's had weighed her down. The constant stares and the low buzz of conjecture hadn't helped either but when someone as rich as Jax married a waitress, who was the mother of his child, people stared and speculated. The wedding had been a strain and her father's confession of wrongdoing had crushed her. It had been the ultimate humiliation to learn that only Kreon's criminal act had made it possible for her to marry Jax.

And yet what could they possibly *do* about it now? Kreon had confessed too late to change anything. If she and Jax were to part this very night, it would cause a major scandal and she knew Jax wouldn't want to invite that media attention, which meant that at the very least they would have to stay married for a few months to make any breakup appear less worthy of comment.

'I can understand that,' Jax conceded, removing his jacket in a lazy fluid movement.

And Lucy watched him with a fast-beating heart,

still wondering what she should do and how she should be behaving. Yet with a good ninety per cent of her being she craved the intimacy that being with Jax would give her. She wanted forgetfulness. She wanted to sink into the comfortable depths of the massive bed and shut the rest of the world out to take refuge in Jax. Even if he wasn't really hers and possibly wouldn't be hers for very long. His dazzling green eyes gleamed in the low-lit room, so bright against his dark bronzed skin, and her mouth ran dry.

Tugging his shirt from his waistband, he came back to the bed and sank down behind her to unzip her dress. She sat there like a little statue, her heart thudding like crazy in her chest as he lifted the garment up over her head, leaving her clad only in the white lace lingerie she had worn with her wedding gown. Sliding upright again, he unbuttoned his shirt, displaying a wide slice of his torso, well-defined muscles coming into view as he shed the shirt.

And she was as entranced by his sheer male beauty as she had once been in Spain, feasting her eyes on him with feminine appreciation. Jax worked out and it showed. He was all lean muscle and controlled power.

'Take the rest off,' he urged. 'I want to look at you.'

Her face burned as she reached behind her back to unclasp her bra. She had never done that before in front of him. Her clothes had once vanished beneath his skilled hands and she hadn't had to think about it or ever feel particularly naked. But there in that silent bedroom she was insanely aware of her body and its deficiencies as she let the bra fall. Most of the pregnancy weight had fallen away but there was no denying that she was curvier at bust and hip and there was an obvious scar low on her belly from the Caesarean she had had to have. Her waist was bigger too, she thought nervously, anxiously cataloguing every flaw. And this was a guy accustomed to the flawless female bodies of underwear models.

Jax studied the pouting swell of her pink-tipped breasts with intense pleasure, arousal flashing through him with storm-force potency. Everything about her daintiness appealed to him because her slender lines became lush in all the right highly feminine places. And he knew exactly what would happen when he touched her. He knew she would respond to him in a way no other woman ever had and that there would be nothing fake or exaggerated about it. Anticipation gave him the ultimate high.

'I'm not perfect,' she warned him tightly as her fingers flirted with the band of her knickers. 'Well, I never was, but—'

A flashing grin flared across Jax's lean, darkly handsome features as he came down on one knee on the bed and yanked her playfully to him by her ankles. 'You're perfect for me...I only want to see you.'

Sharply disconcerted by that teasing assault, Lucy looked up at him with apprehensive eyes of blue. He hooked his hands into her knickers and dragged them off, lowering her back gently against the pillows and then rearranging her to his own satisfaction, her legs parted and her hands by her side.

'I'd love a painting of you looking like this, all spread out and waiting for me, but I couldn't stand the artist seeing you naked,' he admitted thickly, peeling off his trousers and his boxers in an impatient movement.

Lucy lay there feeling like a sacrifice and yet she was quite ridiculously excited by his scrutiny and the thrusting fullness of his arousal. He was so ready for her, was always ready. He made her feel as though her body were flawless and the desire he made no attempt to hide warmed the sore place inside her where her father's betrayal had contrived to undermine her self-esteem.

Jax joined her on the bed and went straight for her mouth with hungry, driving kisses that parted her lips and sent a current of high-voltage expectation flying through her trembling length. Her fingers clutched into his spiky, messy black hair and tears burned behind her lowered eyelids because she wanted him so much that she hurt with the wanting. It felt too intense, too desperate and that wasn't what she wanted to feel. She needed to stay in control, she told herself, remember what was real and what wasn't real. And what they had now *wasn't* real. Why did thinking that drive a knife through her when it was only the truth?

'I can't get enough of you,' Jax growled between the urgent biting kisses that bruised her lips and the devastating plunge of his tongue that made her slight body jackknife in reaction beneath his.

'We've got all night,' she whispered through rosy swollen lips, eyes glazed with passion.

'I've got a hunger that one night won't come anywhere near satisfying,' Jax told her rawly, fisting a hand in her tumbling curls as he snaked a string of kisses down over her collarbone and found a plump, pointed nipple to torment with attention.

'Oh... Jax,' she gasped, a fire trail of tingles lighting up from her breast to her pelvis where a warm damp sensation pulsed.

With difficulty Jax dragged his lips from her writhing body and stared down at her. She was his wife now. Signed, sealed and delivered. In the strangest way, he registered, he *liked* that, liked that ring on her finger that marked her as his and loved the way she was looking up at him as though he had hung the moon.

'You will be very tired tomorrow,' Jax forecast without hesitation. 'I'm planning to take everything you can offer and then some more.'

Without hesitation, Lucy leant up and claimed his sensual, taunting mouth for herself, revelling in the instant rush of hungry need he betrayed. He scored the edge of his teeth across her full lower lip, dallied over the sensitive skin below her ear and then returned to his self-imposed worship of her full breasts. He lashed the hard little tips into swollen, throbbing sensitivity and her hips rose beneath his long, lean physique until he settled a leg between hers, giving her the pressure she craved at the crux of her body.

The demanding ache at the heart of her spread, sending little tingles through every skin cell, building and building her tension. He teased her nipples with his teeth and the heat of a climax simply exploded through Lucy in a glorious rush that made her cry out and jerk under him.

'That's one…' Jax husked with satisfaction.

'You're counting now?' Lucy mumbled distractedly, dragged into brain-dead lethargy by the shimmering backwash of sheer pleasure.

'I always was goal-orientated,' Jax reminded her, working his passage slowly down her quivering length.

Tell him you know about the blackmail, a guilty little inner voice urged her. But that would unleash a very difficult conversation after an extremely long and trying day. In any case Jax was reasonably happy at this precise moment, she decided, and she didn't want to spoil things. Later they would both be more relaxed and less tense. He tugged her thighs apart and buried his mouth there and suddenly her brain didn't have any space left in which to be rational. Suddenly she became a twisting, gasping creature at the mercy of her own sensual responses.

Jax slid a finger through her silky folds. He stroked her, smiling as she moaned and shifted, striving to urge him on, but in bed Jax was always in control, most particularly because Lucy had no control.

'Torture!' she muttered between gritted teeth, a rosy flush and perspiration slicking her skin as she thrashed under his ministrations, gasping as he hit the exact spot where she was most sensitive.

'I love the taste of you,' Jax growled, the vibrations of his dark deep drawl pulsing through her tender flesh.

Involuntarily, her body erupted again, driven to the point of explosive climax by the intensity of her excitement. She screamed his name and jerked and then fell still, wonder creeping over her that anyone could possibly wreak such havoc with her system and give her that much pleasure.

'*Thee mou*, I want you so much,' Jax ground out as he slid over her, his hands strong on her hips to angle her back.

He entered her slowly, urging her tender flesh to open for him and stretch, and the sensation made her dizzy with yearning and wildly impatient for more. He eased back and then pushed in hard and deep and her body convulsed and tightened round him, intense sensation ravishing her. A string of tiny sounds was wrenched from her parted lips as he ground into her and picked up the pace, raw excitement flooding her as she tilted up to meet him, hot, damp and abandoned as the wild roller coaster of sensation raged on and on. He slammed into her with primal force and her body just splintered from the inside out, taking her apart in pieces so that she slumped back on the bed, barely aware of his muffled groan of completion but welcoming the warm, heavy weight of him.

Empty of all conscious thought, Lucy skated her hands over Jax's smooth damp back and then wrapped her arms round him tightly. He was struggling to catch his breath close to her ear and she smiled and twisted her head to kiss him on the cheek.

Jax froze as though she had crossed some invisible boundary line. He refused to do that stuff with her again. Bone and sinew he rejected any show of affection that came from her and he yanked back from her and rolled away. He wasn't buying into that again with her, no way! She had given him that same hugging and petting and apparent warmth in Spain and he knew it was meaningless. He had known that when he saw her in that alleyway having sex with another man. As that cringe-making memory returned, Jax wanted to smash a fist into the wall.

That was better left buried and he knew it, particularly now that they were married. When he thought about it, he felt seething anger and violent. Forgiveness wasn't in his vocabulary and forgetting wasn't in his nature. There wasn't any reason for him to think about that sordid episode, he told himself grimly. All he had to do for his own protection was remember that she was treacherous and watch out when she was around other men.

When Jax jerked away from her and headed for what she assumed was the bathroom, Lucy felt as if he had slapped her in the face. He had recoiled from her as if she were contagious, as if he couldn't *bear* her touch. After such intimacy, that hit hard and hurt, spelling out the message that once he had had sex, he was up and away, any pretence of courtesy or caring set aside and rejected.

She felt hollow and very, very foolish. This was the aggressive male her father had blackmailed into marrying her and this was the payoff, she assumed sickly. Evidently he had taken the only thing he actually wanted from her and now she was like an abandoned toy, a distraction good enough only to be tossed back in the cupboard until the next time he wanted to take her out and play with her.

'You don't like it when I touch you after sex,' she accused baldly.

Jax shot her a winging glance from narrowed green eyes that glittered. 'Because it's fake.'

Lucy sat up. 'It wasn't fake,' she told him but he had already vanished into the bathroom and within seconds she heard the sound of a shower running.

Well, Jax needn't think that was the end of the conversation just because he wanted it that way, Lucy thought angrily. She scrambled out of bed and grabbed up her handbag to extract the letter that Kreon had given her. Whether she liked it or not, it was time to be open and honest. She opened the bedroom door and found their luggage piled outside. She lifted a case and dragged it in, opening it up to remove a light cotton robe. Nothing slinky about her nightwear, she reflected ruefully. Iola had insisted on buying her some stuff and the prospect of Jax gazing in disbelief at her chain-store PJ's had persuaded her. She wrapped herself in the robe, watching out of the corner of her eye as Jax strode naked into what sounded like an en-suite dressing room because she could hear drawers being rammed open and shut and cupboard doors being slammed. My goodness, he was in a bad mood... so much for her assumption that intimacy would bring relaxation and a release of tension!

Jax reappeared, clad in a pair of faded jeans and a black tee shirt that clung to his muscular torso. He headed straight for the trolley and opened it before lifting a plate and piling food on it. 'Would you like anything?' he asked with studious politeness and she wanted to slap him for his tone.

'Not right now, thanks,' she murmured tightly. 'I have something for you... Kreon gave it to me today.'

Jax swung round, fully acknowledging her for the first time, his lean, darkly handsome face guarded until he saw and immediately recognised what was in her hand and he stalked forward to snatch it from her with a profound look of revulsion.

'Were you in it *with* him?' Jax shot at her accusingly, for most ironically that possibility hadn't occurred to him and right there and then he called himself an idiot for not having suspected her active involvement in Kreon's blackmail threat.

Lucy's chest swelled on a stark indrawn breath of shock as she drew herself up to her full unimpressive height. 'Are you certifiably insane?' she demanded in fiery rebuttal of that suspicion. 'Yesterday, *after* the wedding, Kreon told me what he had done to you because he felt guilty. He knew he'd done wrong—'

'*Diavolos...*' Jax derided. 'Kreon felt guilty? You will never know what a comfort that is to me!'

'He did wrong but he's not a bad man and the mistake you made was in not immediately coming to me about my father's threat and the existence of that letter,' Lucy condemned with conviction. 'I believe I could've stopped it because he would have been too ashamed to continue with it once I knew about what he was doing.'

'And pigs fly and there's two blue moons in the sky,' Jax scorned, shaking his tousled dark head in wonderment, green eyes as cutting as sword blades. 'I'll ask you one more time...were you aware of his intentions?'

'No, I blasted well wasn't!' Lucy shouted back at him, her blue eyes flooded with angry, defensive discomfiture. 'How can you even ask me that? I wasn't expecting you to ask me to marry you, wasn't even thinking along those lines!'

Jax cocked his proud dark head back, black curling lashes semi-screening his stunning eyes. 'It's done now.'

'Yes,' she acknowledged uncomfortably. 'But I had nothing to do with the blackmail or any idea of what was going on behind the scenes—'

'But it all worked in your favour, all the same,' Jax spelt out with contempt. 'You got to marry into the Antonakos family.'

'Well, from where I'm standing now, on my wedding night, marrying into the Antonakos family is not the triumph it's purported to be!' Lucy shot back at him furiously, an angry flush mantling her cheeks. 'In fact it feels like hell, most particularly when I seem to have a husband who can happily have sex with me and then virtually push me away afterwards!'

'I don't cuddle...*ever*,' Jax stressed.

'Bella needs cuddles so you'll have to revise your rule and I need them too,' Lucy flung back at him rawly. 'So, if you want sex, you'll do it.'

An unholy flare of rage lit up Jax's eyes, lightening them to the brilliance of sea glass gleaming in sunshine. 'I've put up with a hell of a lot but I won't stand for *that*!' he raked back at her, every word slicing through the air like a knife. 'I married you. Be grateful for it because you're getting nothing else from me but the name and the money and a father for your child!'

And as Lucy stood there staring at him, involuntarily unnerved by the sheer force of his rage, she stilled a shiver, appalled by that assurance. 'That's not enough for me,' she muttered shakily.

'Tough,' Jax enunciated with clarity. 'That's all you'll be getting now and in the future.'

With that final statement of punitive intent, Jax strode out of the room and just left her there. Lucy ate through a whole plate of profiteroles and drank coffee and then felt sick. Her whole world had fallen into pieces round her feet and, with it, any sense of security. She lurched into the bathroom where she was sick and when she felt strong enough to stand up again she went for a shower. She knew she would never look at a profiterole again. She would never look at Jax the same way again either for she had just seen a side of him that he had never shown her before.

Now she knew what she really *hadn't* wanted to

know. He hadn't wanted to marry her. In fact he had absolutely hated and thoroughly resented having to marry her. He had suppressed that fury successfully throughout the day and she had provoked him into expressing it by asking for something more: a stupid cuddle, of all things. Her eyes stung and she looked heavenwards as she struggled to control her wildly see-sawing emotions. As far as Jax was concerned he had already given her more than enough: his famous name, his great wealth, his readiness to be a father. *Your* child, he had called Bella, not *our* child.

Why would he care that none of that would be sufficient to make her happy? Why would he care that she was hurting so bad that she wanted to scream with the pain of it? He hadn't asked her to care about him and she didn't know when or how she had started caring again. In Spain it had begun with a smile, a shared look of understanding and discussion, a touch of his hand, six weeks of breathless excitement and more happiness than she had ever experienced before she lost it all again.

But, Jax had reappeared in her life and somehow shreds of those old feelings had taken root again deep down inside her where she didn't explore very often. *She* cared. Much more than he deserved. But was that a true or fair view? Kreon had been vicious and Jax had been strong-armed by family affection into making a sacrifice he didn't want to make. Sadly, Jax wasn't any keener on the concept of marriage than he had ever been.

So, what did that leave her to work with? Lucy blinked back tears and went to clean up her face again, dashing on a little make-up in a desperate hope of relocating a hint of a lingering bridal glow. Unhappily she looked tired and heavy-eyed and pale and even bronzer didn't help. In the end she washed it all off again before she went to look for Jax.

It was the early hours of the morning but everywhere was lit up. She didn't even know what she was going to say to him but she knew that she had to deal with the situation and make something out of the mess Kreon had created. After all, they had Bella to consider and while Lucy was prepared to let go of her own dreams she wasn't prepared to give up on her dream of giving her daughter a normal family life.

She peered into empty room after empty room on the ground floor and then she found him, sprawled with a glass in his hand on a huge fancy padded lounger sited on a wide terrace from which he was watching the sun come up in a glorious multicoloured reflective rainbow over the dark sea far below the house. She hesitated beside the patio doors and then noticed that the phone he was studying was displaying a wedding photo of their daughter. And that discovery softened her and empowered her in a way nothing else could have done into moving forward.

'Jax?' she murmured uncertainly.

'We have to make a go of it…or at least *try*…for her,' Jax breathed in a raw undertone without turning his head.

'Yes…' It was exactly what Lucy wanted to hear and yet she still felt as though her heart were breaking inside her because she knew that she wanted so much more from him.

'I'm drunk,' Jax confided gruffly, wishing he weren't, wishing he were better at handling his own emotional turmoil. 'But drowning your sorrows doesn't help. It only darkens everything more.'

In the tense silence, Lucy dropped down onto the smaller lounger beside his. She didn't recline, she sat on the side of it, rigid-backed and still. A photo lay on the table between them and she lifted it. It was a picture of another little girl, a little girl who looked similar enough to Bella to be her sister.

'Who's this?' she asked worriedly, immediately wondering if Jax had another child.

'My little sister, Tina. The reason why I didn't need to wait on DNA test results to know that Bella was mine,' Jax explained reluctantly.

'I didn't know you had a sister.'

'Hardly anyone knows. When she died it was hushed up,' he muttered.

Lucy frowned. 'Your father's child?'

'No. From my mother's second marriage to an actor. He was half her age. It fell apart quickly. By then Mariana was accidentally pregnant and as a devout Catholic there was no question of her not giving birth. Valentina was born the summer I was twelve. Mariana was determined to keep her a secret because she couldn't bear the idea that her adoring fans would pity her for being abandoned a second time with a child. Unfortunately, she could never keep household staff for long. I looked after the baby that summer—'

'At twelve years old?' Lucy gasped although she was trying hard not to react to what he was telling her. 'Where was your mother?'

'Zonked out of her skull on prescription drugs...the way she always was,' Jax confided grudgingly. 'I got attached to Tina. She was a sweet kid. Mariana got another nanny before I went back to boarding school and for a couple of years everything was fine. I saw Tina in the holidays. And then Mariana had a fight with the nanny the day before she held a pool party...and Tina drowned because nobody was looking after her. My mother was a legendary star and the studio ensured that the death and the burial were dealt with very discreetly.'

'I'm so sorry, Jax,' Lucy whispered shakily.

'The worst part of it was that nobody ever mentioned Tina again. It was like she'd *never* existed.'

Lucy slid to her feet and settled on the big lounger by his side, one arm draping over him protectively.

'I don't cuddle,' he told her argumentatively.

'You're not cuddling,' Lucy assured him. 'I'm cuddling you.'

'I really don't need *or* like that sort of stuff,' he growled.

'Of course you don't. You're just tolerating me to be polite.' Lucy sighed, feeling the rigid tension in his muscles ease and snuggling into the powerful heat of his long, lean frame. 'You have such good manners, Jax.'

'I *do*?' Jax said in surprise, flipping over to face her, green eyes clear as emeralds in the dawn light.

'Most of the time,' Lucy murmured with amusement, colliding with those gorgeous eyes of his, eyes full of so much hunger and uncharacteristic uncertainty. 'I *wasn't* part of the blackmail plan.'

'I know...' Jax rubbed his dark stubbled jaw against her shoulder as if in apology. 'But I think I preferred you not knowing about what your father did.'

'I would've preferred that too,' Lucy admitted. 'But it happened and we have to deal with it.'

Assertive hands tugged at the edges of her robe and the sash before sliding beneath the crisp fabric. 'Naked,' Jax savoured. 'I like, *glyka mou.*'

Lucy bridled. 'I wasn't thinking about that when I came looking for you. I couldn't be bothered poking through another case to find clothes...'

'Shush...' Jax murmured, long brown fingers rubbing with devastating expertise over the most sensitive spot on her entire body to set off a devastating tingling awareness before sliding down below. 'I want you.'

'Here?' she gasped in consternation even as her slender thighs parted and her hips shifted in a rhythm as old as time.

'I sent the staff to bed when we arrived. Poor Theo had kept them all up,' Jax told her. 'I don't need attention twenty-four-seven...except from you.'

Lucy's rosy lips parted on a helpless gasp. 'Twenty-four-seven?' she framed with difficulty.

'I'll make it well worth your while,' Jax promised, crushing her ripe mouth urgently under his as he unzipped his jeans and shifted over her with urgent intent. 'Let's take this back into honeymoon territory...'

And Lucy, at that moment malleable as clay in his expert hands with her body rising and burning and already defencelessly eager, had no objection to that plan. They had weathered the first storm, learned that for both of them Bella was their main focus. That had to be enough, she told herself urgently, a strangled sound escaping her convulsing throat as he pinned her under him and plunged into her with raw, hungry energy.

Pushing for more would only strain their relationship, which meant that *she* had to learn to settle for what she could get. And if that meant forgiving his suspicion that she could have been involved in her father's blackmail, she had to do it. It was early days, she reminded herself.

Yet how could he suspect her of such dishonest behaviour? And why did he assume that her affection was faked? Was his past so littered with unscrupulous lovers that trust was impossible for him?

CHAPTER NINE

'You were telling me about your adoptive parents,' Jax reminded her as they walked along the deserted beach three weeks later, walking Bella between them to keep the little girl steady.

'Was I? They were good people. I was nine years old and very fortunate to get a home at that age,' Lucy declared wryly.

'I imagine you were a very pretty little girl. I'm sure that helped.'

Lucy shrugged, thinking back to that brief three-year period when she had been part of a family. 'They were very academic. When they took me on they were warned that I'd fallen behind at school and straight off they decided to hire tutors for me in every subject.'

Jax frowned. 'Impatient, were they?'

'No, they were trying to help but it put me under a lot of pressure. I was trying very hard to be everything they wanted and then I failed an important exam, which meant I couldn't get into the school they had set their hearts on and they were really disappointed. I don't think I was the right child for them,' she admitted ruefully. 'But when they died in the car crash, all that ended and I went back into care because none of their relatives saw me as being part of the family. At the end of the day and whether you agree with it or not, blood counts.'

'Yes, doesn't it?' Jax agreed, thinking of his late brother, Argo, a good-natured, indolent young man, who with hindsight had been remarkably dissimilar to Heracles and Jax in nature.

Bella tugged her hand free of her mother's and pulled at Jax's jeans to be lifted. He hoisted her high and she giggled and rested her curly head down sleepily on his bare shoulder. Their interaction was so relaxed and natural now, Lucy thought with satisfaction, that it was hard to believe they had only met a month ago.

She and Jax hadn't lasted a whole week on the island without Bella. Lucy had never been separated from her daughter before and had decided a week was unnecessarily long when there was a nanny on the household staff, willing and able to give the honeymooners a break from childcare: Heracles had prepared for every eventuality when he entertained. But the rumour of a private zoo had proved to be just that—a rumour.

The gardens, however, were spectacular although Jax and Lucy had spent more time on the beach, crunching through the pale sand to the water's edge where Lucy, who could not swim, liked to paddle. Never having enjoyed many such opportunities, she was not keen on trusting her body to either a swimming pool or the sea, but Jax had insisted that her learning to swim was a safety issue more than anything else. So, Lucy had braved swimming lessons with Jax, which they had both found equally trying,

Jax because he was naturally impatient and Lucy because she was nervous.

Over the past three weeks they had learned so much about each other, she acknowledged cheerfully. Jax was a morning person, Lucy was a night person. They had spent a wonderful ten days cruising round the Mediterranean on his father's yacht, *Sea Queen*, docking at different islands to see the sights, dine out and shop. She loved to dance and they had enjoyed several really late nights out at clubs. He had bought her loads of clothes in hip boutiques on Crete and Mykonos and he had had a jeweller flown out to Tifnos for her to choose what he deemed to be the basics. A gold watch now encircled a wrist and gold hoops ornamented her ears. She had a diamond pendant, bracelet and earrings as well, which he had referred to as a 'belated' wedding gift. And Bella had a nursery overflowing with toys and clothing and picture books to go with the designer furnishings.

In fact, Lucy believed she already had almost everything she had ever wanted or ever dreamt of having. Jax had spoiled them both. He was marvellous with Bella, far more patient with her than he was with anyone else. He was making a huge effort to be a dad and she appreciated that when so many of his friends, smooth sophisticates whom they had met in the clubs where he was well known, had yet to even settle down. For a man who had never wanted to marry, Jax was settling down into family life remarkably well, she reflected gratefully.

Yet she couldn't forget that Jax was the same guy who had dumped her for 'boring' him two years earlier, the same guy who had seemed perfectly content with her one day and who had then cut her out of his life only days later. That past still made her insecure because she had no faith that she could accurately read Jax and estimate his state of mind with regard to her and their marriage. Of course, he seemed to do and say all the right things, but then he had done that before in Spain and look how that had ended!

'I'm hungry...' Jax curved a hand to Lucy's shoulder and steered her up the beach towards the buggy that would waft them up the steep hill. 'And I think our daughter needs a nap...and maybe I need one too, *glyka mou.*'

Lucy coloured. Heat licked at her feminine core as Jax sent her a glittering green glance of sensual enquiry. Dampness gathered between her legs, anticipation rising because that side of their relationship was outrageously healthy. He still wasn't doing the cuddling thing the way she wanted. No, with Jax what might start out as a cuddle invariably turned into sex. He said he couldn't be that close to her and touch her without wanting to get naked and energetic. There was nowhere they hadn't made love. They had indulged on the beach, in the pool, in the pine forest, in the labyrinthine privacy of the lush gardens, but most often in the delicious comfort of their own bed. The simmering flare-ups of passion that wound through their days felt so natural to her. It was as if Jax couldn't get enough of her, a thought she kept tactfully to herself, and that made her feel safer. She couldn't help viewing sex as a barometer to gauge the health of their marriage because Jax certainly wasn't any keener to discuss such things than he had ever been.

'It's those freckles. I can't resist them,' Jax said huskily, skimming the bridge of her nose with a teasing finger.

Lucy laughed because she hated her freckles, seeing them as imperfections, but Jax thought they looked delightfully natural, which of course they were. Did anyone draw in freckles? She thought not and smiled as they piled into the buggy. A pang of sadness infiltrated her mood because the honeymoon as such was almost over. Jax was meeting with Heracles about some big project in Athens the following morning and she was accompanying him because she planned to take Bella to visit her father and Iola. She was hoping that the passage of time since her wedding day and Bella's noisy presence would make the occasion less tense and awkward.

In actuality, Jax wasn't looking forward to the next day either. He intended to confront his father with the file Heracles had had sent to him on Lucy two years before. From what he had so far managed to establish the file was full of inaccuracies and outright lies and he needed to know if those lies had been a deliberate attempt to break up their relationship or the simple product of a lazy investigator and a case of mistaken identity. He could scarcely censure Kreon's ethics if his own father was guilty of the same lack of moral scruple when it came to getting the result he wanted most.

Even so, he still could not have said which answer he wanted to hear from Heracles because if the older man actually *believed* the contents of that file, it outraged Jax in a way he could not rationally explain. Yet he, more than anyone, knew Lucy was far from perfect. His mind skipped superfast over that acknowledgement and tucked the memory of that alleyway encounter back into the box where he kept it locked away. She had made an unforgivable mistake and he *had* to live with that…for Bella's sake, he told himself urgently, *only* for Bella's sake.

Bella's nanny took the little girl off to bed. Lucy went for a shower because she was hot and sandy and she wasn't at all surprised when Jax stepped into the shower with her, all lithe, wet bronzed skin and rippling muscles. She ran her hands up appreciatively over his torso and as the water jets shot at them, sprinkling even their faces with droplets, his mouth came crashing passionately down on hers. He tasted her with raw driving need and as always the strength of his hunger for her disconcerted her. He gathered her slippery body up and pinned her against the cold tiles, lifting her thighs round his waist while rocking and grinding against the tender triangle of flesh at the heart of her.

That fast she wanted him intolerably and with every probing plunge of his tongue she wanted him more. Evocative little noises were wrenched from low in her throat as skilled fingers teased and played to prepare her for his entrance. And then he tilted her back and thrust into her with vigour while she clung to his shoulders, her ankles wrapped round him. He grunted with raw male satisfaction, his hand supporting her hips as he pounded her yielding body with delicious force. Excitement writhed through Lucy in an unstoppable surge and she reached her peak with an involuntary cry, convulsive waves of exquisite pleasure rippling through her lower body as an orgasmic flush spread over her sun-dappled skin.

'I didn't use a condom,' Jax groaned in her ear as

he slowly lowered her back to her own feet. 'Is that likely to be a problem?'

'Hopefully not,' Lucy muttered after doing some quick calculations and without looking directly at him as she stepped out of the shower and grabbed a towel. 'It's the wrong time of the month.'

What had he meant by that question? Was he asking her if she was willing to get pregnant again? Or was he worrying that she *would* conceive? And for that matter, was she willing to take that risk? Lucy thought not. She had not had an easy pregnancy the first time around and was not in a hurry to do it again, particularly when she did not yet feel secure with Jax. Even so, if she did conceive she would still welcome and love her baby.

But then what would it take for her to feel truly secure with Jax? she asked herself. Perhaps she was her own worst enemy and had quite unrealistic expectations of a marriage in which only one of them loved. She might not like the reality but their relationship was bound to be unbalanced with one of them wanting and hoping for more than the other.

'Did you know that the contents of that file were a complete fiction?'

'What do you want me to tell you?' Heracles slapped the file on Lucy back onto his desk and sighed heavily. 'I will not lie. I did what I felt I *had* to do.'

Sharply disconcerted, Jax tensed even more, anger roaring through his tall, powerful frame because he had somehow expected the older man to try and evade his very direct question. 'Why did you think you *had* to do anything? Why did you even think that it was your place to interfere? It wasn't as though I was talking about marrying her—'

'Jax...in the space of two weeks, you flew back to Spain *five* times to see her,' Heracles traded defiantly. 'That was enough for me to view her as a serious contender for something and when I discovered that she was the daughter of Kreon Thiarkis, well, to be really blunt...that was that. Thiarkis is a slippery customer, always has been, always will be and I will not apologise for not wanting a criminal's daughter involved with my family.'

'I know Kreon's history,' Jax interposed harshly. 'I know what he is and I can understand your concern but I was twenty-six years old, *not* a teenager, and you had no right to interfere.'

The older man stood his ground. 'I know I had no right but I didn't care. Years ago I watched Thiarkis charm my deluded first wife into paying for his legal representation in court when he was charged with fraud—'

'Two years ago, Lucy hadn't even *met* her father,' Jax pointed out rawly. 'What I had with her was our business alone, nothing to do with your ongoing distaste for Thiarkis. And far be it from me to say a word in Kreon's defence but for over thirty years he held onto a letter that would have made his fortune had he sold it to the press...'

Jax settled the letter Lucy had given him down on the desk. 'Your first wife confessed her sins on paper during her last days.'

His father turned grey before his eyes and dropped down suddenly into his office chair, studying the letter as if it were a cobra likely to strike out at him. 'Sofia was never discreet,' he muttered heavily. 'Are you telling me I have to thank Thiarkis for his restraint?'

'No,' Jax breathed in a driven undertone, having decided not to reveal the secret of Kreon's blackmail. 'But it's time you came to terms with the fact that he is Lucy's father and stopped visiting your experiences and your resentments on *my* life. I'm not Argo—'

'I know you're not,' Heracles acknowledged grimly. 'Argo always did as he was told and you *won't*, which is why I went behind your back in the first place. I assumed she would be wrong for you.'

'She's not,' Jax bit out curtly. 'But because of that file I treated her badly and now I have to tell her why.'

Heracles compressed his lips in disapproval. '*Do* you? I don't think that's a good idea. A wise man shares nothing with his wife but a bed.'

'Three wives and you *still* don't know better?' Jax derided with seething bite. 'Well, I do know better and I will not tolerate your meddling in my life. If you ever do anything like this again, I'm *out*.'

'You can't mean that,' Heracles breathed in consternation.

'I do. Blood counts but family counts more and you were out of my life for too many years to be considered family in the same way that I consider my wife and my daughter. They come first…*always*.'

Simmering with angry frustration, Jax sat in his limo in the heavy Athens traffic mulling over that confrontation. Heracles had finally apologised and at least his father had at last told him the truth. Jax hated secrets. He had grown up in an atmosphere of secrecy, continually urged never to tell anyone that his mother was 'ill', pregnant or involved with a man. As a boy, he had reacted to those warnings by deciding to never tell anyone at school that the famous Spanish movie star was his mother. It had been a rather pathetic ploy considering that the name Antonakos was too well known and just about everyone who was anyone knew his father had divorced Mariana for having an affair with one of her co-stars. But the practice of keeping his thoughts and feelings and personal details strictly private had been taught to him when he was very young and had become a habit he couldn't shake...until he'd met Lucy and told her things he had never told anyone before.

And if he was honest that experience had totally unnerved him two years earlier. He had seen that he was veering into dangerous territory and had feared getting too involved with a woman again. *Feared?* No, obviously he had been in no hurry to admit that to himself. His mother had been frighteningly volatile, constantly ranging between high and low moods while using drugs as a crutch to get her through the day. Freed by Mariana's death from the powerful conviction that it was *his* responsibility to look after her, Jax had decided that emotion was a weakness and that a sensible man steered clear of it. Most of the time that had worked very well for him.

Until he'd met Lucy...

Until he'd met Bella...

Jax poured himself a stiff drink and drank it down. He *had* to tell Lucy. How could he *not* tell her? He reminded himself that she had married him even after what he had done in Spain. He reminded himself that she seemed happy. He didn't have to love her to make her happy. Hadn't he already proved that? Together they had the fathers from hell. Not her fault, not his fault either. He would give her the facts. She would be angry and hurt but she would forgive him. Jax knew he wasn't the forgiving type but he was convinced from recent experience that Lucy *was*. They had signed up to be a family for Bella's benefit. And that would be Lucy's bottom line because more than anything else, Jax reminded himself doggedly, after a life of turmoil Lucy craved security.

And he offered security, he offered a *lot* of security, he reflected with growing assurance. But it still really bothered him that she wasn't clingier and more open with him. The Lucy he remembered in Spain had been distinctly needy and clingy and, although he ran a mile from that trait in other women, for some reason he had liked that attribute in Lucy as much as he had liked her once flaky tell-all chatter. He had liked it when he was the first person she looked for in a room, when he was the only one she really smiled at or noticed, when she wrapped herself round him all night as though she was afraid he might attempt an escape. He had liked being told that he was loved even if in the end it had all turned out to be a lie.

But she didn't do those things any more even though he wanted her to. She was wary. Of course she was, he conceded, struggling to be fair, so, putting the truth out there was a sensible move, he told himself squarely. He would tell her what had really happened and she would forgive him because that was what Lucy did. And what choice would she have? a more cynical voice enquired. After all, she had betrayed his trust too...

* * *

'He's treating you well?' Kreon prompted while Iola was playing in the garden with Bella.

'Yes,' Lucy told her father flatly. 'But I won't discuss Jax with you.'

'A wife should be loyal to her husband,' Kreon remarked equably. 'I simply wanted you to be happy—'

'I can only be happy with a man who is happy to *be* with me,' Lucy countered drily, resisting the urge to remind him that he hadn't thought of that angle.

But with Jax being the very practical but reserved male that he was, he was more likely to make the best of a bad job than try to wriggle out of the commitment, particularly when his daughter was involved. Lucy showered and changed while telling herself that she had absolutely nothing to complain about. Whatever else, she was married to the love of her life. There was nothing she could do about the fact that she had only gained a wedding ring through her father's dirty tricks. But she knew that somewhere in the back of Jax's astute brain he would probably *always* associate her with her father's treachery and would never quite forgive her for his lack of choice and loss of freedom.

'He gave in to me very easily. That is *not* an Antonakos trait,' Kreon argued.

'Obviously he cares about his father.'

'I believe he cares more about you.'

Unconvinced by that startling claim, Lucy returned to the city villa with nerves run ragged by the strain of pretending for Iola's benefit that everything was fine between her father and her. She had been surprised that Jax hadn't objected to her visiting Kreon and Iola and then relieved because her father was still her father even though he was imperfect. *Imperfect?* Manipulative, sneaky, quick to jump on a golden opportunity even if it entailed blackmail, Lucy's brain added unhappily. But until she had met her father and learned about the existence of her sisters, she had believed that her father was her only living relative and his support and acceptance had meant a great deal to her. That he was capable of going to such lengths to secure a very rich husband for her still devastated her because of course it had to make a difference to her marriage and the light in which Jax saw her.

If Kreon hadn't interfered, who knew what might have happened? All right, they would clearly not have got married, she allowed ruefully, but at least Jax wouldn't have felt forced into doing something he didn't want to do.

Lucy had only just finished drying her hair when Jax strode into the bedroom. He paused for a second, appreciating the sight of her small slender figure in a summery blue dress, tumbling ringlets framing her piquant face. 'You look ridiculously pretty,' he heard himself say stiltedly, and he almost winced at that ill-timed opener because he had come upstairs to give her the investigation file.

Lucy angled her head to one side and gave him a questioning look. 'You never pay me compliments. What's wrong?'

He had called her pretty, not beautiful, and she was more than happy with that, well aware that her looks weren't on the beauty level. In marrying Jax, she had boxed above her weight because *he* was the beautiful one in their relationship, standing there in his exquisitely tailored silver-grey suit, his stunning bone structure accentuated by a shadow of black stubble, gorgeous green eyes glittering like stars in his lean bronzed face.

'Never?' Jax was taken aback by her claim, only belatedly recognising that she was right. He thought such things but he very rarely voiced them out loud. 'I have something for you to read.'

He looked so very serious that Lucy's heart gave a sudden lurch inside her chest. 'OK,' she said apprehensively.

He extended the file. 'My father sent this to me two years ago in Spain. It's why I didn't turn up that last night.'

Lucy grasped the slim file and sank down heavily on the foot of the bed. 'Your father?' she queried with a bemused frown.

'He had discovered who your father was and apparently he was determined to break us up,' Jax explained flatly. 'The file is filled with what I now know to be lies about you.'

Lucy lowered her shaken gaze to the file, thoroughly off balanced by what he was revealing because it was coming at her out of nowhere. Suddenly he was talking about what had happened in Spain and admitting that he hadn't ditched her simply because he had got bored. 'You *now* know…?' she questioned with an uncertain questioning glance.

'I had my own investigation carried out,' he admitted smoothly.

And Lucy was even more shaken at the enormous amount of stuff that Jax had been hiding from her, not to mention the lowering reality of just how much his father had not wanted her in his family. She swallowed hard and, breathing in bracingly, she opened the file and straight away she could not credit what she was reading. It was a seriously exaggerated character assassination in print, from the outrageous allegation that she had convictions for drug dealing and soliciting sex to the fact that her age was quoted as being twenty-five.

'But how could you possibly have believed *any* of this?' she heard herself whisper with incredulous emphasis.

'It was in the early stages of my new relationship with my father and I trusted him. I had no reason to be suspicious of his motives because I had no knowledge of his acquaintance with your father or his dislike of him,' he pointed out flatly.

Lucy shook her head very slowly, an almost dazed light in her luminous blue eyes as she focussed on him. 'You misunderstood my question. I'm not asking why you believed your father but how on earth you could believe that kind of nonsense about *me*? Soliciting *sex*? I was a virgin when we met!' she reminded him with sudden resentful heat. 'And you knew that!'

Jax compressed his lips, wearing the aspect of a male who would have liked to be anywhere but where he was at that moment. He shifted his feet uneasily. 'A woman can fool a man over stuff like that. She can pretend,' he began uncomfortably.

'Then you must have assumed my acting ability rivalled your mother's!' Lucy slotted in a little shakily because anger was rising now to cut through the shock of what she was learning. 'I just don't know what to say about all this…*stuff*!' she selected jaggedly, tossing the file down on the floor in disgust. 'I thought you *knew* me—'

'I thought I knew you too until I read that file,' Jax admitted curtly. 'But I had no good reason then to suspect my father of setting me up.'

'So, you're telling me then that he was responsible for me losing my job?'

'I didn't go into that with him... I was far too angry,' Jax confessed. 'But it's probable that he *was* responsible for that and for the manner in which you were treated as you were put off the yacht. If I had stayed long enough to get into that kind of detail I probably would have *hit* him...'

'Oh...' Lucy was a long way from forgiving him for having had so little faith in her but she was certainly mollified by that little speech.

'You were pregnant,' Jax pointed out, still stuck on that offence with an anger she could see making his lean, darkly handsome features rigid. 'You could have been seriously hurt. He could have killed his own grandchild...we could have lost Bella!'

Lucy warmed up to him a little more in response to that additional really quite emotional exclamation. Jax had only known her for six weeks in Spain. Six weeks and a handful of dates. They had finally become intimate during the final two weeks of that time frame. Why would he have distrusted his father? The father then riding high on the wave of finally deciding to accept and welcome the younger son he had once ignored?

Lucy felt that she had to be fair to Jax. After all, she had not distrusted Kreon when she first came to Greece, had she? It occurred to her that Jax was probably feeling much as she had felt on their wedding day, angry and hurt and defensive while wondering how someone he cared about and respected could have done such a thing to him.

'I think the very least you could have done was speak to me about the file and give me the chance to answer those allegations,' Lucy told him firmly. 'There is no excuse whatsoever for you failing to tell me about that file two years ago.'

And Jax's long, lean, powerful physique went rigid, shoulders squaring, legs straightening. 'Actually there is...'

'No, there's not.' Lucy could understand and forgive a great deal but he could not justify his complete failure to tell her what was going on either in the past or the present. 'You didn't even send me a text in Spain to tell me we were finished, for goodness' sake!' she exclaimed.

'I had my reasons,' Jax breathed in a raw undertone, his eyes gleaming like polished gems.

'Unacceptable reasons.' Lucy refused to give way. She often gave in to Jax because he had a very forceful personality but she knew she couldn't go through life without disagreeing with him occasionally. 'You owed me an explanation of some kind—'

'I owed you *nothing*!' Jax shot at her with sudden derision. 'I did come to see you the night after I received that file.'

Her brow had furrowed because she was beginning to feel a little lost in the dialogue, as though she had misinterpreted some crucial sentence. 'You *didn't* come to see me—'

'And do you know why?' Jax's hands knotted into

fists because he felt like a volcano about to spew lava and somewhere in the back of his mind lurked a tiny voice asking him if he *really* wanted to say what he was about to say. But Jax didn't back down, had never learned *how* to back down. He only knew how to come out of a corner fighting and how to win. He had had a hell of a day and it wasn't getting better the way it was supposed to, it was only getting *worse* and that thought did nothing to cool his temper. He had done nothing wrong with Lucy, he was, in his own opinion, the injured party. He was not a vengeful man but he would not be accused of something he wasn't responsible for.

'If I did, I wouldn't be arguing with you or trying to get you to see my point of view,' Lucy parried.

'I bet you don't even remember that night...'

'I remember it very well,' Lucy admitted, lifting her chin. 'What's this all about, Jax? I'm getting confused—'

His eyes narrowed, his mouth flattening. 'I drove over to the bar and before I could get out of my car, I saw you walking down the alleyway in your red dress—'

'It wasn't me you saw,' Lucy sliced in thinly. When Jax had failed to turn up to see her the night before Lucy had stayed in her attic room after doing her shift, frantically hoping that Jax would magically appear with an explanation. Like a child waiting for Santa Claus she had refused to believe he wouldn't show up eventually and she had been terrified of somehow missing him. She had had that much faith in him, that much *trust*...

'It was you. You were with a man—'

'You're mistaken,' Lucy told him confidently.

'I followed you because I assumed you were heading for the entrance that led up to your room but you weren't,' Jax informed her stonily. 'You stayed outside to have sex with the man you were with against the wall.'

Her lashes fluttered up on disbelieving bright blue eyes and she stared back at him. 'You think that I had sex with some guy in the alley?' she demanded with a revulsion she couldn't hide. 'Are you kidding me?'

Lean, strong face shuttered and forbidding, Jax stood his ground because naturally he hadn't expected her to own up to her behaviour. 'You know I'm not kidding and what I saw that night is why you never heard from me again. There was no point in showing you that file when you were already with another man,' he proclaimed harshly. 'I don't need to apologise or make excuses for not approaching you again.'

'I agree,' Lucy said with wooden diction, shattered inside herself but holding it all together out of pride. 'If I had been with another man that soon, you owed me nothing. Clearly, it suited you very well to assume that night that the girl in the alley was me—'

'And what's that supposed to mean?' Jax shot at her suspiciously.

'Well, you'd seen that file and learned that your precious father did not approve of me. It was really incredibly convenient for you that in spite of everything you knew about me you decided to accept that file and *assume* that I was the sort of young woman who would have sex in an alley.'

Lucy could feel her cheekbones ache with the strain of keeping her face composed but there was a much deeper ache of pain inside her chest. She knew he didn't love her. She knew he had never loved her. That wounding knowledge had chipped away at her upbeat outlook on their marriage and she had fought it off, telling herself to settle sensibly for what she could get. But for the first time ever, Lucy decided that Jax was *bad* for her.

Never mind the Antonakos fame, the money and the gorgeous looks. Two years back, she had told Jax that she loved him and she *had*, but he had given nothing back, not the words nor any other form of commitment. He had held back from her, he had always held back from her and now she finally knew why. But she deserved better. She deserved a man who would, at the very least, refuse to *believe* that she would have sex in public with some chance-met stranger. And Jax hadn't had that faith in her and probably never would have. A horrible sense of emptiness spread inside her. *Her* loving him wasn't enough.

'It *was* you. I recognised the dress,' Jax bit out, exasperated by the stretching silence and the strange way she was staring at him.

'Yes...you may have done but it wasn't me *wearing* the dress,' Lucy countered tightly. 'I loaned it to Tara that night because she had a hot date and I imagine she was fooling around in the alley because she could hardly bring a man back to the room we shared when I was there. Not everyone has a private room or a yacht available for these things...'

Jax froze. 'It *couldn't* have been her! Why would she have been wearing the dress I bought you?'

Lucy sent him a weary glance of exasperation. 'Because we shared our clothes. We didn't have much but what we had, we *shared*. Half the clothes you saw me wear that summer belonged to Tara.'

'It couldn't have been her,' Jax repeated again doggedly, struggling to remember her friend before dimly recalling the much more worldly blonde whom Lucy had worked and lived with.

Lucy shrugged a shoulder in a jerky movement. 'Well, it doesn't much matter after this length of time, does it?' she traded.

'It matters to me. And it *must* matter to you,' Jax told her with assurance.

'No, it doesn't,' Lucy responded heavily.

Jax hovered and clenched his teeth hard. He wanted it dealt with and then never mentioned again. But could it have been Tara in that stupid dress? It had been dark and Tara had had long blonde hair too. Between the street lights and the shadows, it was possible that he had been mistaken. And if he had been mistaken, it would be the very first time in Jax's life that he would ever be *grateful* to have made a mistake. Didn't she appreciate that? Didn't she understand what believing she would behave that way had done to *him*? Refusing to look at him, Lucy was staring at the tiled floor instead as if she were expecting it to start showing a movie and frustration racked Jax's tall powerful frame. *Women!* She had gone into a weird mood now and he would probably get nothing more out of her.

'I have a meeting. I was planning to reschedule it and take us back to Tifnos—'

'No, go to your meeting,' Lucy urged, her throat convulsing, and she still wouldn't let herself look at him because she didn't want what she felt in her heart to show.

'We can fly back in the morning,' Jax commented. 'The timing would probably suit Bella better than a late flight.'

Lucy listened to the door close on his exit and continued to sit there with tears rolling silently down her cheeks. Jax had just shown her how he really thought of her and how he saw her and it was...it *was* ugly, uglier than she could bear or forgive or comprehend. To think that all those weeks on the island he had believed that she had been unfaithful to him and yet he hadn't said a word, hadn't even given her the chance to explain or defend herself. It was so cruel, so unfair but you couldn't change a man, couldn't alter what went on inside his head.

Jax didn't trust her, had never trusted even a word she'd said. He had been her one and only lover and he couldn't even believe that. She had been too young and immature at nineteen to recognise how cynical and distrustful Jax was. She had realised that he was pretty jealous and possessive but her awareness had gone no deeper than that. She thought of him seeing Tara in that grubby alley and believing it was her and a stifled sob of pain and regret and humiliation was wrenched from her. That hurt so much and it seemed with Jax at that moment that he did nothing but hurt and disillusion her. She didn't want to stay married to a man like that, she *couldn't* stay married to a man who thought so little of her...

And when the wave of conflicting emotions began to tear at Lucy more than she could stand she dug out her phone and rang her sister, Polly, desperately needing a shoulder to cry on.

Polly was a terrific listener. Lucy let the whole

sorry story of her relationship with Jax and Kreon spill out and, very satisfyingly, Polly was even more appalled by the alleyway accusation than Lucy had been.

'Come and stay with us, Lucy,' Polly suggested warmly. 'You need a holiday. I know you felt that you were happy with him at first but Jax doesn't seem to appreciate you the way a husband should. It's possible that he resents you for what your father did.'

To Lucy in that instant the prospect of walking away into a different environment shone like a bright welcoming light. 'I don't even know where you live, Polly,' she pointed out unevenly.

'In a country called Dharia. It's one of the Gulf States,' Polly explained.

Lucy was flummoxed by that news. 'I don't know how I'd get there or even how I'd get away from here.'

'Don't you worry about that,' Polly told her assertively. 'I will arrange everything. If you leave tonight, we'll be having breakfast together in the morning and I can get hold of Ellie and she could be here by this weekend. We really do want to meet you and your daughter, Lucy.'

'Leave...*tonight*?' Lucy gasped in astonishment, wondering if it would be wrong of her to take her daughter with her as well and then deciding that, just at that moment, losing both of them was what Jax deserved for his distrust.

'I don't think you should waste any more time on the Antonakos family. They don't love or value you but we *will*.'

And Polly's enthusiasm was the deciding factor for Lucy, who usually took more time to decide anything of a serious nature. But at least she didn't feel like crying any longer, she registered with relief, because crying after Jax had gone over her like a steam roller with his nasty allegations seemed feeble. Jax didn't want her and his father didn't want her in his precious family and her own father had seriously disappointed her. A fresh start and the friendship of her sisters looked a lot more promising than her current situation.

'Tonight will be fine,' she assured Polly. 'I'll start packing. I suppose it will be very hot?'

'Yes, but the pal—er...my place is air-conditioned,' her sister informed her.

CHAPTER TEN

JAX WAS STUNNED. He ran through the empty wardrobes again as if he expected to find Lucy curled up below the empty coat hangers in hiding. He wandered back to the empty nursery, stared into the even emptier cot and then hurriedly strode back downstairs again.

'Take me through it again,' he urged Zenas jerkily, struggling to master the kind of emotions he generally never allowed to see the light of day. Emotions like panic, fear and insecurity that could tear a man to pieces as they had once torn apart the boy he had been. Having frequently lived those emotions in childhood and adolescence, he had sworn never to give them space again. But there they were still inside him, he discovered, just waiting their chance to jump on him and either paralyse him or urge him to make fundamentally stupid decisions…

Zenas breathed in deep, a wary eye on Jax, who was visibly pale and stressed. 'A diplomatic limousine with a foreign flag drew up. An Arab man in a suit and a crowd of heavies got out. The man had diplomatic credentials but he spoke neither Greek nor English and was unwilling to engage with my questions. Your wife opened the door with your daughter in her arms. She had a stack of suitcases waiting in the hall—'

'And you just let her *go*...?' Jax repeated incredulously. 'You let a bunch of foreigners *kidnap*—'

'She wasn't kidnapped. She went of her own free will,' Zenas told him apologetically. 'We followed the car to the airport where the whole party proceeded through VIP diplomatic channels to which we were denied access. From what we can establish a private jet flew Mrs Antonakos and the little girl to Dharia.'

The name of that country rang a bell of familiarity with Jax. His brow furrowed. There had been some connection. *Thee mou*, his one-time business partner, Rio Benedetti, was married to the sister of the Queen of Dharia...who was coincidentally called... Polly, just like Lucy's long-lost sister. No, he shook away the suspicion until he thought about that slick diplomatic kidnapping—he refused to accept that Lucy had willingly left him—and then the suspicion lodged deep.

Lucy was making a statement, he told himself grimly. He should do nothing and wait for her to get in touch. Lucy would not walk out on him, he told himself. She was annoyed with him. There was nothing he could do about that. He was merely paying the price for having finally told her the truth and if she didn't like the truth, what was he supposed to do about it? Satisfied that he had reached a mature and measured decision, Jax poured himself a stiff drink.

Within the hour he was back pacing the empty marital bedroom. He should not have been imagining Lucy there because they had never yet spent a night in his Athens villa. Yet inexplicably memories of Lucy were everywhere around him. He pictured her on the bed, the softness of her pouty lips, the delicate paleness of her skin, the silky fall of her hair running between his fingers. He snatched in a stark breath. There was a tiny spiralling blonde hair on the dressing table and the scent of the perfume he had bought her in Mykonos still lingered on the air. The bedding was still creased from where she had sat while they'd talked that very afternoon.

Talked? Well, she hadn't really talked, he acknowledged tardily, indeed had been remarkably quiet for a chatterbox. With hindsight it became clear to Jax that she had been upset, *seriously* upset. And he hadn't picked up on that. How could he *not* have picked up on that?

Still locked in the mindset he had had for two long years, Jax had continued to feel like the victim of her treachery. But what if there had been no betrayal in the first place? What if that ridiculous story about sharing clothes was genuine? What if he had abandoned her in Spain two years earlier without any excuse for doing so? And what if he had blown up his marriage over a stupid red dress and a mindless need to finally confront Lucy?

Jax paced, feeling in dire need of another drink but knowing he shouldn't have one when his brain was already leapfrogging all over the place. Lucy and Bella were gone and he could live with that, couldn't he? A divorce, shared custody, parental access…?

Suddenly feeling very short of breath, Jax froze. There was a tightness in his chest and a dryness in his throat and his heart was thundering in his ears. No, he couldn't live with that option, he decided with dizzy abruptness.

And as so often before when life challenged Jax, anger came to his rescue. He wasn't letting the queen of some tinpot country steal his wife and child! Lucy had been lured away from him and misled and he was going to get her back pronto where she belonged, which was in Greece with him.

'By the sound of it, Jax really doesn't know how to deal with the emotional stuff,' Ellie remarked with a wry smile on her lips.

'That's an understatement,' Polly inputted with a sniff. 'That alley business…accusing her of *that*—'

Ellie laughed and Lucy looked at her red-headed sister in surprise. 'But don't you see? It was all still as fresh as yesterday for Jax, which tells you that he never got over it. Two years on he's still agonising over that alley…yet he still decides to *stay* married to you, he takes you on a honeymoon, acts happy, treats you decently in every other way. It took the equivalent of torture to get the story about the alley out of him because he's *ashamed* that he still wants you, regardless of what he supposedly thinks you did. No, really, Lucy…you can learn a lot from reading between the lines.'

Lucy smiled at that more optimistic viewpoint even if she didn't quite believe in it. She coiled back into her comfortable corner of the sofa in the beautiful room with its impossibly high domed ceiling and wished that she could see what Ellie appeared to see in Jax's behaviour. Her two sisters were so different. Polly was warm and caring, almost motherly, while Ellie was very clever and sympathetic and their children, *her* nephews and nieces, she noted with pleasure, were simply gorgeous.

Polly's boys, Karim and Hassan and Ellie's daughter, Teresina were playing out in the shaded courtyard on trikes. Ellie was feeding her baby boy, Olly, with a bottle while Polly was nursing her newborn daughter, Haifa. Bella was watching the older children scoot around on their bikes while chasing a ball. Karim got off his bike simply to move Bella back a little with her toys, looking out for the toddler in the most considerate way for a small boy.

Lucy was shaken to admit that she would have been crazily happy in her sister's gorgeous royal palace were it not for Jax's absence. The discovery that her eldest sister was a ruling queen with her husband, Rashad, and that Ellie was the working wife of a fabulously wealthy Italian had certainly helped to take Lucy's mind off her own problems. The three women had sat up into the early hours the first night they were all together, exchanging histories, talking about the three rings they had inherited and catching up on a lifetime of different experiences.

Talking about Jax had come later and had sent Lucy's mood plummeting again because, even though she still felt that walking out on Jax had been the only thing she could do, there was a hollow place inside her where her heart had been ripped out.

In the back of her mind lurked the conviction that Jax had been hurt so much in life just like herself yet they dealt with emotions in very different ways. Jax buried his, hid troubling issues and lived in virtual denial of his feelings. Lucy wore everything on the surface and picked herself up again emotionally no matter how often she was kicked. But she hadn't reacted that way at her last encounter with Jax, she acknowledged.

He had hurt her too much and for the first time ever with Jax she had hidden her feelings as well.

In a sense that had been cruel of her and hitting him over the head with something large and heavy might have been kinder. Feelings had to be shoved in Jax's face like placards for him to read them. He had probably been very shocked by her departure and he was probably furious that she had taken their daughter with her. But he still wouldn't understand *why* she had left, which bothered her. The truth was all that had mattered to Jax and he had finally told it without grasping the damage he was doing. He had expected her to excuse him for past events soured by their fathers' machinations. He had not been capable of realising that she had been devastated because everything he had said had spelled out the message that he had never loved, respected or even understood her. How could she possibly love someone like that?

'He's a man. He might as well be from another planet,' Ellie mocked quietly. 'Rio was exactly the same, hiding things, holding onto the past—'

'Rashad too,' Polly admitted ruefully. 'So, perhaps Jax *could* be rehabilitated...'

Lucy studied her linked hands, unable to imagine Jax budging a stubborn inch from his own convictions.

The door opened, framing Rashad, the King of Dharia. Tall and very handsome, he flashed a smile at his wife. 'Polly...we have a visitor. He thinks we kidnapped his wife. What would you have to say to that?'

'Lucy's my sister and I didn't kidnap her...I offered her sanctuary,' Polly declared loftily.

'Sanctuary?' Rashad echoed, visibly appreciating

that choice of word. 'I don't think I would employ that particular word with Jax, Lucy.'

'Jax is here?' Lucy flew off the sofa as though jet-propelled and then stilled, colour rising in her cheeks below her sisters' interested scrutiny.

'Let the rehabilitation commence,' Ellie remarked softly.

'*Have* I been interfering?' Polly asked worriedly.

'No, I was hugely grateful for the support,' Lucy told her warmly.

Lucy couldn't think straight. It had taken Jax less than forty-eight hours to come out to Dharia and she was sharply disconcerted. In the back of her mind, she had feared that he would let her go and write off their marriage as a mistake. After all, how could he possibly *want* to stay married to a woman whom he had such a low opinion of? But then letting her go could well be what he had arrived to discuss, she reasoned unhappily.

Jax was in no better mood after his long flight to find himself in a room decorated like something out of an Arabian Nights' fantasy, which dovetailed beautifully with the royal palace of Dharia. Rashad, the King, had seemed fairly normal though, acknowledging that he too would have been very 'put out' to find his wife and child had staged a vanishing act.

And then Rashad had murmured, 'But now that you're part of the family I should warn you that when the sisters get together, they plot and plan. You're either with them *or* against them.'

'You're my brother-in-law...well, *half*-brother-in-law,' Jax adjusted, recognising that the three sisters had all had different fathers.

'They don't think of each other as half anything,' Rashad cautioned him.

'Catching up?' another voice interposed, a voice that Jax recognised and he tensed, slowly turning round to arrange his thoughts before meeting the eyes of his former business partner, Rio Benedetti. 'Well, isn't this a small world?' he breathed uncomfortably.

'Relax,' the Italian billionaire urged. 'I ran into Franca last year and she brought me up to speed on past events. No disrespect to Franca intended, but I had the lucky escape and *you* had—?'

Jax winced. 'I owe you a wholehearted apology for what happened but let's not talk about it,' he retorted wryly of that sobering experience.

'Let's not,' Rio agreed, leaning closer. 'A word of advice though,' he added in a rueful undertone. 'The word "alley" will be etched on your gravestone...'

Momentarily, Jax froze as if a gun had been angled at him and faint colour rose over his sculpted cheekbones. 'Is that so?'

'The sisters don't keep secrets,' Rio imparted. 'Nothing is too sacred to be discussed. Cross one and you cross all three and none of them are batting for you.'

That was information that Jax could well have done without. He knew he had messed up but everyone else knowing how badly he had messed up made him feel worse. He had had forty-eight hours in which to think and he had done more thinking within that forty-eight hours than he had done in all his twenty-nine years. And having reached obvious conclusions, had even decided what to say.

But Jax's prepared speech flew right out of his head

when Lucy walked into the suite he was wafted off to. Lucy was wearing a long flowing dress in shades of blue and it fluttered round her as she moved and just seeing her again, just looking at her again, made Jax feel stuff he couldn't suppress any longer.

'I came because...' he began.

Jax looking gorgeous as usual, Lucy was noting, striving to be cool and composed after Ellie had advised her to play hard to get. But she couldn't play hard to get with Jax, which was the crux of her problem where he was concerned: she loved him. She had always loved him and what had been rather insta-love in Spain when she barely knew him had turned into something much deeper and more binding the second time around. Jax might be hopeless at some things, like talking about feelings and paying compliments, but he was very, *very* good at other things.

'Yes...you were saying?' Lucy prompted, striving to take control of their meeting.

Jax raked a deeply frustrated hand through his tousled black hair, green eyes glinting from below black lashes, and her heart jumped. 'I don't know what I was going to say. I had it all planned out but now it's gone. This is all new to me,' he muttered in a sudden surge. 'But the only really important thing I have to say is that I love you and I need you and I want you to come home with me...'

And just like that and with the unexpectedness of an explosion, Jax stole the wind from Lucy's sails. She didn't have time to try and work out how to play hard to get. He took the breath from her lungs and the arguments from her brain because what he had just said was what she felt as if she had been waiting all her life to hear.

'I've never said those words to anyone else,' Jax admitted gruffly as the silence dragged. 'I married you, not because of your father's blackmail, but because somewhere deep down inside me I *wanted* to be married to you. My head was telling me I didn't want to get married but my instincts were pushing me in a very different direction. Is that weird?'

'No...' Lucy almost whispered the word, scared to move, scared to speak lest she interrupt him and stop him speaking.

'My father reminded me that over one two-week period I flew back to Spain five times to see you. My attachment *was* obsessional,' he conceded grudgingly. 'I loved you then but I was afraid to accept that. Possibly when you said it suited me to believe that file and...*the other stuff* there was a shred of truth in that. Love has always been something that hurt and damaged me. I loved my mother, my father, my little sister, my half-brother and years before I met you I fell for a woman, who turned out to be a very troubled alcoholic, whom I had to place in rehab for recovery. I was determined not to get hurt again.'

Lucy nodded like a vigorous little marionette, wanting so badly to reach out to him and hug him and cover him in kisses but knowing it was wiser to let him say what he needed to say to explain the past and the present. 'I can understand that—'

Jax released his breath on a hiss. 'How can you? You keep on caring about people even when they hurt or disappoint you. That's brave—'

'Or plain stupid,' Lucy slotted in wryly. 'That's just

me. I tend to look for saving graces in people and stay optimistic but you're a giant pessimist, who always sees the worst possible conclusions.'

'Pretty much,' Jax conceded.

'And thinks the worst,' Lucy added with spirit, thinking about the alley. 'Even if there's no justification for it.'

Carefully avoiding the word Rio had advised him to avoid, Jax straightened his shoulders. 'The alcoholic that I fell for was repeatedly unfaithful to me. She couldn't help herself—she was a mess until rehab. But like my mother before her she conditioned me to distrust women. I'd seen that file. I saw a woman I thought was you and it seemed to fit, it seemed to be exactly the sort of thing that happened to me—I had got in too deep and you weren't who I thought you were—'

'Like with this alcoholic lady? That would be... er... Franca?' Lucy checked. 'Rio told Ellie about her and Ellie told me.'

Jax took on board the second of Rio's warnings. 'Yes, it was Franca. After her I was very wary and cynical with women. I didn't have faith in my own ability to read a woman, to really *know* her and, life being life,' he groaned, 'that meant I screwed up very badly with you. I ran when I should've stayed. I thought I was protecting myself but you had already burned me.'

'Burned you?'

'I never got over you. I kept on thinking about you at random times and reminding myself how bad you were...you know the—?'

'*Alley* stuff?' Lucy enunciated with precision, bright blue eyes gleaming.

'Yes, that,' Jax muttered, desperately keen to move on. 'Obviously I was wrong and I am very sorry that I believed that was you. I just saw the dress and the blonde hair and—'

Lucy moved closer and closed both arms around him. 'It's all right,' she murmured softly because his voice was ragged and too troubled for her to bear without touching him. 'It's all right. I forgive you. You made a mistake. It's over, done and dusted—'

Jax stared down at her with suspiciously bright green eyes. 'I don't deserve you. You probably don't even believe that I love you and that I loved you right from the start and I don't know how to prove it to you.'

But Lucy didn't need any more proof. Jax had wanted to stay married to her even though he believed she had once been unfaithful to him and that spoke volumes on its own. He had loved her warts and all, carefully schooling himself to overlook what any man would have seen as a monumental flaw and betrayal and predictably keeping his thoughts to himself. And then he had come clean and what he had been keeping secret had shocked and distressed her but at the same time it had set both of them free.

'I love you too,' Lucy whispered, planting a flyaway kiss on his freshly shaven jaw line, which was as high as she could reach even on tiptoes. 'So much that when you're not there it hurts.'

Jax carried her hand to his lips and kissed the back of it in the most un-Jax-like tender manner. 'You didn't even leave me a note. I felt sick. I didn't know what to do. I experienced pure panic—'

'I would've phoned eventually,' she confided. 'I was so upset but you were right to tell me. It all needed to come out for us to deal with it and then put it away again.'

'Your departure in a royal private jet was fairly straightforward when it came to tracking you,' Jax admitted ruefully, and then he gathered her up into his arms with the attitude of a male who couldn't keep his hands off her any longer.

'The bedroom's next door,' Lucy told him helpfully.

'I even told myself I was only marrying you for Bella's benefit,' Jax confessed. 'I lied to myself all the way down the line.'

'I persuaded myself I was only marrying you for our daughter's benefit as well, so you're not the only one.'

'How's Bella reacting to being here?' Jax queried.

'She's got six cousins to watch and loads of toys to steal. She's having a whale of a time.' Lucy laughed, blue eyes sparkling, and Jax looked down at her with his heart in his own eyes and adoration there, a brilliant smile on his lean, darkly handsome features.

'You are a very special woman, Tinker Bell,' Jax declared, settling her down on the bed with that same heartbreaking smile dazzling her. 'And the saddest element of all this is that my father is now going to be battering down our doors for invites.'

Lucy studied him in bewilderment. 'How? *Why?*'

'Heracles is the son of a pig farmer,' Jax told her with a chuckle. 'Yes, he keeps that little fact well under wraps because he is an enormous snob. When he discovers that your sister is a queen, he will be horribly friendly. He's very easily impressed in that line.'

Lucy shifted an unconcerned shoulder. 'I can live with that. It's not as though either of us can change our fathers. They are what they are but neither of them is going to get the chance to spoil our happiness again.'

'*Can* you be happy with me?' Jax pressed with touching anxiety. 'You do know I'll screw up again. I won't mean to but I will because I won't always get it right—'

'Neither will I,' Lucy pointed out equably as she struggled to get him out of his jacket and tie and then, when he got helpful, embarked on his shirt, spreading her fingers lasciviously across his muscular torso. 'Love is all about making allowances and compromises. We'll get there. Nobody has to be perfect.'

'I think you are. You have a heart as big as any country, *khriso mou*,' Jax told her with a blissful sigh as she knelt over him, cheerfully stripping him.

'And so have you,' Lucy countered, much amused. 'The difference between us is that you put your heart in a cage to keep it safe—'

'And you still worked your way through the bars of my cage,' Jax reminded her appreciatively. 'You've got more power than you realise.'

Lucy let a small hand stray and he arched up against her as if she had pressed a switch and she laughed as he sat up, wound both hands punitively into her hair and kissed her into breathless, leaping excitement. There was no more conversation then. They were both much too involved in sharing their bodies as they had shared their love.

'I suppose we should get up for dinner...or whatever they call it here,' Jax mused hours later. 'I'm being a very rude guest.'

'No, I know my sisters and they know me. They'll have tucked Bella into bed and gone on as normal.

There's no pressure, no expectations. Everyone's family here and that's just the way it is. I *love* it, especially because you're here too now,' Lucy confided, tucking a sleepy head into the crux of a strong brown shoulder and dreamily taking in the familiar scent of his skin, soothed by his proximity and the glorious high of knowing herself loved at last.

'I love you,' Jax muttered, easing her closer, marvelling at how easy it had become to say those words that he had refused to think about for so long.

'Love you,' Lucy whispered, dropping off to sleep, because she had lain awake sleepless while they were apart.

And Jax smiled in the darkness, recognising that for the first time in his life he was truly, joyously happy.

'This place looks amazing,' Polly carolled as she stood in the marble hall of the house on Tifnos and admired the fabulous Christmas decorations and the glittering tree. 'It's wonderful that you have a home big enough to take us all too, so we can get together like this to celebrate.'

'You can thank my father-in-law, Heracles, for that. He built *big*.'

'Was that the little man who kept on bowing to me?' Polly whispered uneasily.

'Yes, that was him, very subdued at being in the royal presence,' Lucy remarked, stifling her amusement.

In the three years Lucy had been married to Jax a great deal had changed. Her father-in-law was a frequent visitor, their children providing a major draw. Lucy had warmed up to Heracles considerably once she'd realised that he genuinely adored children and his grandchildren most of all. Yes, she had had another baby, a little boy called Dmitri, who was almost two years old. Their lengthy unplanned holiday in Dharia after their reconciliation had extended the family. She had enjoyed her second pregnancy much more than the first because she had had Jax by her side and Jax had been scientifically fascinated by every change she had gone through on the road to producing his son. He had shared everything with her and supported her right through the nausea in the early stages to every medical appointment and finally the birth.

During those three years only Lucy's son had been born but Polly was expecting again, freely admitting that she wanted a large family. Ellie had declared that two children would do her nicely but one never knew with Ellie, who could be prone to saying one thing and then quietly doing another. As for Lucy and Jax, they were still young and, while being quite happy with the children they had, they thought that some day they might plan a third child. Ellie had already lectured them hilariously about birth control, pointing out that *two* accidental conceptions was inexcusable, and her audience had only laughed.

Kreon and Iola were regular visitors on the island and Kreon and Heracles politely avoided each other at family gatherings. Her father had faced bankruptcy proceedings the year before and Jax had bought a small business for him and placed him in it, pointing out that Kreon needed to be kept occupied and independent. His kindness had almost reduced Lucy to tears and she was relieved that Jax had finally begun to see and understand Kreon's essential good-heartedness.

'He's your father and you love him,' Jax had said to Lucy. 'We have to do our best for him. After all, you put up with my father and forgive his foibles.'

Jax was a wonderful husband in every way, Lucy reflected gratefully, feeling very blessed. After spending so many years of craving the feeling of being special to someone she had finally found a safe harbour.

Leaving Polly to get settled in with her children and explaining that Ellie had gone straight to bed after a hospital late night shift, Lucy went off to put Dmitri down for a nap because he got very cross and whiny when he got too tired and with all the children in the house and the excitement of the Christmas season, he needed more sleep. The little boy snuggled into his cot, clutching his toy elephant. He was as blonde as his mother, which had been a surprise to his parents, but he too had Jax's green eyes and olive complexion.

Lucy looked out of the window and saw the older children down on the beach with Rashad and Rio. She could just make out four-year-old Bella in her yellow dress skipping through the surf with Polly's younger son, Hassan, and Ellie's Teresina. The cousins had all become fast friends and playmates, which made family get-togethers run more smoothly.

Recognising that she finally had the family circle she had dreamt of having all her life, Lucy vented a contented sigh and went to freshen up before dinner. She was in the shower when another body stepped in beside her and she spun round with a delighted smile of welcome.

'Jax...thought you were going to be late tonight!' she gasped.

'No, I looked round my office, thought of you all here enjoying yourselves without me and decided I was needed at home. I saw the children down on the beach as we flew in.'

'Dmitri's having a nap. He was throwing tantrums all over the place,' his mother confided ruefully.

'I swear he's got my mother's temperament,' Jax said worriedly.

'No, don't be silly,' Lucy soothed, aware that he had that little fear that he might somehow pass on some troublesome gene. 'He's a toddler with a short temper and he hasn't learned to control it yet. When he's not tired he's very good-natured. And, hey, did you join me in the shower to talk about the kids or—?'

'Or, *agapi mou*,' Jax chose, plastering her back against the shower wall and tasting her lush mouth with hungry urgency.

Lucy melted every time he called her his love. He was hot and wet and gorgeous and all hers. Excitement rippled through her in seductive sensual waves.

'Birth control,' Jax growled, lifting her out of the shower and throwing a heap of towels down on the tiled floor as he dug into a drawer for the necessary.

Lucy arranged herself on the towels and giggled like a drain. 'Ellie really got to you with that lecture, didn't she?'

'Ellie knows how to make a man feel irresponsible,' Jax responded. 'And I will *never* be irresponsible with you again but don't tell her that.'

'I promise I won't.' Her amusement dying as they joined, Lucy lifted tender fingers to stroke his jaw line. 'I love you, Jax Antonakos...I love you so much.'

He was too otherwise engaged to speak at that moment but his emerald eyes telegraphed love and passion and need and that was more than sufficient for Lucy, who knew a good man when she found one and held fast to him because he gave her so much happiness.

* * * * *

PROMOTED TO
THE GREEK'S WIFE

CHAPTER ONE

'FORGET ABOUT THEM,' the family lawyer had advised. 'Should a problem arise in the future, provision has been made. Your inheritance is ring-fenced. There is no reason why you should concern yourself with this issue.'

Even today at the newly opened London HQ of Stefanos Enterprises, where the proof of his own exhilarating rise to success should have put him in a very different mood, Aristaeus Stefanos couldn't get that unscrupulous little speech out of his head. Only a month had passed since his father's death. A renowned philanthropist and business mogul, Christophe Stefanos had been a much-admired figure. A loving son, Ari had been devastated by his sudden death, and in all the years he had known his father, he had never once doubted his essential decency.

In retrospect, that complete trust now struck him as ludicrously naive for a male of twenty-eight years of age. Death had, after all, cruelly exposed his parent's darkest secret and had shattered Ari's faith in him. Ari had been forced to acknowledge his father's feet of clay and to make a decision that he might some day regret even while accepting that he could not *live* with any other option. Fierce conflicting emotions still bubbled uneasily beneath Ari's controlled surface. Angry shame and disbelief still rose uppermost whenever he reflected on his father's choices.

Life, however, was too short to agonise over what could not be changed, Ari reflected grimly. For that reason, rather than taking advantage of the many social invitations that had come his way since his return from his father's memorial service in Greece, he had decided to do something he had never done before: get to know some of his employees. It wasn't Ari's style to get close to his workers. A billionaire shipping tycoon and resort developer, he hired professionals to monitor his staff and kept his distance. His need for a distraction, however, had won out, and what could be more of a diversion than his participation in a company retreat to be staged in the wilds of Norfolk?

The new HQ of Stefanos Enterprises brought staff together from several different sites, and his HR director had suggested the retreat as a means of bringing down barriers and improving communication. Ari wasn't quite sure he believed in the value of company retreats. He understood the concept and the potential benefits, but he also suspected that many of his executive staff would view the retreat as a nice little holiday on company time.

His handsome mouth quirking, Ari left his office just as an eruption of giggles sounded from the reception area. His hard, dark gaze arrowed in that direction, and exasperation flooded him at the sight of a security guard flirting with the receptionist, who irritated the hell out of him. What was her name again? Cleo, he recalled, and even the name was inappropriate for a female with a mop of blonde curls and blue eyes. Cleo, short for Cleopatra, was, in Ari's highly experienced opinion, the name for a tall, dark beauty, *not* an undersized one with the curves of a pocket Venus and the dress sense of an eighties swagged and ruffled floral curtain.

It was fair to say that Ari had no time at all for Cleo the temp. But then she had blundered badly on her first day by letting Ari's stalker-type ex, Galina Ivanova, walk into his office unchallenged. Of course, she had apologised. *Thee mou*—had she apologised! While Ari never used two words if one would suffice, Cleo was a hopeless chatterbox and capable of utilising fifty words to do the work of two. She had apologised to him for five solid minutes, staring pleadingly at him with those huge blue eyes of hers that made her look more like a cherub than a grown woman. Having been made aware by Human Resources that he could not simply sack her out of hand, he had grudgingly accepted the apology, but her presence in his vicinity offended him.

'Have a nice afternoon, Mr Stefanos!' Cleo called cheerfully, not having the wit to pull a low profile after being caught in the act of distracting the security guard from his job.

Ari struggled not to respond with something derisive and told himself off for letting so minor an incident darken his mood. But Ari liked absolutely everything in his life shipshape and *tidy*. He had placed things in neat little groups since he was a child. Back then he had found security in making and restoring order. The testing times of his childhood were unforgotten, although he chose not to dwell on them. His wardrobe was colour-coded, his bookshelves alphabetically arranged, his desk immaculate. In his world, there was no clutter and everything and everybody had a place. When anything was out of place, it set Ari's teeth on edge, which was exactly why the receptionist irritated him, he reasoned in exasperation.

Cleo didn't 'fit' Stefanos Enterprises. She lacked dress sense and sophistication. She was too visible, too chatty and too friendly. She smiled too much. Spend five minutes in a taxi rank with Cleo and she would divulge her entire life story without the smallest encouragement. That kind of verbal licence gave Ari the chills. Thrusting her from mind, he reminded himself that he had a Norfolk-bound helicopter waiting for him…

Cleo clambered into the minibus with her overnight bag.

A lot of the staff were travelling to the retreat by car, but she hadn't made any close friends at Stefanos Enterprises and she hadn't been offered a lift. People rarely made much effort to get to know temporary employees and she was accustomed to being somewhat invisible at work when others were socialising. Even so, she had been thrilled to be included in the retreat, which was probably because she would be working at Stefanos Enterprises for another eight months.

She suppressed a grimace, thinking of the incident on her first day that she suspected had ruined any hope she had of ever stepping into a permanent position at Stefanos Enterprises. An enviably confident sleek dark beauty, dressed to the nines in designer fashion, had approached Reception to announce that she was lunching with Mr Stefanos and would go straight through to his office. Cleo hadn't even thought of questioning the woman further. She had simply assumed that the woman was a regular visitor, possibly even a family member. She hadn't been shown the banned list of visitors before she began her shift. She hadn't been told that the boss's lovers never had access to him during working hours either by phone or by personal appearance. And nobody had been more shaken than her when she saw the furious woman escorted off the premises by two security guards and one of his personal assistants came running to ask what on earth had she been thinking when she had allowed that 'madwoman' into Mr Stefanos's office. An ex, a stalker-type ex, apparently, who refused to take no for an answer and kept on showing up in the hope that he would change his mind. Cleo felt that she should have been warned the minute she took over the desk that her employer's adventurous, ever-changing love life included such a deceptive personality.

Cleo suppressed her unproductive thoughts. She preferred to concentrate on positive things. A night away from the cramped little studio apartment she shared would be very welcome. Although she had been grateful to find city accommodation that she could share, she often longed for the peace and quiet of her own space, but with the cost of rents in London and her less-than-stellar earning power, that was a luxury she could only dream about. In any case, she reminded herself, she was lucky enough that her landlady, Ella, spent a couple of nights a week at her boyfriend's place, leaving Cleo in sole possession of the mezzanine bedroom space and the tiny living area they had to share. Ella's parents had bought the property for their daughter and it really wasn't large enough for two people. Ella, however, was a student, who was struggling to get by, and she needed Cleo's rent.

The retreat was being held at a boutique country hotel, situated deep in the countryside and surrounded by woods and fields. The bus arrived late, after an accident caused a long, slow tailback of traffic. As they waited for their key cards at Reception, several remarking on the fact that their belated arrival excluded them from joining the team chats, Lily, one of the clerical staff, turned her head to say to Cleo, 'Come on... You're sharing with me.'

Cleo forced a smile, able to see that her companion was no keener on the arrangement than she was. No sooner had they arrived in the comfortable hotel room than Lily was excusing herself to join her friends. 'We'll be in the bar after dinner... You're welcome to join us,' the pretty blonde told her with a pleasant smile. 'The more the merrier.'

And a strange face was easier tolerated in a crowd,

Cleo reflected ruefully. She was pleased about the invitation, just a little worried that she would not truly be welcome and was only being asked out of politeness. 'I'm going downstairs to see what I can sign up for.'

'The yoga classes are supposed to be very good,' Lily informed her on the way out of the door. 'And they've got one on first thing…'

Cleo wasn't fond of yoga. Having once signally flopped at twisting her body into a pretzel shape at a class and having felt an absolute failure, she had decided that she simply wasn't bendy enough.

After freshening up, she went downstairs to explore the other options on offer. Breathing in deep and mustering her courage, she signed up for paintballing and stand-up paddleboarding the following day. Although she was not remotely athletic, she was a firm believer in moving out of her comfort zone when the opportunity was presented, and goodness knew, she thought ruefully, she was unlikely ever to receive another opportunity to try out such activities free of charge. At the very least, it should be fun.

Throwing herself in head first was Cleo's way when she felt intimidated. Growing up with a single mother perpetually fretting and expecting disaster had taught her to be fearless. Lisa Brown had always had a pessimistic outlook, while Cleo preferred to look on the brighter side of things.

Getting changed for dinner, she tugged out a stretchy comfy dress and heels. The bright colours of the jungle-palm print made her smile, whisking her back to her childhood with a mother who habitually wore black, believing that colours were less elegant. A lot of good that dark, colourless wardrobe had done her poor mother, Cleo reflected wryly. The man she loved, Cleo's father, hadn't loved Lisa Brown back and hadn't wanted a child with her either. Lisa's pregnancy had eventually concluded their clandestine relationship.

Cleo went down for dinner, glancing round the dining room and seeing only a handful of vaguely familiar faces. She was keeping an eye out for Ari Stefanos, who was reputedly joining his staff for the retreat. That had surprised her, Ari not being the most approachable of employers, and true to form, Lily had mentioned that he was not staying in the hotel, but in some separate luxury property in the woods, well away from the hoi polloi. No, Cleo was looking out for Ari simply because it was always a treat to feast her eyes on him. Those cheekbones, that unruly blue-black hair, that piercing dark-as-night gaze set below level ebony brows, not to mention the lush pink of his eminently kissable mouth.

The first time Cleo had met her employer had been the same day she had attempted to tender an apology for the woman she had allowed to walk unchallenged into his office. That had been her first glimpse of him, and sheer fascination had mesmerised her because there was just something about the precise arrangement of his perfect features that had made her stare like an enraptured schoolgirl. Her tongue had tripped over words, her mouth had dried up and her brain had closed down in that same moment. Ari Stefanos exuded irresistible appeal with every breath that he drew.

He was Cleo's secret addiction. It was a harmless piece of fun. All the women in the office treated Ari Stefanos to more than one glance: he was shockingly good-looking and smoulderingly sexy. He cast ordinary men in very deep shade. But he was a safe target for appreciation because his distaste for office flings was incorporated in her employment contract. In any case, Cleo knew that she didn't have the looks to attract such a man.

Cleo had never been in love and had no desire to fall in love either. Her mother had loved her father and it had ruined the best years of her life. No, Cleo would only allow herself to fall in love with a man when it was clear that *he* was keen enough on *her* to make a commitment. That was where her mother had gone wrong, trusting promises made in the heat of the moment, making the assumption that deep feelings were involved when they were not. Cleo had no plans to make the same mistake.

And in the short term, admiring Ari Stefanos from a safe distance was an amusing, perfectly prudent and private source of enjoyment.

Unaware that anyone received entertainment simply by looking at him, Ari led a discussion on the company vision for the future before heading for the bar, determined to have one drink and be sociable before he retired to his own quarters.

For some inexplicable reason, his attention immediately landed on Cleo and stayed locked to her. She was seated with a group, engaged in animated discussion, her mop of golden curls glinting in the low lights as she moved her head. She stood up to walk to the bar and he almost winced at the sight of the vivid giant-palm-leaf print she was sporting. A large blue butterfly was stretched across her curvy behind and, like the leaf cupping her full breasts, the loud design somehow accentuated the lush fullness of her glorious curves. In that instant he understood perfectly why she continually attracted his notice. She might be barely over five foot, but she had a superb figure. Pretty good legs too, he noted absently, watching her at the bar, catching her gurgling laugh and the brilliance of her smile as the bartender surged to serve her.

'She's very pretty and very young,' his senior PA, Mel, commented at his elbow as she looked in the same direction.

Ari tore his gaze from Cleo, faint colour edging his high cheekbones as he registered the throb at his groin, and shifted uneasily. 'She talks too much.'

'Yes, but she's very good on Reception,' Mel countered. 'Friendly, helpful, welcoming. In my opinion, she's a big improvement on that frozen fashion doll out on maternity leave.'

Ari gritted his even white teeth. 'She dresses badly.'

Mel frowned and gave him a surprised look. 'So, let someone give her the advice to tone down the colours a little and look more…er…professional.'

Tiring of the conversation, Ari tipped back the whisky brought to him without savouring the vintage. 'I'm going to turn in now. It's been a long day.'

Cleo didn't spend the whole evening with Lily and her pals, just an hour to be friendly. She went to bed smothering a yawn, wondering where Ari Stefanos had disappeared to, because she hadn't seen him. She woke and went down to breakfast alone because Lily had gone to the yoga class. Clad in a long-sleeved top and cargo pants, she ate and then followed the signs to the wooded, fenced area that held the paintball operation. She was a little embarrassed to see that only one other woman had chosen the activity and she was an athletic former soldier, whom Cleo had met the night before in the bar, and she was jogging on the spot with eagerness. Cleo put on her mask, helmet and protective vest and grasped the gun after it had been demonstrated for her benefit, and then she tried to strike a fit pose as if she too were fizzing with pent-up energy.

Ari Stefanos strode into view with a small group of other men. His black hair was tousled and in need of a cut. Cleo curved back into the shadow of the wall the better to watch him before he disappeared into the equipment shed. She wondered what it was about those features of his that continually locked her attention to him. The dark deep-set eyes, the rawly masculine hard jawline and faint shadow of stubble? The thin aristocratic nose? That beautiful mouth, which she had never seen smile? With the recent death of his father, she supposed he didn't feel he had much to smile about. He was very tall, spectacularly well built, all lean muscle from his wide, strong shoulders, flat stomach and narrow waist to his long, powerful legs.

The group was split into two teams and the game began. Cleo was ambushed behind a tree when she was least expecting it. Three of her own team, young and boisterous types, cornered her and literally sprayed her with paintballs, laughing uproariously as they did it. As the balls struck and spattered over her, she was startled by the force of each hit and by how much it hurt. She cried, 'Stop it!' as she felt the stings of pain and the pressure that would surely bruise her, but they were still laughing hysterically as they ran off again.

When they were gone, Cleo was left in a rage. Her own team members had attacked her, presumably because she was a temp, a safer target for a prank than a permanent staff member and an easy mark! And she was hurt, aching all over from the assault as she began clumsily picking herself up again, furious tears blinding her.

'You're out... Take yourself off to the dead zone,' a curt voice instructed.

'I'm not out! My own team ambushed me!'

'Got witnesses? If not, you're out,' the voice told her without sympathy.

'I'm going to get my own back,' Cleo countered furiously, recalling how turning her back on unkind behaviour aimed at her at school hadn't won her any favours. When anyone deliberately set out to injure Cleo, she had learned to always fight her corner in self-defence. It didn't pay to let people walk over her. If she allowed such treatment, it would be more likely to reoccur.

'That's against the rules. Neither is that attitude in the spirit of proper gamesmanship,' her unwanted companion informed her in a lofty tone of superiority.

'Oh, shut up!' Cleo said sharply. 'If they can ignore the rules and attack me, I can do it back!'

Below Ari's disbelieving gaze, Cleo shimmied up the tree behind her like a miniature ninja warrior. 'They won't even see me up here. I'm going to get them!' she hissed.

'Did you listen to anything I said?' Ari enquired drily. 'Did you even read the rules? You're not supposed to climb the trees or attack from above. Once you're hit, you're out and you should leave the field immediately.'

'A lot of good it did me reading the rules when nobody else is following them!' Cleo shot back, unimpressed. 'Go away and leave me alone. You'll draw attention to me and that'll wreck my plan.'

'Get down and I will see you get off the field safely,' Ari breathed impatiently.

'Like I need your help!' Cleo snapped. 'Anyone ever told you to mind your own business?' Reaching up to a higher, sturdier branch, she clutched the gun awkwardly below one arm. 'I'm about to teach those guys a lesson!'

Ari had never had an employee simply ignore his commands before. Undoubtedly, the helmet and the mask were a better disguise than he had appreciated. Ari was a stickler for rules, and while he understood her burning desire for retribution, he could not condone it. Stretching up, he closed his hands around her small waist, and from that angle, he really could not avoid noticing that in the close-fitting pants her derrière jutted out like a particularly ripe and luscious peach. Disconcerted by the instant swell of arousal against his zip, he tugged her down from the tree and brought her carefully down to ground level again. Of course, he knew who she was. Cleo was unique amongst the top-floor staff. She was too tiny to be mistaken for anyone else.

'What are you *doing*?' She gasped in disbelief.

As she staggered, he bent down to steady her and the faint scent of strawberries emanated from the golden hair curling out from beneath her helmet: he was too *close*. Ari took a sharp and deeply conservative step back from her as he spun her round to face him. The cornflower depth of blue that distinguished her eyes was distinctive. He tensed while he censured himself for his overt physical reaction.

'I'm taking you out of here,' Ari told her curtly. '*Before* I lose my temper with you.'

'Just because you have a different take on how to play games—'

'Breaking the rules could lead to the game being stopped for everyone,' Ari warned her curtly. 'There are safety concerns here. Please...'

And it was his accent, roughening the edges of his vowel sounds with a growl that made her steal a longer frowning glance at him. In one fell swoop she rose above her rage sufficiently to recognise the clothes that he wore and the dark golden eyes flaring like a shower of sparks behind the mask. *Oh. My. Word.* She was fighting with the boss, the great rule upholder!

'I'm so sorry, Mr Stefanos,' she murmured flatly. 'I didn't realise it was you.'

'Maybe I should have worn a warning label,' Ari riposted as he retained a controlling hand on her shoulder and steered her towards the boundary fence and the area marked out for the paint-spattered losers.

As the first arrival in the losers' corner, Cleo gritted her teeth on a snarky reply and compressed her lips, saying stiffly, 'Thank you. I'll head back to the hotel to change.'

Ari leant down to her level from his great height. 'I promise you… I'll cover those bullies in paint!' he murmured fiercely.

'Don't exert yourself on my account, Mr Stefanos,' Cleo remarked thinly as she walked away. 'After all, it's only a game…'

Ari snatched in a sudden sustaining breath, incredulous at her insouciant gall, and he stood there for several taut seconds watching her disappear from view, defiance in every line of her shapely, sexy body. The natural sway of her hips stole his masculine attention. He gritted his teeth and swung away, furious at the fact that she evoked a visceral sexual response from him. She was an employee. Such a reaction was unacceptable.

Still furious, Cleo stomped back to the hotel and straight into the shower, unhappy until she had rinsed the last speck of paint from her body. Faint pink circles of bruising marked her arms, her neck, her legs and stomach. It was her own fault for not wearing thicker clothing and for not taking advantage of the extra protective gear on offer in the equipment shed out of a fear of looking naff. Now she was suffering from an attitude adjustment and a growing retrospective horror about her unfortunate encounter with Ari Stefanos.

Talk about a clash of opinions! She shouldn't have been arguing with anyone in the game, considering that she was the most junior member of staff on the retreat. She couldn't afford to foolishly offend anyone higher up the ladder than she was...and what had she done? Only attracted the wrong kind of attention to herself *again* with the boss! She winced as she donned her swimsuit and got dressed again. Ironically, she was no longer in the right mood to try out a paddleboard following her unfortunate experience with the paintballing. But Ari Stefanos was truly the most infuriating guy! So bossy, so confident and bold in his conviction that only his way was the right way and, while Cleo had never considered herself a rule-breaker, his strictures had made her madder than a hornet.

In the end she decided the encounter didn't much matter in the scheme of things because she had probably already given him the very worst possible impression of herself and her talents on her very first day at work. No point crying over spilt milk, she told herself firmly, reminding herself that at least nobody else had witnessed their exchange of words.

Consoled by that reflection, she went downstairs to an obligatory first-aid class and accompanied Lily's group into lunch. Everyone talked about what a beautiful day it was to go out on the lake. Cleo's spirits lifted when one of the women insisted that you didn't need to be especially fit to succeed at paddleboarding. Words like 'slow' and 'peaceful' increased her optimism as she clambered awkwardly into a wetsuit in the changing rooms. They all helped each other do up the back zips and there was much laughter as they added the life jackets and compared their bulky images.

Ari almost smiled when he saw Cleo walking down to the edge of the lake with her friends. There was nothing sexy about Cleo in her current apparel. Indeed, Ari felt wondrously safe looking at her, and he told himself that he had imagined his former response to her. The instructor stood on the wooden pier to see everyone safely disposed onto their boards. Cleo stepped onto the board like someone stepping onto hot coals, an oddly frozen expression on her face as though she was forcing herself to do something she didn't want to do.

As she used the oar to push away from the pier, it caught on something, jerked and fell from her hand, and she immediately lurched off balance. For a split second, Ari glimpsed the sheer terror on her face, and then he was instinctively moving forward because the instructor had already moved away while he adjusted someone's life jacket for them. Cleo plunged face first into the water with a tremendous splash and scrabbled frantically for the board. Ari recognised the pure panic in her reaction and the ineptness of her flailing hands. The board was right beside her, but she seemed to be too alarmed actually to see it. Someone was laughing, but Ari had already seen more than enough. He dropped down into the water beside her and grabbed her, lifting her above the water with easy strength.

'Relax, the water is barely a couple of metres deep at this point—'

'I'm not a couple of metres tall!' Cleo gasped, spitting out lake water in disgust. 'I'll drown at that depth—'

'No swimmer could drown in water this shallow,' Ari informed her forcefully, capturing her flailing hands. 'And calm down... You're not in any danger—'

'I *can't* swim!' Cleo hissed in a desperate undertone. 'I know I've got the jacket on and I'm sorry, but I'm very nervous—'

Ari dealt her an arrested appraisal. He lifted her up onto the side of the pier and hauled himself bodily up beside her. 'You can't swim? You actually went out on the water without being able to swim?' he demanded in a rising crescendo of incredulity.

'I've got a life jacket on,' Cleo protested.

'Have you a death wish? The minute you hit the water you panicked! Have you any idea how many people drown because they panic?' he raked down at her wrathfully.

'I wasn't likely to drown unless someone deliberately held me down under the water!' Cleo slung back at him in furious denial. 'And while you may not be my biggest fan, I doubt if you were about to do that—'

'You're an absolute bloody idiot and you should stay away from water!' Ari flamed back at her, dark eyes brilliant with anger, kissable mouth hard as granite. 'What you did was stupidly dangerous!'

Alerted by his wrathful volume, every eye in their vicinity had now turned to them, and Cleo cringed.

She was shivering with cold and the aftermath of fright. Ari Stefanos was standing over her in a rage and it was too much to be borne in the mood she was in. Cleo swallowed the lump in her throat, but her stricken eyes still flooded with tears of hurt and mortification.

A woman broke the horrible silence in which everyone on shore had fallen quiet and hurried forward to wrap a large towel round Cleo. 'Let me take you back to the hotel,' she urged. 'You've had a shock.'

'Thank you, Mel,' Ari breathed in a compressed undertone. 'But I'll take care of Cleo.'

CHAPTER TWO

Cleo scrambled awkwardly upright and, because she felt shaky, she removed the life jacket very slowly while breathing in deep.

'Let me help you... You're swaying,' Ari murmured, scooping her up into his arms and striding away from the pier before she could object to his high-handed behaviour.

'I'll be fine when I get back to my room,' Cleo insisted tightly, shivering within the damp towel and closing her eyes to envision a blissfully warm shower and privacy. 'But I hate you...'

Ari released his breath on an audible hiss because he was well aware that he had screwed up. 'I kind of hate me too at this moment.'

Eyes wide with surprise, Cleo turned her head to really look at him as he settled her down into the front seat of an open-topped buggy. 'You disrespected me... You humiliated me,' she condemned thinly.

'It was an overreaction and I apologise. I saw my twin sister drown when I was a child. It...er...upsets me when people take risks in the water, but I shouldn't have taken that out on you,' he breathed, taking a split-second decision to drive on past the hotel sooner than face the challenge of escorting a wet, distressed and tear-stained woman through a busy reception area.

Cleo was stunned by that very private admission. Curiosity had made her look him up on the internet and that information about his sister had not appeared in his history. Of course, what she had read had related to his education, his business prowess and his sex life, which had been encyclopaedically covered. All his exes had struck her as being of a particular type: tall glitzy brunettes, socialites and models, spiced with the occasional up-and-coming actress.

Scolding herself for her wandering thoughts, she concentrated instead on what he had just told her. Naturally, he would have been traumatised by the experience of seeing a sibling drown, and even she, who didn't like him, could begin to understand and forgive what he had termed an overreaction. For the first time she recognised that Ari Stefanos, the gorgeous, wildly successful billionaire, was not omnipotent and, indeed, was as human and prone to errors of judgement as she could be.

Ari shot the buggy to a halt outside an opulent two-storeyed and balconied wooden cabin surrounded by trees and got out. 'Come on. You'll feel better once you have a shower and warm up—'

'But why did you bring me here instead of back to the hotel?' Cleo demanded, climbing out of the buggy at a much slower pace, an uncertain look on her heart-shaped face.

'It's more private.' Ari raked lean brown fingers through his wind-tousled black hair in a gesture of frustration and gave her a rueful look. 'You were crying. The hotel is very public.'

'I'm not crying any more. It was just a momentary thing...caused by shock,' Cleo pointed out defensively. She squelched up the steps to the front door and, in embarrassment, kicked her sodden footwear off to leave it outside before she stepped indoors barefoot.

'There's a shower through here,' he told her, pushing open a door.

'You didn't think this through, did you?' Cleo said uncomfortably. 'I have no clothes to change into and I'll need a hand to get out of the wetsuit.'

'Trivial,' Ari pronounced, tugging her forward and turning her round to attack the back zip of the wetsuit. 'I'll have our clothes brought here.'

He unzipped the suit, blunt fingertips grazing the smooth, soft skin of her back, and she shivered, shockingly aware of him. She tugged loose her locker key and spun round to hand it to him.

The confines of the bathroom suddenly seemed very small and tight, and breathing felt like a challenge when she glanced up uneasily to meet the lustrous dark gold of his black-lashed gaze. Those ridiculously lush long black lashes of his had gold tips, she thought crazily, locked there in stillness.

'I suppose I should ask you to perform the same service for me,' Ari murmured.

'I suppose...unless you're a natural contortionist,' Cleo mumbled thickly through her dry mouth, ducking her head to move behind him and stand on tiptoe to reach the zip on the back of his suit. Every brain cell in her head felt as though it had died as a long slice of golden satin-smooth brown back showed through the parted edges.

Cleo backed off to the side and tugged at the sleeve of her suit to start removing it, reminding herself that she was wearing a perfectly respectable swimsuit underneath. Yet she was feeling as awkward as a woman forced to perform a strip in public.

Catching a glimpse of Cleo's full rounded breasts cupped in smooth, stretchy material, her movements accentuating the luscious depth of her cleavage as she struggled with the sleeve, was not to be recommended, Ari decided when he went as hard as a rock, every libidinous instinct sparking instantaneously. In an effort to distract himself, he reached for the edge of her sleeve and gave it a sharp yank, enabling her to get one arm free.

'Thanks,' she said, warm colour blossoming in her cheeks as she began peeling her other arm free of the flexible fabric.

His wetsuit hung down round his waist, exposing a flawless bronzed masculine torso and the lean muscular perfection of sculpted abs and pecs. In her haste to draw back and put some space between them, she almost collided with him.

'Not enough room in here for the two of us,' Ari pointed out jerkily, backing away in turn to step back into the hallway. 'I'll sort out the clothes and leave them outside the door for you.'

'Th-thanks,' she heard herself stammer while still staring at him as if he had dropped down in front of her from the moon.

Her palms were sweating, her skin had come out in goosebumps and she was running out of oxygen. He was beautiful, like a glossy picture in a book and just as unreal and untouchable. An odd clenching sensation thrummed between her thighs and she knew what it was—oh, yes, she knew what it was, and it was absolutely *not* anything she should be feeling around her employer. Her face burned hotter than ever.

'Can you get out of that suit alone?' Ari pressed in a roughened undertone.

'Yes, of course,' Cleo declared, hurriedly shutting the door, turning the lock, flinching in even deeper embarrassment when it made a noisy click.

But that instant when she had recognised just how powerfully she was attracted to Ari Stefanos had thrown her back in time to her first love, Dominic, and that could only send chills through her. She didn't want to feel like that again about anyone! Dominic hadn't been her boss or a colleague, though, just a salesman who came into the office occasionally. She had fallen for him like a ton of bricks, although with hindsight she reckoned it had only been an infatuation. He had been young, good-looking and full of easy banter. There had been nothing suspicious about him and, as far as was possible for her, she had checked him out before deciding to commit to their relationship and sleep with him. He would have become her first lover had his girlfriend not turned up on her doorstep clutching their toddler.

To be fair, Imogen hadn't been nasty. She had just said, 'Dominic does this... He gets bored with us and strays... But he always comes back again. It's not your fault. He tells lies and he's very convincing, but he will get bored with you too.'

And Cleo had realised to her horror that she had almost fallen into the same trap as her mother. Her mother had only been a convenient outlet for her father, who had also had another woman in his life. Cleo had been badly burned by the experience she had had with Dominic. The fear that she might place her trust unwisely in a man haunted her whenever she dated and made her very wary.

Irritated by thoughts of her less-than-successful dating past, Cleo managed to remove the wetsuit and her swimsuit and rummage for towels on the open shelves before she stepped into the shower.

The warm water combatted the shivers running through her. She shampooed her hair, thinking that she shouldn't be feeling guilty when nothing had happened between her and Ari. Attraction was normal, but people didn't always act on it, and in any case, she doubted very much that he was equally attracted to her. She had seen the sleek, expensively dressed and giraffe-legged females he dated on the internet, women with the kind of beauty that she had never had. On a good day in her very best clothes and all done up, she could shoot at being pretty, but she wasn't distinctive or particularly sexy, and she didn't have classic features.

He had classic features and yet that description severely understated the ability of his features to linger inside her head. She always wanted to stare at him, to linger with pleasure on the full curve of his lower lip, the clean-cut perfection of his angular jaw, the blue-black luxuriance of his hair and his spectacularly noticeable eyes.

Such reflections were ridiculously immature and foolish, she conceded as a knock sounded on the door and Ari informed her that her clothes had arrived. She wondered how he had achieved that miracle at such speed and she reckoned that it was probably something to do with the fact that he was very, very rich and people seemed to fall over themselves in their eagerness to please the very, very rich.

Wrapped in a towel, she opened the door and ducked back inside with her bag, quickly pulling on her jeans and long-sleeved top, regretting that she had worn her supposedly waterproof shoes down to the lake because now she had nothing else for her feet. Without her miracle styling spray that suppressed frizz, she would also have to leave her hair to dry naturally.

Cleo emerged into the silent hall and went straight for the front door to leave, but it was locked and the key had been removed. Rolling her eyes in frustration, she walked quietly down the hall into the large sitting room and sat down on a comfortable sofa to await the reappearance of her careless host. A wave of tiredness engulfed her because she hadn't slept well the night before with Lily just across the room from her engaged in constant texting with her boyfriend.

Ari strode downstairs, his black hair still damp from the shower, and stared in surprise at Cleo, who was curled up in a ball on the sofa fast asleep. He studied her, struggling to identify what it was about her that roused his libido to such an extent. She wasn't his style, and yet when she had turned those big blue eyes on him, lust had roared through him in a surge of heat that had left him thunderstruck. He breathed in slow and deep, steadying himself. Of course, that urge was not something he would ever succumb to, he reasoned confidently.

Ari was as organised and restrained in his sex life as he was in everything else. He had a select band of willing lovers in his life with whom he spent occasional casual nights and he had never had an exclusive relationship. Sex was a release from tension, a sporadic pastime, something enjoyable rather than exciting. Perhaps that was the secret of Cleo's appeal, he mused. She excited him and he could not recall when a woman had last had that effect on him. Possibly actual excitement in that field had evaded him since he'd left the adolescent years behind.

Wry amusement tilted his mobile lips. He was well aware that he was spoiled in the female department, never being asked for anything more than he was willing to give because women wanted him to continue to call. He received endless invitations and selected only the most tempting from women he viewed as 'suitable'. Cleo wasn't and never would be suitable, he conceded calmly.

He was hungry. He swept up the phone and glanced at Cleo's tumbled mop of guinea-gold curls over the back of the sofa. He would order dinner for her as well, make up for his outburst down by the lake by being sociable with an employee for a change. He was very much a loner, he acknowledged. But then he had been an only child born to two only children, so there never had been much of a family circle to enjoy, which was naturally why the family lawyer's revelations had been so very intriguing.

Ari viewed his slumbering guest with amusement. There was something impossibly sweet about that innocent lack of intent. Women never fell asleep in Ari's radius because they were invariably keen to utilise every possible moment to impress him. Certainly, he could not imagine any other woman he had ever met cheerfully telling him that she hated him, as Cleo had done without hesitation. She was outspoken, again not a quality he was accustomed to because people were not honest around him, not if there was the smallest risk that that honesty could offend or indicate anything that could prove to be personally prejudicial. Cleo didn't guard her tongue or pay lip service to his position even as her employer.

As she shifted and stretched like a little cat in wakefulness, Ari leant over the sofa to say quietly, 'I'm ordering dinner—'

'Ah!' Cleo squealed and shot off the sofa and upright, huge blue eyes locking to him in consternation. 'You gave me a fright!'

'My apologies... What would you like for dinner? Or should I ask what would you *not* like?'

'Dinner?' Cleo gasped, backing away in apparent dismay, wide blue eyes pinned to him as though he were a ghost.

Ari was hugely entertained. 'I'll just order for you,' he decided, lifting the phone to contact Reception and order steak with all the trimmings for two.

'Why would you offer me dinner?' Cleo framed as he replaced the phone again.

Ari gave her a slanting smile that unleashed butterflies in her already tense tummy. 'I don't know. Do you think it could be an attempt to make amends for being rude to you?'

'That's not necessary, Mr Stefanos,' Cleo declared woodenly, her discomfiture unconcealed as she contemplated her bare toes digging into the plush luxury rug beneath her feet.

'I think it is,' Ari asserted. 'So, sit back down and relax...'

He had to be joking on that front, Cleo thought, incredulous at the idea of sharing a meal with a billionaire, who was also her boss. Even so, if he was trying to be nice when he was so obviously *not* a nice person on her terms, it would be mean of her to deny him the opportunity. Grudgingly, she sat down very stiffly in an armchair.

'You've had a pretty rotten day of it,' Ari pointed out quietly, determined not to smile at his recollections. 'You got ambushed at the paintballing and you fell in the lake when you tried to go paddleboarding.'

Stony-faced at those unwelcome reminders of her lack of athletic talent and physical grace, Cleo nodded. 'I'm not an outdoorsy person, but I like to give things a go—'

'That's an admirable trait,' Ari remarked, thinking that she was about as 'outdoorsy' as an exotic plant plunged into the frost, but he was impressed that she had been willing to try.

'Except when it comes to activities in the water,' she dared to remind him of his opinion.

'I may be in a minority, but I did think that your participation in those circumstances was dangerous and, worst of all, the experience gave you one hell of a fright,' Ari told her drily, letting her know that he hadn't changed his opinion of her daring in the slightest. 'Would you like a glass of wine?'

'Thank you.' Cleo nodded again and tucked her restless hands between her thighs because she had never been more conscious of a man's scrutiny. Those dark golden eyes that lit up his lean, darkly handsome features held her fast as glue.

Cleo watched him uncork a bottle of red wine and fill glasses, his every move smooth and dexterous, his polished assurance as much of a draw as his devastating good looks. Cleo had never met a male that confident and there was something oddly reassuring about that quality. 'I suppose I should have panicked when I found the front door locked,' she confided abruptly.

Ari glanced back at her with a raised brow of enquiry.

'Locked in a house with a strange man...' Cleo clarified in a belated attack of mortification because she could see that that aspect had not once crossed his mind. And why would it have? she asked herself ruefully. Women rarely wanted to escape from young, rich and very handsome men.

'I'm sorry. It didn't occur to me that you would wish to leave immediately,' Ari countered, walking away from her and back to the door to replace the key that he had removed in an act of personal security that came to him as naturally as breathing. 'There, it is possible for you to leave now whenever you like...'

In receipt of that demonstrative response, Cleo had turned as red as a ripe tomato while secretly cursing his decision to take her word so literally. She took a strong glug of her wine.

'Is the wine okay?'

'I don't drink much, so I don't have an opinion to offer,' Cleo admitted tautly.

'I thought everyone in your age group indulged,' Ari remarked.

'I don't like the feeling of being out of control. I remember my mother...' Just as she voiced those words, her lips compressed. 'Sorry, you don't want to hear about that—'

Ari elevated a brow, deciding that yanking Cleo out of her shell could take more effort than he was capable of awarding her. For all her bubbly friendliness on Reception and her surprising backbone and defiance in adversity, she was amazingly shy. Clearly, only fear of losing her employment had turned her into a chittering chatterbox in his office the day they had first met.

'I do. I'm trying to get to know you. Did your mother have a problem with alcohol?' Ari prompted with deliberate boldness.

Cleo paled, shrugged. 'Only for a while, when I was younger and I didn't really understand what had happened. She had broken up with my father and obviously she was upset for a time because she knew she wouldn't see him again.'

Ari angled suddenly intent eyes on her troubled face. 'You grew up without your father?'

'Yes. He had a relationship with my mother, but not with me.' Cleo winced.

'And how did that work?' Ari Stefanos asked her with apparent interest, his entire focus on her, which was a rather unnerving experience.

Indeed, the sudden intensity of those black-lashed burnished bronze eyes of his was mesmerising and her skin broke out in goosebumps of awareness. She shifted uneasily in her seat, mortified by her reaction to him.

'I can't see how you would be interested in that,' Cleo commented edgily, not knowing a polite way of telling him that the subject was too personal since he seemed to be clueless in the empathy stakes.

'I have very good reasons for asking such questions,' Ari declared. 'There is a situation in my life at present which appears to bear some resemblance to *your* childhood experiences.'

'Oh...' Cleo drained her wine and set the empty

glass down on the coffee table with a snap, demurring when he offered her a refill. Her brain was concentrated on striving to work out what situation in his life could possibly lead to such questions.

In the dragging silence the doorbell rang.

'That will be the food.' Ari strode off to answer it.

I'm dining with a billionaire, Cleo reminded herself, pinching a slender denim-clad thigh to reassure herself that she was not dreaming while the buzz of voices, the sound of a trolley and the chink of china and glass sounded in the background.

'Cleo!' Ari called, and he sounded just like a boss and she grinned then, her discomfiture vanquished by *that* tone.

She crossed the hall into the dining room and sank down at the table, her chair pulled out by a hovering waiter.

'If you answer my questions, I would be very grateful,' Ari informed her once the front door thudded closed again on the waiter.

Cleo had to swallow hard on her mouth-watering steak because she was unable to imagine any situation in which her input could possibly be helpful to Ari Stefanos. 'What relevance could my very ordinary life have to do with anything in yours?' she asked quietly.

Ari studied her. 'Is it possible for me to trust you not to run to the nearest tabloid newspaper to sell a story?'

Cleo stared back at him in wonderment. 'You've had someone do that to you?'

Ari gave her a brusque nod of confirmation.

'I wouldn't sink that low!' she declared with convincing sincerity. 'I *swear* I wouldn't!'

Ari reached a decision and set down his cutlery. 'Okay. Recently I learned to my astonishment that, through my father, I have half-siblings...'

'My goodness...' Cleo almost whispered. 'So have I, although I've known about them since I was a teenager...'

Ari dealt her an amused look. 'Which in your case is not exactly a hundred years ago. Tell me about what it was like growing up without a father, which I assume is what happened?'

'Yes. Mum worked with my father and had a long affair with him. It ended when I was about three. I'm afraid I have very few memories of him. He wasn't married but he did live with another woman with whom he had already had two children. When I was fifteen she admitted that in her late thirties she decided to get pregnant before she missed out altogether on having a family of her own.'

'Then you weren't an accident...'

'No, but she *may* have told my father I was,' she confided with a wrinkled nose. 'I didn't like to ask too many painful questions because she was a brilliant mum, apart from that period after she and my father broke up and I think she was depressed and that's why she was drinking then.'

'Probably. Did your father take any interest in you?'

'He paid maintenance but there was no visitation. He wasn't interested obviously in having a relationship with me and I can accept that—'

'But do you *really* accept it? And how does it make you feel that you were rejected?'

Cleo winced at that rather cruel question. 'Try for a little tact, boss.'

'Don't call me that when we've strayed so far from workplace boundaries.' Ari pushed away his empty plate. 'There's desserts somewhere...possibly in the kitchen—'

'Not for me. That steak filled me up.' Cleo stood up. 'I'll have coffee, though.'

Cleo set out the coffee cups on the top tray of the trolley and proceeded to pour for both of them before walking back into the sitting room. 'You asked me how I felt about my father? Rejected about sums it up. It hurt a lot when I was growing up when I saw other kids with their dads. And then years later I saw my father again with a woman and two children in the park. They seemed happy. It was only then that I truly understood my background. That woman and those kids were his *real* family, while I was only the by-product of his affair—'

Ari frowned. 'That's harsh.'

'It's reality,' Cleo contradicted quietly. 'It was healthier for me just to accept that that's how it was. I gather your half-siblings come from a similar set-up?'

Ari expelled his breath in a sharp hiss. 'A long-running secret affair, yes. I was shattered when I found out—'

'Shattered?' Cleo queried in surprise.

'I believed that my parents had had a very happy marriage—'

'Yes, but you were on the outside,' Cleo pointed out gently, reflecting that, in the realm of personal relationships, Ari seemed rather naive. 'I assume that this affair was your father's and that you only found out about it because he had...er...passed away?'

Ari released a heavy sigh as he paced. 'Yes... Do you mind me asking if you've ever contacted your half-siblings?'

Cleo twisted to look at him and frowned. 'No. Why would I do that?'

It was Ari's turn to look surprised. 'They're your flesh and blood.'

'Yes, but I've always assumed that they don't know about me and probably have no idea that their father cheated on their mother with another woman. Why would I want to upset them with that knowledge?' Cleo asked ruefully. 'Yes, I'm curious about them, but approaching them would probably hurt them by revealing stuff they don't need to know. I doubt that I would get a very positive response.'

His level ebony brows pleated. 'All the same—'

'No, Ari,' she cut in, using his name for the first time because she was so caught up in the discussion. 'Look at how *you* are feeling now. You said you were shattered when you discovered that you had siblings and that it's trashed your belief in your parents' happy marriage...'

As Cleo made those deductions, Ari angled admiring dark golden eyes over her and sank down on the hide sofa beside her. 'You really understand all this stuff... You see, I don't. The whole thing just came at me out of nowhere and I'm not sure how to handle it—'

'But you're on the *other* side of the fence from me. You are the *accepted* child. What about your half-siblings? What do you know about them?'

'I've got a private investigation team trying to trace them, but nothing that I have so far discovered is reassuring. I don't know when the affair ended or even how it ended, but my father appears to have left the woman and the children without money, which very much shocked me,' Ari imparted in a driven undertone. 'The very *least* he should have done was ensure their financial security.'

'I suppose I respect you for caring and not just thinking about yourself,' Cleo told him truthfully.

'I feel bloody guilty. I had an idyllic childhood. I have never lacked anything I wanted in life.' Ari breathed rawly, his disquiet unhidden. 'I have had every educational opportunity and advantage handed to me on a plate...while my father's other three children have had next to nothing in comparison—'

'There are *three* of them?'

'A boy and girl set of twins and a younger girl,' he proffered curtly.

Compassion filtered through Cleo. She was staggered by the amount of emotion he was revealing, because she had always assumed he was as self-contained and cool and calm as he appeared to be on the surface. The revelation that he was not at all that way humanised him and erased her awareness of their differing status while touching her heart. His spectacular golden eyes were liquid with emotion and she lifted an instinctive hand and rested it in a soothing gesture against his jawline, fingertips lightly grazing his stubbled skin.

'It's all right,' she whispered softly. 'It's not your fault. Nor is it your duty to carry the responsibility either. It was your father's choices that made it that way for his other children. I can't believe that they would blame you for his oversights.'

That this tiny young woman was actually striving to comfort him knocked Ari sideways. No female had ever approached him in that light since his mother had died several years earlier and it drew him like a fire on a winter's day, his dark eyes flaming pure glittering gold as he tipped up her chin with a flick of his fingers and brought his mouth down on hers.

It was like sticking her finger in a light socket, being hit by lightning, taking a ride on a shooting star, Cleo thought crazily as her whole body pulsed and lit up with a burst of heat and longing that blew her away. Nothing had ever tasted as good as that beautiful mouth of his, about which she had fantasised so often. Hard and yet soft, his lips caressed hers with lazy sensuality, and then, as her own parted to let him inside, the stab of his delving tongue kick-started an infinitely more primitive response. A needy ache stirred between her thighs and her nipples tightened, pushing at the lace of her bra while her heart thundered inside her chest.

'Are you okay with this?' Ari husked in her ear as

her hands clung to his shoulders as if he were the only stable thing in a collapsing world.

And in a way, he was, because she knew exactly what he meant, only there was no time to think about the many, many things she knew she would normally be thinking about. She knew that any perceptible hesitation would end the opportunity. She also knew she definitely didn't want that. She didn't want to be a virgin any longer either, she conceded grudgingly. For goodness' sake, she was twenty-two years old and had held on to her innocence, her *ignorance*, whatever people might choose to describe it, for longer than most in her age group. For once, too, she didn't want to play it safe; she wanted to tear up the rule book and take a risk. After all, with every man she had ever spent time with, she had always been waiting for the magic moment when passion sparked and swept away every other concern, giving her that shot of adrenaline-driven desire that other women had described. So what if her magnetic irresistible lure was Ari Stefanos? Surely she was as capable of having a one-night stand and walking away afterwards as any other woman? After all, there was nothing surer than that *he* would be walking away...

A guy who lived in a world utterly removed from her own. *Are you okay with this?* He took it for granted that every woman was prepared to consider travelling from a mere kiss to full sex when he asked! Hiding her reluctant amusement, Cleo pressed her face into his shoulder, drinking in the divine scent of him and quivering with an awareness absolutely new to her. 'I'm fine with this,' she framed shakily.

Ari was refusing to think. That kiss had powered him up like a rocket. He hadn't ever felt *that* before with a woman and he could not overcome the temptation to explore it even though every brain cell in his head was telling him 'no'.

'Let's go upstairs,' he heard himself say in defiance of his shrewd brain.

'You had better not get me pregnant,' she warned him in a near whisper, because that was her biggest fear relating to sex. She didn't want to be a single parent as her mother had been with no other adult to rely on. 'I'm not on the pill.'

'I don't make mistakes like that,' Ari assured her while trying not to laugh at the gaucheness of that warning.

Cleo was wondering whether to mention that she was a virgin, but she decided he didn't need to know that and would hopefully not notice. She was also afraid that if she admitted that truth it might make him think better of what they were doing. He closed a bold hand over hers and headed for the stairs, and she got all breathless and incredulous about what she was doing. But this was the guy who had haunted her dreams from the first moment she laid eyes on him, and there was no way she was willing to deny herself the chance to be with him just once. She *could* handle the 'just once', she told herself squarely.

The bedroom had a wooden cathedral ceiling and a massive divan bed. Ari tugged her gently back to him and lifted her top off her so smoothly she only fully registered what he was doing as he freed her from the sleeves. Cheeks colouring as he eased round her to appreciate the fullness of her breasts in a bright scarlet bra with deep cleavage, she only forgot to be self-conscious when he kissed her again, and—*my goodness*—he could kiss. He made her head swim and her body hum like a purring engine. She didn't notice the bra dropping to the floor or the loosening of her waistband, only reconnecting with reality when her loose jeans dropped round her ankles and he lifted her out of them and brought her down on the bed instead.

'You have gorgeous breasts,' he husked.

In the act of trying to cover them like some shy maiden, her hands dropped again and she lifted her chin, striving for a confidence that she did not have in her body. She had always thought that her boobs and her hips were too big for the rest of her, and that if by some miracle it were possible to stretch her to a much greater height, she might have had a terrific figure. As it was, she had always felt dumpy in stature and top-heavy.

He sank down on the bed beside her and curved his hands to the full firm globes, his heavily lashed dark golden eyes colliding with hers. It was as if a shower of sparks went flying through her and suddenly she was leaning forward and finding his gorgeous mouth again for herself. It had not even occurred to her that she could ever feel anything as powerful as the instincts driving her now with him. He tasted so good and the scent of him was even better, ensuring that one kiss led to another and that his hands were all over her just as hers were equally all over him. She had never felt that fierce urge to touch and explore before. But the smooth flex of muscles below his shirt, the tented evidence of his arousal beneath his trousers, held an extraordinary pull of attraction for her. He groaned beneath her touch, hunger blazing in his dark golden eyes as he gazed down at her.

'You are so incredibly sexy,' Ari husked feverishly, rearranging her to close his lips round a pouting pink nipple and tug on it until she gasped out loud.

A river of molten fire snaked through Cleo's veins as he simultaneously stroked the delicate folds between her legs. A fingertip dipped, a thumb skilfully brushed her clit and her body raced from zero to sixty in seconds as a flood of reaction gripped her. A croak of sound was torn from her lips, her back arching, a spasm of such raw response travelling through her that she was mindless in that moment, a being controlled by wild want and need.

'Never wanted anyone as much as I want you right now,' Ari growled, peeling away what remained of his clothing. He was entranced by her passion. She couldn't seem to keep her hands off him any more than he could keep his hands or his lips off her: she was more than the object of his desire; she was a partner, and for him it was an exhilarating experience.

Yet on another level of his shrewd brain Ari could not quite credit what he was doing. He did not mix business and pleasure, yet he was in bed with an employee—an absolute no-go in his rule book. But

Cleo's innate allure for him, he conceded, overpowered every misgiving and smashed his control.

Cleo was way beyond the ability to speak, pulling him closer, finding his sensual mouth again for herself, hands roaming down over his long, smooth back and spreading there while she remained feverishly attuned to her awareness of the erection pressed against her thigh. For an instant there was a pause as he drew back to don protection. Her breath was feathering in her throat, her heart pounding as he came back to her and suddenly he was *there*, where she most wanted him to be, nudging against the most sensitive spot, pushing in, stretching her in the most remarkable way, somehow answering the overpowering need coursing at the very core of her.

A sting of pain made Cleo jerk and grit her teeth. For an instant she tensed and then the discomfort was gone, washed away in the tide of amazing sensation that followed. He shifted his lean hips and a wave of elation gripped her as the pleasure began to build with every driving motion of his powerful body on and in hers. A sense of wonder rose within her as her heart hammered and the piercing need that had controlled her only minutes earlier returned with a vengeance, forcing the level of excitement to a pitch she could hardly bear. Ultimately, she reached the heights, and white-hot electrifying pleasure shot through her every limb as her body seemed to splinter in a shower of physical and mental fireworks that left her falling back against the pillow in shaken wonder.

A wicked grin slashing his sensual lips, Ari sat up

and feasted golden bronze eyes on her dazed face. 'We need to talk,' he declared unnervingly.

'We've got nothing to talk about!' Cleo told him in a defensive rush, clawing the duvet to her and sitting up. Had he guessed that he was her first? How would he have guessed that? There was no way on earth he could have guessed, she told herself urgently.

'Think about it,' Ari urged softly, springing out of bed and disappearing into the bathroom.

There was blood on him, and he knew, he simply *knew*, that she had been a virgin, but he could see that she was ready to deny it. And how did he fight that? Admit that her lack of sensual sophistication had been an equal betrayal? Yes, a seeming critique of her performance would really raise him in her estimation! Frustrated, because he was a male who always preferred honesty in place of other less presentable approaches, Ari switched on the shower. All he could realistically think about at that moment was how soon he could have her again…and he knew that was out of the question so soon, only that didn't stop him recollecting how absolutely amazing the encounter had been. He had never felt passion like that; he had never had sex that good…

The scent of her skin, the feel of her, her ability to stay natural and her lack of desire to impress him, all combined with her effortless sexiness, were a temptation he could not resist. As a rule, women didn't tempt Ari. He felt like sex and he had sex and it was usually that basic in that no one particular woman had special appeal for him. Yet Cleo attracted him like a magnet, and in surrendering to that attraction, he had not been sated, as was the norm for him. In fact, he was already wondering how soon he could be with her again...

Distract him, Cleo was thinking in consternation. The last thing she wanted was any kind of intimate discussion, not following on from the biggest mistake she had ever made in her life! She had to get out of the cabin and back to the hotel just as soon as she possibly could, write her ghastly error off to temptation and inexperience and never ever think about it again. In a frantic race she located her dropped clothing and hastily got dressed again.

Ari emerged from the bathroom, a towel knotted round his lean waist because he suspected that too much nudity would freak her out. He was utterly taken aback and unprepared to find her fully clothed again. Women didn't usually rush away from him. *He* did the leaving, not the other way round. Shock stilled him in his tracks.

'So,' Cleo stated rather abruptly. 'You never did get around to telling me what you were planning to do about these siblings you've discovered you have.'

Ari shot her an arrested appraisal, that having been the very last thing he had expected her to mention at that moment. He shook his tousled dark head slightly and regrouped. 'I'm trying to track them down with a view to getting to know them...if that's what they want.'

Cleo gave him a bright smile of approval that struck

him as incredibly fake while she sidled closer to the door with the air of someone not wishing to be noticed. 'That's a lovely idea—'

Ari stepped between Cleo and the door. 'Going somewhere?'

'Yes, I want to get back to the hotel before my roommate wonders where I am,' she pointed out stiltedly.

'Staging a cover-up is unnecessary,' Ari intoned with conviction. 'This is a private matter.'

Cleo tilted her head back, because she was barefoot and he was so tall that she couldn't look him in the eye any other way. 'Well, that's one way of putting it. I'd call it a huge mistake, but fortunately, we can forget it ever happened,' she told him even more brightly, seeking and expecting his approval. 'As far as I'm already concerned...it *didn't* happen—'

His well-shaped black brows pleated. 'It *did* happen, and why should you want to run away from it? I have no regrets whatsoever—'

'It was wrong. We both got carried away—'

'I'm not a teenager and neither are you. I'm way past the age where I get carried away. We started out being inappropriate and then somehow it began feeling right and *being* right,' Ari imparted with level emphasis, revealing far more than he usually did with a woman because everything felt different and new and fresh with Cleo.

'How can something so absolutely wrong be right?' Cleo demanded fiercely, reaching past him for the door handle.

Ari rested a lean brown hand down on hers to forestall her. 'I can make it right. I can make it possible. I will find you employment somewhere else—'

It was the perfect solution, Ari reflected with satisfaction. They would no longer be working in the same place, which meant that he could cherish his rules of office conduct again. A voice in his brain queried that, even though he had already thoroughly *broken* his own rules by getting intimate with an employee. But what was done was done, he ruminated, and he already knew that he didn't want it to be only a casual hook-up. For the first time ever with a woman, he was willing to sign up for a repeat experience, and in the light of that, it would be infinitely wiser to move Cleo into another job.

'No...you don't get to do that and interfere!' Cleo gasped, stricken. 'I'm not like my mother... I won't change my life or base my decisions on what some man wants!'

'I'm not asking you to do that,' Ari incised tautly as she ignored his attempt to reason with her and yanked the bedroom door open. 'I'm only offering to remove any obstacles which you may feel prevent us from being together like this—'

Cleo stalked out onto the landing. 'You're crazy but you're also my boss. I want to forget this happened and never have it mentioned again.'

'That seems rather like overkill,' Ari commented drily. 'We're young and single. We haven't harmed anyone.'

'Thanks for dinner,' Cleo pronounced awkwardly.

'*Cleo...*' Ari breathed in fierce frustration as her

bare feet slapped down the wooden staircase, her golden curls a messy mop that glimmered in the fading daylight, her slender spine rigid in its rejection. The solid thud of the front door closing on her heels was the only answer he received.

Cleo didn't trust herself to say another word, particularly when Ari had forcefully disagreed with every word she had said. But every inch of her rebelled against the secret sordid fling she believed he was offering her. *My goodness.* Had the sex been *that* good on his terms?

CHAPTER THREE

ARI WAS STILL recalling that exasperating conclusion with Cleo when his limousine dropped him off at his London Headquarters. He had been out of the country for five days, negotiating the purchase of an exclusive Portuguese beach resort that had unexpectedly come on the market. He hadn't been able to contact Cleo because he didn't have her phone number, and using his status to acquire that number had struck him as beneath his dignity. In any case, he was keen to believe that a few days to cool off would have put Cleo into a more reasonable frame of mind.

For that reason, Ari was taken aback to see a strange face presiding over the reception desk when he arrived on the top floor. 'What happened to Cleo?' he demanded of his PA, Mel, when his personal staff joined him in his office.

Everybody's surprise that he should even ask that question about a junior staff member made him bite back further comment.

Mel shrugged. 'She quit and the agency replaced her the next day with profuse apologies.'

Ari knew that he had much more important matters to handle than Cleo's disappearance, but he also knew that workplace ethics would not, in this instance, stop him from discovering her address. He had an appointment with the family lawyer at lunchtime. Apparently, the private detective agency he had engaged had lodged a timely and pretty comprehensive report, although enquiries were still ongoing. Receiving information about his siblings was definitely something to look forward to, he reflected confidently.

By mid-afternoon, Ari's sense of anticipation had died in receipt of a truckload of bad news. Indeed, he had learned things about his siblings' lives that would most likely give him sleepless nights. One fact in particular had hit him very hard and he left the office mid-afternoon to seek out Cleo. He could not imagine discussing such personal stuff with any of his friends but, somehow, Cleo was in a different category in his mind. She had impressed him as practical rather than overly emotional and he liked that trait. Somewhere in the back of his brain, he was querying that immediate wish to discuss the situation with a woman he barely knew, but Ari was not accustomed to questioning his own decisions or to stifling urges that might impress some as unwise. Nor was he the sort of male who dwelt overlong on the mysteries of life and his connections to other people.

Cleo was tired. With her free hand she massaged the ache in her back, acknowledging that she had forgotten how exhausting bartending could be when it was busy. Mercifully, the rush was over, and she was thinking longingly of the end to her shift because her feet were killing her in the high heels she so rarely wore. But then she had had no choice because without the heels she wasn't tall enough to reach for certain items.

The office temp agency had been furious with her for breaking her contract, but Cleo had no doubt that she had done what she *had* to do when she resigned from Stefanos Enterprises. She was mortified by her own behaviour and it had been easier to leave than risk an even more complicated and embarrassing situation developing. And yet on another level, which she did not wish to examine, she was also grieving the reality that she would never see Ari Stefanos again, and feeling like that against all common sense just made her hate herself all the more!

After all, she had barely been a blip on Ari's radar even to begin with. He had scarcely registered that she was female or indeed shown any sort of interest in her until events thrust them together and somehow—she didn't honestly know *how*—they had ended up in bed. She should have said no. She was well aware that she *could* have said no, because he had given her that opportunity, but she hadn't and there was no denying that. She had made the wrong choice, put *herself* out of a good job and a reference, and she could not find an excuse to hide behind.

When she glanced up and saw Ari Stefanos in front of the bar counter, she could not initially believe the evidence of her own eyes. 'How did you find me?' she croaked in horror.

'Your flatmate—'

Her eyebrows airlifted. 'You found out where I live?' she condemned resentfully, because walking away from him had been a challenge and she was proud she had managed to do it. Ari seeking her out and showing up again was way more temptation than she needed and it felt very unfair. 'That's not...er... very professional, is it?'

Pleased with that sally, Cleo turned away to draw a beer for a customer and ignored him. But then Cleo didn't need to look more than a second at Ari Stefanos to see him inside her head in all his perfection. Dark grey designer suit cut to outline every muscular angle and line of his tall, powerful body, a white-and-grey pinstripe shirt teamed with a royal-blue tie. Ari didn't believe in dressing down for work and there were no casual-wear days in his offices. He was a formal guy, who laid down pretty demanding conservative rules to be followed in the workplace. Rules, however, that he had chosen to ignore in her case.

Sam, her current employer, stretched above her to retrieve a glass and murmured, 'With your friend here, you can take your break now if you like.'

Cleo turned brick red at the concept of Ari Stefanos being any kind of a friend. He was more like a nuclear submarine who had sneaked up on her, blown her sky-high and destroyed her nice quiet life. But she supposed she had to speak to him, to act normally instead of angry and resentful, before he worked out that she had had a lowering sort of immature crush on him before they had become intimate. How humiliating would that be? He wasn't stupid. He would soon guess too if she kept on behaving as though he were some serious threat instead of simply a man she had once slept with. 'Thanks, Sam.'

'Ari...' she muttered, glancing up only to be ensnared by rich tawny eyes semi-veiled by black curling lashes, and her heart literally clenched in her chest. 'Why are you here?'

'When do you finish?' he pressed, his keen gaze scanning the colourful geometric top she sported, the fitted skirt exposing her shapely legs, the strappy shoes accentuating her slender ankles. Hunger punched through him with raw vigour, disconcerting him because he had believed, *genuinely* believed, that some weird combination of reactions had coalesced in him at the retreat and made him act out of character. Only now he was looking again at Cleo in the flesh, the guinea-gold curls surrounding her heart-shaped face, the big blue eyes striving to avoid his, the delicate flush of her pale skin, and his response was almost instantaneous, setting up a throb of almost painful arousal.

His lean, darkly handsome face gripped her gaze. 'I need to talk to you—'

Cleo struggled to drag her hungry eyes from him. But it was as if he were a magnet and she were made of metal. Compulsion made her gaze cling to his sinfully gorgeous face. 'We've got nothing to talk about—'

'I've had some news about my siblings, but not anything I want to share in a public place,' Ari intoned drily. 'When will you be free?'

She knew her own vulnerability as her heartbeat quickened and a shimmer of prickling awareness sifted wickedly through her taut body. He was still making her feel things she had never felt before, but even worse, he was making her feel them when she was striving not to be affected. He broke down her every defensive barrier and she didn't know how he did it.

'Six. But—'

'I'll have you picked up,' Ari incised, and turned on his heel.

Cleo wanted to smack him for his arrogance even while curiosity was tugging crazily at her because she was almost as inquisitive about the unknown relatives he had discovered as he was. She bristled at having been taken by surprise. Would she have acted any differently had she been prepared for his appearance? She suppressed a sigh and tried to be honest with herself. Truth was that, on the spot and in the flesh, she found Ari Stefanos downright irresistible.

Only a few minutes after she walked out of the bar, a luxury car purred into the kerb. A male she recognised from the office as belonging to Ari's security team emerged from the vehicle, tugged open the rear passenger door and called, 'Miss Brown?'

Cleo settled into the car as it pulled back into the traffic and didn't really draw breath again until the vehicle purred through a select city square of Georgian town houses and finally drew to a halt outside one of them. She had expected some penthouse apartment, not an actual house, she reflected in surprise as she climbed out and mounted the steps to the front door. The car departed again just as the door opened and an older woman murmured, 'Mr Stefanos is waiting for you, Miss Brown.'

Her slender spine stiff with self-consciousness, Cleo walked through an echoing tiled front hall, becoming belatedly aware that the house was a rare double-fronted town house of enormous size and grandeur. Her surroundings were like a shock wake-up call to her. This was Ari's true milieu, the rich and opulent environment of a male born with an entire silver service in his mouth, never mind a single silver spoon! What did he know about scrimping to survive in a city as expensive as London? What did he know about shopping with coupons and buying clothes in charity shops? How on earth had she ended up in bed with a male with whom she had so very little in common?

She was shown into an unexpectedly airy sunroom where tall exotic plants offered filtered shade from the sunshine. Comfortable seating overlooked a secluded rear garden that was a glorious oasis of greenery. The sound of a sliding door sent her flipping round. Ari strode in from outdoors, more casually clad than she had ever seen him in faded jeans and a forest-green sweater. Although his lean, dark features were clenched with a brooding tension she had not seen there before, he still looked younger and even sexier than normal in that get-up. The instant that bold thought raced through her head, she squashed it flat and reddened.

'Cleo...sit down,' he urged. 'Coffee?'

'No, thanks. I'm on a caffeine high by the time I leave the bar,' she confided.

'It's time we exchanged phone numbers,' Ari decreed.

Cleo breathed in deep, on the brink of refusing, and then, belatedly, she acknowledged that she wanted that link, and she dug out her phone.

The woman who had ushered her indoors reappeared with a laden tray, which she set down on the low table before withdrawing again. Cleo was relieved to see a pot of tea on offer.

'Help yourself,' Ari urged, passing her a plate. 'I thought you might be hungry...'

'Only a little,' Cleo confided, tempted by the delicious snack foods into selecting a couple and then setting down her plate to pour the tea. 'I get a pretty good lunch at midday.'

'It's none of my business, but why would you leave a decent position in an office to do bar work?' Ari shot at her with a frown.

'If you take tips into account, I actually earn more at a busy city bar,' Cleo explained apologetically, glad to employ an excuse that glossed over her real reasons for leaving Stefanos Enterprises. 'My stepfather runs a pub. Thanks to him, I'm experienced behind the bar.'

'I think we both know that the salary is not why you chose to jack the job in,' Ari murmured softly.

Cleo stiffened. 'Let's not get into the personal stuff. What did you want to talk to me about?'

'You're the only person apart from my lawyer who

knows about my father's second family. It seems wiser to keep it that way,' Ari explained heavily. 'Tragically, I received bad news on that score today.'

'Oh...' Cleo framed in dismay on his behalf. 'What did you discover?'

'That their mother died over ten years ago and that the three children went into foster care because there were no other relatives. So far, the investigation agency has only been able to trace one of them... Lucas, the elder twin and the kid brother, whom I was *so* eager to meet,' Ari breathed through clenched teeth, a muscle tightening at the corner of his unsmiling mouth, his amber gaze dark with suppressed bitterness and regret. '*Dead* at the age of twenty-two from a heroin overdose, both him and his girlfriend—'

'What hideous news to receive,' Cleo responded in a shaken whisper, leaning closer, wanting to offer comfort but not sure how to do it without crossing the imaginary line that imposed the boundaries she felt that she needed around him.

'Their bodies were found together in a squat. I feel sick with shame that something like that could have happened to my own flesh and blood!' Ari admitted in a savage undertone. 'How could my father neglect the needs of the children he had brought into the world to that extent?'

Cleo frowned at that searing condemnation. 'You take such a negative view of things,' she scolded softly. 'You don't know all the facts, do you? And unfortunately, with both your father and the woman he had the affair with dead, you may *never* know the facts.

A hundred and one different things could have happened. Maybe the woman broke up with your father and refused his support... Nobody knows their own future. Maybe they lost contact and she was too proud to ask for help. It was a secret relationship as well, so there was probably nobody else able to inform your father that the children had lost their mother. Until you know for sure what happened, you must *try* not to make harsh judgements.'

'When you receive news of that nature, it is difficult *not* to judge! My siblings went into the care of the authorities. My little brother dropped out of school at fifteen and ran away from his foster home to live on the streets. He had a string of convictions for drug-dealing before becoming an addict. He was identified by his criminal records—'

Cleo reached for his hand, where his fingers were biting angrily into the arm of his seat. 'Ari...it's *not* your fault. None of this is. You didn't even know Lucas existed. But it's very sad that you never had the chance to meet him and that he seems to have lived what sounds like a pretty unhappy life—'

'I haven't even told you the *whole* story yet,' Ari admitted heavily. 'There was a baby found with my brother and his girlfriend, a baby girl on the brink of starving, whose birth hadn't even been registered. She may be their child... She may not be. DNA tests are being done to identify her and to establish whether or not she is of my blood. She's still in hospital and then destined for foster care—'

'A baby?' Cleo repeated, with frowning eyes of

concern. 'It breaks my heart to think of a poor little baby suffering like that...but, all the same, it's *good* news—'

'Good?' Ari repeated rawly as a warm smile chased the shadows from her face. 'How can it be good news?'

'If she's your brother's child, she's your niece and you should have a say in what happens to her, unless there are other, closer relatives involved—'

'I have given a DNA sample and requested a meeting with the child,' Ari admitted. 'But what do I know about babies? What would I do with her even if she does prove to be my brother's kid?'

'That's for you to decide in the future. One step at a time. Don't waste energy even thinking about what hasn't happened yet,' Cleo murmured calmly.

Ari locked stunning dark eyes highlighted with flecks of gold on her and studied her from below his curling black lashes.

Cleo flushed. 'What?' she pressed uncomfortably.

'You're a remarkably soothing woman in a crisis,' Ari murmured with frank appreciation.

'My mum used to flip at the smallest thing going wrong. I learned to be quieter, more practical,' she muttered defensively. 'It's just how I react when there's trouble.'

'It helps,' Ari breathed, his rich drawl dark and deep in tone as he closed a hand round the small fingers still engaged in stroking the back of his hand. She was very touchy-feely and he wasn't used to that, because in his family they had all been of a stand-offish bent, rarely touching and certainly not embracing.

There was no denying that her natural warmth and sympathy attracted him in some bizarre way.

Cleo gazed down uncertainly at the hand gripping hers. Ari tugged on it and she glanced up warily to be engulfed in smouldering dark golden eyes. 'Come here...' he murmured, soft and low and intense.

Something dangerously hot curling low in her pelvis, Cleo half stood up and hovered nearby rather than immediately accepting his invitation. 'Not a good idea,' she muttered shakily, inwardly fighting herself to keep her distance from him.

'Stay with me tonight,' Ari urged.

And that fast, she thought, where was the harm? That ship had already sailed and she no longer worked for him. It was the most freeing thought she had had in days, and the weight of her guilt, regret and insecurity fell away even faster, leaving a wonderful lightness in its place.

'Yes,' she murmured with a sudden shy smile of agreement.

With a flashing smile, Ari tumbled her down on top of him and claimed her readily parted lips with raw, breath-stealing hunger. Her fingers speared into his thick black hair and held him fast. A rush of heat surged at the heart of her and she swallowed back a moan as he groaned into her hair. 'Upstairs before I shock my housekeeper...'

'I assumed that you would be living in a modern apartment,' Cleo confided, feeling the heat rise in her face as he led her up the imposing main staircase, and she hoped like hell that nobody would see them.

For goodness' sake, she wasn't a misbehaving teenager breaking rules, she told herself, irritated by that sneaking-around sensation and her adolescent lack of confidence.

'I was and then my father died. I didn't want this place lying empty and I didn't want to sell it, so I put the apartment on the market instead.' Ari thrust open a door and drew her into a very large bedroom, splendidly decorated with gleaming inlaid furniture. 'Tomorrow evening, we'll go out to dinner—'

Cleo swivelled startled eyes in his direction, taken aback by that announcement. 'No,' she told him without hesitation.

'No...to dinner?' Ari prompted in wonderment, suddenly falling still.

'No to dinner... Yes to everything else,' Cleo qualified with hot cheeks.

'Why no?' Ari pressed for further clarification even as he scooped her off her feet and settled her on the side of the bed before crouching down to loosen the ankle straps on her shoes.

'I don't want to be seen out with you!' Cleo told him in a rush. 'This...*us*...it's a crazy fling. Let's keep it under the radar.'

His flaring black brows elevated. 'I don't think I've ever met a woman who was ashamed of me before—'

'For goodness' sake, it's not like that!' Cleo protested. 'I just don't think this is a relationship meant for public consumption. You know that you and me won't last for five minutes, so why bother? I don't want the media attention either. When I go for another office job, it wouldn't do me any favours if I've been labelled as one of your cast-offs on the internet.'

'Why am I the one feeling like a cast-off right now?' Ari enquired drily.

'Because you're so used to being marched out and shown off like a trophy by women that you now think you're being slighted,' Cleo told him squarely. 'But no insult was intended.'

Ari laughed, helplessly amused by her blunt and irreverent outlook. Cleo was new and fresh in a way that consistently grabbed his interest. And his desire for her and hers for him were off-the-charts hot. Her careless designation of their intimacy as being a fling had sharply disconcerted him, but, in truth, he was probably in agreement with that sentiment. Presumably, what they had would burn out and die as quickly as it had started, and in the short term, why should they need to complicate that? He lifted her small curvy body up to him and ravished her parted lips with his, his tongue delving deep.

Cleo shuddered in his grasp, her nipples tightening, damp infiltrating the heat building between her thighs. He came down on the bed with her, reaching behind himself to haul off the sweater he wore in a very masculine movement. Muscles flexing, he cast it aside and studied her, tawny eyes ablaze with hunger, and her tummy flipped as if she were on a big dipper.

'I wanted to eat you alive again the instant I saw you standing behind that bar, *koukla mou*,' he growled. 'I don't know what it is about you—'

'Or I you,' Cleo cut in, slender fingers stroking

down over his bronzed torso and the cut lines of his muscles with a tactile delight that she could not help savouring.

Ari lifted her top over her head and embarked on her skirt. She wriggled out of it, her heart racing with wicked anticipation. As her bra fell away, he cupped her full breasts and groaned, pressing her back on the bed to explore her lush curves, lingering on the stiff little buds of her straining nipples and then lowering his mouth there. As he captured a straining peak between his lips and gently tugged, she gasped out loud and her back arched. He lingered there, grazing her with the edges of his teeth, licking the hard buds with hungry energy before he shifted down the bed to pay attention to an even more sensitive area.

Cleo's head whipped back and forth on the pillow as her breath sobbed in her throat. Waves of increasing delight were gripping her pelvis. Her fingers were locked into his black hair, shock at what she was allowing silenced by the amount of pleasure flooding her. And then it came, the ultimate wash of sensation that lit her up like a firework display, and she cried out, her body convulsing and writhing in ecstasy. Liquid heat and relaxation surged in the moments afterwards.

'No, you're not going to sleep on me now,' Ari warned her, lifting her with strong hands and turning her over, urging her up onto her knees before reaching for the top of the nightstand to grab a foil wrapper and tear it open with his teeth.

He tugged her hips back to him and plunged boldly into her tingling damp channel in almost the same movement, and a charge of indescribable excitement roared through her as her body stretched to accommodate him. She felt possessed, dominated, and it was a huge turn-on that added to an already intense experience. His hands firm on her hips, he quickened his pace. Claiming her with fierce thrusts, he made her body hum and pulse with raw hunger and impatience for the satisfaction that only he could deliver. As the sensual tide of sensation swelled and overwhelmed her on every level, another orgasm engulfed her and she cried out his name, helpless in the hold of that thundering charge of elation.

As she slumped flat on the bed beneath him, Ari snatched in a shuddering breath and flung himself back on the bed beside her. He snaked out an arm and gathered her to him. 'That was amazing,' he muttered thickly.

'I should go home,' Cleo announced with conviction, spooked by a sudden clingy craving to turn into the shelter offered by that arm of his and embrace that closeness.

His hold tightened. 'Stay—'

'I have a shift in the morning. I need a change of clothes—'

'I'll take you home early to change,' Ari spelt out insistently.

But Cleo had already made up her mind. They were having a fling. They were not in a relationship. The way she saw it, that meant she shouldn't stay overnight. Observing those limits would keep everything tidier and ensure that she never forgot where she stood with him. She couldn't afford to get too comfortable with Ari Stefanos. She didn't want to get attached to him and then get hurt. Sleeping over was a step too far in the wrong direction. Her warning was that dangerous desire to cuddle him! Best to keep everything casual, she reasoned ruefully, troubled by her craving to stay with him longer.

'No, I've got to go,' Cleo spelt out briskly in defiance of an instinct that she interpreted as weak. She slid out of bed, still half concealed by the sheet, and reached for her discarded clothes.

'You're not even staying for a shower?' Ari shot at her.

'I can freshen up at home,' she told him firmly.

Seated on a corner of the bed, she dressed, only as she stood registering that the silence that had spread was leaping and bouncing with hostile undertones. She turned her head and encountered brooding dark golden eyes that glittered like the heart of a fire.

'If you walk out of here now, you don't come back...*ever*,' Ari framed in a deceptively quiet voice.

Cleo froze in shock at that warning. 'I don't respond well to threats—'

'Then be reasonable, rather than offensive,' Ari advised, pulling himself up against the pillows.

He looked so beautiful lounging there against the white bedding that he stole the very breath from her lungs. Black hair wildly tousled by her clutching hands, she recalled in mortification, dark deep-set eyes fiercely intent on her below his slashing ebony brows, his bronzed muscular perfection never on more magnificent display.

A knot formed in her throat, threatening to choke her, and tension held her fast. 'You don't mean that—'

'Walk away and find out,' Ari invited in a raw undertone of challenge she had never heard from him before.

'Why are you behaving like this?' Cleo demanded in consternation. 'I haven't done anything offensive!'

'You won't be seen out in my company. You won't spend the night either? That's offensive,' Ari contradicted without hesitation.

'Are you telling me that you a-always spend the night with the women you—?' she began, stumbling over the words that she did not wish to say out loud, and even that sensitivity inflamed her. Ari Stefanos didn't belong to her. She had no right to feel remotely possessive about him.

'We're not talking about me right now. We're talking about you and your hang-ups,' Ari cut in smoothly.

Cleo bridled. 'I don't have hang-ups—'

'Maybe I should have called them *trust issues*,' Ari countered drily. 'But yes, it doesn't take a rocket scientist to see that you definitely have those.'

Outraged at her insecurities being read that accurately, Cleo thrust her feet into her shoes.

'The car will be waiting outside for you,' Ari completed quietly.

For a split second, she sat there, her every instinct at war and plunging her into conflict. She didn't want to leave him, which only persuaded her that she *should* overcome that weakness and leave at speed. In a quick movement, she rose and left the room without a backward glance because she wouldn't allow herself to look back at him. She hurried downstairs to collect her jacket from the sunroom. She was furious with him for cornering her and furious with herself for surrendering to her anxieties.

CHAPTER FOUR

Ari emerged from an erotic daydream in which Cleo was splayed across his bed like a sensual enchantress and he gritted his even white teeth at that unlikely image.

Two long weeks waiting for Cleo to apologise had sharpened his temper because intelligence was warning him that Cleo would sit him out. Even that he should guess that about a woman's reactions unnerved him because generally he didn't really get to know his lovers on a deeper basis. With women, Ari had always been more of an easy come, easy go guy. He was heading down a very unfamiliar path, he acknowledged grimly, and yet he could not overcome the visceral desire to see Cleo again. Cleo was stubborn and proud. He was equally stubborn and proud.

But wasn't it fortunate that one of them was feeling generous enough to offer a face-saving escape from their current deadlock?

Ari sent a text.

A very discreet dinner? No witnesses?

Cleo's heart jumped inside her chest as she read the text and quickly plunged her phone back into her bag. She breathed in slow and deep. Then out came the phone again.

At your house?

She wished she could inject a sarky note. Surely his own home was the only place he could hope to offer her that kind of privacy?

And the phone started actually ringing in her hand and she stood there paralysed, staring down at it, her heart rate pounding crazily before she surrendered and answered it.

'Not at my house. A restaurant, a surprise,' Ari specified, smooth as glass.

'What happened about the baby?' she almost whispered, revealing her intense curiosity with some embarrassment.

'It's complicated. I'll tell you over dinner,' Ari murmured, smiling as he recalled the way she had lit up with interest when he told her about the baby two weeks earlier. Cleo *liked* babies. He had picked up that much just from her expression at the time.

'When?' Cleo pressed, mouth running dry while she told herself that she wasn't going to agree even while she somehow knew that she had already made that decision from the moment that dark, deep drawl of his had sounded in her ear. He had made the first move, she reasoned feverishly, so she could afford to be magnanimous. Or was she just making pathetic excuses for herself? Cleo winced.

'Tomorrow evening. I'll pick you up at seven.' It would take that long to organise a venue, Ari acknowledged wryly, wondering if he had ever gone to so much effort to see a woman again and why he was doing it for her. Why was she a challenge that he could not ignore or forget? Why wasn't he simply walking away as he had done a hundred times before?

A huge smile tugging at her tense face, Cleo dug her phone back into her bag. She knew she had been guilty of an overreaction at their last encounter. Refusing to consider either a date or an overnight stay had been excessive. Panicking over an entanglement that seemed to have sneaked up on her and caught her unawares with her defences down, Cleo had wanted to run away. Unhappily, her attitude had allowed Ari to see just how hard she found it to trust a man and that was humiliating. He had also been offended and she could hardly blame him for that, considering that he had, from the start, been honest with her. He hadn't told her any lies, hadn't given her any unrealistic expectations or any excuses. He hadn't argued either when she had declared that they were having a fling that wouldn't last longer than five minutes. Clearly, his opinion was similar, she reflected tautly.

Her bar shift flew past while she mentally thumbed through her wardrobe for a suitable outfit and decided that she owned nothing smart enough. She was off the following day and she went shopping, trawling through charity shops until she found her best option, a short fringed blue dress that had a dash of style and was a little less colourful than her usual choices. Turning in front of the wardrobe mirror that evening, she watched the fringes glide silkily across her thighs with every movement, revealing glimpses of her legs, and realised that for the first time in her life she felt sexy. Ari had done that for her ego, she acknowledged ruefully. She had never felt sexy in her life until he had come along and enabled her to accept that side of her nature.

Ari wasn't in the car that picked her up and that disconcerted her. When the vehicle entered a tight network of narrow streets and she was finally ushered out into what appeared to be an alley, she surmised that Ari's surprise could be more of a splash than she had expected. As soon as she was guided through a narrow corridor past a busy kitchen area, where hatted catering staff peered out at her with intense curiosity, she appreciated that she was being brought into the restaurant through a rear entrance as though she were a celebrity desperate to escape the paparazzi. A discomfited veil of colour had swept across her face by the time she was led into the low-lit restaurant, which was unnervingly empty of other diners.

'Cleo…' Ari rose to greet her from a corner table, effortlessly elegant in a dark designer suit, cut to mould his wide shoulders and broad chest, his long, powerful legs outlined by narrow black trousers.

'Where is everyone else?' she almost whispered as a waiter whisked away the jacket she was laying down on the back of a chair and hurried to usher her into her seat.

'Tonight, it's just us. I promised discretion and here it is.' Ari moved a lean brown hand to indicate the unoccupied tables surrounding them. 'We're alone, aside of the servers.'

With that staggering admission, Ari settled back down at the table opposite her and reflected that every effort he had made to achieve such privacy had been worthwhile because Cleo looked incredible in a sapphire-blue dress that accentuated her eyes and revealed tantalising glimpses of slender thigh as she walked. He wondered why it was that no matter how often he had her he wanted more of her, as though she had some weirdly addictive flavour. But, in truth, at that moment he didn't care. He was relishing the surge of sensual anticipation gripping him, the newness of it, the very exhilaration of such an unusual feeling with a woman.

'How can we be here alone? I mean, why would the owner exclude other diners?' Cleo queried nervously as Ari ordered wine.

'I made it worthwhile for the owner to reschedule his other bookings,' Ari explained.

And sudden comprehension sent pallor climbing up her throat into her troubled face. 'You bribed him just for my benefit?' she almost whispered in horror.

Ari frowned. '"Bribed" isn't the word I would employ in these circumstances. I offered a business proposition, which the owner accepted. Nothing wrong with that,' he declared with unblemished assurance.

'The world turns every day on questions of profit and loss. I assure you that the proprietor is not making a loss…and *here you are*. Would you be here if I had not promised you this option?'

Mortification seized her. He had offered and she had accepted, and she had not spared a thought as to how he could achieve such a phenomenon for her benefit, had she? Any criticism would be unjustified and, what was more, did she want to criticise? For the first time in her life, a male had gone to considerable lengths simply to see her. Did she really want to diminish that compliment or criticise it? She glanced around the empty restaurant and finally understood that Ari wielded the kind of power with money that she could barely imagine. Ari didn't play games and he didn't offer false promises. He had met her demand for privacy, and if she shrank from the means he had chosen to utilise, that was her problem, *not* his.

'I didn't think through what I was asking properly,' Cleo conceded uneasily. 'Considering who you are, it wasn't a reasonable request. Your social life is always in the gossip columns. People are interested in your life and your companions—'

'Let's order our meal,' Ari cut into her troubled observations quietly as the waiter extended a handwritten menu. 'And let's forget about how we got here.'

Perhaps that was easy for him, but it wasn't easy for Cleo, who was ridiculously conscious of their quiet surroundings and his admirable ability to behave as though eating in an empty public dining room was normal for him. She selected her menu choices, sipped at the rich wine that arrived and tried not to stare at Ari.

Only that was a challenge she could not meet, for he was breathtakingly beautiful no matter what angle she looked at him from. The way his black luxuriant hair fell across his brow, the exotic slash of his high cheekbones, those perfectly moulded lips surrounded by a faint shadow of dark stubble, but most of all she was enthralled by his eyes, a dark and volatile mix of bronze, gold and caramel, accentuated by glorious black lashes longer than her own. She looked at him and it was his spectacular eyes that captured her every time.

'Tell me,' Ari urged quietly as he glanced up after the appetisers had been delivered. 'Why, after we were first together, were you so dismayed by my suggestion that I help you find other office employment?'

Cleo tensed and tried to savour the tiny sliver of wild mushroom on her fork. She pondered for a moment and then murmured, 'My father meddled with my mother's employment choices and it was to her detriment. I grew up with her bitterness. To protect his position in the same company, he persuaded her to resign hers. She agreed to keep him happy and because she believed they had a future together,' she advanced ruefully. 'But, of course, they didn't have a future and, unluckily for her, she never got that high up the career ladder again.'

'A sobering tale,' Ari remarked thoughtfully. 'Only we don't have a similar history and why would I wish to damage your prospects?'

'I have to be sensible and look out for me because nobody else will,' Cleo parried, refusing to get into the topic because it would be embarrassing. Nobody would take her seriously in any new job if she only got the job in the first place on Ari's personal recommendation. She would have to be stupid to think otherwise.

'I don't like feeling responsible for your resignation from my HQ,' Ari admitted bluntly.

Cleo shrugged. 'I was only a temp. It's not that big a deal, but I did the right thing when I left—'

'Only it didn't work,' Ari pointed out silkily. 'After all, here we still are...together.'

'And it's *still* against all common sense,' Cleo said roundly.

Ari lounged back in his chair and grinned, that slashing charismatic smile making her heart clench inside her chest. He looked utterly gorgeous and utterly unrepentant. 'That's a risk I'm prepared to take.'

'Will you tell me what you've found out about the baby?' Cleo pressed inquisitively as the first course arrived.

'She's only recently left hospital and she is still receiving medical attention in foster care. She's suffered a lot in her short life...but yes, she is, according to the DNA tests, my flesh and blood. Her mother was also an orphan. I am presently the only relative waiting in the wings, although her aunts are obviously still out there but it will take time to track them down,' Ari conceded. 'I have expressed an interest in meeting my niece—'

'When?' Cleo prompted with interest.

'Possibly later this week. I was hoping that you would consider accompanying me—'

Cleo was taken aback by the suggestion. *'Me?'*

'I know nothing about babies, and your presence would make me more relaxed—'

'I spent years babysitting as a teenager. That's my only experience of young children,' Cleo confessed in a rush, but she was pleased by his request. 'I would love to meet her, though. How old is she?'

'They think she's ten months old, but apparently she's very small and she has developmental delays, which makes it hard to be more accurate.'

'Does she have a name?' Cleo asked.

'Someone came up with Lucinda by contracting her parents' first names... Lucas and Cindy,' Ari proffered wryly. 'Considering that their addiction almost killed her, I'm not sure how happy an association that is to give their daughter.'

'They were still her parents, and I think that until you know all the facts, it's probably better not to make judgements,' Cleo suggested quietly. 'Particularly when you're hoping to find your other siblings, because it's possible that Lucas's sisters may have a very different outlook on what happened to their brother.'

Ari nodded. 'A fair point,' he commented with a smile. 'Making snap judgements is a habit of mine—'

'You're an only child. You've never had to bite your tongue to keep the peace. I haven't either,' Cleo remarked reflectively. 'But I saw what it was like when my mother married my stepfather, who has three adult children. Watching them interact was an education.

You and I had nobody to argue with us and challenge us as kids.'

'It doesn't even occur to me to think about stuff of that nature,' Ari admitted. 'When did your mother meet and marry your stepfather?'

'When I was seventeen. He's a kind man and she's very happy with him.'

By the time they were leaving by the rear entrance, Cleo was on a high following a relaxing evening. Ari was letting her into his life, trusting her with secrets and taking her opinions on board. Of course, she felt a little giddy and had a sense of accomplishment. When he curved an arm round her in the back of the limousine that collected them, her cheeks blazed as she voiced the awkward words that had been in the back of her mind all evening. 'I can't stay with you tonight...'

'No expectations here, *glykia mou*,' Ari responded.

'It's just...er... It's just that—'

Ari laughed. 'It's fine, Cleo. You're dealing with a fully grown adult male...but, to be frank, you're a welcome guest in any condition.'

Cleo's face was beet red and she dropped her head, knowing that she would never take the risk of having to hug a hot-water bottle to ease cramps in his radius. Long fingers tipped up her chin to meet her troubled blue eyes, and without warning, he kissed her breathless. A piercing surge of sweet heat arrowed through her quivering body, setting her alight wherever it touched. That quickly, she ached shamelessly, wanting what she couldn't have, reliving their last encounter with every sense thrumming and her body throbbing.

'I'll call you,' Ari told her as he saw her right to the door of the building where she lived.

She floated into bed that night feeling as light as a breeze and resolved not to sink into negative 'what if?' thoughts that would make her feel as though she were doing something wrong. It was an insane attraction and it wouldn't last for ever—she knew that... *Of course* she did. Maybe she would never hear from Ari again. There were no guarantees in her future, but she could live with that, couldn't she?

Ari called the following day to tell her that his meeting with his niece was scheduled for the Thursday afternoon. Cleo rearranged her shift to make herself available, agreeing to work that night instead, and Ari picked her up. He looked tense, his lean, dark features taut.

'Why are you stressing about this?' Cleo asked him quietly. 'All you need to do is smile and be gentle and unthreatening.'

Ari settled troubled dark golden eyes on her and his lips took on a wry curve. 'I'm stressing because I really don't know where I'm going with this and I'm not used to that. I like to plan ahead.'

'Stop trying to conquer the mountain before you even start climbing,' Cleo told him. 'You can't pre-plan everything. Maybe you're just curious to see your brother's child. I don't think that's a sin if that's all it is. She's a baby. You're not harming her by visiting her one time.'

'I hope not,' Ari breathed as the limousine filtered to a halt outside a bleak municipal building.

An older woman greeted them in the reception area and discussed her role as the baby's caseworker. Ari introduced Cleo as his girlfriend, which disconcerted her. His girlfriend... Was she really? Or had that merely been a convenient label to excuse her presence? They were shown into a meeting room and invited to sit down. Impervious to that suggestion, Ari paced restlessly in front of the window until another woman arrived with a baby in her arms. Ari strode eagerly forward to get a first look at his niece. Not wishing to muscle in, Cleo remained seated. Ari sat down beside her and the baby was handed to him.

Lucinda was tiny but her eyes were bright and huge in her tiny face. As Cleo finally got a proper look at the baby, she was betrayed into an exclamation. 'Ari... she's got your eyes!'

And it was true. Lucinda had eyes just like Ari, a golden mixture of browns, heavily fringed with black lashes that matched the wayward strands on her little head.

'Yes,' he said heavily. 'I've seen a photo of my brother and we looked alike. The Stefanos genes seem to be strong.'

Keen to angle his thoughts in a more positive direction and away from the premature death of his half-brother, Cleo murmured, 'She's a very pretty baby.'

'And so she should be,' the social worker chimed in.

'I believe her mother was a model and quite a looker before substance abuse destroyed her career.'

'Would you like to hold her?' Ari asked.

Cleo swallowed hard and opened her arms. The baby was a slight, warm weight curled into her arm and gazed up at her with Ari's tawny eyes. 'She's beautiful,' she whispered.

'She doesn't cry much,' the foster parent proffered. 'But she likes her bottles.'

'She probably became used to her cries not getting a response,' the social worker opined. 'She is gaining weight steadily, though, and getting stronger.'

As the little rosebud mouth opened, Cleo gently rocked the child to soothe her again. The long lashes drooped and a thready little sigh sounded. Ari reclaimed his niece with visible awkwardness and sat in silence gazing down at her. A few minutes later, he passed the child back to the foster parent and, after organising a further meeting with the social worker, they returned to the limousine.

'What do you think you will do?' Cleo asked.

'I believe that I will try to adopt her. She deserves a loving home… I only hope that I can provide that,' Ari murmured tautly. 'Do you want to join me for dinner now?'

'No, drop me off at the bar, please. I'm working tonight. I swapped shifts so that I could come with you this afternoon,' Cleo explained.

Ari sighed but, contrary to her expectations, he made no critical comment. 'I'll see you at the weekend,' he told her.

But indeed, Cleo saw him much sooner than that. Someone hammered on the door before nine the next morning. Ella had already left for her classes and Cleo clambered up with a groan, straightened her pyjamas and hurried down to answer it. The last person she was expecting to see was Ari Stefanos, who shook a newspaper in her startled face and strode in past her.

'I trusted you!' he shot at her in furious condemnation.

Cleo leant back against the door to close it and stared at him. Unlike her, he was fully dressed, all designer chic in a silver-grey fitted suit, dark grey tie and shadow striped shirt. He looked drop-dead gorgeous from the gleaming black crown of his head to the toes of his hand-stitched shoes. But his expression was murderous. He was pale below his bronzed complexion, his eyes were dark and as hard as iron, his mouth compressed and his hard jawline heavily shadowed with stubble as if he had not yet shaved.

'What did you say...about trusting me?' Cleo prompted, because she was only just beginning to wake up properly. 'And what are you doing here this early in the day?'

Ari slammed the newspaper down on the breakfast bar of the tiny galley kitchen for emphasis. 'I'm here about *this*!' he stressed with savage distaste.

He could never recall being in such a rage before, and a bitter sense of betrayal ran hot as a lava flow through his veins. His suspicions had zeroed in on Cleo first because it was so rare for him to share confidences with another individual. He had trusted her and she had let him down. Why hadn't he kept his own counsel? Why had he put his faith in a complete stranger? He had never before taken a risk like that. *Thee mou*, what quality did she have that had contrived to come between him and his wits? Had his libido persuaded him that she was a safe harbour for his secrets? The suspicion that he could be that basic, that stupid, outraged his pride.

Cleo padded closer in her bare feet and picked out the headline in the colourful tabloid newspaper that evidently had Ari breathing fire.

Billionaire baby almost dies from neglect!

Beside it they had run a large photo of Ari. Beneath ran a story about Lucinda's mother, Cindy, stating that she had been a model and an ex of Ari's before heroin became her downfall. The item described how the baby had been found starving in a squat beside the body of her mother. Ari was named as the baby's father.

'Well, they've got the story very wrong,' Cleo pointed out. 'What I don't understand is why you should think that this nonsense has anything to do with me...'

'I imagine that if I checked your bank account I'd find the proof that you were paid for that story by a journalist, who decided to put his own, more interesting twist on Lucinda's background! It's much more newsworthy if I'm cast in the role of a neglectful father!'

'I can assure you that you won't be checking my bank account any time soon,' Cleo retorted crisply. 'But I'm not responsible for this article. I haven't told anybody about Lucinda or your father's second family—'

'Perhaps you decided to keep my father's affair and the children born from it a secret as a special favour to me. I don't know,' Ari grated with distaste. 'I only know that you were the *only* person who knew about my niece and her unsavoury beginnings, and now here it is, spread across the newspapers for all to read about, and now *I'm* being accused of having abandoned her vulnerable mother and left my child to starve and suffer.'

Cleo folded her arms. 'Well, the article's nine tenths rubbish, so I don't know why you're so bothered about gossipy conjecture when you know the truth and the authorities do as well. You didn't even know Lucinda's mother, never mind have an affair with her,' she pointed out with quiet common sense. 'But while I understand that you're upset to see this kind of stuff being printed, I don't understand why you're bringing it to my doorstep when I had nothing to do with it—'

'It has to be you who leaked certain facts... There are no other possible profiteers in the picture!' Ari slammed back at her accusingly.

Cleo refused to be intimidated, although her temper was steadily climbing and had she had the physical strength she would literally have thrown him out of the apartment. Even so, she could already feel the sharp piercing sting of hurt and disappointment that he could believe her capable of breaking his trust and profiting from his family's tragic secrets. But she buried that vulnerability as fast as she could and refused to acknowledge it. 'Don't be so naive, Ari. There must be dozens of people who know enough about Lucinda to have sold this story,' she parried curtly.

'What the hell are you trying to say?'

'Well, a lot of people have been involved in Lucinda's life because of her near-death experience. Start with your lawyer and those who work for him—that's one set of people in possession of facts you would prefer to keep confidential. Then there's the private investigation agency you hired to find your siblings, who identified Lucinda as potentially being your brother's child... That's another set. What about the paramedics and the police who found Lucinda and her parents? Or the medical staff, who cared for your niece in hospital? Or even the DNA-testing facility you used to find out whether or not you and her were related? Then there's the social services staff involved in finding a home for her and her foster carers. Why don't you start counting up just how many different people already know enough about Lucinda's background to cause you grief?'

Ari stared back at her in brooding silence. Cleo looked so tiny standing there, even with her slight shoulders thrown back and her body stretched to its maximum, not very impressive height as she squared up to him. She was wearing pyjamas with horrendous zebra stripes on them, her mop of curls an explosion of gold round her face, her bright blue eyes wide and shocked. She didn't look remotely like a young woman who had been caught out in a shameful money-grabbing exercise. 'I—'

'No, don't you accuse me of anything more,' Cleo warned him in a brittle tone as she struggled to hold her composure together. 'I'm not responsible for this stupid story, and I would suggest that you concentrate your energies on finding out who *is*.'

With that advice, she lifted the newspaper, folded it and thrust it back at him before walking back to the door and yanking it open to encourage his departure. She slammed it shut behind him even as he began swinging back to say something else. In all her life she had never felt more exposed or more hurt. With a few simple sentences Ari Stefanos had trashed her every hope and belief, revealing his true opinion of her character.

She was poor, which apparently meant that she was also untrustworthy and a potential gold digger without a conscience. Tears stung her eyes. Ari had encouraged her to develop a false impression of their relationship. He had emptied a fashionable restaurant for her benefit just in an effort to see her again. But what had that been worth? He was an incredibly wealthy man, a man accustomed to doing exactly as he liked, regardless of cost. It hadn't meant that he set a high personal value on her or her character. Nor had his confidences about his father's second family meant anything more concrete. She had simply been in the right place at the right time at the retreat when he had been in the mood to talk to someone.

But she *had* made a big mistake, hadn't she? The mistake of thinking that she was somehow special in Ari's eyes.

Only now that pathetic conviction had fallen down around her ears like a collapsed house of cards, warning her that she had been vain and foolish to overestimate her importance to him. The instant someone had talked to the press about Ari's private life, she had become his prime suspect! Yet if he had thought it through, he would have realised that had she been guilty she would have made much more money from selling the *real* story, which he had shared with her. And not a story that merely twisted a tiny part of the whole to falsely depict him as a mean-spirited, neglectful father who had failed to look after his illegitimate child's well-being.

So, lesson learned the hard way as always, Cleo reflected unhappily. She was nobody and nothing in Ari's eyes, just a girl he had slept with a couple of times. Everything else had been icing on an empty cake and she had been an absolute idiot to believe that it could ever be anything more.

CHAPTER FIVE

'THESE ARE GORGEOUS!' Ella chorused in wonderment over the extravagant arrangement of tiger lilies in the vase that had been delivered with them. 'You can't put these ones in the bin as well.'

'Well, I've nobody left to give flowers to,' Cleo pointed out, having handed out the previous bouquets to neighbours and workmates. 'And I don't want to look at them here and be reminded of him.'

'I wish you'd tell me what he did that is *so* unforgivable,' Ella said and not for the first time. 'He is certainly saying sorry with style.'

'He can say it until he's blue in the face... It won't change anything,' Cleo said, her generous pink mouth suddenly tight and flat as a steel bar. Ari Stefanos had wronged her in the most unforgivable way. He should never have risked sharing his wretched family secrets in the first instance if he was so ready to suddenly flip and blame her for selling them to the press.

'If you're sure you don't want them, I'll give them to my mother when I meet her for lunch. She'll be thrilled,' her flatmate declared. 'Are you certain?'

'Completely certain,' Cleo asserted as she finished her make-up and gave her reflection a cursory glance in the mirror.

'You don't even want the vase?' Ella checked. 'It's crystal.'

'Not even the vase,' Cleo confirmed.

'He's gorgeous, Cleo,' Ella remarked abruptly, having got a look at Ari when he called at the flat to find out where Cleo worked. 'In your shoes, I think I'd cut him some slack.'

'Looks aren't everything,' Cleo parried, grabbing up her bag to leave, wondering exactly how long it was likely to take for that hollow sensation of loss that she had been nursing inside her to dissipate. Ten days had passed and that awful feeling hadn't yet faded even a little bit. 'And he's already had a second chance and he blew that as well, so I'm not about to put myself out there again.'

The bar was quiet when it opened, and she was up on a stool dusting shelves when the doors swung and she flipped her head expecting to see a customer and seeing Ari instead. Ari, devastatingly spectacular in a dark suit that fitted him like a glove, his bronzed and handsome face unusually grave. She froze and then lurched down off the stool clumsily, almost turning her ankle, wincing as she made contact with the ground again.

'How can I help you?' she asked in a frozen voice as he approached the bar.

'Have you blocked me on your phone?'

'Of course I have. Why would I want to hear from

you?' Cleo asked, genuinely surprised by that question as she bent down to rub her aching ankle.

'Did you hurt yourself?' her boss, Sam, asked from the other end of the bar. 'I warned you about getting up on that stool... It's dangerous—'

'I'm fine,' Cleo insisted with hot cheeks as she limped away to put the stool back.

'Take a break,' Sam urged her across the counter. 'Give the leg a rest for a few minutes.'

'I'll have coffee with you,' Ari murmured very quietly, watching her like a hawk and marvelling at the rapidity of the changing expressions on her heart-shaped face. She had given her boss a genuine smile, but the one she had given him had been fake. That infuriated him. Yet she still looked astonishingly pretty, her halo of curls burnished by the low lighting, her eyes blue as violets against her pale porcelain skin, her sexy little mouth tight with constraint.

She had blocked his calls as if he were a nuisance caller, Ari reflected bleakly. That had *never* happened to him before with a woman. Nor had the attempt to apologise with flowers got him anywhere as he'd waited in vain for her to contact him. Of course, he had never got in deep enough with any woman to the extent that he was having arguments with her and trying to apologise, he acknowledged impatiently. He was disturbed by the suspicion that he was behaving clumsily because he had absolutely no experience of ever being in such a position. There was something to be said for sticking to one-night stands, only no one—

night stand had ever had the effect on him that Cleo had. And it was Cleo and Cleo alone whom he wanted.

Ari breathed in slow and deep. Hunger slivered through him and bit deep enough to make him wince as his pants tightened across his groin. He couldn't sleep for thinking about her. She had got him obsessed. He didn't know how, he didn't know why, he only knew that she tied him up in knots and her absence took every spark of excitement and anticipation out of his life. And now that he needed a favour from her, he didn't know how the hell he could persuade her into helping him out of a tight corner.

Cleo's head flew up, angry words on her tongue until she realised that Sam was watching and that, as far as he was concerned, Ari was a customer to be served. She gave Ari a bright meaningless smile. 'No problem, sir,' she said and watched his beautiful face tense at her formality.

As she made the coffee she tried to eradicate that image of his beautiful face and wilful, wonderfully sensual mouth from her mind, but it was too big a challenge. She saw Ari and a sharp little arrow of hot, desperate craving shot through her, scrambling her brain and ensuring that she just wanted to rip his clothes off and climb him like a vine. There was nothing mature or controlled about that reaction. It was a primitive urge that she struggled to suppress every time she met his extraordinary eyes.

'I'm trying very hard to apologise,' Ari proffered when she brought the coffee to the table. 'Why won't you listen?'

'You hurt my self-respect. I can't forgive that,' Cleo advanced as she sat down opposite him, eyes very bright and level, her chin at a challenging angle. 'I thought you knew me. I trusted you. Then I find out that just because I'm a nobody without money, I was your one and *only* suspect. That tells me all I need to know about the way you think and about exactly where I stand with you.'

'It wasn't like that... I flew off the handle—'

'You have a short fuse,' Cleo condemned. 'And this isn't the first time we've been at odds. We don't match, Ari. You live in a different world—'

'I made assumptions, assumptions I had no good reason to make. I think I've tracked down where the leak came from—'

Cleo waved a dismissive hand, which set his even white teeth on edge. 'No need to explain...as long as you know it wasn't me. I wouldn't have betrayed your trust in me like that. I do have standards and you trusted me with secrets, and I haven't shared a word of them with anyone!'

'I was uneasy about the confidential matters which I had shared with you because I don't make a habit of confiding in people,' Ari bit out tautly.

'I guessed that, but I still don't understand why you're approaching me again.'

'I'm in a bind,' Ari admitted grimly. 'I may have somehow given social services the impression that you live with me and, now that I've expressed an interest in adopting Lucinda, they want to come out and interview us together in my house.'

Cleo stared back at him with parted lips of dismay. 'How on earth could you have given them the impression that we live together?'

'I think the lady simply assumed, when you came with me to see the baby the first time, that we were a couple—'

'But we're not,' Cleo cut in, sharp as a knife.

'That's not to say that we couldn't be,' Ari sliced back at her with determination. 'I will do literally *anything* to be considered as my niece's adoptive parent. If that means doing whatever I have to do to gain your willing participation, I *will* do it.'

Ari was thinking about the echoing emptiness of the giant house in Athens where he had grown up with his parents. He had been a lonely child, only making friends at school. There had been no family circle of relatives aside of a few remote cousins whom his parents had not encouraged to visit. He had visited Lucinda only the day before, but he had felt constrained without Cleo's soothing presence, although he had been ridiculously thrilled when he had managed to get his niece to smile at him. He had realised then that he was more ready to have a family than he had ever suspected.

Surprise engulfed Cleo because she had not appreciated that he was already prepared to make such a serious commitment to the little girl.

'Giving my niece a home means that much to me,' Ari admitted in a driven undertone. 'Her parents were unable to take care of her and do what was best for her.

Until I can track down my half-sisters, there's nobody else in the world likely to be as interested in that little girl as I am. I can't let her down the way her parents did. I can't turn my back on her just because I'm single and inexperienced with children. I can rise to a challenge as well as any other man. Bringing her up as a Stefanos is the only thing I can do now for the little brother I never had the chance to meet.'

Involuntarily, Cleo was impressed. Ari had thought the situation through in depth and acknowledged the difficulties ahead, but he was still keen to give his niece the advantages that his own father had chosen not to offer the children born of his second family.

'If you move into the house, I promise not to try and take advantage of the situation,' Ari declared. 'And *you know* I want you and that it will be a battle to keep my distance...'

Cleo flushed to the roots of her hair, awareness shimmering through her in a heady swell, but she was shocked by the suggestion that she actually *move* into his house. She understood why he was asking, because if she lived under the same roof nobody in authority was likely to question the veracity of their relationship. Even so, it was a huge ask for him to make. Her nipples prickled and tightened and, as she connected with his spectacular tawny eyes, her heartbeat thundered and a bolt of sensual heat surged between her taut slender thighs. The wanting, she was painfully conscious, was *not* one-sided. Unfortunately for her, being angry with Ari didn't stifle her desire for him. It never had. He made her angry, but he still inflamed her.

'But I will do nothing to make you uncomfortable,' Ari swore, his lean, dark features taut. 'If you decide to agree to this arrangement, you will have your own bedroom, your privacy, whatever else you require. You will have no bills, nothing to worry about. I will take care of everything.'

Cleo gazed back at him in astonishment at the suggestion. Live in that fabulous house without expense or expectations being attached? For anyone in her precarious financial position it was a prize-winning proposition. It would allow her to build up some savings, something that she had always wanted to do but had never achieved, living as she did from job to job, just about managing to keep her head above water on a day-to-day basis. 'How long would I have to live there for?' she asked abruptly.

'At least a few months,' Ari replied. 'Right now, I can't be more accurate than that.'

Cleo frowned. 'That's a long time and I'd lose the accommodation I have now—'

'I'll help you find somewhere else when the time comes for you to move on,' Ari slotted in.

'I don't want to be put in a position where I'm expected to lie to anyone—'

'Let's not worry about what hasn't happened yet,' Ari urged.

'I'm only considering it for Lucy's benefit,' Cleo warned him defensively.

'Lucy?' Ari queried.

'She's too little to be called Lucinda yet,' Cleo opined in a rush, her cheeks colouring. 'At least, I think so.'

'I suppose you'll want to think about this for a while,' Ari breathed, pushing away his untouched coffee and rising to his full height.

Intimidated by his even more commanding height while she was still sitting, Cleo quickly followed suit and stood up. Her brain was a morass of conflicting urges and needs, all trying to jerk her in different directions. She blinked rapidly, thought even faster. She had to protect herself. She knew that. But she still wanted to help out for Lucy's sake. In the set-up he had outlined, she could not lose, could she? She had loved that house of his, too. That shouldn't count in the scheme of things, but she was human and she could be tempted like anyone else at the idea of her own bedroom and possibly even a bathroom and a garden as well. Those were the kind of luxuries she had never had.

'When do you finish?' Ari prompted. 'I'll pick you up and we can discuss this more.'

Holy moly, those eyes of his, Cleo thought wildly, momentarily lost in his smouldering dark golden gaze and an intensity that revved up every nerve cell in her body and left her feeling both dizzy and confused. 'I don't need to discuss this more...but it'll be a struggle for me to keep my distance too,' she heard herself confide inanely and almost cringed for herself.

Ari muttered something in Greek as he stood staring down at her and the fluctuating colour in her triangular face. Hunger lanced through him and settled into a fierce pulse at his groin.

'B-but we're adults. We'll keep our distance because it's the sensible thing to do. I'll move in as soon as it can be arranged... I'll do it for Lucy,' Cleo informed him shakily.

'I'll make the arrangements.' With a sudden flashing smile lifting the tension from his lean, darkly handsome features, Ari strode off.

Mission accomplished, he thought fiercely. Cleo would move in. Unfortunately, he didn't feel remotely sensible in her radius, but he knew what she was trying to tell him. In such a situation he *had* to be cautious. He had a friend who had ended up with a live-in girlfriend he didn't want in the wake of a wild weekend. False expectations had been fostered by careless comments and compliments made in the heat of passion. Misunderstandings had followed. It had taken weeks for the male involved to regain his freedom and the unfortunate woman concerned had been very upset.

Ari was not that clumsy or naive. Nor was he foolish. He wouldn't make those mistakes. He thought Cleo was fantastic in bed and out of it, but nothing would persuade him to express those sentiments out loud. This time around, he would keep his hands off her and respect the boundaries. How hard could that be?

CHAPTER SIX

FIVE DAYS LATER, Cleo scanned her beautifully appointed bedroom and suppressed a sigh of appreciation. She had moved out of Ella's tiny apartment less than forty-eight hours earlier and already she felt as though she were living in a different world. A world in which meals were made for her and where nothing was too much trouble. Gracious living at its best, Cleo reflected, shaking her head in wonderment.

Her suggestion that she provide her own meals had been received with dismay by Ari's housekeeper. Mrs Thomas had insisted that she would be glad to have someone to look after because the house was often empty. Since she had agreed to move in, Cleo had only talked to Ari on the phone because he was in Paris on business.

A limo had arrived to collect her, her suitcases and her single box of mementos. Cleo had learned young not to acquire too much stuff because there had rarely been much storage in the apartments she had shared with her mother and she had had even less space to enjoy since she left home. Her mother had moved frequently when she was young. It wasn't until her mother had married her stepfather and settled in Scotland with him when Cleo was seventeen that Cleo had felt that she too had a permanent base.

Her phone rang and she stiffened at the name that appeared, answering it with reluctance.

'So, how are you doing?' her stepbrother Liam asked in a hearty tone.

He then announced that he was coming down from Scotland to look for work in London and he asked if he could stay with her. Wincing, Cleo told him that she was sorry but she couldn't help.

'But you gave your mother your new address this week and I assumed that you would have more space now that you've moved,' Liam commented accusingly.

'I do, but it's not my house and I couldn't invite you here to stay.' Cleo hesitated awkwardly in the strained silence. 'I'm living with my boyfriend now, Liam—'

'I didn't even know you *had* a boyfriend!' Liam complained angrily. 'And you certainly didn't tell your mother that you were moving in with some guy!'

'Well, I don't tell my mother everything,' Cleo answered quietly. 'And I'd be grateful if you could keep that fact to yourself until I see whether or not the relationship is going to go the distance.'

Her stepbrother was annoyed and made no attempt to hide his feelings. She was tempted to tell him to mind his own business when he began questioning her about Ari and demanding to know how long she had known him. Ducking his invasive questions as best she could, she remained pleasant, reminding herself that Liam was her stepbrother and that falling out with him would cause grief for her mother.

Liam was the reason why Cleo rarely went to Scotland to see her parent. Her stepbrother had announced within hours of first meeting Cleo after he left the army that she was the woman of his dreams. Sadly, he was *not* the man of Cleo's dreams. But he currently lived with his father and her mother and worked in the pub they ran, and avoiding Liam when she visited was impossible. Unluckily for her, nobody seemed to understand why she couldn't date Liam and at least give him a chance. He was an attractive, decent enough guy, who worked hard and had no obvious bad habits, but Cleo didn't find him remotely fanciable and for that reason she had refused to go out with him. Teased and ultimately criticised for her resistance to her stepbrother's charms, Cleo had found it easier by far to avoid visiting her mother's Scottish home. Sometimes, her stepfather and mother came down to London to see her and she always visited them for Christmas and birthdays. In truth, she resented Liam for coming, however unintentionally, between her and the mother she loved.

Now, keen to avoid any further controversy, she made suggestions about where Liam could stay in London and reluctantly agreed to meet him for a meal on the weekend that he arrived. The knowledge that she would have to put up with Liam's flirtation, heavy-duty persuasion and criticisms purely to keep the family peace made her tense and anxious. Getting off to sleep was a challenge and at two in the morning she surrendered and got back out of bed to go downstairs and grab a snack from the well-stocked fridge.

Mrs Thomas lived in an apartment in the converted stables behind the house and was not disturbed by anyone getting up at night. Clad in shorty pyjamas because Ari's house was always kept at a comfortable temperature, Cleo switched on the low lights in the kitchen and dived into the refrigerator, laying out eggs and broccoli and cheese, thinking hungrily of an omelette. Locating a suitable pan, she almost dropped it when she heard a sound from the door behind her and she whirled round, clutching the frying pan like a weapon.

Ari grinned at her and lounged in the doorway. 'You could batter me to death with that,' he remarked.

Her wrist aching from the weight of the pan, she set it down on the hob. 'I didn't know you were back.'

'About an hour ago. My meetings finished early and I decided to move up my flight, even though it was late,' Ari imparted smoothly, faded jeans clinging to his lean hips, the top button undone, his impressive brown torso as bare as his feet. 'Are you cooking?'

'I was about to make an omelette. Are you hungry?'

'I wouldn't say no to something to eat,' Ari replied lightly. 'How are you finding it here?'

'How could I complain? I've never been so comfortable in my life,' she told him truthfully. 'You said that we had that interview with the authorities the day after tomorrow. Is there anything else I need to know?'

'We have another meeting with Lucy tomorrow

morning. I was hoping you would want to come to that as well.'

'I wouldn't miss it,' Cleo said with an easy smile, striving not to be so conscious of his presence or of her own state of undress.

For goodness' sake, they were adults, not feckless teenagers to whom an inch of bare flesh could be an incitement. She was wearing shorts and a loose tee, not a bikini. Why, then, was she alarmingly aware of his gaze on her slender thighs? He wasn't staring. No, Ari was far too polite and controlled to betray himself like that. She chopped ingredients while stealing feverish glances at him where he sat at the island, one long leg braced on the floor, a powerful muscular thigh flexing below the worn denim that emphasised the bulge at his crotch. Her face burning scarlet, she dragged her attention from him and threw together the omelettes without further ado.

'This is good,' Ari remarked as he ate heartily, allowing himself only a brief glance in her direction because he was ridiculously aware of the curvy, highly feminine little body concealed by her pyjamas. The level of his awareness astounded him. He was accustomed to regular exposure to half-naked female bodies in clubs, on yachts, beaches and at parties. Wherever he went he met women who wore less clothing than she did, and he shouldn't be susceptible to even the smallest show of Cleo's body...but he *was*. Cleo only had to move for her full breasts to shift beneath her top, pert nipples poking out beneath the cotton, and he was as mesmerised as a teenage boy.

'It's a quick, easy option. Your housekeeper is treating me like royalty. This is the first time I've cooked since I moved in.'

'I'm glad you're here. I have a party to attend on Saturday evening. It would seal our couple status if you appear with me in public. I'm not sure we can be very convincing without a public appearance or two.'

'No can do. I'm meeting someone for dinner on Saturday night.'

Ari stiffened, a shard of outrage flaming through him, even though he knew that he was not entitled to that reaction. 'You have a...*date*?'

'Wrong word for it, although *he'll* probably treat it like a date,' Cleo replied ruefully, her mouth tightening with resentment. 'My stepbrother is down in London and, much though I'd prefer not to, I have to be friendly to keep the family happy.'

'If he's family, he can attend the party with us,' Ari suggested.

Cleo cringed at the prospect. 'No, that wouldn't do. He might be rude to you. I told him that we were living together and he was furious. It's none of his business but he pulls the big-brother act when it suits him and reserves the right to criticise. I don't want a truckload of misinformation going back to my mother if I can avoid it.'

'If you don't like this guy, you shouldn't have to spend time with him,' Ari asserted.

'I wish it were that simple, but I'll use my living situation to put some more distance between me and

Liam,' Cleo confided. 'If I talk about us like we're a proper couple, it'll put him off...hopefully.'

'Or if he's the average male, it might only make him try harder.'

'I can handle Liam,' Cleo said ruefully. 'I just wish I didn't have to and that the family would accept that I'm not interested in him.'

'Why do your family want you to be together?'

'Because he decided that he wants to be with me and the family approve. To be fair, other women find him fanciable.'

Reluctant amusement glimmered in Ari's gorgeous eyes. 'I may not come from your world, but at least you fan—'

Cleo leant across the gap between them and rested her fingers against his parted lips to silence the words she could see ready to tumble off his tongue. 'Don't you dare say that I fancy you!'

A slanting irreverent grin illuminated his darkly handsome features and he nipped at her lingering fingertip, making her jump. 'Even if it's true?'

'Don't be vain,' she urged, leaning back from him, overpowered by his masculinity that close. The scent of him was tugging at her nostrils, an intoxicating combination of musk, mint and the faintest hint of some exotic cologne. Even the smell of Ari Stefanos made her fill her lungs like an addict and left her dizzy.

'I was being frank,' Ari countered huskily.

'And don't be provocative either,' she added jerkily, stiffening in the midst of a sizzling encounter with his glittering dark golden gaze. With an effort she dropped her head only to find herself looking instead at the impressive pecs and abs delineating his chest and stomach below his sleek bronzed skin. Her mouth ran dry, hunger stirring in an almost painful surge, her breasts swelling and her nipples pinching taut while a hollow ache throbbed at the heart of her. She pressed her bottom down hard on the stool in an effort to ward off that craving.

'I wasn't trying to be provocative.' Ari breathed in slow and deep, his chest swelling. 'But I take just one look at you when I get this close and all I can think about—'

'Me too,' Cleo cut in, instinctively leaning forward to close the gap between them, on such an edge of anticipation that she could barely breathe.

'I promised not to make you feel uncomfortable here,' Ari reminded her in a frustrated undertone.

'I'm only uncomfortable because you're not touching me,' Cleo mumbled, craving his mouth so badly she ached.

'Is that an invitation?' Ari growled as he slid off the stool to stand in front of her.

In answer, Cleo succumbed to temptation and rested her palms against his warm chest, letting her hands slowly trace down over the ridged planes of his abdomen. Her heart was racing, her breath coming in short choppy waves, her body tight with an urgent tension that literally hurt to withstand.

Without further hesitation, Ari knotted long fingers into her sleep-tousled curls and crushed her soft pink lips under his. Her tongue tangled with his as a big hand curved to her hip to urge her into connection with the urgent hardness pushing against his zip. Excitement leapt and flared inside her and a hot melting sensation in her pelvis turned her body boneless.

Desire simmered and boiled through Ari. He remembered the boundaries he had sworn to observe, the caution he had planned to exercise, and he marvelled at the effect Cleo had on him. None of those reservations could stand against the charge of unfamiliar recklessness powering him. Her hands ran lightly down his body to his thighs, scorching him wherever her exploring fingers touched. She dropped to her knees and pure anticipation ran riot through him.

She unzipped his jeans, found him with her stroking fingers, tracing the powerful heat and urgency of him. He wanted more, he wanted more before she even got properly started. And she was definitely a little clumsy at what she was doing, but her sheer enthusiasm could have levelled entire cities. The fleeting graze of her teeth didn't have the slightest impact on the wild flare of excitement flaring through Ari and expanding at an exponential rate. He exulted in the satisfying suspicion that he could be the first male she had dared to appreciate in such a way.

Long brown fingers smoothed through her tumbled hair and he groaned out loud with pleasure. Cleo glowed with a sense of achievement and then he was pulling her up, lifting her up onto the granite counter behind her to peel off her pyjamas.

'Remind me to buy you some proper lingerie,'

Ari husked as he spread her thighs and bent his dark head, shifting with predatory grace to utilise his carnal mouth on the tiny bundle of nerve endings screaming for his attention.

On the brink of telling him that he would not be buying her any clothing and that any he did buy would not be worn, Cleo lost her concentration. She lost it so completely that the heart-pounding, pulsing wave of bliss that seized her utterly consumed her, and for a few timeless moments in the grip of that powerful climax she honestly felt as though she had left her body.

'I need to go upstairs and get protection,' Ari breathed raggedly.

'I'm on the pill now,' Cleo told him. 'After what happened at the retreat, I decided it would be safer to protect myself, but if there's a risk that *you* may—'

'I was tested last month and I haven't been with anyone but you since.'

That information pleased Cleo enormously and she smiled at him.

Mere seconds later, Ari lifted her and sank into her hard and deep, and her spine arched and she moaned, because her swollen flesh was already so exquisitely sensitive. The pleasure was intense, and excitement roared through her afresh as Ari ensured that she did not have time to begin worrying. As another exhilarating surge of pleasure rocked her, she gave herself up to the moment, suddenly rejoicing in the freedom to do exactly as she liked.

With every lithe erotic thrust, sensation piled on sensation and she quivered at the shocking intensity of what she was feeling. Her heart was pounding, her pulses racing, and suddenly she was in a fever of excitement for the finishing line again. And she was there in the heart of the flame, fireworks flaring inside her and the colours of the rainbow in her dazed eyes as the wild fevered hunger rose to an agonising peak and then slowly brought her down to earth again.

Ari felt intoxicated by pleasure as he began to pull back from her. He had never wanted anyone as much as he wanted her, had never dreamt that he could go from day to day reliving intimate moments with one particular woman and counting the hours until he could see her again. In truth, he had flown back late the previous evening purely to ensure that he could have breakfast with Cleo. What had transpired since that modest goal inflamed him all the more.

As Ari stepped back, Cleo slid naked off the counter, shocked by her surroundings, and she stooped to grab up her pyjamas. Long fingers closed over her wrist. 'Where are you going?'

Cleo breathed in deep. 'I thought—'

'No, you're staying,' Ari incised succinctly as he bent down to lift her up into his arms, naked and flushed. 'Tonight, I don't want to feel like a one-night stand whom you can't wait to escape again.'

'I didn't mean it that way. I just thought—'

'You think the wrong things sometimes, especially around me,' Ari told her lethally. 'I want you here in the morning, so that I can have you again...although I could always grab you out of your room at a mutually agreeable hour—'

Cleo grinned. 'Seems a little complicated...but like this...er... It's totally casual, no strings...okay?'

'You're quite happy for me to be with other women?' Ari intoned in apparent surprise. 'I'm sorry, but I'm not happy to offer you the same freedom—'

'I didn't say that.'

'So, not so totally casual, after all,' Ari murmured in soft and sweet conclusion.

'Why does everything have to get so complex? Why does everything have to have a label?' Cleo lamented.

'Does it matter as long as we're both content with the status quo?' Ari dropped her down on a big bed in a low-lit bedroom.

Cleo abandoned her crumpled pyjamas and curled up into a tight ball of anxiety. She didn't want to get content with him or used to him. She didn't want to get hurt again. Ari made demands and then got annoyed when she failed to deliver. If she had more backbone, she would return to her own room.

While she considered that defiant option, Ari ran a hand down over her hip and flipped her round and back into his arms. 'Go to sleep. I can feel you stressing from here.' He sighed. 'What time do you start work? I'll drop you off after we've seen Lucy.'

An hour later, aware that Ari had fallen asleep, Cleo crept out of bed to go back downstairs and tidy up the mess they had left behind in the kitchen. Ari hadn't even switched off the lights. She stacked the plates in the dishwasher, restored the work surfaces to sanitised perfection, doused the lights and crept back upstairs.

Now, at least, nobody would suspect the shenanigans that had taken place there. Her face burned at the X-rated images still locked in her memory banks. There was no need to advertise her total inability to resist Ari Stefanos.

As she slid back into bed, Ari murmured, 'Where were you?'

'Cleaning up the kitchen. You didn't even switch the lights off!' she told him in a scandalised whisper.

Ari laughed out loud and curved an arm round her. 'Why are you worrying about that?' he asked in wonderment.

Cleo marvelled at his masculine incomprehension.

The next morning, Lucy was very quiet when they arrived for the visit. Cleo got down on the floor and propped the baby up with cushions and began to roll the electronic toy she had persuaded Ari to purchase. As the coloured sections lit up and a nursery rhyme sounded, Lucy began to smile and show interest. Ari joined them, kept the flashing lights going and lifted Lucy's little hand to press the button down to change the tune playing. The baby grinned and Cleo felt her heart clench at that smile and could no longer resist those bright brown eyes in that tiny face. She lifted her up for a cuddle and told her what a wonderful little girl she was, and the way the baby reacted, it was as if she knew that she was being praised to the skies.

Ari was fascinated by the warmth of Cleo's cheerful interactions with his niece. She was so natural and confident with the child that a baby who did suffer from being rather timid and wary positively glowed in her presence, attracted by her sure handling and affection. Lucy, he registered, needed a loving mother figure like that to feel properly secure.

'My turn...' Ari gently eased Lucy into his arms and wondered how Lucy would handle being cared for by a nanny and how she would cope with his absences, practicalities he had not previously considered. His single status was not an automatic bar to adoption, but he also knew that it was not an advantage. And there was Cleo right in front of him: great with kids, fabulous in bed, absolutely not a gold digger. Could it get much better than that for him? He wanted to keep Cleo and what better way would there be?

The appointment passed unbelievably fast and another was arranged while Lucy yawned and yawned, exhausted by all the one-to-one attention and ready for another feed and a nap. Ari dropped Cleo off and she warned him that she would be working later to make up for her late start. He frowned but made no comment, and she looked at him and marvelled that Ari Stefanos was, however temporarily, hers. In jeans and a long-sleeved top in line with her suggestion that he dress more casually for his meetings with his niece, he was heading home again to put on a suit before he went into the office.

Hers, she savoured helplessly. The guy with the colour-coded wardrobe that had sent her into whoops of laughter only hours earlier. He was terrifyingly tidy and organised and...she *wasn't*. He hadn't learned yet how to be flexible, how to compromise. She had watched an expression of appalled disbelief freeze his lean, darkly handsome features when she emptied her capacious handbag to find something and he glimpsed the conglomeration of disparate articles she dragged around with her every day, everything from a mini first-aid kit to a bottle opener.

Hers? Of course, he wasn't, not in any meaningful, durable sense, she acknowledged, only hers in a weird and incredible time-out-of-time way. She remembered him strolling out of his en suite first thing stark naked, like some glorious Greek god and infinitely more sexy. She had been tempted to pinch herself to check that she wasn't dreaming, only the ache of her still humming body the evidence that she was not. And he had dragged her out of bed, displaying all the irritating characteristics of an energetic early riser who put punctuality on the same level as godliness. Yes, what they had, she reflected tautly, was very, very real, but it wasn't likely to last and it would hurt when it ended. As long as she didn't forget that she would be fine, she reasoned as he dropped her off at the bar and made yet another comment about finding her a more suitable job, which she totally ignored.

At lunchtime, Liam turned up and got chatting to her boss. Sam had a friend in need of a temporary bar manager at a Soho pub, and before Liam left again, he had secured an interview that afternoon. Cleo wasn't surprised because her stepbrother had considerable experience in the bar trade. When he showed up at finishing time and pressed her to join him for a drink, she agreed because she could see that he was dying to talk about his interview.

Liam, convinced he had the job in the bag, was in an ebullient mood, and he was annoyed when she said she had to leave at seven.

'Ari's picking me up outside,' Cleo protested when he endeavoured to persuade her to stay longer.

As she grabbed her coat to leave, Liam trailed out after her.

'What's this guy got apart from money and a big house?' Liam demanded argumentatively.

'I'm not with Ari because of his bank balance!' Cleo told him angrily.

'I looked him up online. He's nothing but a womaniser, Cleo. He'll use you and dump you again. He's never had a serious relationship in his life!' Liam proclaimed loudly. 'He's a Greek playboy, who doesn't want to grow up like the rest of us—'

'Will you stop raising your voice?' Cleo hissed at her stepbrother, noting passing heads swivelling in their direction and wishing Liam would calm down. 'And lay off Ari. You don't know anything about him!'

'Except that he dresses like some fancy-dancy model,' Liam quipped nastily, his attention on the tall, dark male drawing level with them.

'Keep your opinion to yourself,' Ari told him curtly.

And without the smallest warning, her stepbrother swung a wild punch at Ari.

Ari ducked and was coming back up to return the attempted blow when Cleo caught his arm. 'No, please... He's drunk and jealous—'

His lean bronzed face taut, Ari stepped back. 'The car's parked round the corner,' he murmured evenly while studying her swaying, pugnacious stepbrother grimly. 'As you heard, Cleo's very loyal to me. That's why we're getting engaged. I may have been labelled a playboy in the past, but Cleo has changed me for the better—'

'Engaged?' Liam repeated in thunderous disbelief.

'Engaged?' Cleo queried incredulously, twisting her head round to focus on Ari's granite-hard profile.

'So, you see, I'm not *playing* with Cleo. This is the real thing,' Ari breathed curtly, closing a taut hand over Cleo's and urging her away.

CHAPTER SEVEN

'HAVE YOU GONE CRAZY?' Cleo hissed at Ari as he led her round the corner of the crowded street and into the comfort of the limousine.

'No. Hopefully I've got him off your back now *and* without having to brawl with him in the street,' Ari parried without an ounce of regret. 'You shouldn't see him again on Saturday when he can behave like that. I don't trust him—'

'You shouldn't have told him we're engaged, and you can't tell me who I can and cannot see!' Cleo slung back at him sharply.

'He was drunk. You couldn't handle him,' Ari countered.

'He was drunk because he's landed a job and he was celebrating,' Cleo retorted. 'Believe me, that's not the norm for him. He wouldn't last long in the bar trade if it were.'

'I don't trust him with you,' Ari responded with finality. 'He lacks boundaries. Although you've never been with the guy, he's already making you very uncomfortable. It's none of his business if you choose to be with me. It's time someone *made* him back off.'

'*Not* you!' Cleo lanced back. 'That's just salting the wound. You're rich, you're good-looking, you're successful, everything most men want to be. Have some compassion.'

Ari's beautifully shaped mouth quirked and he studied her with glittering tawny eyes full of naked appreciation. '"Everything most men want to be"? *Really?*' he queried with amusement.

Cleo flushed to the roots of her hair and punched his shoulder in mock retaliation. 'You know what I mean... What the heck possessed you to tell him that we were engaged?'

Ari lifted his chin. 'It struck me as a good idea.'

'Well, it was the worst idea imaginable! Liam will tell my mother and then I'll have to come up with a whole story about how we broke up and everyone will feel sorry for me and assume you did the dumping,' she complained bitterly.

'But what if we don't break up? What if we *make* it real?' Ari murmured silkily just as the limo drew up outside the town house.

Cleo frowned and fell silent as she preceded him into the house. 'What were you trying to say in the car?' she prompted.

Ari pressed open a door into a room obviously used as an office. Lined with pale bookshelves and dominated by a desk, it had a contemporary aspect very different from the rest of the house and she suspected that Ari must already have had it redecorated. Now he leant back against the solid desk, his lean muscular body taut, sunlight behind him gleaming over his blue-black hair and bronzed skin, his spectacular eyes vibrant.

'Close the door,' he instructed.

'Ari...' she began impatiently.

'I'm asking you to marry me. No more pretending, no need for us to fake or lie about anything.'

Cleo was stunned by the concept. Her upper lip lifted as though she was about to speak and then met with her lower again as she thought better of the hasty refusal ready to tumble off her tongue. 'But you're not in love with me... Why would you ask me to marry you?' she asked stiffly, as though she were afraid that he could be pranking her for some nefarious reason of his own.

'I don't do the love thing...*or* the love thing doesn't do me,' Ari murmured calmly. 'I'm almost twenty-nine and I've never been in love. I've met women I like more than others, but I've never wanted to keep one of them. But you're different.'

'How am I different?' Cleo pressed tightly, and she felt as if her world were riding on his response. His opinion shouldn't matter that much to her, but she was discovering that it did—indeed, that his opinion mattered very much.

Ari had grown up expecting to fall in love, but it had never happened to him. He had decided that possibly he was too grounded to focus that amount of emotion on another human being. Or perhaps it was because he had never witnessed that kind of love in his adolescence. His parents had not been demonstrative with each other, although he had read love in the looks they often exchanged. Now he was asking Cleo to marry him, and even as he did it he was shocked that he was doing it. Yet the commitment he was suggesting didn't scare him in the slightest, which he marvelled at because he had always thought that even thinking about marriage would condemn him to sleepless nights worrying that he was making a mistake. But then Cleo *was* different in his eyes from other women.

'You get on great with Lucy and she needs you. I can be a lot of things for her benefit, but I can't be a mother,' Ari intoned wryly. 'She deserves a mother after her poor start in life, and even though she's not your child, I believe you are capable of loving her. Not every woman could offer that to a little girl who is not her own. The minute I decided that I wanted to adopt Lucy, I realised that I would have to be very careful about any woman I brought into her life.'

Cleo focused her attention on a corner of the desk to the far side of him and her eyes prickled with stinging tears. He was giving her the truth, but it was a truth that could only hurt. He was asking her to marry him for his niece's benefit. He needed a wife, whom he could trust to be kind to Lucy. And on one score he was correct. She was very capable of loving that little girl and would be eager to take up the opportunity, if only it didn't entail marrying a man who didn't love *her*.

'I'm quite sure that there are other women who

would be equally caring with Lucy,' Cleo declared, striving to rise above her instincts. Instincts that cruelly told her to immediately accept Ari's proposal because she wasn't likely to get him any other way. And she was realising for the first time that she wanted Ari, like really, really, *really* wanted Ari for much more than a casual affair. When had that happened? When had feelings crept in to weaken her objectivity? Why had she kidded herself that she could stay uninvolved when every scrap of evidence had indicated the opposite?

'No doubt there are other women, but I doubt if any of them would attract me to the extent that you do. We share dynamite chemistry—'

'And you would marry me just for that?' Cleo questioned in disbelief.

'Sexual compatibility is pretty high up my list of non-negotiable necessities,' Ari acknowledged without embarrassment. 'I have no plans to play away outside my marriage like my father did. No child of mine will ever have to deal with the situation I've found myself in.'

Cleo sealed her lips on the urge to tell him that he was too rigid in his viewpoint. Had his father planned to have a second family? Or had that been something that just happened?

'And of course, eventually, I would like children of my own with you,' Ari informed her levelly. 'I'm suggesting a perfectly normal marriage—possibly one built on a more practical foundation than most, but that doesn't mean that it couldn't be a good and successful marriage.'

Silence fell while her thoughts raced like trapped animals running in circles inside her head. She wanted to say that she would think about it for a while, but she knew she would only be saying that for the sake of her pride. She had always assumed that some day she would marry and have a family. She had also assumed that the man she married would love her, but nobody got everything they wanted, she thought ruefully. With Ari, she was boxing above her weight. He was rich and gorgeous and very honest about his expectations. He wanted what she wanted and she very much wanted him *and* Lucy. She had fallen headlong in love with that little girl and needed to be involved in bringing her up. Ari could make them both happy, was already making Cleo happy, if she was honest with herself, only that happiness had felt very, very risky and short-term in nature because she had naturally assumed that what they had together would not last for long. Now Ari was offering her something permanent and secure and she was discovering right there in that moment that she wanted that chance with every breath in her body. She wanted him and she wanted Lucy and it really was that simple.

'Okay,' Cleo said shakily. 'I'll marry you.'

His exotic caramel eyes glittered gold below his lush black lashes and her heart skipped an entire beat. 'Right, let's go and get a ring—'

'Aren't you being a bit hasty? It's after closing time too!' Cleo reminded him.

Ari pulled out his phone, and a moment later, he was talking to a jeweller. Within minutes he was herding her out of the house again, pausing to speak to his housekeeper to tell her that they would return for dinner. 'Or do you want to eat out to celebrate?' he asked Cleo suddenly.

'No, no, I'll be perfectly happy to eat here,' she assured him, feeling more than a little light-headed at the speed with which events were moving.

Two hours later, seated in a private room in the opulent jeweller's in Hatton Garden, she sipped champagne and contemplated the magnificent pear-shaped palest blue diamond on her engagement finger in fascination. Blue diamonds were rare and she loved it, simply because Ari had expressed interest in it and admired it on her finger. As he walked her back out to the limo in the fading light, he murmured, 'We'll get married in Greece and fly your family out to join us. What do you think?'

'I'm thinking about how much there is to organise beforehand,' Cleo muttered weakly, dazed by how quickly he made plans. 'Like a dress and invitations and—'

'Mel will organise all that for us,' Ari incised with satisfaction as he referred to his senior personal assistant. 'She was a wedding planner before she came to work for me and she's amazingly efficient.'

'I'd better phone Mum,' Cleo said, surprised that her head wasn't spinning with the stream of changes that was suddenly threatening to turn her world upside down.

'We'll go and see Lucy before we leave and we won't stay away long,' Ari stipulated, single-minded as always, and Cleo's romantic haze cleared a little at that point because, however unintentionally, Ari was reminding her *why* he was marrying her.

'Ari didn't really notice me until we were at the retreat, and then, after he'd hauled me out of the water, he took me back to the house he was staying at and... er, well, that's when we got to know each other,' Cleo revealed in an embarrassed rush to her mother.

'I can see why Liam didn't make the cut,' remarked Lisa Brown, a small blonde woman with her daughter's blue eyes and generous mouth. 'Ari's very, very good-looking.'

'I had a bit of a crush on him from the day I first saw him,' Cleo admitted with a sigh. 'It went from there...'

'I just want him to make you happy. At the end of the day the fancy frills don't matter,' her mother opined. 'It's only feelings that count. But my word, this place is out of this world.'

Lisa's blissful sigh of appreciation as they sat outside the luxury suite made Cleo grin. The opulent cabins of the Stefanos beach resort enjoyed the most beautiful view and they fronted a world-renowned hotel. Best of all, the twinkling turquoise sea and the smooth sandy beach lay only yards away, and both women were barefoot after a refreshing walk through the surf. With the sun beating down on them below a bright blue sky, Cleo's mother, an inveterate sun lover, was in seventh heaven.

'This is the holiday of a lifetime and I get to see you married as well,' Lisa murmured, squeezing her daughter's hand affectionately. 'And you'll be nearby for most of it, which is even more wonderful—'

'But she'll be on her *honeymoon*,' Cleo's stepfather, Davis, reminded his wife gently as he emerged from the cabin to join the two women, a greying, still trim older man in swim shorts. 'We'll go to the wedding and then work on our suntans. If Cleo gets a spare minute, I'm sure she'll try and drop in to see us before we fly home again.'

'Of course I will,' Cleo said warmly.

Ari's father had built an exclusive beach resort at the far end of the private island of Spinos and it had been Mel's idea for most of the guests to stay there. Ari had flown her family out in his private jet. With her mother and stepfather, her stepbrothers and their partners all attending, Cleo had felt much more grounded and comfortable with the arrangements. She was also relieved that Liam had opted to stay home and look after the pub to allow his father and stepmother to come to the wedding and enjoy their first proper holiday in years.

'Just one thing I wanted to ask you before we join the others,' her mother murmured in an undertone. 'How much does it bother you that your father isn't here for your big day?'

Cleo sent the older woman a look of astonishment. 'But he's never been part of my life,' she pointed out.

Lisa grimaced. 'Yes, but in recent years I've come to believe that I may have given you a false impression of him when you were a child. I was still very bitter, you know, when he ended the affair and returned to being faithful to the woman he had been living with all along,' she confided awkwardly. 'To be honest, he told me then that it would break his heart to walk away from his child and that he was deeply ashamed but that my pregnancy had made him appreciate how much he loved the family he was already with. The only reason he didn't visit you was that he couldn't face telling the woman he loved about his infidelity and he didn't want any more lies between them.'

Cleo studied her mother in shock because what she was hearing was a very different version of what she had previously been told. Her mother had not told her any lies, but Lisa had given her a much more negative image of her absent father.

'I'm sorry that I let my bitterness over his rejection colour my judgement. It's not fair for you to have to judge your father badly for a relationship that I freely entered. I *knew* he was with her. I *knew* he had kids. But I made the mistake of believing that because he hadn't married her, he was not committed to them.' Lisa breathed out audibly. 'There—I've got that confession off my chest and I can relax now and we need never discuss it again.'

Cleo nodded twice, taken aback by the information she had received and knowing that she needed to mull it over in private. She felt sad at what she had learned, but she also better understood her father's choices. He had chosen to be true to the children he had presumably planned to have rather than the unexpected pregnancy that her mother had presented him with. Could she really blame him for that? That he had admitted that he was ashamed to walk away from her gave her a much more positive image of the man.

Two crazy weeks of high-octane wedding preparations during which Mel had consulted her about every possible bridal preference had already left Cleo dizzy and very much aware that her bridegroom enjoyed an extremely privileged lifestyle. Time and time again she had had to swallow her misgivings and embrace the art of compromise. Just as often, she had taken Mel's advice and chosen to go with more upmarket options. Neither she nor her family had been allowed to pay for anything. Of course, they couldn't have afforded to pay for anything that would have passed muster in Ari's elite world. In a battle between her pride and her common sense, practicality had won. But Cleo had, however, picked her own wedding gown and her mother had paid for it.

And tomorrow was her big day, Cleo acknowledged in wonderment. The one downbeat note in her life was that she missed Ari. She missed him much more than she had expected to miss him. When Lisa had asked her to spend some time with her family, she had wanted that precious time with her mother but, unfortunately for her, she wanted Ari too. And with him having been in Brussels on business and their separate travelling arrangements, she had only seen him when they visited Lucy together shortly before her departure. They were hoping that on their return to the UK they would be allowed to foster Lucy until such time as it was possible to adopt her.

After an evening spent over a long dinner, Cleo's phone buzzed as she climbed into bed at midnight, and she answered it, surprised that it was Ari. *Oh, my goodness.* He wasn't getting cold feet, was he? She came out in a cold sweat of horror at the suspicion.

'I thought you were with your friends tonight,' she said tightly.

'I am, but I don't want a hangover tomorrow, so no wild partying for me. I know it's late, but I want to see you—'

'It's bad luck for us to see each other before the wedding,' she told him gently.

'You can't be that superstitious,' Ari censured.

Cleo winced. 'I am...and I want a good night's sleep.'

'Okay,' Ari conceded, although she knew him well enough to know that it wasn't okay with him, but then Ari was not accustomed to refusal.

'I want you back in my bed where you belong,' Ari admitted in a roughened undertone.

Cleo flushed and felt heat surge in her pelvis. 'Tomorrow night... My mum is enjoying having me here with her.'

She lay back on the bed, perspiration on her upper lip and a wrenched feeling tugging at her loyalties. She knew exactly what would have transpired had she met up with Ari. As her face burned, the ache between her thighs intensified. He had transformed her into a wanton hussy. And there was nothing wrong with that, she reminded herself, as long as she didn't get carried away and start advertising what a pushover she was for him. In her opinion, Ari didn't value anything that came to him too easily and she still needed to offer him an occasional hint of challenge.

Flying in that afternoon, Cleo had noticed the imposing Greek Orthodox church built on the hill above the village. It was a much larger and more elaborate building than one would have expected to find on a small Greek island. Apparently, Ari's grandfather had built the church to commemorate his wife's passing.

The following morning, as the car that had collected her mother and her from the resort drew up outside the church, Cleo breathed in deep and stepped out into the sunlight. She shook free her dress. The iridescent beaded and intricately embroidered bodice shaped her full breasts. It rejoiced in a vee neckline, bell sleeves and a layered and tiered tulle skirt, which flowed softly round her feet. Worn with a short veil, the gown had a romantic bohemian vibe, which she had fallen in love with. On her head she wore the superb sapphire-and-diamond tiara that Ari had had delivered to her the night before.

'You look like a princess today,' her mother had sighed in contentment.

A loud buzz of voices carried from inside the church. By the sound of it, the interior was packed. Ari had said most of the guests were business acquaintances and friends, with only a handful of his distant cousins sprinkled through the mix. Cleo, on the other hand, only had her stepfamily and a couple of old schoolfriends who had elected to come but who hadn't arrived until late the night before.

Now as she walked down the aisle with her mother she was insanely conscious of the number of heads turning to look at her, and her first impression was that there was an inordinate number of very beautiful women in the pews, all staring at her so intently that a veil of colour turned her pale cheeks a soft pink. And there was Ari waiting for her at the altar. He looked amazing in a formal morning suit, very tall and dark and extravagantly handsome, his spectacular eyes locked to her with unhidden appreciation.

And that was that for Cleo. Evidently, Ari liked how she looked, and a cast of thousands in the pews couldn't have daunted her from that point on. He didn't need to speak. His brilliant and attentive gaze told her everything she needed to know.

'You look like a fairy queen,' he murmured softly, his breath fanning her cheek, and a ripple of powerful awareness shimmied through her taut body. 'Or like you belong in a field of wildflowers.'

A narrow platinum band studded with diamonds eased onto her finger some minutes later and the short and sweet ceremony was done. She was Ari's wife now, for better or for worse, she reflected headily.

The reception was being staged at the hotel at the centre of the resort. Gathering her skirts, Cleo settled into the SUV that would take them there along the island's single road, which wound along the sandy shore. 'It's gorgeous here. How long has the island been in the family?'

'My great-grandfather bought it for peanuts in the days when such acquisitions were not considered desirable. Ironically, he did it to prevent tourist development. He didn't have an eye for the future or the people who live here and need employment.'

'But your father built the resort,' Cleo recalled.

'Yes. The family home used to stand where the hotel now is in the bay. After my sister died, my father demolished the house, had the resort built and built a new house at the far end of the island, but my parents only ever made fleeting visits here after that. Losing Alexia here on the island devastated them and they never got over that. My mother was heartbroken because she had always wanted a daughter. I know that they tried to have another child because my mother went into hospital with a miscarriage a couple of years later. I think she had a breakdown after that.'

'That was really tragic after they had lost your sister.' Cleo sighed with sympathy. 'The last thing your parents needed was another hard blow.'

'I know.' Ari compressed his sensual mouth.

'You've never told me how your sister drowned.' Cleo almost whispered the reminder.

Ari tensed. 'We were very close. Alexia was a tomboy, the perfect playmate for me. On the day that it happened, she dived into the pool and struck her head on the side. I tried to get her out of the water, but I'm afraid she was too heavy for me to lift.' Tiny muscles pulled his strong profile taut with the regret he couldn't hide. 'Sadly, I hadn't had lessons in life-saving either. By the time help came, it was too late… Alexia had gone—'

'So, the two of you were playing without supervision in the pool?' Cleo gathered in some surprise at the idea.

'Yes, we both swam like fish and it was assumed to be safe. But we were only six years old. My parents' guilt over that decision probably made it worse for them afterwards.'

'The trauma of that loss may also be why your father got involved with another woman in the first place,' Cleo suggested with a wince. 'Grief doesn't always pull people together. Just as often, it pushes them apart.'

Ari was frowning at that comment. 'The dates would tally with that possibility,' he conceded reluctantly. 'I haven't looked at the situation in that light before.'

'It makes sense. I doubt that your father deliberately went out to have an affair, unless that sort of behaviour was the norm for him.'

'As far as I know, it wasn't. He was a conservative man. Why are we even talking about this on our wedding day?' Ari demanded with a frown as he grasped her slender hand and squeezed it in emphasis.

'I was being nosy.'

Ari laughed, his tension vanishing, his dark golden eyes gleaming. 'You look incredible in that dress,' he told her. 'I like the fact that it's more casual. It suits you.'

In a very grand function room, they greeted their guests. Cleo saw very few recognisable faces around her, but her impression that there was a great number of beautiful women increased, particularly once she had identified four, not from personal acquaintance but by the fact they were celebrities who were often in the newspapers. Two were models, one was a soap actress and another a very rich socialite. And from the amount of snooping she had done into Ari's private life on the internet, she was also aware that at some stage he had been linked to all four women.

'You invited ex-girlfriends,' she remarked in a mild tone that could not be interpreted as censorious for she was reluctant to register an objection to that decision.

'Most remain friends and discreet about our past connection,' Ari parried without batting a magnificent curling black eyelash at her comment.

'There seem to be quite a few of them,' Cleo pointed out, very much aware of the extra degree of critical curiosity such ladies subjected her to and of their often overly familiar manner of greeting Ari. An avalanche of sultry looks, kisses and lingering touches had come his way, every woman vying with the next to claim that revealing physical bond. Their enthusiasm for touching him was a dead giveaway. Body language did reveal a great deal, Cleo conceded unhappily, far from content that Ari had chosen to invite so many of his former lovers to attend their wedding. Shouldn't *her* feelings have been taken into account? What had happened to the bride's right to enjoy a tranquil day of happiness?

'How come they're all still friends with you?' she enquired, unable to swallow back that obvious question.

'Why wouldn't they be? I never promised them anything that I didn't deliver.' Ari parried that further question with perceptible impatience at her continuing interest in the subject. 'Nothing was ever exclusive. It was casual. We'd go out, have a good time, enjoy a few intimate hours together. It was meaningless.'

Just as *she* might have been had Ari not developed a greater hunger for her after their single encounter, Cleo found herself thinking wretchedly. Troubled by his entitled attitude, she visited the cloakroom to freshen up before they took their seats. She was in a cubicle when she heard several female voices belittling the bride and she stayed put, reluctant to embrace the embarrassment of meeting the rude guests but guessing that she was undoubtedly listening to Ari's former lovers dissecting her. It was jealousy, envy, she told herself soothingly, but she could not forget that Ari was only marrying her to improve his credentials as a prospective parent for his niece, Lucy. That was a sobering slap in the face lest there was a risk of her getting too big for her boots.

'I think she's pregnant. She barely sipped the champagne and that hippy dress of hers is cut loose at the front,' a woman chimed in confidently. 'It's the oldest trick in the book, but it *would* explain why he's marrying her.'

A door opened and then another, and the voices

faded away. Cheeks flushed with temper and mortification, Cleo emerged from her hiding place, annoyed that she had remained concealed but all too conscious that Ari would not have thanked her for confronting friends of his about their nasty outlook and cruel comments.

It didn't help her mood to return to the reception and find a lithe brunette in a daringly styled cerise-pink dress flirting like crazy with Ari. The bright smile already fixed to her generous mouth stiffened a little more at the sight.

As the brunette grudgingly gave way to her for them to take their seats at the top table, Cleo murmured, 'Before you met me, you lived like a sultan with a harem, didn't you?'

Straight ebony brows lowering over his spectacular tawny eyes, Ari shot her an incredulous glance. 'What are you trying to say?'

'All those women vying for your attention, nobody daring to complain lest you lose interest, nobody demanding fidelity or anything else that might curtail your freedom,' Cleo clarified with acid sweetness. 'Marriage promises to be a big boring shock for you. How on earth are you planning to manage without your harem?'

Ari gazed back at her in disbelief. It had never once crossed his mind to see his sex life in such a light. He reckoned he could see some point in her censure. He had virtually picked women out of a wide selection of willing contenders, but what was that to do with Cleo now? At the point when he had been admiring Cleo's wondrous lack of vanity, competitiveness and drama in comparison to other women he had known, she chose to blindside him with an attack he hadn't foreseen, and he was very much taken aback.

CHAPTER EIGHT

'So what if it *was* like that?' Ari countered with a lethal cutting edge to his dark, deep drawl and a careless shrug of dismissal, as though his bride's opinion of his past mattered not in the smallest way. 'How I conducted my sex life prior to our marriage is, thankfully, not your problem.'

Cleo went white at his derisive tone, but she tilted her chin up in challenge. 'You made it my problem when you chose to invite every darned one of them to the wedding,' she retorted in a terse undertone.

Silence fell then and Cleo busied herself chatting to the elderly cousin who had been chosen, as Ari's most senior surviving relative, to sit by her side. Ari's best man made a very amusing speech, but that was the only speech, as her mother had had no desire to speak up amongst strangers and Cleo hadn't had any bridesmaids. As the bridal couple stepped onto the dance floor to open the dancing, the silence between them thundered, but she could see that as long as they both spoke to other people and smiled readily, nobody was the slightest bit suspicious that the bride and groom might already have fallen out.

Beneath the show, however, she could feel Ari's tension in the tautness of his lean, powerful body against hers and in the tightness at the corners of his sculpted lips. He held her lightly and did not pull her close, and as soon as the dance was over, he went off to socialise and Cleo joined her family. It was a ridiculously *civilised* row, she conceded ruefully.

The sunshine was fading softly into dusk when Ari suggested they leave. A full-scale party was taking place by then. Her family had gone down to the beach, where a barbecue was burning, a bar was operating and Caribbean music was playing.

'I should get changed,' Cleo said awkwardly.

'I'm afraid you can't yet. All your luggage has already been transferred to the house,' Ari informed her, long fingers brushing her spine as he urged her in the direction of the exit.

Cleo had taken her leave of her mother when the whole group chose the informality of the beach party. Another SUV awaited them outside the hotel with the rear passenger door wide for their entry. Ari strode round the bonnet and climbed into the front passenger seat.

Clearly, she wasn't exactly flavour of the month, Cleo acknowledged, but, rather than her feeling rebuked and put in her place, Cleo's annoyance was growing. How dared he behave as though what she had said was unreasonable? Prior to meeting her, Ari had behaved exactly like a sultan with a harem, cherry-picking whichever willing beauty he chose from a wide pool of choice as and when he wanted without any need to offer anything more than a fun few hours. He had no experience with ordinary relationships. He was unable to see why she should feel angry and hurt by the presence of his previous lovers at what should have been *her* special day. So, she would have to show him in terms that he could understand.

After a drive along the sea road, the SUV cut down a lane surrounded first by dense oak woods and then by orchards. She saw orange and lemon trees and other fruit trees she couldn't identify before the car moved back into the fading sunlight to approach a very large and long stone-and wood-built house overlooking a secluded bay. It was a beach house, she reckoned, going by the many open patio doors and the wide surrounding terraces, but it was a Stefanos property and therefore it was a beach house on steroids.

They walked into the house, where Ari shared a brisk exchange in Greek with the older woman awaiting them. He introduced her as Delphine, who then took her leave.

'There's a cold meal and snacks prepared for us, but she's happy to come back and cook us a hot meal if we want,' Ari told her smoothly.

'Cold will be fine,' Cleo responded, strolling into an airy reception room with a glorious view of the sea and the surrounding hills. 'I wasn't expecting something so contemporary.'

'I had it renovated a couple of years ago,' Ari retorted. 'My father rarely came here, and he signed the island over to me on my twenty-fifth birthday.'

'We need to talk about our difference of opinion,' Cleo told him quietly.

'No, we don't. Let it go,' Ari countered curtly.

'That's not how I operate,' Cleo said apologetically. 'I want you just to picture another scenario. Imagine if I had invited all *my* past lovers to attend our wedding—'

Ari actually rolled his eyes. 'Let's be real. You haven't *had* any other lovers,' he pointed out very drily.

Cleo's blue eyes blazed like sapphire bolts. 'That's not relevant,' she sliced back at him with hot cheeks. 'You can still use your imagination to picture how you would have felt had I paraded my past lovers in front of *you*.'

'I did not parade—'

'You did,' Cleo cut in. 'You invited a lot of women, who were not well-wishers and who spent our entire wedding loudly speculating about why on earth you had married someone as ordinary as me. I found it offensive. You didn't think about my feelings and you should've done.'

'I—'

'No, don't you say that it wouldn't have bothered you if I'd trailed a load of exes in front of you,' Cleo protested. 'You didn't like me spending time with Liam, even though you knew I'd no interest in him.'

'I'm possessive...about you,' Ari added jerkily, because it wasn't the norm for him and he didn't like admitting it. He didn't get attached to women, although he had to confess to having somehow become somewhat attached to Cleo, he allowed grudgingly. When it came to emotions, having grown up in a family where emotion was not freely expressed or shown, Ari had learned to conceal his feelings. That had become his default setting in every situation, he recognised belatedly.

Cleo curved a small hand over his arm. 'I'm possessive too...'

Ari breathed in deep and looked out to sea as the sun sank in a blaze of glorious colour. Peach, gold and scarlet rays radiated out into the darkening sky. Slowly the fierce knot of tension inside him eased. He got her point. He remembered how flirtatious some of those women had been, the inviting glances and touches, the hints that they would still be available were he to get bored, and he was suddenly amazed at how thoughtless he had been. Cleo, he recognised then, operated on an entirely different mental wavelength from him.

'I assumed it wouldn't matter to you because you were my wife, which gives you an unassailable role in my life that no other woman has ever come close to achieving,' he admitted. 'But perhaps that was arrogant...and I was careless and unkind.'

'Or perhaps I lack sufficient confidence to see myself in that lofty light,' Cleo allowed thoughtfully. 'But you do need to consider your attitudes before Lucy grows up.'

'Lecture over yet?' His mouth quirking, Ari gazed down at her, his extraordinary tawny eyes gleaming pure mesmeric gold in the light of the sunset over the bay. 'You're already trying to change me.'

'Polish up the rough edges a bit,' Cleo contradicted softly. '*Not* change you. You're not used to considering other people's feelings. It's not that you're rude. You're—'

'I get it,' Ari interposed before she could expand more on the topic. 'Now can we eat something? That crack about sultans and harems killed my appetite earlier.'

'Show me the kitchen,' Cleo told him with a relieved grin that lit up her delicate face like sunshine.

For a split second, Ari wanted to grab her, flatten her to the nearest horizontal surface or plaster her up against a wall and sink into the warm, wet heat of her curvy, sexy little body, but that kind of impetuosity could be deemed inconsiderate, he calculated, and he desisted from that libidinous urge with the greatest difficulty.

'I have quite a hot temper,' he muttered between bites of the snacks she piled in front of him. 'But I didn't want to argue with you on our wedding day or say anything that might upset you more.'

'So instead you simmered like a cauldron of oil on a fire and went silent on me. Good to know,' Cleo teased.

Ari snaked out a long arm and drew her between his spread thighs. 'Mrs Stefanos, you are sassy.'

Her blue eyes danced. 'You're only just noticing?'

He leant forward and claimed her parted lips with unashamed hunger. 'Last night, I would've killed to have you here with me.' He breathed that frank admission rawly.

'Last night,' Cleo whispered, drinking in the warm, wonderfully familiar scent of him like an addict as her hands wound round his neck, 'I said no when I really wanted to say yes...'

With a growl of response, Ari vaulted upright and grabbed her hand to lead her into the hall. 'Time to give you a tour of the upstairs.'

A wicked little spark of anticipation curled low in her pelvis.

He walked her up into a huge bedroom with patio doors opening out onto a balcony. The room was decorated in pale aqua colours, providing a fitting frame for the glorious panoramic view of the starry night sky above the dark shadowy ocean below while the white sandy beach glowed even in moonlight.

'Help me with the hooks,' she urged him, shifting her slight shoulders.

Ari undid the dress and she shifted her arms and let it drop to the rug beneath her. Hearing the catch in his breath, she smiled and turned round, refusing to allow herself to be self-conscious in a lingerie set she had chosen to wear.

Ari took a step back to fully appreciate the short peacock-blue corset cupping her plump breasts, the silk panties lovingly moulding the rounded swell of her derrière and the suspenders adorning her slender thighs.

'You were worth waiting for...the perfect wedding present to unwrap,' Ari husked. 'No sultan could greet his harem favourite with greater appreciation than I at this moment, *glykia mou*.'

Cleo sent him a speaking glance, amused and not at all surprised at the way he was throwing her crack back in her teeth like a challenge. He cast off his jacket, jerked loose his cravat and began unbuttoning his dress shirt, a sliver of bronzed muscular torso catching her eye as he shifted his lean hips to kick off his shoes. His exotic eyes connected with hers and he grinned. 'I love the way you watch me.'

Cleo went red as fire. 'I can hardly avoid watching you when you're right in front of me...'

'You watch me the way I watch you. With desire,' Ari contradicted, dropping down to his knees in front of her. 'I like it.'

He made that confession as he gently tugged her panties down her slender legs and her breath caught in her throat as she stood there, willing herself not to go into embarrassed retreat. There was nothing to hide, she reminded herself irritably, when he was already familiar with her body and all its flaws. He had none of her innate inhibitions.

'I'd take off your shoes, but that would make you too short for me to appreciate like this,' Ari muttered intently.

'It's all right,' she said in a voice that sounded as though her vocal cords were being squeezed, even though her fancy bridal shoes were torturing her toes, because when Ari smiled up at her, she was as much *his* as if he had branded her. She was discovering that she really liked being needed and wanted. His hunger for her made her feel empowered, *necessary*.

He ran his hands lightly up and down her thighs, gently spreading them, and she quivered. His lips grazed her heated core and she jerked, suddenly the party most wanting, most needing, and as he ran his tongue through that honeyed heat, she moaned his name. A jolt of feverish pleasure gripped her as he flicked her sensitive bud. Her hips bucked as he continued his sensual assault. Her legs trembled as the flaming heat at the juncture of her thighs roared higher. Her hands lifted in a silent seeking gesture of unbearable arousal and then her body detonated in an explosion of wild, seething delight.

Catching her up in his arms while she was still quivering, Ari spread her on the bed, flipping off the shoes and the stockings, unzipping the corset and then bending over her to capture a straining bullet-hard nipple in his mouth. She gasped out loud, liquid and boneless. He paused only to strip off what remained of his clothes, leaving them lying where they fell with uncharacteristic untidiness.

He came down to her hungry and urgent, tipping her legs over his shoulders, rising above her to penetrate her with one fluid stroke. She cried out in response to that sudden fullness, hips writhing as heavenly longed-for sensation shimmied through her pelvis, bringing a wash of heated excitement in its wake. He tilted her back even further, thrusting deep and sending her pleasure to an unholy height. Her body surged with the sheer thrill of it, and in the passionate minutes that followed, she finally plunged over the edge into another climax.

'I'm never going to move again,' she mumbled weakly as he hauled her with him under the sheet.

Ari leant over her and dropped a careless kiss on her cheekbone, tawny eyes smouldering over her with immense masculine satisfaction. 'You're my personal kryptonite.'

'Not feeling too much like a superhero right now… but my goodness, I'm starving,' she confided.

Stark naked, Ari sprang out of bed within seconds of that announcement. 'I'll go and fill a tray.'

'You're in a helpful mood,' she remarked in surprise.

'Maybe I don't want you flagging in energy this early in the evening,' Ari contended.

Sitting up, Cleo swallowed a yawn. 'Weddings are incredibly exhausting,' she warned him.

'I'm as hungry for you as you are for food,' Ari explained almost apologetically.

He knew she was tired. She was pale and her eyes were shadowed. But he had told her the truth. He had a hunger for her that seemed to have no limits and it had made him a little uneasy before he married her. Now, however, that he had acquired Cleo on a permanent basis, that amazing hunger for her no longer bothered him in the same way. There was nothing dangerous or worrying about lusting after his wife. In fact, he now thought it was healthy.

That comment of hers about harems had hit him harder than she could even appreciate. His sex life *had* been highly organised, he acknowledged grimly. He had been careful not to spend too much time with any one woman, not to favour one over another, and for years that cool, logical approach had paid dividends by keeping his life smooth and free of strife. Of course, there was always the occasional hiccup in even the smoothest, slickest schedule, he reflected wryly, recalling Galina, the gorgeous but slightly unhinged Russian supermodel, who had revealed stalking tendencies after only one dinner date.

He had backed off fast, blocked the woman's repeated phone calls and ignored her appearances in his favourite haunts. To the best of his ability, he had protected himself from that kind of nuisance. And now he was married, and he felt remarkably content with the bargain he had struck with Cleo, but possibly rather more aware now that his niece, Lucy, would not be the only party to benefit from their official status as a couple. A wife who attracted him as much as Cleo did was a find, a huge and wonderful *find*...

Thinking that he was now a married man still shook him. In a matter of weeks his life had changed course to an extraordinary degree. Lucy had come along, of course, a totally unexpected but decidedly cute development in his world, but before her had come *Cleo*. Ari struggled to choose food and concentrate at the same time as he thought about Cleo.

Two weeks later, the afternoon before their return to London, Cleo stretched in the warmth of the shade.

She was reclining on a shaded and padded lounger in more comfort than she had ever known, and she had a wonderful view of the beach in front of her.

After the first couple of days of their honeymoon on Spinos, Cleo and Ari had reached an agreement that covered their radically different approaches to what constituted a break. Ari always had to be *doing* something, while Cleo liked to sunbathe with a good thriller or go for a not-too-strenuous stroll. It had had to work after Ari had dragged her huffing and puffing in the heat to see the remains of the Greek shrine at the top of the island's only hill. She had been on the brink of expiring on the peak of that hill, while Ari had barely broken a sweat. Now, one day they went out and did *physical stuff*—as she termed it—and the next she got to be lazier, aside of the daily swimming lessons he insisted on, and that combination worked. She had finally learned how to swim and she was hugely proud of herself for conquering her former fear of deep water.

Today, Ari was out diving in the bay.

'Isn't that dangerous?' she had said to him anxiously.

And he had laughed, but he had also liked that she was worried about him. He had confessed that it felt like a very long time since anyone had worried about him, and with prudent probing, she had gained a view of his childhood that she didn't like and which he would probably dispute out of loyalty to his mother and father.

There was no doubt that his sister's death had

ripped the heart out of Ari's family. Instead of cherishing the child who had survived, however, his parents had retired to separate corners to grieve for the child they had lost. Ari had been left very much to his own devices after he lost his twin, yet his involvement in that tragedy had damaged him as well. Even so, his parents had spent little subsequent time with their son and had sent him off to boarding school at eight years old. That detachment and distance had influenced Ari, making him too much of a loner who lacked understanding of normal relationships either in or outside the family circle.

On her family's last night on the island, they had enjoyed a dinner together at the resort. Ari had emerged shell-shocked from the chattering closeness of her mother and stepfamily, with everybody talking at once and the children alternately playing and then squabbling. The relaxed and yet warm informality he had witnessed had surprised Ari, but, ultimately, charmed him.

Only the day before, she and Ari had flown to Corfu for a day of sightseeing that had ended with dinner on the beach and a late night at a fancy club. Cleo fingered the diamond platinum pendant Ari had casually handed her over the meal, touched the diamonds in her ears, glanced at the delicate watch on her wrist and smiled, dazed by the heat and a growing sense of security. Ari liked giving her stuff. He liked giving her stuff so much that it got embarrassing. She knew he would go out of his way to spoil Lucy as well.

Lucy. Briefly, her smile dipped. She missed that baby so much, and occasional bulletins from her caseworker didn't replace actual bodily contact. Ari's lawyer was working on their fostering application but had warned them to be patient because the authorities dealt slowly with such matters. She watched as a motorboat came to shore and Ari vaulted out into the shallow water. Clad only in swim shorts, he was stunning, tall, bronzed and muscular as he strode up onto the beach, dripping wet and gorgeous.

You watch me the way I watch you.

He had nailed that observation to perfection.

But then, Cleo conceded ruefully, she had watched Ari from the very first day she saw him. The attraction for her had been instant, visceral, while with Ari she had proved to be more of an acquired taste. Fortunately for her, he *had* acquired that taste, but she didn't kid herself that that was anything deeper than sexual chemistry. Yet, in comparison, she had become very conscious that she was in love with the man she had married. Indeed, she had probably taken the first crucial steps along that path that first evening together, when he had chosen to confide in her about his father's second family. Now he was her obsession, she allowed, her mouth running dry and a zing of excitement curling between her thighs as he strode up the beach path with her firmly in his sights and a wolfish smile curving his sensual mouth.

'Were you waiting for me?' Ari intoned huskily.

'Don't you just wish?' Cleo mocked, insanely conscious of his gaze welded to her lips and straying down to the full breasts moulded by the rather brief bikini she wore. 'No, I was just reading and lazing—

'You're wet!' she shrieked as he grabbed her.

'You should've lied and said you were waiting for me this *once*!' Ari complained. 'You're bad for my ego.'

'You don't need any more compliments,' Cleo told him, running a small hand down over his washboard-flat abdomen and feeling him shiver in response, noting the thrust of the erection the shorts couldn't hide. 'Can we be seen from here?'

'No,' Ari confirmed, coming down over her with hungry sexual intent etched in every angle of his lean, darkly handsome features and his strong, muscular body. 'I wouldn't risk any other man seeing you naked, *kardoula mou*.'

Some minutes later, they were both naked and intent on each other. Cleo went up in sensual flames as he surged into her and sated the fierce craving he had lit inside her. In the aftermath, she lay limp in his arms, blissfully at peace and not a single shadow in her world, barring the absence of Lucy. She was incredibly happy, happier, she acknowledged, than she had ever known she even could be.

Ari ran a hand down over her spine, pure satisfaction engulfing him. He found the strangest sort of peace when he was with Cleo, rather as if she were the missing puzzle piece that made him whole or, at the very least, he adjusted, somehow *more* than he had been without her. She made him see the world and the people who surrounded him in a different light. She *wasn't* changing him, though.

'Tell me about your ex, Dominic,' Ari murmured, startling Cleo, who had not expected that question. 'You mentioned him in passing but never told me why you broke up.'

With a recollective wince of her generous mouth, Cleo explained about Dominic's girlfriend and child showing up at her door.

'What did he say when you confronted him?' Ari prompted with interest.

'I didn't confront him. I just cut all contact with him, and I was moving on to work at another office, so I didn't run into him again,' Cleo confided, wondering what he was getting at and why in his estimation she would have put herself through such a humiliating confrontation.

'Didn't it occur to you that *she* might have been the liar?' Ari pressed with a frown of bemusement as he stared down at her, his extraordinary eyes holding her full attention. 'Easy enough to borrow a child to make such a visit on a rival and see her off.'

Cleo blinked rapidly. 'I never thought of that... I have to admit that that suspicion never once crossed my mind—'

'You didn't do *anything* to check out her contention that she was living with him?' Ari stressed in wonderment, and he shook his tousled dark head slowly. 'You just condemned him out of hand on her word.

Maybe she was telling the truth, but maybe she wasn't. Whichever, you should have checked it out, not simply assumed that he was guilty as charged. Please be a little more thorough in your approach if I ever get on your wrong side.'

Cleo swallowed hard, taken aback by his very different reading of the situation while seeing her own skewed reasoning process at the time. Her innate distrust of the opposite sex had fuelled her willingness to believe that Dominic had been lying to her and she had never given him the chance to defend himself, which really hadn't been fair, she belatedly acknowledged.

Ari's mobile phone rang as he was pulling on his shorts. It was his London lawyer, a stuffy old-fashioned sort of man, who tended to talk in a confidential murmur and preferred face-to-face meetings to phone consultations, but he was very wily and knowledgeable, which was why Ari retained his services.

'I'll be back in London tomorrow,' Ari confirmed. 'What sort of news?'

Regrettably, the sort of news that Oliver Matthews didn't wish to discuss on the phone. Ari suppressed a groan and mastered his impatience as he agreed to see the lawyer the following afternoon.

'Oliver's being cagey as usual, which means that what he has to tell me is unlikely to be good.' Ari sighed, his lean, dark face shadowing as Cleo asked him what was happening. 'It can only relate to my sisters. *Thee mou*, surely one of them can't be deceased as well—not at their age!'

Cleo closed a hand over the clenched fist that betrayed his tension. 'I'm coming with you to see the lawyer,' she said soothingly. 'Don't be such a pessimist.'

CHAPTER NINE

'Lucy remembers you,' the caseworker commented.

'Thank goodness,' Cleo responded cheerfully. 'I was worried she would forget our faces after two weeks.'

Lucy was smiling widely at her, showing the tooth that had finally emerged during their absence and which had, apparently, given her foster carer some sleepless nights. She lifted her hand to Ari's jaw and giggled.

'He feels just like a hedgehog, doesn't he?' Cleo quipped, because they had come straight from the airport and Ari hadn't yet shaved. A shadow of dark stubble surrounded his wildly sensual mouth.

'But it's sexy,' Ari informed her with all-male confidence.

And Cleo smiled as widely at him as his niece did. She was hoping the lawyer had some encouraging news for him, rather than the kind of depressing information he had received about the brother he had never met and now never would meet. Instead, he was hoping to raise his brother's child, striving to make up for what he viewed as his late father's neglect. Ari had a lot of heart. He mightn't like to show the fact, but his search for his father's second family was the proof of his compassion.

When they entered the senior lawyer's imposing office, Cleo immediately saw that the older man was disconcerted by her arrival with his client.

'Mrs Stefanos may—' he began tightly.

'Cleo and I have no secrets from each other,' Ari imparted with scorching assurance.

Feeling embarrassed by the suspicion that she was unwelcome at the consultation, Cleo took a seat beside Ari, and only moments later she had to battle to keep her face composed because the older man plunged straight into the matter he wished to discuss. Sadly, Cleo would very much have preferred *not* to be present once she realised what the issue encompassed.

'A *paternity* claim?' Ari repeated in a flat tone of emphasis in which no discernible emotional expression could have been read. 'From whom?'

Cleo had gone rigid in her seat, her spine straight, her hands clasped tight on her lap, not a muscle moving in her small face. She had insisted on accompanying Ari to the appointment and pride would not allow her to show how distressed she was by the very idea of another woman giving birth to Ari's first child.

They had discussed having children but had decided it would be a year or two before they did because, at present, Lucy had needs that could well demand a lot of time and attention and she had to be their priority. Furthermore, they needed to adjust to being Lucy's parents before they could consider extending the family. But that Ari could still become a father *without* Cleo had never once struck Cleo as even a possibility! And now she was deep in shock at the discovery that the sex life prior to his marriage, which Ari had dared to say was none of her business, was promising to impact on both their lives in a way neither of them could have foreseen.

She sat in silence while Ari and his lawyer discussed prenatal DNA testing and the necessity of obtaining the birth mother's agreement to the non-invasive procedure. It only required a cheek swab from Ari and a blood test for the expectant mother. Ari sounded so calm and yet she felt sick to the stomach! How could he be so *calm*? Had he suspected that there could be a potential pregnancy risk with some woman? Was he one of those men who could occasionally be careless with precautions? He had not been irresponsible with her. But how was she to know how he had behaved with other women in his bed? That thought made her feel even more nauseous and distanced from him because Cleo was now at a stage where she could not bear even to *think* of Ari having bedded other women, and now she was being faced with the prospect of having to deal with the evidence of that fact for the next twenty years.

Forget twenty years, she thought almost hysterically. Any child would be around and part of her life as well for the whole of their marriage and lives. Children grew up but they did not go away. Ari was very responsible. He would be a supportive father to *any* child that was *his*. Such devastating news was a huge and cruel blow to receive in the very first weeks of their marriage.

Ari glanced at Cleo by his side, registering that she had not said a single word since her arrival. But then what did he expect after such an announcement? A paternity claim, his first. He was in shock, striving to hide it because Cleo was silently freaking out and he did not want to encourage her to feel that way. But he knew that, no matter how careful any male was, there was always the risk that a baby could be conceived. But to have a baby with that *particular* woman? Ari gritted his teeth while acknowledging that thinking negative stuff about his potential baby's mother was a very bad idea. He needed to stay off that fence until he knew more.

'Ready?' Ari was standing, looking down at her with an enquiring gaze because the appointment was over.

Cleo blinked rapidly, struggling to come out of the turmoil of her anguished thoughts and her sense of betrayal, but it was a serious struggle to pull herself together again. Shock, panic and dismay were all pulling at her simultaneously. Her image of Ari with a child who was not hers clawed at her like salt scattered on an open wound…

Yet Lucy was not her child, she reminded herself, sanity attempting to intrude on her intense mental upheaval. But Lucy *was* different, she reasoned. Ari had not been involved with Lucy's mother and Cleo was as much in love with tiny smiley Lucy as Ari was.

If only Ari had not been such an unrepentant man whore, she found herself thinking helplessly, angry resentment assailing her because suddenly her shiny new marriage no longer seemed half as appealing as it had only hours earlier.

Not that that mattered, Cleo conceded unhappily. She loved Ari, flaws and all, and she was growing to love Lucy as well, and no way could she consider walking away from either of them for good. At the same time, however, she felt that she had to have some space to come to terms with what she had just learned. As it was, she felt utterly trapped by undesirable circumstances that couldn't be changed. It was painful too to be forced to accept that, although she would suffer much from the development, she had no rights whatsoever in such a situation.

'Just say what you're thinking,' Ari urged in a raw undertone in the back of the limousine, stunned by Cleo's ongoing lack of either questions or comment about a development that had knocked him for six.

Nor did it help that the prospective mother was Galina Ivanova, who could quite correctly declare that he had refused to have anything more to do with her. Had the woman truly been chasing him in an effort to tell him that she had fallen pregnant? Had he so misread the situation *and* the woman involved that he had inadvertently put himself very much in the wrong? He was appalled by the suspicion and determined to play his every next step by the book.

Cleo swallowed hard and breathed in deep. 'I

didn't sign up for this,' she mumbled bitterly, half under her breath.

'Neither did I, but we're married now. Difficult issues must be faced together and dealt with together,' Ari murmured with a cool distance that she was painfully aware of. 'Are you with me or against me on this?'

The silence stretched because Cleo truly didn't know how to respond to that question in the state she was in at that precise moment.

'In this instance, silence is not golden,' Ari said very drily.

'Who *is* this woman?' Cleo asked tightly, having to force the question past her lips because she knew that she didn't really want the answer. She didn't want any image inside her head, particularly when she was thinking that it could be one of the bitchy wedding guests.

Ari frowned in astonishment. 'You weren't listening to what Oliver told us?'

'I sort of zoned out,' Cleo admitted grudgingly.

'Galina Ivanova, the woman you let into my office on your first day…and I censured you for it,' Ari reminded her doggedly. 'It sounds as though that was, very much, my mistake.'

'That brunette?' Cleo was horrified because the woman had possibly been the most stunning woman Cleo had ever seen, with a mass of tumbling silky black hair, cut-glass cheekbones, huge sultry brown eyes and a slender figure straight out of a fashion magazine adorned with legs as long as rail tracks.

'Yes,' Ari confirmed. 'If her claim is true, I will have to make amends for having asked her to leave my office. I cannot risk being on poor terms with her now.'

'No...of course not,' Cleo muttered sickly, sick to the stomach at the prospect of his having an ongoing relationship with the woman and merely reaching a new high of misery at his explanation.

'It was only one night—' Ari gritted with startling abruptness.

Cleo jerked up a hand to silence any such recollections and directed a blazing glance of reproach at him. 'No, no details, *please*!' she slung back at him in condemnation.

'You are not handling this in an adult way,' Ari rebuked her.

'I wonder how adult you would feel were I to tell you that I was pregnant by another man a few weeks after we had married. That is the *nearest* approximation I can make to your current position,' Cleo framed bitterly.

'In no way would that be the same, but I would accept it because you are my wife. Such things happen, Cleo, whether we want them to or not. Sometimes, nature or fate is in control, not us. Anyone who has sex must recognise such contingencies,' he bit out in a savage undertone.

Contingencies—the same word the lawyer had used at one point, Cleo dimly recalled, nicely sidestepping all more personal and intimate references to the child that was to be born. She recognised that Ari was now furious with her, as though she were the one who had brought this nightmare down on them, and that infuriated her. But it also scared her because she knew she loved him, and she didn't want this child to fatally damage their relationship. He expected her to stand by him and she *would* stand by him because she loved him…but that didn't mean she had to *like* it.

Still in a state of passionately rejecting their plight, Cleo resolved to go home for a visit. A trip to Scotland made sense, she reasoned. Her mother would talk sense to her and calm her down, drag her out of the turbulent feelings and urges that she could not afford to direct at Ari.

She needed time away from him to deal with the situation and come to terms with their altered future. *Stand up and grow up*, she told herself irritably, thoroughly ashamed of the emotions she was drowning in. She was so jealous, so bitter at the concept of another woman carrying Ari's child, particularly a woman as very beautiful as Galina was. No normal woman, she consoled herself, would want a Galina on the sidelines of their life, particularly not as the mother of an all-important eldest child.

Ari would be in regular contact with Galina from now on. He would be looking after the mother of his child, being supportive…and how could she fault him for that? Wasn't that what a decent man was supposed to do? Step up and accept full responsibility? Do whatever was in his power to support the expectant mother?

Gripped by yet another wave of anguish, Cleo fled upstairs to their bedroom to pack an overnight bag.

She didn't pack anything more than jeans and tops. She wanted to be anonymous.

Ari filled the doorway. 'What the hell are you doing?' he gritted incredulously.

'I'm going to visit Mum…only for a few days,' Cleo responded stiffly. 'I think it would be the best thing for us both to have some space from each other for a *little* while.'

'The first bump on the road that we hit, you abandon ship and run!' Ari slashed back at her furiously.

He was losing his English. He would never have mixed up clichés like that in a normal mood. His beautiful eyes were scorching gold with anger and her tummy flipped and the breath shortened in her throat, making her chest feel tight. 'It's not like that,' she argued vehemently. 'I have to have some time alone, but I'm coming back.'

'Bully for you!' Ari bit out angrily. 'That makes me feel a whole lot better!'

'I'll get the train—'

'No, you won't. You'll fly there,' Ari countered squarely. 'As my wife, you have security needs. When are you planning to return?'

'Just the rest of this week…back Sunday,' Cleo promised, thinking fast because they had a visit scheduled with Lucy only a day later.

Ari dealt her an angry fulminating appraisal. 'I don't agree with this tack. Walking away doesn't deal with this… It's *running* away,' he condemned.

'No, it's not,' Cleo protested, turning away from the disturbing image of him in the doorway, all lean and dark and beautiful and absolutely everything that she loved. Tears prickled her eyes in a stinging lash. She didn't want to go, but she didn't want to stay either and say the wrong things, and she was terribly afraid that, in the resentful frame of mind she was in, she would totally say the *wrong* things to him. And he definitely did not deserve that, she reckoned wretchedly.

Nothing more was said. Cleo went to the airport, climbed on board the jet for the short flight and worked at drying the tears trickling down her face. She felt betrayed...but was that *his* fault? Or the fault of her ingrained habit of distrusting men? She supposed it had begun when her mother first poisoned her view of her father and had settled in hard after her infatuation with Dominic had been destroyed by his seeming lies. But then Ari had come along, and Ari was very honest and just about perfect, she reflected miserably. He hadn't pretended that he had fallen miraculously in love with her. He had asked her to marry him for Lucy's benefit. That was a praiseworthy act for his niece's welfare, but it was also an act and a level of honesty that increasingly cut Cleo to the quick. Loving Ari had made her more sensitive.

How did one trust a man with a woman like Galina when he didn't love his wife? Galina was ten times more beautiful and sexier than Cleo would ever be, and once she had Ari's child, she would have magnetic appeal for him. Cleo knew that. Ari set a deep value on blood ties and he would be very keen to spend time with his child. Only witness what he was willing to do for his half-brother's daughter! What might he wish to do for his *own* child with Galina? Wasn't there a very strong chance that what had initially attracted him to Galina would revive once he saw her with his child? And wouldn't it make sense that he could want to eventually marry Galina for the sake of his own flesh and blood?

And where would Cleo be then? His *practical* choice? Not the woman he loved, who could at least have felt secure in that love at such a testing time. Cleo didn't have that stability, that sense of safety, to ground her in their relationship. As a result, that first bump in the road that he had mentioned had been a complete car crash for her...

'Cleo...nothing's perfect.' Lisa Brown sighed at the kitchen island of the house attached to the pub that she and Cleo's stepfather ran. 'Not life, not people, not marriage. You can't blame Ari because he burst your fantasy bubble... He's right. These things do happen, whether we want them to or not. I thought you loved him—'

'I do!' Cleo proclaimed uncomfortably.

'Then why are you here with me?' the older woman prompted gently. 'He must be upset about this as well and you have to sort this out with him. Can you live with this child being a part of your life as well? It's that basic.'

'Maybe the DNA test will reveal that it isn't his kid,' Cleo opined, looking hopeful.

'Do you have cause to suspect that it may not be his?'

'No. I don't know anything about the woman, don't

want to either!' Cleo confided in a distressed rush of honesty.

'In this scenario, you can't afford to take that attitude.' Lisa sighed. 'If you can't learn to cope with this, it could mean the end of your marriage—'

In receipt of that warning, Cleo lost colour. 'I don't want that.'

'Learn to cope with it, then,' her mother advised ruefully, sliding off her bar stool. 'Sorry, love, I have to get back to work.'

'That's fine. Just forget I'm here,' Cleo urged guiltily.

It was Sunday and she was due to fly home that evening. She had had several days and several sleepless nights to think stuff through. The blinding resentment, anger and turmoil *had* receded somewhat, leaving her facing the reality that she had to handle the situation as it was, not as she wished it could be. Pessimism had already convinced her that, of course, the baby would prove to be a Stefanos baby.

The doorbell buzzed and she slid off her stool, glimpsing her reflection in the hall mirror as she passed and grimacing because she hadn't bothered to put on any make-up and she was wearing 'comfort' clothes from her teenage years that consisted of a pair of lounge pants, a stretched, already oversized pullover and slippers.

To say that she was shattered to open the door and find Ari standing there would have been an understatement. One glimpse of his familiar tall, lean and powerful figure and a complex tumble of emotions washed over her. Joy, consternation and annoyance that he had taken her by surprise and found her clad in her rattiest, oldest clothes.

'Ari...' she whispered shakily once she had found her voice again.

'We have some serious talking to do,' Ari intoned coolly, his gaze raking over every inch of her, noting the tender valley of smooth skin visible at the neck of her jersey, the curve of her hip as she turned towards him, blue eyes widening, golden curls tangled.

And both that announcement in that tone and the forbidding expression on his lean, darkly handsome features made Cleo's heart sink to her very toes.

CHAPTER TEN

'WE'LL TAKE THIS discussion to the hotel I'm staying in locally,' Ari decreed.

'I'm not going anywhere dressed like this.' Cleo sighed. 'Give me twenty minutes to change.'

His beautifully moulded mouth firmed. 'I'll wait in the car.'

Cleo fled back to the bedroom she had been using and stripped at the speed of a maniac before rushing into the shower. The whole time her brain was crackling with frantic frightened thoughts. Perhaps Ari had already decided that a divorce was the best way forward. Would he risk such a move in the midst of their application to foster Lucy? Or was it possible that the news of the baby that had been conceived with Galina could now take precedence over his niece? She supposed anything could be possible because she had run away rather than talk about that baby with him. Shame filled her as she frantically dried her hair and dabbed on some make-up to conceal her reddened eyelids. She *had* run home like a little girl rather than stand her ground and act like a grown woman, she conceded in mortification.

Clad in jeans, a stylish red top and sneakers, Cleo walked out to the car with her heart pounding very fast in her chest.

'I wasn't expecting you,' she admitted, filling the silence when she joined him.

Ari said nothing. A fierce rage had settled inside him as the days of her absence crept past on leaden feet. He couldn't initially credit that Cleo had run home to her mother until common sense kicked in and he contrived to imagine how he might have reacted to such a situation at her age. His bride was still very young, and if she did not have his life experience and greater maturity, that rested on *his* shoulders, because he had married her, hadn't he? In any case, none of that mattered when he was so hopelessly relieved to be back with Cleo again. At that moment nothing else really seemed to matter.

Predictably, Ari was staying at a madly grand country-house hotel with turrets, luxury suites and awesome service. Too twitchy to stand still or sit down, Cleo crossed the vast reception room with its ornate antique furniture and elaborate curtains and stood at one of the windows, which overlooked an immaculately kept lawn and trees. Ari offered her a drink and she asked for water.

As he slotted the glass between her fingers, she glanced up at him mutinously. 'I *was* planning to catch that flight tonight and come back to London,' she told him squarely.

'I wasn't prepared to wait that long,' Ari parried without skipping a beat.

The gleam of his dark golden eyes below curling black lashes ensnared her and the heat rose in her pale cheeks. 'I shouldn't have left in the first place,' she muttered reluctantly. 'But I… I just didn't know how to handle it—'

Ari lifted a straight ebony brow in challenge. 'And you think that *I* did?'

Cleo reddened even more, her discomfiture pronounced.

'I was as shocked by the information as you were,' he admitted quietly. 'But it also bothers me to see a pattern in your behaviour…'

Her brow indented as she shifted from one foot to the other. 'What pattern?'

'It worries me that we're in conflict again over a past that I cannot change,' Ari confessed levelly. 'We had an argument on our wedding day about my exes—'

'Not about their existence,' Cleo disagreed, lifting her head high. 'About you inviting them all to our wedding! As for this baby—'

'I had a normal sex life in which I took every possible precaution to ensure that there were no accidental conceptions,' Ari slotted in, his lean, darkly handsome face grave. 'No male can do more than that. Yet I feel that you are *blaming* me—'

'That's…that's just human nature in a tight and unpleasant corner,' Cleo protested uncomfortably, taking his point but not admitting the fact. 'And our wedding did make it rather obvious that your...er...past is rather extensive in comparison to mine.'

'Unfortunately for me, I didn't appreciate that I would end up married to a woman who would find my past so distasteful,' Ari breathed harshly.

'That's not fair. I'm not judging you. In fact, I would never have thought about your past sex life at all had it not been for all those women at our wedding,' Cleo pointed out truthfully, standing her ground. 'You're the one who put a spotlight on your past for my benefit.'

Ari felt rather less certain of his position than he had once been. A married friend had remarked after the wedding on *his* wife's comments concerning that inconsiderate guest list. He had shot himself in the foot, Ari recognised, owning his mistake but typically reluctant to acknowledge it.

'I'm not remotely concerned about your past history with other women unless it impinges on our marriage,' Cleo declared steadily, meeting his gorgeous eyes calmly. 'And sadly, this baby does, and it threw me for a loop, I'm afraid. You need to try and view this development from my point of view—'

'I have—'

'No, you haven't,' Cleo responded, with bitter certainty in that accusation. 'This isn't a *real* marriage, not the way others are. You married me for Lucy's sake. I don't have the security of knowing that you love me, so I felt more threatened than many women would by the idea of a former lover having your child and the constant contact between you that will obviously follow on from that continuing relationship.'

'I'm possibly not the most emotionally intelligent guy you will ever meet,' Ari breathed tautly. 'Well, we already know that from the wedding guest list...but I'm not totally stupid. When I wake up in the morning and you're not there and I miss you. Well, that's never happened to me before with a woman—'

'You missed me?' Cleo slotted in brightly.

'And I'm not used either to thinking about a woman all day, because that *seriously* interferes with my concentration, but I can't get you out of my head,' Ari complained. 'I look at you, and as far as I'm concerned, you're the most beautiful and sexy woman in the world, which means that I truly don't see anyone but you now...'

By that stage, Cleo was simply staring back at him in shock at that unexpected rambling speech.

Ari sent her a wolfish smile of achievement. 'I believe it's called love. So, yes, you do have the security of knowing that I love you and that, as far as I'm concerned, this is a *very* real marriage.'

Not quite able to jump that fast from her assumptions to what appeared to be her new reality, Cleo trembled and frowned. 'Do you mean that?'

'Hey, I'm the guy who couldn't wait until tonight to see you,' Ari pointed out without hesitation. 'And no, I don't know when exactly I fell in love with you or how it happened in the first place. I only know that we forged bonds at the very beginning that first night, and the minute I had you in my bed, I wanted you back there again in the worst way. And absolutely nobody else would do as a substitute.'

'Is that so?' Cleo queried as she finally shook free of her paralysis with the craziest, fiercest happiness circulating through her in an enervating surge. Nothing at all mattered at that moment but that he loved her. Everything else, she thought warmly, would just fall naturally into place. She was no longer second-best, no longer the practical choice of wife. In fact, she found herself suspecting that Ari would have married her anyway once he understood how he felt about her.

'That is so,' Ari confirmed, resting both hands on her slight shoulders, flexing possessive fingers over her fine bones, dark golden eyes aglow with more emotion than she had ever hoped to see there.

'Well, you were way behind me,' Cleo informed him teasingly. 'The first time I laid eyes on you, I wanted you. That's how I ended up in bed with you that first time. You were my fantasy.'

'I like being your fantasy, *kardia mou*. But I did notice you from the start. I thought it was because your clothes were too colourful for me,' he admitted. 'Only I think it was because you were so different from my usual type...and now I only have one type and it's you.'

'I like that,' Cleo confided sunnily. 'You do realise that I fell for you on our honeymoon?'

'I was ahead of you there,' Ari asserted with pride. 'I knew when you walked down the aisle towards me in the church. You looked magical and I was so excited that you were mine.'

Cleo frowned. 'But you never said that you loved me!' she censured.

'I'd made all those speeches about Lucy, and changing tack that fast made me feel a little lame,' he explained. 'But the way I was behaving, I think you should have guessed how I felt about you. I was jealous of every man that looked at you, possessive beyond reason, and I couldn't get enough of you in bed or out of it. If that's not love, what is?'

Cleo rested tender fingers against his hard jawline. 'I do love you very much and I'm so sorry I ran away. I always knew I was coming back, though—I should get points for that, shouldn't I?'

'I was worried you wouldn't come back,' Ari confessed in a driven undertone as he closed both strong arms round her and literally lifted her into close contact with his lean, powerful body. 'Do you think I didn't appreciate that that news from Galina Ivanova was a body blow?'

'I don't have much to say about that yet,' Cleo admitted honestly. 'I'll get used to the idea, though. Time will help—'

Ari froze and looked down at her with a sudden grimace. 'It's *not* my baby she's carrying,' he told her bluntly.

'*Not* your baby?' Cleo whispered in shock.

'No. The DNA test proved that the child isn't mine. I think I was the richest bet Galina had and she just hoped that I would turn out to be the father, but obviously I wasn't her only lover at the time—'

'You should've told me it wasn't your child *first*!' Cleo exclaimed in rampant disbelief at that oversight.

'No. I wanted to wait. I needed to know that you

were willing to accept me as I am, flaws and all...because it *could've* been my kid. I'm very grateful that it's not. It's not how I would want to have my first child, but if it had been mine, I would have stood by her, and that would have been a major challenge because I don't like her—'

Her brow furrowed. 'You don't like her?'

'Not when she was behaving like a stalker. She was a little weird with me,' he confided, his mouth tightening. 'I was with her once and never again. Then she began constantly phoning, turning up places I went, showing up at the office uninvited. It was all too much.'

'But you're safe now from those kinds of mistakes,' Cleo said with a wicked grin. 'I won't let you out of my sight very often. You are truly off the market now, Mr Stefanos.'

'Is that supposed to be a threat?' Ari husked, running his hands up below her top and levering it off her with the slick skill that only he could contrive. Her bra followed. He lifted his hands to cup her ripe curves and backed her towards the bedroom next door. 'Right now, seeing more of you feels more like a very exciting promise.'

With thrilling impatience, he bent down and swept her up into his arms to carry her into the bedroom and lay her down on the wide, comfortable bed. Clothes were tossed aside and silence fell, broken only by little moans and mutters as they made love, satisfying the gnawing sense of insecurity that had attacked them both when they were apart. In the aftermath of all that excitement, Cleo lay in the circle of Ari's arms, feeling gloriously content and safe at last.

'I wanted my baby to be your first child. I suppose that was sort of childish and mean,' she conceded ruefully.

'I don't think so. I wanted the same thing, but I also knew that, even if you stood by me, it would damage our relationship. How could a child with another woman do anything else when we were so newly married?' Ari murmured grimly, his arms tightening their hold on her slight body. 'We'll go and pack your clothes and catch up with your mother. Since I assume you told her about the baby that isn't mine, we'll have to explain that it was simply a con. And when we get back to London tomorrow morning, I have a surprise for you...'

'What sort of a surprise?' Cleo prompted, twisting her head to look at him, loving those gorgeous tawny eyes of his.

'Something unexpected. It's up to you to decide whether it's a positive or negative development,' he framed mysteriously.

'I don't like mysteries.'

'It won't be a mystery for long.' Ari ran a soothing hand down over her spine and grabbed her to kiss her again, and all thought of the surprise vanished under the sensual onslaught of his mouth on hers.

On the flight back to London the next day, he explained that her father had seen a picture of their wedding in a newspaper and had contacted him to ask if they could meet.

'I told him that you were away and I suggested we meet for coffee,' Ari explained. 'You may think that was interfering of me, but I wanted to *vet* him for you lest he was only getting in touch because you had married a rich man.'

In shock, Cleo gazed back at him. 'My father?' she gasped. 'Why would he get in touch?'

'Because he would like the chance to get to know you. He parted from the woman he was originally with several years ago and tried to track you down then. He was unable to find you because of course your mother has moved on, married and changed her name. He is in regular contact with the son and daughter he has and he has now told them about you. He seems pleasant enough and genuine in his interest in you and a little nervous as to his reception with you,' Ari told her levelly. 'But it's up to you what you choose to do.'

'Do we look alike?' Cleo demanded curiously.

'You're almost a doppelganger for your mother,' he reminded her with amusement. 'But you do definitely have your father's big wide smile. Would it bother your mother if you had contact with him?'

'No. He's old history, as far as she's concerned.'

Cleo smiled sunnily and looked at Ari. 'I will see him. Our contact may not amount to anything more than a couple of meetings, but I would like the chance to get to know him. It's a chance I never thought I'd have.'

'As long as it doesn't cause you distress,' Ari commented, his protectiveness touching her heart. 'You've got by without him all these years and I don't want you upset.'

'I've got you now...and hopefully Lucy some day soon,' Cleo pointed out gently. 'My world is a secure one. I'm very curious about my half-brother and sister as well. I would like the opportunity to meet them if...if I like him and, of course, if they want to meet me. Now that we're all grown up, it doesn't seem as controversial as it seemed when I was a teenager.'

'It struck me the very first time we met that we had a lot in common.' Ari curved her into his arms as the limo wafted them through the traffic on their homeward journey. 'And it really is a challenge to keep my hands off you...'

'*So* romantic, Ari,' she whispered cheekily.

'I've organised a special dinner for your homecoming,' he announced with a smile of pure one-upmanship. 'And a gift.'

'And you're such a trier,' Cleo pronounced with a helpless giggle and sheer joy bubbling up through her. 'Always determined to take top billing...'

EPILOGUE

Two years after that conversation took place, Cleo was on the island of Spinos in Greece. It was summer and a bunch of young children were playing a noisy game on the grassy space in front of the terrace where Cleo was enjoying tea with her mother.

'I love staying at the resort. Tell Ari thanks,' Lisa said happily. 'You know he won't let me thank him for all the free luxury holidays we get here.'

'We enjoy the company,' Cleo responded lightly, and it was true. Her stepfamily were lively company for her own little family and she got to enjoy spending time with her mother at the same time.

Lisa snorted with laughter. 'Like you couldn't find company with this place and Ari behind you! You're living the dream, my love. You and those babies of yours are going to have a wonderful life.'

'I certainly hope so.' Cleo contemplated the huge mound of her pregnant tummy, being at that stage of pregnancy where she could no longer see her feet and when she felt as though she had been pregnant for ever, rather than a mere seven months.

She was carrying twins: two little boys she couldn't wait to meet. And considering the fuss she had made about the unplanned conception Ari's ex had tried to lay at his door, she did not have a leg to stand on when it came to her own. They had decided to wait for two years before starting a family, and then, over a year into their marriage, they had had a romp late one hot night in the swimming pool when Cleo had been ready to expire from the heat and... *Boom*. Cleo had conceived and twins were on their way, with Ari claiming that he was delighted, regardless of that conception having been an accident.

Ari might continue to insist that he hadn't changed, but he had definitely mellowed. His wardrobe was no longer colour-coded, and he had learned to live with the clutter of a toddler's life, not to mention a wife who was infinitely less organised and tidy than he was, Cleo reflected fondly.

And having observed her husband with Lucy, who was almost three years old now, for they had picked her birthday as the date she had been found and rescued, Cleo was pretty sure Ari *was* delighted about the little boys soon to join their family. He was brilliant with Lucy, who had recovered from her poor start in life slowly, reaching the milestones other children took for granted at her own pace. Luckily for her, Lucy had no lingering medical issues. Now she was a happy, healthy toddler with a shock of black hair and she still had Ari's eyes, except hers were full of mischief most of the time. Those dancing dark eyes full of love and trust had walked so easily into Cleo's and Ari's hearts. Lucy had finally become officially their adoptive daughter only a couple of months earlier, but they had become her foster parents within a few months of that first meeting.

Now watching Lucy walk up from the beach with her little fingers possessively clinging to the leg of Ari's denim shorts, Cleo smiled because father and daughter, uncle and niece, however you wanted to look at them, were very close. And Lucy couldn't wait for the babies to come, the little brothers she would undoubtedly fuss over and boss around.

'It's idyllic here,' her mother sighed happily.

She watched Ari come to a halt to answer his mobile phone. Lucy abandoned him and ran up to the house, ducking the other children, who were all older than her, and rushing up the steps to Cleo to climb straight onto her lap. Unfortunately, it was a lap no longer in existence since pregnancy had altered Cleo's shape, and she sat up to accommodate the little girl more comfortably.

'Sleepy,' Lucy grumbled, slotting her thumb into her mouth.

'I'll take you upstairs for a nap,' Cleo promised.

'Love you, Mum-mum,' Lucy sighed.

Cleo's mother stood up and lifted the little girl. 'I'll take her up. You're supposed to be staying off your feet in the afternoon,' she reminded her daughter as Lucy snuggled her head into her grandmother's shoulder. 'And I'll be a while. I like reading her a story.'

'I only do that at night.'

'Well, when Granny's here, it's naps as well,' Lisa said cheerfully.

'Thanks, Mum,' Cleo murmured, thinking about how grateful she had been for her mother's laid-back attitude towards her getting to know her long-lost father.

Gregory Stevens was not the selfish, uncaring man Cleo had once imagined he would be. She saw her father when she was in London and she liked him, although she doubted that they would ever develop a truly close relationship. She had also met her half-brother, Peter, who was a medical student and very down to earth. Her half-sister, Gwen, hadn't yet agreed to meet up with Cleo and clearly wasn't sure she wanted the connection, and that was fine with Cleo. She had no desire to upset anybody and thought it was sad that Gwen's loyalty to her mother should have made meeting Cleo contentious. But Cleo was so happy in her own life that she had no need to put pressure on anyone.

Ari, having been cornered to settle a dispute in the kids' ball game, mounted the steps into the shade. He scrutinised Cleo, lying there all golden and ripe and so damned sexy it made him smile, because he knew that if he told her she looked like some sensual fertility goddess in her current condition, she would threaten to slap him. Unlike her husband, Cleo was way *past* finding pregnancy sexy.

He sat down in the seat his mother-in-law had vacated. 'Oliver's got information on the whereabouts of Lucas's twin sister,' he told her in an excited surge, his gorgeous dark eyes golden and bright with satisfaction, for he had been chasing dead ends in his search for his siblings for the whole of their marriage.

Cleo sat up. 'No bad news?' she checked.

'Well, Oliver said it's a mix. She's healthy, not an addict or anything like that. Clever girl, has a business degree, but, as Oliver put it and, no, I don't know what he means by it, she's had a lot of bad luck.'

'Oh, dear... You'll have to be careful about how you deal with her,' Cleo warned him. 'No bull-in-the-china-shop approach. You've seen how differently my siblings have reacted, so you have to accept that you may not be a welcome arrival in her life.'

Ari raised a cynical ebony brow and said drily, 'Beware Greeks offering you a small fortune?'

'Ari! There's much more to it than the bottom line of an inheritance!' Cleo framed worriedly, fearful that he would be tactless and would destroy the potential relationship before he even got the opportunity to have one.

Ari just laughed, all sun-bronzed and gorgeous and smiling, his spectacular eyes glittering. 'I was only teasing you. I'll find out what Oliver has to tell me about her "bad luck".' His handsome mouth took on a sardonic twist at that phrase. 'And I will act accordingly, but you have no idea how relieved I am just to find her and know she's alive and healthy.'

'I do understand,' Cleo protested, linking her fingers with his to tug him down to her. 'Now, just one kiss...'

'Just one kiss could lead to more,' Ari warned her

thickly, leaning down, closing his beautifully moulded mouth to hers and saying huskily, 'Do you have any idea how much I love you?'

'Possibly just as much as I love you,' Cleo whispered as she gave herself up to that passionate kiss.

* * * * *

THE SICILIAN'S STOLEN SON

CHAPTER ONE

Luciano Vitale's London lawyer, Charles Bennett, greeted him the moment he stepped off his private jet. The Sicilian billionaire and the professional exchanged polite small talk. Luciano stalked like a lion that had already picked up the scent of prey in the air, impatience and innate aggression girding every step.

He had tracked her down...*at last*. The thieving child stealer, Jemima Barber. There were no adequate words to convey his loathing for the woman who had stolen his son and then tried to sell the baby back to him like a product. It galled him even more that he would not be able to bring the full force of the law down on Jemima. Not only did he not want his private life laid open to the world's media again, but he was also all too aware of the likely long-term repercussions of such a vengeful act. Hadn't he suffered enough at the hands of the press while his wife was alive? These days Luciano very much preferred the shadows to the full glare of daylight and the endless libellous headlines that had followed his every move throughout his marriage.

Even so, Luciano still walked tall and every female head in his vicinity turned to appreciate his passing. He stood six feet four inches tall, with the build of a natural athlete, not to mention the stunning good looks he had been born with. Not a single flaw marred his golden skin, straight nose or the high cheekbones and hollows that combined to lend him the haunting beauty of a fallen angel. He cared not at all for his beautiful face, though, indeed had learned to see it as a flaw that attracted unwelcome attention.

As it was, it was intolerable to him that in spite of taking every precaution he had almost lost a *second* child. Instantly he reprimanded himself for making that assumption. He could not know for certain that the boy was his until the DNA testing had been done. It was perfectly possible that the surrogate mother he had chosen for the role had slept with other men at the time of the artificial insemination. She had broken every other clause of the agreement they had signed, so why not that one as well?

But, if the baby was his as he hoped, would it take after its lying, cheating mother? Was there such a thing as bad genes? He refused to accept that. His own life stood testament to that belief because he was the last in a long ruthless line of men, famed for their contempt for the law and their cruelty. There could be no taint in an innocent child, merely inclinations that could be encouraged or discouraged. He reminded himself that on paper his son's mother had appeared eminently respectable. The only child of elderly, financially indebted parents, she had presented herself as a trained infant teacher with a love of growing vegetables and cookery. Unfortunately her true interests, which he had only discovered after she had run from the hospital with the child, had proved to be a good deal less respectable. She was a sociopathic promiscuous thrill-seeker who overspent, gambled and stole without conscience when she ran out of money.

Time and time again he had blamed himself for his decision not to physically meet with the mother of his child, not to personalise in any way what was essentially a business arrangement. Would he have recognised her true nature if he had? He had not expected her to want to see him either, when he came to collect the child from the hospital after the birth, but in the event he had arrived there to learn that she had already vanished, leaving behind only a note that spelt out her financial demands. By then she had found out how rich he was and only greed had motivated her.

'I must ask,' Charles murmured in the tense silence within the limousine. 'Do you intend to tip off the police about the lady's whereabouts?'

Luciano tensed, his wide sensual mouth compressing. 'No, I do not.'

'May I ask...' Choosing tact over frank frustration, Charles left the question hanging, wishing that his wealthiest client would be a little more forthcoming. But Luciano Vitale, the only child of Sicily's once most petrifying Mafia don, had always been a male of forbidding reserve. A billionaire at the age of thirty, he was a hugely successful businessman and, to the best of Charles's knowledge, resolutely legitimate in all his dealings. And yet his very name still struck fear into those who surrounded him and they paled and trembled in the face of his displeasure. His loathing for the paparazzi, and the ever lingering danger of his criminal ancestry making him the target of a hit, ensured that he was encircled by bodyguards, who kept the rest of the world at bay. In so many ways, Luciano Vitale remained a complete mystery. Charles would have given much to know why a man with so many more appealing options had chosen to pick a surrogate mother to bring a child into the world.

'I will not be responsible for sending the apparent mother of my son to prison,' Luciano said without any expression at all. 'There is no doubt in my mind that Jemima deserves to go to prison but I do not wish to be the instrument that puts her there.'

'Quite understandable,' Charles chimed in, although it was a polite lie because he did not understand at all. 'However, the police are already looking for her and notifying them of her location could be done most discreetly.'

'And then what?' Luciano prompted. 'The elderly grandparents receive custody of my son? And the authorities are forced to enter the picture to consider his welfare? You have already warned me that surrogacy arrangements receive a divergent and uncertain reception within the UK court system. I will not take any risk that could entail losing all rights to my son.'

'But the Barber woman has already made it clear that she will only surrender the boy for a substantial sum of money...and you *must* not, you *cannot* offer her cash because that would put *you* on the wrong side of British law.'

'I will find some acceptable and legal way to bring this matter to a satisfactory conclusion,' Luciano breathed softly, lean brown fingers flexing impatiently on his thighs. 'Without damaging publicity or a court case or sending her to prison.'

Warily encountering his client's cold dark eyes, Charles suppressed a shiver and tried not to think about how Luciano's forebears had preferred to clear their paths of human obstacles: with cold-blooded murder and mayhem. He told himself off for that imaginative flight of fancy but he could not forget that chilling look in Luciano's gaze or his notorious ruthlessness in business. He might not kill his competitors but he had never been a man to cross and was known to exact harsh retribution from those who offended him. He doubted very much that Jemima Barber had the slightest comprehension of the very dangerous consequences she had invited when she had reneged on her legal agreement with Luciano Vitale.

Sì, Luciano brooded, he would achieve his goal because he *always* got what he wanted and anything less was unthinkable, particularly when it came to his son's well-being. If the little boy proved to be his, he would take him whatever the cost because he could not possibly leave an innocent child in the care of such a mother.

Jemima tidied the flowers on her sister's grave. Her crystalline blue eyes were stinging like mad, her heart squeezing tight with misery inside her.

She had loved Julie and hated the reality that she had never got the chance to get closer to her natural sibling and help her. Born to an unknown father and a drug-addicted mother, the twin girls had ended up in separate adoptive homes. Julie had briefly been deprived of oxygen at birth and had required major surgery soon afterwards. Her sister had not been available for adoption until her treatment was complete a full two years later. Jemima, however, had been much more fortunate in every way, she thought guiltily. Her middle-aged adoptive parents had adored her on sight, adopted her at birth and given her a wonderfully happy and secure childhood. Julie had been adopted by a much wealthier couple but her developmental delays and problems had disappointed and embarrassed her parents. Ultimately the adoption had broken down when her sister was a wayward teenager and Julie had ended up back in care, rejected by the parents she'd loved. It was no surprise to Jemima that from that point everything in her twin's life had gone even more badly wrong.

The twins had not met again until they were adults and Julie had tracked Jemima down. Right from the outset Jemima and her parents had been captivated by her lively charming twin. Of course that had gone wrong as well for *all* of them, Jemima acknowledged reluctantly. But perhaps it had gone worst of all for little Nicky, who would now never know his birth mother. Her misty eyes rested on the eight-month-old baby in the buggy on the path and predictably brightened because Nicky was the sun, the moon and the stars in Jemima's world. He studied her with his big liquid dark eyes and smiled from below the mop of his black curly hair. He was the most utterly adorable baby and he owned his auntie's heart and soul and had done so since the moment she'd first met him when he was only a week old.

'I saw you from the street. Why are you here again?' a worried female voice pressed. 'I don't understand why you're torturing yourself this way, Jem. She's gone and I say good riddance!'

'Please don't say that,' Jemima urged her best friend, Ellie, whom she had first met in nursery school. She turned to face the taller, thinner redhead with determination.

'But it's the truth and you have to face it. Julie almost destroyed your family,' Ellie said bluntly. 'I know it hurts you to hear me say it but your twin was rotten to the core.'

Jemima compressed her lips, determined not to get into another argument with her outspoken friend. After all, when times had been tough during the Julie debacle Ellie had regularly offered Jemima and her parents a sympathetic shoulder as well as advice and support. Ellie had proved her loyalty and the depth of her friendship many times over. In any case, it would be pointless to argue now that Jemima's twin was dead. Even so, the pain of that loss still made such judgements wounding. Only a few months had passed since Julie had carelessly stepped out in front of a car and died instantly. Julie's adoptive family had refused even to attend the funeral and the cost had been borne by Jemima's parents, although they could ill afford the expense.

'If we'd had more time together, things would have turned out very differently,' Jemima declared with a bitterness that she struggled to hide.

'She ripped off your parents, stole your identity and your boyfriend and landed you with a baby,' Ellie reminded her drily. 'What could she have done as an encore? Murdered you all in your beds?'

'Julie never showed any tendency towards violence,' Jemima argued back through gritted teeth. 'Let's not talk about this any more.'

'Let's not,' Ellie agreed wryly. 'It would make more sense to discuss what you're planning to do with Nicky now. You've got quite enough on your plate with a full-time job and helping out your parents.'

'But I'm more than happy to look after Nicky as well. I love him. He *is* my only living relative,' Jemima pointed out with quiet fortitude as the two women walked out of the graveyard and down the road. 'Obviously I'm not planning to give him up. We'll manage somehow.'

'But what about his father? Surely you have to consider his rights?' Ellie countered impatiently and, seeing her companion stiffen and pale, she groaned. 'My shift starts in an hour—I have to go. I'll see you tomorrow.'

Parting from her friend, who lived in an apartment on the same street, Jemima walked away at the slow pace of someone exhausted—Nicky still only slept a few hours at a time. She had expended a great deal of thought on the worrying topic of Nicky's paternal ancestry. Other than the fact that Nicky's father was supposedly a very wealthy man, she knew nothing about him or, more importantly, why he had chosen to father a child through a surrogacy agreement. Was he a gay man in a relationship? Or were he or his partner unable to have a child? Julie had not cared about such details but Jemima cared about them very much indeed.

There was no way she could ignore the reality that Nicky had a living father somewhere in the world, a parent who had paid for and planned his very conception. But she didn't know his identity because Julie had flatly refused to divulge it and there was therefore nothing that anyone could expect Jemima to do about tracing the man, she reflected with guilty relief. Her sole concern was, and always had been, Nicky's well-being. She wasn't prepared to hand the little boy over to anyone without first seeing the proof that that person would love and nurture her nephew. That was her true role now, she conceded unhappily: to step into the untenable situation Julie had created and try to ensure that Julie's son was not damaged by his mother's rash choices.

Jemima still marvelled that her twin had not even recognised that she was literally agreeing to bring a child into the world for a price. Incredibly at the time she had signed up, Julie had only viewed the surrogacy agreement as a job that paid living expenses at a time when she was short of cash and needed somewhere to live. She had admitted to loathing what pregnancy did to her body and she had not changed her mind about handing Nicky over after the birth. No, Julie had simply decided that she had not been well enough rewarded for suffering the tribulations of nine months of pregnancy followed by a birth, particularly once she had learned that Nicky's father was rich.

And what were the chances that the man would prove to be a caring, compassionate father? The sort of man who would love and cherish Nicky to the very best of his ability? Jemima believed that there was little chance of that being the case when the man concerned had not even wanted to *meet* the mother of his future child. From what little she had read most surrogacy agreements encouraged some kind of contact between the various parties involved, at least initially. After all, Nicky was half Julie's flesh and blood as well. He had not been conceived from a donated egg but from her sister's body, which meant he was very much Jemima's nephew and a part of Jemima's small family, a little connected person whom Jemima felt it was her duty to love and protect.

Jemima let herself into the small retirement bungalow that was her parents' current home. It had two bedrooms and a small garden and she was very grateful that there was enough space for her and Nicky to stay there. Her father was a retired clergyman and her mother had only ever been a clergyman's wife. Sadly, the careful savings her parents had made over the years had gone into Julie's pocket when she had pretended that she'd wanted to rent a local shop and start up her own business. Or maybe that hadn't been a pretence, Jemima conceded, striving not to be judgemental.

Quite possibly, Julie had genuinely intended to set up a business when she'd first floated the idea to Jemima's parents but Julie had been tremendously impulsive and her plans had often leapt enthusiastically from one money-making scheme to the next within days. Her sister might have seemed to have good intentions and might have uttered very convincing sentiments but she *had* told lies. There was no denying that, Jemima reflected unhappily.

Regardless, the Barbers' financial safety net was now gone and her parents' lifelong dream of buying their own home was no longer possible. In fact the only reason her parents still had a roof over their heads was Jemima's decision to come back home to live and help to pay the rent and the household expenses, which were exceeding her father's small pension. Faced with bills they couldn't afford to pay, the older couple had begun to fret and their health had suffered.

With quiet efficiency, Jemima changed Nicky and settled him down for a morning nap. Screening a yawn of her own, she decided to lie down too, having learned that napping when Nicky did was the only sure way to get her own rest. She peeled off her tunic top and winced when she caught an accidental glimpse of her liberally curved bottom in the wardrobe mirror.

'Your backside's far too big for leggings! Always wear a long top to cover your behind,' Julie had urged her.

But then Julie had been thin as a willow wand and tormented by bulimia, Jemima reminded herself ruefully. Her twin had had serious issues with food and self-image. On that unhappy reflection, Jemima fell straight to sleep, still clad in her leggings and vest top.

When the shrilling doorbell wakened her, Jemima scrambled up in surprise because most visitors were family friends and aware that her mum and dad were currently staying in Devon with a former parishioner.

That was the closest her parents could get to a holiday on their restricted income. She peered into the cot, relieved to see that her nephew was still peacefully asleep, his little face flushed, his rosebud mouth relaxed.

From the hall she could see two male figures through the glass.

'Yes?' she asked enquiringly, opening the door only a fraction.

An older man with greying hair dealt her a serious appraisal. 'May we come in and speak to you, Miss Barber? My card…' A business card was extended through the narrow gap and she glanced down at it.

Charles Bennett, it read. *Bennett & Bennett, Solicitors.*

Instantly fearing yet another problem linked to her twin's premature death, Jemima lost colour and opened the door. Julie had left a lot of debts in her wake and Jemima just didn't know how to deal with them. She shrank from the prospect of telling the police that her sister had stolen her identity to the extent of contracting debts in her name, travelling on her passport and even giving birth in Sicily as Jemima Barber. She was very much afraid that revealing that information would make her current custody of Nicky illegal and she was frightened that the minute she admitted that he was *not* her child he would be taken from her and placed in a foster home with strangers.

'Luciano Vitale…' the older man introduced as his companion stepped forward and Jemima took yet another step back from her visitors, all her senses now on full apprehensive alert.

And when she focused on the taller, younger man by

his side she froze, for he was a man like no other. His movements were fast, smooth and incredibly quiet as if he were a combat soldier slinking through the jungle. He was poetry in motion and pure fantasy in the flesh. Indeed he was very probably the most breathtakingly beautiful man Jemima had ever seen in her life. The shock of his sudden magnetic appearance was hard to withstand. Her chest tightened as she struggled to catch her breath and not stare as the compellingly handsome lineaments of his lean bronzed features urged her to do. It made her feel frighteningly schoolgirlish and she hurriedly turned her head away to invite them into the living room.

Luciano couldn't take his eyes off Jemima Barber because she was so very different from what he had expected. His very first sight of her had been her passport photo application in which she had looked blonde, blue-eyed and a little plump, indeed so ordinary he had rolled his eyes at the idea that such a commonplace woman could give him a child. His second view of her two months earlier on security-camera footage from a London hotel had been far more indicative of her true nature. Blonde hair cut short and choppy, she had sported a very low-necked top, a tiny silver skirt and sky-high hooker heels that had showed off her slim figure and the rounded curve of her breast implants. She had been acting like the slut she was, giggling and fondling the two men she was taking back to her hotel room that night.

Now that image was being replaced by another, even more challenging one for evidently Jemima Barber had reinvented herself yet again. Possibly that big change in appearance was a deliberate element of her con tricks, he conceded. The short hair was gone, exchanged for hip-length extensions, which provided her with a glorious mane the colour of ripe wheat in sunlight. Her heart-shaped face seemed bare of make-up, his keen gaze resting suspiciously on the succulent pout of her pink mouth, the faint colour blossoming in her cheeks and the pale ice-blue eyes, an unusual shade that he had initially assumed was a mere accident of the photographic lighting. She wore a drab pair of black leggings and a tight vest top, which accentuated the sumptuous swell of her breasts.

With difficulty he dragged his attention from that surprisingly luscious display, acknowledging that the camera shots of her chest must have been unflattering, because in the flesh she looked much more natural. Even so, she was distinctly curvier. Had she simply put on weight? The plain clothing was a surprise as well but, of course, she hadn't been expecting visitors and it was possible that she dressed more circumspectly in her elderly parents' radius. In fact at this moment she looked ridiculously wholesome and young. It made him wonder who Jemima Barber really was below the surface. And then he questioned why he was wondering about her at all when he already knew all that he needed to know. She was a liar, a cheat, a thief and a whore without boundaries. She sold her own body as easily as she planned to sell her son.

Hugely self-conscious below the intensity of Luciano's appraisal, Jemima could feel her face getting hotter and hotter but, because he unnerved her, she kept her attention on the older man and said, 'How can I help you?'

'We're here to discuss the child's future,' Charles Bennett informed her.

At that news her heart dropped to the soles of her canvas-clad feet and her head swivelled, eyes flying wide as she involuntarily looked back at Luciano. Looked and instantly saw what she had refused to recognise seconds earlier, finally making the terrifying connection that set a large question mark over her hopes and dreams for Nicky. Nicky was like a miniature carbon copy of Luciano Vitale. Luciano wore his hair a little longer than was conventional. It fell below his collar in glossy blue-black curls that flared luxuriantly across his skull. He had a straight nose, spectacular high cheekbones, winged brows and deep-set eyes the colour of tawny tiger's eye stones—eyes as hard and unyielding as any crystal.

Stray recollections of her late sister's remarks on the topic of Nicky's father echoed in the back of her head.

'If he met me, he would want me... Men *always* do,' Julie had trilled excitedly. 'He's exactly the sort of man I want to marry—rich and good-looking and madly successful. I'd make the perfect wife for a man like him.'

And, of course, Luciano Vitale wouldn't be too impressed right now when, instead of the slim, fashionable Julie, he got the fatter, plainer twin, a little voice whispered in Jemima's shaken head. Was that why he was staring? But he didn't *know* that she was Julie's sister and he had never even met her sister. As far as she was aware he did not even know that Julie had an identical twin nor was he likely to know that Julie had stolen Jemima's identity. Did he even know that her sister was dead?

Jemima assumed not. Had he known, surely that would have fuelled the lawyer's first words because Julie's death now changed everything. A cold little shiver shimmied down Jemima's spine at that awareness. As Nicky's mother, Julie had had rights to her son even if those rights could be disputed in court. As Nicky's aunt, Jemima had virtually no rights at all. The only thing that blurred those boundaries was the fact that Julie had given birth in her twin's name and it was Jemima's name on Nicky's birth certificate and not his real birth mother's. It was a legal tangle that would have to be sorted out some day.

But not on this particular day, Jemima decided abruptly as she collided with Luciano's chilling dark eyes, which were regarding her with as much emotion and empathy as a lab specimen might have inspired. Nicky's father was angry, distrustful and ready to make snap judgements and decisions, she reckoned fearfully. He was not visiting in a spirit of goodwill and why indeed would he? Julie had given birth to his child and had then run away with that child, leaving behind an unabashed demand for more money.

Jemima tilted her chin up as if she were neither aware of nor bothered by Luciano's scrutiny and concentrated on the lawyer instead. The tension in the atmosphere was making her tummy perform nauseous somersaults and suffocating her vocal cords. She knew that she needed to get a grip on herself and do it fast because she had no idea of what was about to happen and for Nicky's sake she had to be able to react fast and appropriately. It disturbed her, though, that one major decision had somehow already been made and that was her willingness to pretend to be Julie for as long as she could pretend while she assessed Nicky's father as a potential parent. If she admitted who she really was, her nephew could be immediately removed from her care and her heart almost stopped at the mere thought of that happening. For that reason alone she would lie...she would *pretend*...even if it went against all her principles.

Luciano was very still, his entire attention engaged by the strange behaviour of the woman in front of him. Women did not stick out their chins and ignore Luciano when they were lucky enough to gain his attention. They smiled at him, flirted, treated him to little upward glances calculated to appeal. They never *ever* blanked him. Yet Jemima Barber was blanking him.

'I want DNA testing carried out on the child so that I know whether or not he is mine.' Luciano spoke up for the first time, startling her. His dark, deep accented drawl trailed along her skin like a fur caress and awakened goosebumps.

As the ramifications of what he had said sank in Jemima went rigid at the insult to her sister's memory. 'How *dare* you?' she shot back at him angrily, her temper rising and spilling out without warning and shaking her with its intensity.

His perfectly modelled mouth took on a derisive

slant. 'I dare,' he said levelly. 'There must be no doubt that he is mine—'

'In any case, mandatory DNA testing after the birth was a clause in the contract you signed,' the lawyer chipped in. 'Unfortunately you left the hospital before the test could be completed.'

The reminder of the contract that Julie had signed in Jemima's name doused Jemima's anger and covered her with a sudden surge of shame instead. She was about to lie. She was about to pretend that she was her sister when she was not and the knowledge cut her deep because, in the normal way of things, Jemima was an honest and straightforward person who detested lies and deception. Her desire to look out for Nicky's needs, she registered unhappily, had put her on a slippery slope at odds with her conscience. She should be telling the truth, no matter how unpleasant or dangerous it was, she thought wretchedly. Two wrongs did not make a right. This man was Nicky's father. But *could* she simply stand back and watch Luciano Vitale take her baby nephew away from her?

She knew she could not. There had to be safeguards. Nicky was defenceless. It was Jemima's job to carefully consider his future and ensure that his needs were met. But she had to be unselfish about that process too, she reminded herself doggedly, even if the final result hurt, even if it meant standing back and losing the child she loved.

'DNA testing,' Luciano repeated, wondering if his worst fears were being borne out by her pallor and clear apprehension. Maybe the child *wasn't* his. If that were the case, it was better that he found that out sooner rather than later. 'The technician can visit the child here. It is a simple procedure done with a mouth swab and the results will be known within forty-eight hours.'

'Yes,' Jemima muttered, dry-mouthed, nerves rattling through her like express trains as yet another fear presented itself to her.

All bets were off if he intended to have her tested for DNA. Did twins have the same DNA? She had no idea and worried that she would be exposed as an imposter. She lowered her feathery lashes. Well, she would just have to wait and see what happened. She was not in a position to do anything else. Arguing against the need for such testing would only muddy the waters. It wouldn't achieve anything. It would only increase the animosity and uncertainty about her nephew's future.

'So, you will agree to this?' Luciano said softly.

Involuntarily, Jemima glanced at him and connected with liquid dark eyes surrounded by black velvet lashes as lush as his son's. Her heart went *bang-bang-bang* inside her and she felt incredibly dizzy, as if she stood on the edge of an abyss gazing down at a perilous drop. Something tugged and tightened low in her pelvis and she was unexpectedly alarmingly aware of her body as if her prickling skin had suddenly become too tender to bear the weight of her clothes. 'Yes...'

'In fact you will agree to all my demands,' Luciano told her without skipping a beat while he silently marvelled at the translucent perfection of her pale blue eyes. 'Because you are not stupid and it would be very stupid to refuse me anything that I want.'

Brows pleating, Charles Bennett turned to study his client in astonishment and then his attention skimmed back to the young blonde woman staring back at Luciano as if he had cast a magic spell over her.

CHAPTER TWO

'AND WHY WOULD you think that?' Jemima fired back in sudden bewilderment, shaking her head as though to clear it.

'Because I hold pole position,' Luciano informed her with chilling assurance. 'I have security-camera footage of you stealing credit cards and using one of them in an act of fraud. If I should choose to pass that evidence to the police, I—'

'You're threatening me!' Jemima interrupted in shock.

Stolen credit cards? Was he serious? Was it possible that Julie had sunk that low while she was working in London? Jemima did recall wondering how her sister was contriving to stay at a fancy hotel. She had asked and Julie had winced as though such a financial enquiry were incredibly rude and had sulkily refused to explain.

'My client is *not* threatening you,' Charles Bennett interposed flatly. 'He is simply telling you that he has footage of the theft.'

But Jemima had turned pale as death and did not

dare look in Luciano's direction again. Proof of theft? My goodness, he could have her arrested right here and now! *Forcibly* parted from Nicky! Her lashes fluttered rapidly as she struggled to think.

'So you *will* agree to the DNA testing?' Luciano queried once more.

'Yes,' she agreed shakily.

'We will endeavour to be civilised about this matter.'

In receipt of that unpersuasive statement, Jemima's palm tingled. Never in her life had she wanted so badly to slap someone for lying. But that richly confident, patronising assurance from Luciano Vitale sent violent vibes of antagonism coursing through her and, daringly, she turned her head to look at him again. It was a grave mistake. As she fell into the hypnotic darkness of his gaze shock gripped her, tensing every muscle with sudden bone-deep fear for in Luciano she sensed a propensity for violence that made a mockery of her own softer nature. He was a man of extremes, of dangerous emotions and dangerous drives, and for a split second it was all there in his extraordinarily compelling eyes like a high-voltage electrical pulse zapping her with a stinging warning to back off or take the consequences. Seemingly he hid the disturbing reality of his true nature behind a chillingly polite mask.

'Yes, we must try to be civilised,' she heard herself say obediently while she shrank from the terrifying surge of ESP that had enveloped her in an adrenaline-charged panic mere seconds earlier.

'I can be reasonable,' Luciano declared, smooth as

polished glass. 'But I will do nothing that could put me on the wrong side of British law. Be clear on that score.'

'Of course,' she conceded, wondering why she didn't feel reassured by that moral statement.

He wanted to stay on the right side of the law. She quite understood that. Only, where did that leave her? Julie had committed her crimes in Jemima's name and the only way for Jemima to clear her name was to own up to her sister's identity theft. Unfortunately doing that would also mean that she lost the right to care for Nicky. How could she bear that loss? How could she risk it? All she could do in the short-term, she thought in a panic, was fake being Julie until she was confronted by the police. At that point she would have to come clean because she would have no other choice.

Luciano studied his quarry, his gaze instinctively lingering on her ripe mouth and the porcelain smoothness of the upper slopes of her full breasts. He was a man and he supposed it was natural for him to notice her body, but the pulse of response at his groin and the sudden tightening there infuriated him. He turned away dismissively, broad shoulders rigid below his exquisitely tailored charcoal-grey suit jacket.

'The technician will call to take the sample this afternoon,' he delivered.

'You're not wasting any time,' Jemima remarked gingerly.

Luciano swung back, eyes narrowed and cutting as black razors. 'You have already wasted a great deal of my time,' he told her with brutal bluntness.

Jemima clenched her teeth together and glanced at

his companion, whose discomfiture was unhidden. There was civilised and civilised, she guessed, and Luciano Vitale had no intention of treating someone like her with kid gloves. It was clear that he saw her as inferior in every way. She would have to toughen up, she told herself urgently, toughen up to handle someone who disliked and distrusted her without showing weakness. Weakness, she sensed, he would use against her.

Shell-shocked as Jemima was by Luciano's visit, once he had left she followed her usual routine with Nicky. She had looked forward to spending the long summer holidays with the little boy before she had to make childcare arrangements to enable her to return to work at the start of the new term. Now she was wondering if she would lose custody of him before then. She was down on the floor playing with Nicky when the doorbell went again.

It was the technician from the DNA-testing facility. The woman extended a consent form on a board for her to sign and then asked her to hold Nicky. The swab was done in seconds and Jemima waited for the technician to use the same procedure on her but instead she packaged the swab and departed, her job evidently complete. Heaving a sigh of relief that she herself had not been asked to give a sample, Jemima was in no mood for further company and she suppressed a weary groan when yet another caller turned up at the door.

Her face stiffened when she recognised her ex-boyfriend. Yes, she was still friends with Steven because her parents liked him and she had had to deal with the awkwardness of continuing meetings whether she liked it or not. Steven was a big mover and shaker in the church she attended and ran a young evangelical group to great acclaim.

'May I come in?' Steven pressed when the polite small talk about her parents' little holiday had dried up and she was rather hoping he would take the hint and leave.

'Nicky's still up,' Jemima warned him.

'How's the little chap doing?' Steven enquired with his widest, fakest smile.

'Well, his father may have turned up,' Jemima heard herself say without meaning to. That she had admitted that much to Steven was evidence of how much emotional turmoil she was in because once she had realised how much he disapproved of her taking responsibility for Julie's son she had stopped confiding in the tall blond man.

Steven took a seat with the casual informality of a regular visitor. A handsome dentist with a lucrative line in private patients, her ex was well liked by all. Jemima, however, was rather less keen. She had believed she loved Steven for years and had fully expected to marry him before Julie came into their lives.

'Yes, he's good-looking and he could give me some fun but he's *your* boyfriend. I'm not poaching him,' Julie had told her squarely.

But Jemima hadn't wanted to keep Steven by default and once she'd realised how infatuated he was with her twin she had set him free. Of course, as a couple, Steven and Julie hadn't suited, as Jemima had suspected at the outset. Her sister and her ex had enjoyed a short-lived fling, nothing more, and Jemima genuinely did not hold Steven's defection against him. How could she possibly blame him for having found her colourful, lively sister more attractive? No, what annoyed Jemima about Steven was that he was smugly convinced that he could talk his way back into Jemima's affections now that Julie was gone. Steven had no sensitivity whatsoever.

'His father?' Steven echoed on a rising note of interest. 'Tell me more.'

Jemima told him about her visitors but withheld the information about the stolen credit cards and the underlying threat, reluctant to give Steven another opportunity to trash her sister's memory.

'That's the best news I've heard in weeks!' Steven exclaimed, his bright blue eyes lingering intently on her flushed face. 'I admire your affection for Nicky but keeping him isn't practical in your circumstances.'

'Sometimes feelings aren't practical,' Jemima countered quietly.

Steven gave her an earnest appraisal. 'You know how I feel about you, Jem. How long is it going to take for you to forgive me? I was foolish. I made a mistake. But I learned from it.'

'If you had really loved me, you wouldn't have wanted Julie—'

'It's different for men. We are more base creatures,' Steven told her sanctimoniously.

Jemima gritted her teeth and resisted the urge to roll her eyes. It amazed her that she had failed to appreciate how sexist and judgemental Steven could be. 'I've moved on now. I'm fond of you but I'm afraid that's all.'

'Tell me about Nicky's father,' Steven urged irritably.

'I only know his name, nothing else…'

Steven started looking up Luciano Vitale on his tablet and fired a welter of facts at her.

Luciano was an only child, the son of an infamous Mafia don. Jemima did roll her eyes at that information. He was filthy rich, which wasn't a surprise, but much that followed did take her aback. In his early twenties Luciano had married a famous Italian movie star and had a daughter with her before tragically losing both wife and child in a helicopter crash three years earlier. Jemima was shocked, *very* shocked by that particular piece of news.

'So there you have it…that's *why* he wants a kid… his daughter died!' Steven pointed out with satisfaction. 'How can you doubt that the man will make a good parent?'

'He's still single. How much actual parenting is he planning to do?' Jemima traded stubbornly. 'And maybe Nicky's supposed to be a replacement but he's not a girl, he's a boy and a child in his own right—'

Steven pontificated at length about the immorality of the surrogacy agreement and how it went against all natural laws. Jemima said nothing because she was too busy looking at photographic images of the exquisite blonde, Gigi Nocella, Luciano's late wife and the mother of his firstborn. Luciano had matched Gigi, she reflected abstractedly, two beautiful people combined to make a perfect couple. He had already lost a child, she thought helplessly, and she was filled with guilt at her own reluctance to hand over Nicky. Who was she to interfere? Who was she to think she knew everything when she was already painfully aware that her sister had made so many bad choices in life?

'Vitale *needs* to know what Julie did to you and your family,' Steven said harshly. 'After all, if he'd kept better tabs on her, Julie would never have come here and caused so much grief.'

'That's very much a matter of opinion, Steven,' Jemima said stiffly and, deciding that she had been sufficiently hospitable, she stood up in the hope of hastening his departure.

'You're not thinking this through, Jem,' he told her in exasperation. 'Nicky's not your child and you shouldn't be behaving as if he is. If you pass him on to his father...'

'Like a parcel?'

'He *belongs* with his father,' Steven argued vehemently. 'Don't think that I don't appreciate that that child is preventing us from getting back together again!'

'Only in your imagination—'

'You know how I feel about you keeping Nicky. Why are you trying to do more for the kid than his own mother was prepared to do? Let's be honest, Julie was a lousy mother and not the nicest—'

'Stop right there!' Hot-cheeked, Jemima wrenched open the front door with vigour. 'I'll tell Mum and Dad that you called in when I phone them later.'

She closed the door again with the suggestion of a

slam and groaned out loud in frustration. But grateful as she was to see Steven leave, he had left her with food for thought. She played with Nicky in the bath and stared down at his damp curly head with tears swimming in her eyes. He wasn't her child and all the wishing in the world couldn't change that...or bring Julie back. Luciano Vitale had lost a much-loved daughter. She must have been loved, for that could be the only reason her father had gone to such lengths to have another child. Jemima wrapped Nicky's wet, squirming figure into a towel and hugged him close.

Luciano had searched for eight months to find his child. He wanted Nicky. She had to stop being so selfish. She had to take a step back. Was she prejudiced against Luciano because he had chosen a surrogacy arrangement to father a second child? She was conservative and conventional and she supposed she was a little bit disposed to prejudice in that line. The admission shamed her. How could she have accepted Julie and Nicky but retained her bias against Nicky's father? Of course, what if Luciano Vitale wasn't Nicky's father?

Two days later, however, she received the results of the DNA testing, which declared that her nephew was Luciano's flesh and blood, and she had barely settled the document down when the landline rang.

'Luciano Vitale...' Her caller imparted his identity with a warning edge of harshness. 'I would like to meet my son this evening.'

Jemima reminded herself that there was no room for her personal feelings in her dealings with Luciano and she breathed in deep. 'Yes, Mr Vitale. What time suits you?'

They negotiated politely for an earlier time than he first suggested because Jemima knew that the later he arrived, the more tired and cross Nicky would be. And she wanted the first meeting between father and son to go well because it would be downright mean and malicious to hope otherwise. The small living room was spick and span by the time she had finished cleaning, but Nicky was teething again and cried pathetically when she tried to put him down for his afternoon nap. Ellie had been texting her constantly with queries since she had told her friend about Luciano and was reacting to his proposed visit with as much excitement as a famous rock star might have invoked.

'Are you sure I can't come round and sort of hover on the doorstep?' Ellie pleaded on the phone. 'I'm gasping to see the guy in the flesh. He looks hotter than the fires of hell!'

'It's not the right moment, Ellie. He has a right to his privacy.'

'Not looking like a walking, talking female temptation, he hasn't!'

'He may look good in photos but he's not the warm, approachable type,' Jemima reminded her friend.

'Well, why would he be? He thinks you're Julie and Julie ripped him off! When are you planning to tell him the truth?'

'When I find the right moment. Not tonight because in the mood he's probably going to be in he's likely to just scoop up Nicky and walk straight out of here with him,' Jemima admitted with a grimace.

'Whether Luciano Vitale knows it or not, he owes you,' Ellie said loyally. 'Julie couldn't cope with Nicky and you've been caring for him since he was only a week old. Your parents will miss him terribly, though, when he goes.'

When he goes, Jemima repeated inwardly, her heart sinking as she was finally forced to face that certainty. Nicky was about to be taken away from her and there was not one blasted thing she could do about it. She was not Nicky's closest relative, Luciano was.

Jemima was very tense while she waited for her visitor. Nicky looked adorable in a little blue playsuit but he was teething and in a touchy temperamental mood in which he could travel from smiles to tears in the space of seconds.

Jemima heard the cars arrive and rushed to the window. The equivalent of a cavalcade had drawn up outside on the street, a collection of vehicles composed of a black limousine and several Mercedes cars, all with tinted windows. As she watched several men emerged from the accompanying cars and fanned out across the street while clearly taking direction from ear devices. All the men wore formal suits and sunglasses and emanated an aggressive take-charge vibe. Finally the rear door of the limo was opened and Luciano slid out, instantly casting everyone around him in the shade. He wore well-washed jeans and a long-sleeved black sweater…and still, he took her breath away.

The well-cut denim outlined long, powerful thighs

and lean hips, while the dark sweater somehow enhanced his blue-black hair and olive skin. Her mouth ran dry while she stared and smoothed damp palms down over her own, more ordinary jeans, wishing she had the same sleek, fashionable edge he exuded with infuriating ease. As she began to back away from the window a movement behind him attracted her attention and she stared as a slim blonde woman climbed out of the car. Instantly, Luciano turned to speak to the woman and a moment later she got back into the car, evidently having thought better of accompanying him. Who was she? His girlfriend?

It's none of your business who she is, a voice reproved in Jemima's mind and she moved through to the doorway and breathed in deep, struggling to bolster herself for what was to come. She opened the door briskly. 'Mr Vitale…'

'Jemima,' he said drily, stepping inside, his sculpted lips unsmiling, an aloof coolness stamped across his lean bronzed face like a wall.

'Nicky's in here…' Jemima pressed the living-room door wider to show off Nicky where he sat on the floor surrounded by his favourite toys.

'His name is Niccolò,' Luciano corrected without hesitation. 'I don't like diminutives. I would also like to meet my son alone…'

Jemima glanced up at him in surprise and dismay but he wasn't looking at her. His attention was all for Nicky, no, Niccolò, and Luciano's lustrous tiger eyes were gleaming as he literally savoured his first view of his son with an intensity she could feel. Jemima stared, couldn't help doing it, noting with relief that the forbidding lines of Luciano's lean dark face were softening, the hard compression of his beautifully sculpted hard mouth easing.

'Thank you, Miss Barber,' Luciano Vitale murmured, deftly planting himself inside the room and leaving her outside as he firmly closed the door in her face.

With a sigh, Jemima sat down on the phone bench just inside the front door. Of course he didn't want an audience, she reasoned, striving to be fair and reasonable. Who was the woman waiting outside for Luciano? If she was his girlfriend, did he live with her? Was it possible that the girlfriend was unable to have children and that she and Luciano had entered the surrogacy agreement as a couple? And what did any of those facts matter to her? Well, they mattered, she conceded ruefully, because she cared a great deal about Nicky's future but ultimately she had no say whatsoever in what came next.

As a whimper sounded from the living room Jemima tensed. Nicky was going through a stranger-danger phase. She could hear the quiet murmur of Luciano's voice as he endeavoured to soothe the little boy. Sadly, a sudden outburst of inconsolable crying was his reward. Jemima made no move but her hands were clenched into fists and her knuckles showed white beneath her pale skin as she resisted the urge to intervene. The sound of Nicky becoming increasingly upset distressed her but she knew she had to learn to step back and accept that Luciano Vitale was Nicky's father and his closest relative.

When Nicky's sobs erupted into screams, the living-room door opened abruptly. 'You'd better come in... He's frightened,' Luciano bit out in a harsh undertone.

Jemima required no second invitation. She scrambled up and surged past him. Nicky's anxious eyes locked straight on to her and he held up his arms to be lifted. Jemima crouched down to scoop him up and he clung like a monkey, shaking and sobbing, burying his little head in her neck.

Luciano watched that revealing display in angry disbelief. Niccolò had two little hands fisted in his mother's shirt, his fearful desperation patently obvious as he hid his face from the stranger who had tried to make friends with him. As Jemima quieted the trembling child Luciano registered two unwelcome facts. His son was much more attached to his mother than his father had expected and Jemima was very definitely the centre of his son's sense of security. It was a complication he neither wanted nor needed. His attention dropped to the generous curve of Jemima's derrière in jeans and he tensed, averting his gaze to the back of his son's curly head as he felt himself harden. So, he liked women to look more like women than slender boys and she had splendid curves, but he abhorred that hormonal response that was so very inappropriate in Jemima Barber's radius.

'He's teething, which always makes him a bit clingy,' Jemima proffered in Nicky's defence. 'And this is the wrong end of the day for him because he's tired and fractious—'

'He's terrified. Isn't he used to meeting people?' Luciano pressed critically.

'He's more used to women.'

'But your parents must've been looking after him for you while you were in London,' he pointed out, momentarily depriving her of breath as he reminded her of the lie she was living for his benefit. After all, nobody could be in two places at once and while Jemima had been teaching and covering Nicky's childcare costs at a local nursery facility, Julie *had* been in London.

'Dad's retired but he's still out and about a lot, so Nicky would've seen less of him,' Jemima muttered in a brittle voice, crossing her fingers at a lie that made her feel guiltier than ever because Nicky adored his grandfather.

Nicky stuck his thumb in his mouth and sagged against Jemima with a final hoarse whimper. 'Sorry about this...' she added uncomfortably. 'But in time he'll get used to you.'

Luciano compressed his lips. He didn't have time to waste.

'Is that your girlfriend outside waiting in the car?' Jemima asked abruptly, keen to know and to change the subject about Nicky's lifestyle in recent months.

Luciano frowned, winged ebony brows pleating above hard dark eyes fringed by lashes as dense and noticeable as black lace. 'No, the nanny I'm hiring.'

Jemima stopped breathing. 'A nanny?' she gasped in dismay.

'I will need some support in caring for my son,' Luciano countered drily, wondering what he was going to do about the problem his son's mother had become.

Well, he certainly wouldn't be marrying her as Charles Bennett had ludicrously suggested after the results of the DNA test had been revealed.

'A paper marriage,' Charles had outlined. 'In one move you would legitimise your son's birth, tidy up any future inheritance issues and gain a legal right to have custody of your son. As an ex-wife you could also give her a settlement without breaking the law. It would be perfect.'

Perfect only in a nightmare, Luciano reflected grimly. No way was he linking his name to a woman who was no better than a thieving hooker, not in a paper marriage of any kind.

He was employing a nanny, Jemima thought wretchedly as panic snaked through her in a cold little shiver of foreboding. Clearly Luciano was planning to remove Nicky from her care as soon as he could.

Luciano surveyed his infant son, who was engaged in contentedly falling asleep against his mother's shoulder. He could rip him away from Jemima as he himself had once been ripped away from his own mother. All right, he had been almost three years old but he had never forgotten the day he was torn from his mother's loving arms. Of course there had been a lot of blood and violence involved and naturally he had been traumatised by the episode. He would not be doing anything of that nature. He despised Jemima Barber but he did not wish her dead for having crossed him. At the same time, however, he deeply resented her hold on his son.

'Nicky's very emotional,' Jemima remarked cautiously. 'He does get upset quite easily.'

'I'm surprised he's so fond of you. You've spent most of your time in London and left other people looking after him,' Luciano condemned.

'I've spent much more time with him than you appreciate,' Jemima protested, tilting her chin. 'Of course he's fond of me...'

'But you always planned to give him away,' he reminded her coolly. 'As long as the pay-off was sufficient. Shouldn't you have prepared him better for the separation?'

An angry flush illuminated her pale porcelain skin. 'I didn't know if there was going to *be* a separation!' she fired back awkwardly.

'I would let nothing prevent me from claiming my son. Since you disappeared there has not been a single day that I haven't thought of him,' Luciano proclaimed, dark honey-rich eyes glittering with challenge. 'He is mine—'

'Yes...' she conceded raggedly, her breath catching in her throat below the onslaught of his extraordinarily compelling gaze. 'But handing him over isn't going to be as simple...er...as I once thought it would be.'

Luciano shrugged a broad shoulder without interest. 'You convinced a psychiatrist that you knew what you were signing up to do and could cope with it.'

Desperation slivered through Jemima's taut frame. 'Things change...' she whispered.

'I want my son,' Luciano told her bluntly.

The germ of a wild idea burst into being inside Jemima and flew straight from brain to tongue without the benefit of any filter or forethought. 'Couldn't *I* be your nanny? Even for a little while?'

Luciano studied her in disbelief. 'My nanny? *You?* Are you crazy?'

'Only until he settles into his new life. You'd be getting a trained infant teacher to look after him. I'm well qualified with young children.'

'But you've never worked with them?'

'Of course I have work experience.'

'Before you decided that you much preferred earning easy money as an escort?'

Jemima froze. 'An...*es-escort*?' Her voice stumbled over the mortifying word. 'That's a dreadful—'

Luciano sighed. 'I know everything about you. You can't lie to me. You were working as an escort in London and you were very popular with older men until you began to steal their wallets. I spoke to the agency that made your bookings for you before deciding to dispense with your services.'

Her lips parted and then closed again. She had turned white as snow, shock thudding through her, her heart thumping loudly in her eardrums. She didn't want to believe him but she did because Julie's love of money had been much stronger than her self-respect. An escort? An escort offering extras? Jemima squirmed, raw humiliation bowing her head. Working as an escort had given her twin the chance to steal. And sadly, the stolen credit cards had only been the tip of the iceberg, she acknowledged wretchedly. Seemingly Julie had been as willing to sell herself as she had been to sell her son.

'It was an exclusive escort service,' Luciano conceded, recognising her mortification and less gratified by it than he had expected to be.

'So I wouldn't be quite what you want in a nanny,' Jemima breathed, stricken, receiving that message loud and clear from his attitude.

'I'm afraid not. My security team will pick Niccolò up tomorrow and bring him up to London for the day. I'll send the nanny with them.' Luciano read her consternation with ease. 'Naturally I want to spend time with my son.'

'Before you do...*what*?' Jemima pressed helplessly.

'Before I take him home to Sicily with me,' Luciano fielded. 'You know how this must end, Jemima. Why make it more difficult for all of us?'

Jemima subsided like a pricked balloon. Julie had accepted payment and signed the agreement. There was no escape clause unless she was willing to run screaming to the media with her sad story. And where would that get her? More importantly, what would it gain Nicky? Notified of the circumstances of Nicky's birth, the social services would probably step in to take charge of Nicky and decide his future and there was no guarantee that Luciano would get him either. In fact there was every chance that Nicky would be placed in an adoptive home and neither Jemima nor Luciano would ever see him again. Seeking outside help would be the wrong thing to do, she decided in despair. The very fact she had lied and faked being

Julie to hold on to her nephew would be held against her by the authorities…and by Luciano if he ever found out the truth.

CHAPTER THREE

'So could I have a lift with you up to London?' Jemima asked the nanny cheerfully. 'I assure you that a lift is all I want, but my being in the car will make it easier for you to get to know Nicky and I can run through his routine with you as well.'

'Er... I...' Nonplussed, the nanny, who had introduced herself as Lisa, hovered on the doorstep and looked at the tall, broadly built bodyguard standing behind her for direction.

The bodyguard dug out a cell phone and punched in a number and Jemima got the obvious message: nothing could be done because no plan could deviate in the smallest way without Luciano Vitale's permission and approval. She scolded herself for thinking that she was being clever when she had come up with the idea the night before. Yet she truly wasn't trying to interfere with Luciano's day with Nicky. She simply wanted to be more accessible if anything went wrong.

'I just thought I could take the opportunity to do some shopping,' she fibbed nervously as the bodyguard's conversation in staccato Italian continued at length.

'Mr Vitale makes all the arrangements,' Lisa told her with an apologetic smile. 'I don't want to screw up my first day on the job. It would be handy, though, to know a little more about your son.'

'Miss Maurice?' The bodyguard handed the phone to the nanny.

Jemima watched the woman stiffen, straighten her shoulders and pale as she evidently received her instructions while answering yes and no several times. She then extended the phone to Jemima.

Realising that it was now her turn to receive her orders, Jemima laughed out loud, stunning her companions.

'So glad you've found something to laugh about today,' Luciano drawled, sharp and swift as a stiletto stabbing at her down the line.

'Oh, please don't take it like that,' Jemima babbled in dismay. 'I promise you that you won't see or hear from me today. I just want to be in London…to…er… shop—'

'I can hear the lie in your voice—'

Her blood ran cold in her veins.

'You got a sixth sense or something?'

'Or something. Tell me the truth or I will not consider the idea,' he told her coldly.

'I wanted to be within reach…you know, in case you needed me. That's all.'

At his end of the line, Luciano gritted his perfect white teeth. Where the hell did she get the nerve to bug him like this? He expelled his breath in a hiss of impatience. 'Why would I need you?'

'Not you, *him*,' Jemima stressed. 'And dial back the tension, Luciano. Nicky can be very temperamental. He works best with calm, quiet and soothing—'

Luciano was incredulous. 'Let me get this straight—*you* are telling *me* how to behave?'

'But not in a rude way, in a *helpful* way,' Jemima emphasised.

'You are irritating me,' Luciano growled soft and low.

'Ditto.' Jemima groaned out loud, having forgotten her audience. 'Less of the growly stuff would be nice but not if you replace it with the rave-from-the-grave voice.'

The rave from the grave, Luciano mouthed in silent disbelief. She was actually telling him that he irritated her. How dared she? A thieving whore...but the *mother* of his *son*...

'You can travel to London with them and accompany Niccolò back again at five today. Pass the phone back to Rico...'

Jemima did as she was bid, handing Nicky's baby bag to the second bodyguard who had appeared before tucking her nephew under her arm to lock up the house.

'What a fuss about nothing,' she wanted to remark to the nanny as she climbed into the limousine and the two women together secured the baby into the very fancy car seat awaiting him, but caution silenced her. Luciano was an intractable tyrant supported in his moods and habits by his intimidated employees. Presumably standing up to Luciano meant instant dismissal. Jemima suspected she wouldn't last five minutes working for him because she had too much a mind of her own, so it was probably fortunate that he hadn't jumped on her nanny offer. At the same time, however, she was relieved he had agreed to let her catch a lift to London and travel back with Nicky at the end of the day. She had been a tiny bit afraid that Luciano wasn't planning on letting Nicky return to her again and now that looming fear could be set aside for at least one more day. Having passed her cell-phone number to Lisa, she asked to be dropped at the entrance to a Tube station.

The attraction of browsing round shops where she could not afford to buy anything held little appeal for Jemima. In recent months she had grown accustomed to being stony broke, to questioning every single purchase and asking herself if she really needed the item. And although she would have adored some new clothes and the chance to replace cosmetics that had run out, she was happy to make those sacrifices to keep Nicky and give her parents peace of mind in their retirement. A desire to make the best of whatever life threw at her had always driven Jemima and she took the same approach to her day out, heading to the first of her free attractions—the British Museum—before enjoying a picnic lunch in Kensington Gardens and a walk round the Tate Modern. She was on the banks of the Thames when her phone rang and she snatched it out.

'Nicky's ill... Where are you?' Luciano demanded thinly. 'I'll have you picked up.'

Her frantic questions elicited no adequate response beyond the assurance that the baby was not in danger. Luciano was much more intent on retrieving her as soon as possible so that she could comfort the little boy. Jemima was perspiring with stress and anxiety by the time a limousine lifted her at the agreed pick-up point and drove her across London to an exclusive block of apartments. There, flanked by two enormous bodyguards, she got into a glass lift to be swept up to the penthouse.

'I thought you were going to stay within reach!' Luciano roared at her as she came through the front door.

Jemima was accustomed to dealing with distraught and often angry parents whose child had become upset at school or had suffered injury and at one glance she recognised that Luciano fell into that category. He was a powerful man who controlled everything around him but Nicky's illness had made him feel powerless and that anger was the fallout. She could hear Nicky's distressed choking wails echoing through the apartment and was not in the mood to waste time sparring with his anxious father. 'Where is he?'

'The doctor's with him,' Luciano gritted, closing a managing hand to her spine to herd her in the right direction. He was the most alarmingly dominant man and, even worse, she thought ruefully, it seemed to come entirely naturally to him, as if an autocratic need to trample over the little people had been programmed into him at birth. 'Not that he's been much use!'

Lisa was pacing the floor with a wailing Nicky and looked as though she had been through the wars. Earlier that day she had looked immaculate. Now her long hair was falling down untidily and her shirt was spattered with food stains. An older bespectacled man, who could only be the doctor, overlooked the scene with an air of discomfiture.

'What's wrong with Nicky?' Jemima asked worriedly.

The doctor studied her anxiously. 'A touch of tonsillitis...nothing more—'

'My son would not be making such a fuss over so little,' Luciano began wrathfully.

'Oh, yes, he would.' Jemima threw Luciano a wryly apologetic glance. 'He makes a real fuss when he's sick. He's had tonsillitis a couple of times already and I was up all night with him.'

With a yell, Nicky unglued his reddened eyes and, focusing joyously on Jemima, he gave a frantic lurch in Lisa's hold. The other woman crossed the room in haste to settle him into Jemima's arms. 'It's obvious he wants his mum.'

'Perhaps you could explain to...er...Nicky's father that this is not a serious condition. The baby has a mild fever and a sore throat and possibly some ear pain.' Exhausted, Nicky moaned against Jemima's shoulder, his solid little body heavy against her as he slumped.

'Try to get him to drink some water to keep him hydrated,' the doctor advised with a wary glance in Luciano's smouldering direction. 'Within a couple of days and with the medication he'll soon be back to normal.'

'Thank you,' Jemima pronounced quietly as she

sank down on a comfortable leather seat and accepted the baby bottle of water Lisa helpfully extended. She studied Nicky and glanced across the room at Luciano. So, she finally had first-hand evidence of whose genes had dealt Nicky the theatrics and the fireworks, she thought wryly, ignoring Nicky when he twisted away his mouth from the bottle. 'Do you want your cup?' she asked.

Nicky looked up at her, dark eyes cross and shimmering with tears.

Jemima dug the baby cup out of the bag and proceeded to pour some water into it while still cradling Nicky.

'Seems that he is one little boy who knows what he wants,' Lisa remarked.

'You're spot on.' Jemima watched the baby moisten his lips and then try a tiny sip. Forced to swallow, he grimaced and sobbed again while she praised him and told him what a brave, wonderful boy he was.

Luciano watched the performance unfolding with blazing dark golden eyes, angry frustration assailing him. He knew when he was facing a fait accompli. Jemima handled Nicky beautifully, clearly knew him inside out and responded smoothly to his needs. He himself and the highly qualified nanny had failed utterly to provide the comfort his son had needed. He wondered if little boys were programmed to want mothers over father figures. He wondered tensely how his son would cope without a mother, particularly with her sudden disappearance. Bemused by that flood of concern and the sort of deep questions he normally suppressed, Luciano grated his teeth together in frustration and called someone to show out the doctor.

'It *is* only a mild illness,' Jemima remarked quietly. 'Relax.'

'How the hell am I supposed to relax when my son is suffering?' Luciano lashed back at her in fierce attack.

'Sometimes you *can't* fix things and the normal childhood illnesses fall into that category,' Jemima pointed out gently.

Well, he *cared* about Nicky; he was quite accidentally revealing that with his behaviour. Of course, he had to be aggressive even in that, but then he was an aggressive man. And intelligence warned her that Luciano Vitale would not voluntarily share anything with her that he considered to be private or personal. Obviously his feelings about his son would fall squarely into that territory and it was not for her to pry, she told herself doggedly as Nicky snuffled into an exhausted sleep on her lap.

Luciano strode to the door, raking an impatient hand through his blue-black glossy hair. A dark shadow of stubble outlined his sculpted mouth and strong jawline. He was obviously the sort of man who had to shave twice a day. He had loosened his racy red tie at the collar, unbuttoned the top button of his white shirt. He looked a little more human and a little less perfect than at their previous meeting and she censured her selfish sense of satisfaction that he was finding his son more of a challenge than he had expected. Such a feeling was mean and ungenerous, she reminded herself angrily. Nicky was Luciano's flesh and blood and she should be pleased that he was so keen to get to know his child.

Lisa reappeared and hovered.

'The nanny will put my son in his cot for a nap now,' Luciano announced. 'We have to talk.'

Talk? What about? A frown indented Jemima's brow as she passed her nephew carefully over to the young woman and the door closed in their wake.

'What do you want to discuss?' she asked stiffly.

Luciano shot her a chilling appraisal. 'Oh, please, don't come over all naïve on me now. I prefer honesty. You've made it clear that you want to make the most profit you can from having brought my child into the world,' he pointed out with unconcealed contempt. 'But I simply want what makes my son happy and it is patently obvious that in the short-term at least Niccolò will not be happy if you suddenly vanish from his life.'

Jemima studied him, surprised he was willing to admit that possibility.

'Although there is nothing I can like, respect or admire about you, Jemima...my son *is* attached to you,' he conceded in a grim-mouthed tone of finality. 'I do not want to damage him by immediately forcing you out of his life. He deserves more consideration from me. After all, he did not choose the unusual circumstances of his birth—*I* did.'

His ringing assurance that he did not like, respect or admire her cut Jemima surprisingly deep and yet she was wryly amused by her apparent vulnerability towards his low opinion of her morals. He thought she was Julie and while she faked being Julie she had to own her sister's mistakes and pay the price of them too.

Luciano watched her porcelain-fair skin wash a guilty pink that simply accentuated the ice-blue eyes, which reminded him of very pale aquamarines he had once glimpsed in his mother's jewellery box. Those eyes and that full, soft pillowy mouth were snares that any man would zero in on, he told himself, his attention widening its scope to encompass the full, buoyant swell of her breasts below the simple tee she wore. He wondered what colour her bra was and marvelled at the ludicrous thought. What was he? A randy schoolboy? He had access to many sexual choices and almost any one of those women would be classier, safer and more beautiful than Jemima Barber, he reminded himself impatiently. Even so, it was his son's mother who was making him hard and taut and needy where it mattered, when he was all too often indifferent to female fawning and flirtation.

But then possibly what annoyed him most about Jemima was that he had yet to see any sign that she was making the smallest effort to sexually attract him. She did not appear to be wearing make-up and her plain denim skirt came to her knees while she sat with her pale slim legs neatly and modestly folded to one side. It was like a simulated virginal act, he reasoned in exasperation. Possibly she had already worked out that hooker heels and too much exposed female flesh were not his style.

Sex was no big deal, he thought impatiently. That was a truth he had embraced long ago. He didn't make time for sex, though, and perhaps that explained his reaction to his son's mother. Possibly any reasonably appealing woman would have given him the same response. But the nanny did nothing for his libido, he conceded, and neither did any of the very attractive female staff he employed. No, Jemima Barber had something special about her, something insidiously sexy he had yet to pin down and label, and it drew him like a very strong magnet. And he loathed it, loathed it like poison in his system, because she was everything he despised in a woman.

The silence smouldered like a simmering pot on a gas hob. Jemima could feel heat striking through her, spreading up from the warmth in her pelvis. *He* did that to her. *He* made her tummy fill with butterflies. *He* made an embarrassing hot, slick sensation pulse between her thighs. *He* made her nipples tighten and push against the barrier of her bra.

That reality mortified and shamed her and reminded her of her first crush as a teenager when her body had gone haywire with a physical longing she hadn't understood and hadn't really been ready to embrace. But this was different because those responses were now attacking her adult body. She found herself studying that gorgeous face of his even though she didn't want to stare, didn't want to notice the perfection of his sleek cheekbones, the classic jut of his nose or the strong line of the jaw cradling that superbly masculine mouth. And then she fell into the dark and dangerous enticement of his deep-set eyes that were tigerish gold in the light from the window and once she looked she couldn't breathe, couldn't think, couldn't even function, she thought in bemused dismay.

The door opened and an older woman came in carrying a tray. Coffee was poured. Luciano took his black and without sugar. Jemima took hers milky and sweet, their differences as pronounced in coffee as in everything else.

Cradling his cup in one elegant, long-fingered hand, Luciano murmured, 'I've decided that I want you to accompany us to Sicily as the nanny you offered to be...'

Shock made Jemima's lower lip part from her upper and she breathed again and a little faster, her eyes widening at that bombshell of a suggestion.

'It would ease the transition for my son but it would be on the strict understanding that you would begin stepping back from him while allowing others to step forward to take your place in his little world,' Luciano spelt out coolly. 'He must learn to do without you.'

Jemima tried and failed to swallow as he described the role. He had delivered the killing blow of truth by telling her what he ultimately expected and wanted from her. Sicily and the nanny job would be very temporary for her and would come at a high cost for a woman who loved the child she cared for. She lost colour, pain knotting inside her at the prospect of walking away from Nicky, but at the same time with every word Luciano Vitale spoke she saw that whether she liked it or not he was worthy of her respect as a father. He detested her yet he still recognised the strength of her bond with his son and he was keen to protect Nicky from getting hurt. How could she judge him badly for that? A more gradual process of parting Jemima from her nephew *should* work much better than a sudden break, she reasoned unhappily. Luciano was taking the sensible, cautious approach to the problem.

Her silence perturbed Luciano, who had expected instant eager agreement. Didn't Jemima Barber worship money and the high life? Wasn't she a fish out of water in her parents' modest home? He had assumed that was why she had made the strange offer to take on the role of acting as her son's nanny. After all, only that position would grant her entry into Luciano's wealthy, exclusive and privileged world. She was also broke, in debt and had to be afraid of the police catching up with her, so a trip abroad should have all the appeal of an escape hatch.

'Have you changed your mind about that offer?' Luciano asked in surprise.

'Well, it was an impulse of the moment offer,' Jemima admitted ruefully. 'I didn't really think it through. It was provoked by the prospect of parting from Nicky—'

'Sicily may make the process a little less traumatic,' Luciano commented tongue-in-cheek, reckoning that a few little treats like shopping trips round the fashion houses would quickly improve her attitude. Of course, he knew she wanted more and he was prepared to give her more to oil the wheels of persuasion. 'If you agree, I will naturally settle your debts here in the UK and compensate the men whose credit cards you stole so that they will drop the charges. That would remove the threat of arrest as well.'

In shock at that smoothly outlined proposition, Jemima snatched in a stark breath of astonishment and studied him with frowning eyes. 'But it wouldn't be right to let you pay those bills.'

Luciano raised a cynical brow. 'Of course you will be happy for me to settle your debts,' he countered forcefully. 'That is the sort of woman you are. Why are you trying to pretend otherwise?'

At that direct and unsettling question, Jemima flushed and hurriedly dropped her eyes. Julie would never have argued against such a benefit. In that he was quite correct. Her twin had always happily taken money to settle her problems and fulfil her dreams and not once had she protested or done anything that would have worked against her own natural interests. So, if Jemima was still set on pretending to be Julie, she had to bite her lip and go with the flow. She tried to take a sensible overview of her situation. The debts Julie had acquired in Jemima's name were a major source of worry to both her and her parents. To be free of that pressure would be wonderful, she acknowledged guiltily.

'And quite naturally *I* don't want my son's mother dragged into court over debts or dishonesty,' Luciano pointed out without hesitation.

But I'm *not* your son's mother, she suddenly wanted to tell him, because the web of her deceit was getting thicker and harder to justify. And what would happen if she simply told him the truth now? Would he still take her with them to Sicily? Still offer her the chance to learn how to part gently from the baby she loved? Jemima thought not. She stole a glance at him from below her lashes. She had *lied* to him. If he found that out, he would be so angry he would snatch up his son and walk away. He wasn't a forgiving or understanding or tolerant man. Furthermore the only thing she had to offer on his terms was that she was supposedly the mother of his son. Shorn of that borrowed status, she would have no standing whatsoever in his eyes.

'Obviously not,' Jemima conceded tightly before she could lose her nerve again. 'I'll come to Sicily with Nicky—'

'Niccolò,' Luciano corrected without hesitation.

'He'll always be Nicky to me,' she fielded quietly, refusing to give ground.

Something bright flashed in his dark gaze, lighting his eyes gold like the dawn sky, and she stiffened, like a small animal suddenly faced with a predator.

'Doing what I tell you to do would be a wise move now,' Luciano spelt out softly, his intent gaze raking down over the fullness of her pink lips, the swell of her tantalising breasts and the slim legs on view. He had never lusted after a woman of her ilk before. What did that say about him? But lust was healthy and indifference was not, he reasoned fiercely, all too reluctant to banish the sexual energy infusing him when for the first time in much longer than he cared to recall he felt *alive* again.

Suddenly restless, Jemima uncoiled her legs and stood up. 'You're trying to intimidate me.'

The golden gaze grew ever more intense. 'Am I?'

'I'll do everything that is reasonable but I won't be intimidated and I won't grovel,' she framed tautly, extraordinarily aware of the darker, deeper note in his rich drawl and the warning flare of his brows.

'You *won't*?' Luciano's intonation was soft and slippery as silk brushing her skin as he stalked closer, all predator, all threat.

And she should have backed away, she knew that was what she should do, but a current of inexplicable excitement was quivering up through Jemima and working its own seduction. 'I won't,' she confirmed shakily, her own voice dropping in volume and, to her annoyance, emerging breathily.

'But the idea of you grovelling at my knees is appealing, *piccolo mia*,' Luciano confided huskily, eyes golden and predatory as a raptor's locked to her upturned face. 'The image of you giving me pleasure while you're doing it gives me a high…'

At first, Jemima just couldn't credit that he had said that to her and then she told herself that he couldn't possibly have meant that sexual innuendo. A surge of embarrassment and uncertainty caused a burst of colour to fly into her cheeks and she blinked, trying to close him out, trying to rescue her brain from the sudden erotic imagery he had filled it with. That wasn't something that had ever happened to her before in a man's presence. She didn't imagine doing sexual things with men as a rule, but maybe if she had, a little voice whispered, Steven would not have been so stupefied by her infinitely bolder twin. Something about Luciano Vitale got to her on a primal level she had never experienced before.

'Did you really just say what I thought you said?' she mumbled unevenly.

CHAPTER FOUR

A HUSKY LAUGH escaped from Luciano. 'Is that how you work this spell with men who should know better? You flutter your lashes and blush at will and act naïve? Let's hit the bottom line and save some time. I don't *want* naïve or shy or fake virginal, Jemima. I like women who aren't afraid to be women…just as I am a man unafraid to admit when I feel like sex.'

Jemima was out of her depth and didn't know where to look or what to say. She couldn't admit that she wasn't a fake virgin and she couldn't admit to being naïve or shy when Julie hadn't had a shy or modest bone in her entire body. Julie had treated sexual invitations as ego boosts and had revelled unashamedly in male admiration. For just a moment, Jemima longed for the cool to emulate her late sister, who had taken her looks and sensuality for granted. *He felt like sex?* Involuntarily she glanced up at him again and a tiny little hot frisson ran up from her feminine core to pinch her nipples taut when she collided with his gleaming golden eyes. She felt the pull of his magnetic force then, the potent, compelling awareness of a powerful sexuality.

'And equally unafraid to act,' Luciano imparted, every predatory instinct in his big powerful body fired by her masquerade of innocence as he reached for her, determined to smash that façade that was so very foolish in the circumstances when he knew so much about her true character.

Jemima regained the strength to move a little too late, her paralysed legs moving her clumsily backwards in the unfamiliar room. He had knocked her off her usual calm, rational perch and wrecked her composure with that blunt sexual come-on. He had truly shocked her but he had excited her as well because, on a level Jemima didn't want to examine, she was hugely flattered by the idea that a male as gorgeous as Luciano Vitale could find her attractive.

As he spoke Luciano reached for her and propelled her back against the door she had almost reached, one hand closing round her shoulder, the other rising to curve to her chin. 'I like the chase. You're right about that, *piccolo mia*,' he told her incomprehensibly as if she had spoken. 'But this is the wrong time to run away.'

She was entrapped by his gaze, her chest swelling as she snatched in a needy breath, her throat tight with tension. Luciano Vitale wanted her. *Her?* The very concept turned her inside out because he was drop-dead beautiful in a way she had never dreamt existed. From the crown of his luxuriant black hair to his stunning eyes and flawless bone structure, he mesmerised her.

'Your pupils are dilated...' Luciano breathed, stroking a strand of golden hair back from her brow to tuck it below her ear, shifting closer, bending his dark head.

'Are they?' She was so insanely aware of how much taller and stronger he was, she was frozen with her hips welded against the solid wooden door. The lemony scent of his cologne assailed her nostrils. He smelled amazingly good and a ball of heat warmed in her pelvis.

'I scare you, don't I?' Luciano laughed again, startling her. 'I don't want to scare you...not any more.'

His breath fanned her cheek and she shivered, feeling the press of his long, powerful thighs and the hard, thrusting fullness at his groin against her stomach. Her whole body seemed to overheat at that point of contact. He was aroused and she had made him that way...she, Jemima Barber, without cosmetic witchery or fancy clothes. Who would ever have believed it? She felt like a real woman for the first time since Steven's betrayal. She didn't understand what possible appeal she could have for Luciano Vitale, but she didn't much care during that instant of exhilaration. As he lowered his head a little more and his lips brushed whisper soft across hers, it felt like *her* moment and it felt crazily like something she had been waiting for all her life.

Long fingers laced into her hair to hold her steady and the pressure deepened. She opened her mouth and he took immediate advantage with a dominance that thrilled rather than annoyed. His tongue darted into the moist interior and tangled with hers and she kissed him back with an eagerness she couldn't suppress. Her body took flight on new sensation, excitement rising like a tide inside her, drowning out every objecting voice in the back of her head. Every inch of her was suddenly tender and supersensitive, so that firm brush of his hand across her covered breasts made her straining nipples prickle in reaction and the trail of his fingers up her thigh as he lifted her skirt set her on fire with tingling impatience and longing. That passionate kiss held her utterly spellbound, her senses excited beyond bearing, and the throb of awakening between her thighs was almost unbearable in its intensity.

He stroked a fingertip across the tight triangle of fabric stretched between her legs and her knees turned to water. 'You're wet,' he told her thickly.

She couldn't breathe for shock at the tiny tremors of response quivering through her while the heat at the heart of her stoked higher. She had never in her life before wanted to be touched so badly and she was ashamed of the desire until his hungry mouth found hers again with bruising force and all thought fled in the same instant. One kiss and he dragged her under again while his skilled fingers strummed beneath her panties and stoked the hunger higher, sliding into the moist cleft and caressing the slick tissue before returning to the tiny bud that controlled her entire being.

She trembled and a strangled moan was wrenched from low in her throat as he rubbed her tormentingly sensitive flesh and suddenly her body was racing out of her control and she was jerking helplessly and gasping mindlessly beneath his mouth in a sudden explosive climax that blew her away. Her legs gave way and she would have fallen had he not lifted her and settled her down on the nearest seat.

Limp and shaking, she wrenched her rucked skirt down in a desperate movement. Shock was blasting through her and her heart was still racing. She couldn't believe what had just happened. She couldn't believe that she had let him do that to her...something so intimate, so inappropriate, so wanton...

'You were ready for that,' Luciano purred, staring down at her with smouldering dark golden eyes. 'You're a passionate woman.'

But Jemima had *never* been a passionate woman. Steven had told her that passion was for sluts and she had always been careful not to seem too keen in that line because that had seemed to be what he expected from her. When he had plunged into a wild fling with Julie she had been shattered at how quickly he had changed his attitude. Luciano, however, wanted that passion, *thrived* on it, she sensed in confusion, forcing herself to look at him, her face hot and flushed, her sated body still somehow feeling like a wanton stranger's.

'Let's not...talk about it,' she mumbled unsteadily.

'Let's not... I prefer to *do* rather than talk,' Luciano murmured, wondering why she was still acting so oddly. Touching her had been a mistake. He wanted more. Given the smallest encouragement he would have dragged her off to bed and eased the burn of his libido. He didn't want to wait. He wasn't used to waiting but he was suddenly very conscious of who she was. His son's mother. It would be most unwise to rock the boat before they reached the security of his Sicilian home, Castello del Drogo.

'It shouldn't have happened,' Jemima breathed tightly, rising from her seat and snatching up her bag. 'I don't know how it did—'

Luciano was not amused. 'It's simple. I wanted you. You wanted me—'

'I forgot where I was and who I was with for a moment,' Jemima corrected stiffly, still carefully evading his eyes. 'I was out of control.'

'I liked it.' Luciano could not understand why she was in retreat. With his knowledge of her, she should have been making the most of the situation and trying to please him. And he was very much in the mood to be pleased.

'You were talking about Sicily and...er...settling bills,' she reminded him stonily.

Ah, business first. He perfectly understood her change of focus. 'I will take care of them. You will have to sign a confidentiality agreement first. You will not be free to talk to anyone, and that includes the media, about the surrogacy agreement or about me or my son,' he informed her with forbidding cool.

'That's not a problem. I'll go and see if Nicky is awake yet. It'll be time for us to leave soon,' she said with scarcely concealed eagerness as she checked her watch.

Luciano stood watching the door swing shut on her exit. A black winged brow quirked. Was it some sort of a game she played with men? Give a little and then back off? Some men would want her all the more after that type of will-she-won't-she uncertainty. But Luciano was in no doubt that she would ultimately share his bed and her withdrawal irritated him. He hardened even more at the prospect of spreading those soft, rounded thighs and plunging between them until he had attained his pleasure. One night would probably be enough, he decided with a dark smile. He wanted her horizontal. For that single night he wanted her every which way up he could have her. That would work her back out of his system and possibly by that stage he would grasp what had attracted him in the first place.

At least there would be no complications with Jemima, he reflected as he phoned his housekeeper to make household arrangements. Never mind Jemima's little ploys, she knew the score. He would reward her richly for sex, for sharing physical pleasure without emotion or strings, and she would be quite happy to walk away again.

'I'm a close friend of Jemima's and her family,' Steven Warrington declared smugly as he walked into Luciano's office. 'And with respect, I'd like to know why you think it's necessary for her to accompany you and your child to Sicily.'

Luciano surveyed the smaller blond man with shrewd, unimpressed eyes. 'That's my personal business, Mr Warrington. But I see no reason not to tell you that my son is attached to Jemima and I'd like to minimise his sorrow when she moves on.'

'Taking Jemima to Sicily with you seems a strange

way of letting *her* move on,' Steven opined with another smile. 'I'd prefer it if you simply removed your son now and left Jemima to get on with her life unencumbered.'

'Happily your opinion doesn't count,' Luciano fielded.

'It soon will. She's the woman I intend to marry.'

Luciano almost rolled his eyes at the idea of Jemima, with her decided preference for the wilder side of life, anchored by a wedding ring to the highly conservative male in front of him, but his lean, dark features remained unrevealing. 'Congratulations,' he responded smoothly.

The information he had already requested on Steven Warrington was finally rolling up on Luciano's computer screen as the younger man departed. Had Luciano the patience, he would have received that information *before* agreeing to see Warrington but curiosity had driven Luciano to depart from his habitual caution. So, Steven was an ex and there was a very, *very* long list of exes in Jemima's chequered past. Did she leave them all longing for a raunchy repeat? Although not the ones whose wallets she had lifted, Luciano conceded, while wondering why that aspect of her nature didn't bother him more. She was a thief. Why did he want to bed her? He had never knowingly wanted to bed a deceitful woman before. Having grown up in the shadows of a crime-fuelled household, he was not drawn to the dark side in any way. Unlike his late father he was temperate and controlled.

Maybe he had been too ascetic in his habits for too long, he reasoned in frustration, because he was still struggling to understand the key to Jemima Barber's appeal. Even so, he wanted her and on those grounds he would have her simply because remarkably few things in life gave Luciano genuine pleasure. Steven Warrington's self-righteousness amused him. Jemima had no plans to marry Steven. He was quite sure of that.

But somehow that didn't eradicate an almost overwhelming temptation to smash a fist through Steven's blindingly white teeth. Luciano didn't comprehend the urge and he suppressed it, thoroughly off-balanced by that sudden lurch towards violence. He had felt it before, of course he had, with his very genes drenched in the violence and corruption of his forebears. But never ever had he had that experience where a woman was concerned and that awareness unsettled him. One night. He would have her in his bed for only one night, he assured himself grimly.

In any case, he reflected thoughtfully, it was not as though he could be at any real risk with Jemima, because Luciano didn't do emotional connections with anyone. His son would be the sole exception to that rule. Loving and caring for a child was pure and it wouldn't damage him or anybody else.

'I think it's the best solution for everybody,' Ellie declared bravely while Jemima was trying to console her weeping mother and her deeply troubled father as the four of them sat round the kitchen table over mugs of tea.

Jemima was feeling sick with shame at having hidden so much from her adoptive parents and she still did not feel up to the challenge of telling them the truth. They would have been horrified if they knew that she was pretending to be her dead sister and faking being Nicky's mother. No argument she could make would persuade them that such dishonesty was justified. In any case her parents were already dealing with quite enough. The older couple had returned from Devon only that morning to learn that their daughter and Nicky would be leaving the next day for a trip to Sicily, following which Jemima would be returning home *alone*. Unfortunately Julie's son had become as dear to Jemima's parents as any grandchild. They too had been part of Nicky's life almost from birth.

'Nicky is Luciano's son and the poor guy's been searching for him all these months,' Ellie pointed out, trying hard to support her friend's arguments in favour of the trip to Sicily and the inevitable surrendering of Nicky to his sole surviving parent.

'I believe he'll be a good father. He's only asking me along because he knows Nicky's attached to me and he doesn't want him to be hurt by me suddenly disappearing from his life,' Jemima explained afresh.

'Mr Vitale *is* being responsible,' her father conceded thoughtfully. 'Although I could never condone the agreement he made with Julie. That was rash and she was the worst possible candidate he could've chosen—'

'Yes, but don't forget it wasn't Julie he really picked. He believed he was picking Jemima.' Ellie was quick to remind the older man that Julie had applied to be a surrogate using her twin's identity rather than her own.

'True and you've certainly stood by the little chap,

giving him what he needs to flourish,' Jemima's father said to his daughter with warm approval. 'I suppose we'll simply have to wait until our daughter gives us a grandchild to fuss over, my dear,' he said to his wife.

Jemima paled beneath that look of approbation. She knew just how shocked her parents would be if they ever learned about the deceit she had employed in her dealings with Luciano.

That same morning, Charles Bennett made a return visit with a colleague in tow. He read through the confidentiality agreement with Jemima and explained every clause while his companion informed Jemima that he was there on her behalf to protect her interests. He spoke up on several occasions, pointing out that a lot of money could be made from selling stories to the media but that choosing to abide by Luciano's rules would be financially rewarded by a bonus once she had finished working for him. Jemima signed on the dotted line and was grateful when the lawyers left.

Later that same day, Ellie stood by grinning while Jemima patiently stood and obediently posed while all her measurements were taken and carefully noted down by the middle-aged female tailor and her assistant who had also called at Luciano's request.

'So, he's planning for you to wear a nanny uniform?' Ellie remarked teasingly after the women had departed.

Jemima pulled a face. 'Obviously,' she pointed out ruefully, far from looking forward to the prospect of being dressed in some starchy formal outfit in the Sicilian heat.

'I suppose it's one good way of ensuring that you

don't forget that you're one of the workers rather than a guest... I mean, it could be a bit awkward with you supposedly being Nicky's mother,' her friend opined with a wince. 'When are you planning to tell Luciano that you're Julie's sister?'

Jemima grimaced. 'Probably not until I'm leaving Sicily, which will be the end of August at the latest because term starts the following week and I'll be starting teaching again,' she reminded the other woman. 'It would be a bit of a risk admitting my true identity any sooner than that because Luciano could just ask me to leave immediately but by late August it's hardly going to matter to him.'

'Stop beating yourself up about it. You're not doing anyone any harm—'

'It's not that simple, Ellie. Every time I'm with Luciano I'm *lying* to him,' Jemima pointed out heavily, wishing she had found it possible to confide in Ellie about how much more complicated her relationship with Luciano had recently become. The problem was that she was too ashamed to admit that their strained relationship had suddenly—inexplicably, to her—dived into the kind of intimacy she had always held back from.

Only three days had passed since that day in London and she still lay in her bed at night unable to quite accept that she had fooled around with Luciano to the extent that she had forgotten not only the tenets that she had been raised by, but also everything she could not afford to forget about her current predicament. She was acting as Julie, not herself, and, although she was convinced that her late sister would also have succumbed to the advances of a gorgeous billionaire, she knew she couldn't grasp at that as an excuse for her behaviour. In reality she had lost control and had allowed herself to be swept away on a roller coaster of sexual sensation new to her. She had acted like a giddy teenager rather than a grown-up, had lived in the moment, had *rejoiced* in the moment without any thought of what it would be like to meet Luciano again or to work for him in an official capacity.

'You're lying *solely* for Nicky's benefit,' Ellie told her with loyal reassurance. 'And by going to Sicily with Nicky you're making all these changes easier for him—'

Jemima gave her friend an anxious look. 'So you think I'm doing the right thing?'

'I always thought that the best solution for Nicky was to be with the father who arranged for him to be born. He's a lovely child, I can see that, but he's not *your* child. I hate to agree with Steven about anything but I do want you to get your own life back,' her friend told her ruefully. 'Be young, free and single again. You deserve that. Nicky was Julie's mistake.'

Jemima compressed her lips and said nothing. She could not think of Nicky's bright, loving existence as a mistake on any terms and being single and free had proved a less fun-filled experience for her than she had been led to expect. Nicky was part of her life now and she loved him. She had not carried her nephew through a pregnancy but the little boy felt as much a part of her as though she had. She knew that walking away from him was going to hurt her a lot, but, if that was truly what was best for Nicky in the long run, she would have to learn to live with that.

The next morning, Jemima, Nicky and their luggage were collected by a limousine accompanied by a car full of bodyguards. The trip to the airport was accomplished in record time and even boarding the private jet awaiting them was a fairly smooth and speedy experience. Jemima was surprised that Luciano was not on board and that, indeed, she and Nicky appeared to be the only passengers aside of the security staff, who took seats at the rear of the plane. The cabin crew made a big fuss of Nicky and were unceasingly attentive.

Luciano boarded in Paris, where he'd had a meeting, and the first thing he noticed was Jemima, curled up fast asleep in a reclining seat with Nicky out for the count beside her in his fancy travelling seat. Her mane of hair was braided when he wanted to see it loose again…even though he knew much of that hair was fake? He shook off that awkward question and scanned the worn jeans and casual washed-out top she sported with a frown of incomprehension forming between his dark brows. Why had she not yet made the effort to dress up for him…even once? No woman had ever been so sure of her hold on Luciano's interest that she would show up garbed almost as poorly as a homeless person! Or was this deliberate dressing down and this avoidance of glamour merely Jemima's highly effective way of ensuring that he bought her a new wardrobe?

Jemima wakened slowly, comfortably rested after having endured a final nervous, sleepless night in her parents' home. Luciano now sat across the aisle. Drowsily she studied his perfect profile, thinking that no man should have lashes that long, that dark or that lush or a nose and a jaw that would not have disgraced a Greek god. Butterflies found wings in her stomach and fluttered. Luciano turned his handsome dark head and she encountered dark golden eyes as lustrous as melting honey. A little quiver ran through her like a tightening piece of elastic, unleashing far less innocent responses that made her squirm with self-consciousness.

'We'll be landing in thirty minutes.'

'Right...er...I'll go and freshen up,' Jemima muttered, sliding out of her seat.

For a split second he gazed up at her, scanning the bloom of soft pink warming the porcelain complexion, which merely enhanced the ice-blue-diamond effect of her unusual eyes and the full softness of the lips he had already tasted. And his body reacted as instantly as a starving man facing a banquet, urgency and hunger combining in a mind-blowing storm of response. His strong jaw line clenching, Luciano gritted his even white teeth angrily and looked away, schooling himself to coldness again.

He didn't like losing control. He had never liked losing control. He had often seen his father lose his head in temper and living through the experience unscathed had been a challenge for everyone around him. Luciano had little fear that he himself would erupt into mindless violence, but he was absolutely convinced that reactions like passion and anger twisted a man's thinking processes and made bad decisions and human errors more likely. She would be in his bed this very night, he reminded himself soothingly. He would have what he wanted, what he increasingly felt he *needed* from her, and then this temporary insanity would be over and done with, decently laid to rest between the sheets. It astonished him, it even slightly unnerved him, that sexual desire could exercise that much power over him.

Jemima concentrated on the mechanics of feeding and changing Nicky while stubbornly denying herself the opportunity to look back in Luciano's direction. He was gorgeous and he had to know he was gorgeous. After all, he saw himself every time he shaved, she thought wildly. But that was not an excuse to stare and blush and act all silly like an adolescent who didn't know how to behave around a man. Absolutely not any sort of an excuse at all, Jemima reminded herself doggedly as she abstractedly admired how much Nicky's glossy black curls resembled his father's and resisted the urge to make another quite unnecessary visual comparison.

Suddenly the thought that she would be in Luciano's vicinity for the rest of the summer was a daunting one. She could never act polite and indifferent in the company of such a dynamic and passionate male. He lit her up like a fire inside but she ought to be fighting that tooth and nail. She was *lying* to Luciano and he was Nicky's father, which meant that there was no possibility of any normal relationship developing between them. Keeping her distance and resisting temptation were what she needed to do. Intellectually she knew that…but knowing and actually doing were two very different things, as she had already discovered. Unfortunately for her peace of mind, Luciano's attraction yanked at her on every possible level…

CHAPTER FIVE

Luciano's phone buzzed into life after they landed, shooting out a string of text messages and missed calls, every one of which hailed from his British lawyer, Charles Bennett. His mouth quirking as he wondered what could possibly have prompted the relaxed Charles to such an uncharacteristic display of urgency, Luciano phoned the older man as soon as he stepped inside the airport.

'I have the worst possible news for you. We've all been conned,' Charles announced with rare drama the instant the call connected. 'Jemima Barber is *not* the mother of your child—'

Luciano froze and waved an impatient hand at his bodyguards to silence their chatter while he listened. 'That's not possible,' he declared.

'I haven't got all the details yet and I won't waste your time with speculation but I believe that the mother of your child was one of an identical set of twins. She died when she was struck by a car a couple of months ago,' the lawyer explained curtly.

Luciano was frowning darkly. 'Which would mean—'

'That at best our Jemima is an aunt to the boy and

a con artist,' Charles framed drily. 'I have a top-flight set of investigators digging into this right now and I expect to have the whole story for you by this evening at the latest.'

'How sure are you of these facts?' Luciano prompted, watching Jemima detach his son's clinging fingers from her hanging golden braid. *Not* Niccolò's mother? How could that be? His brain, usually so fast to adapt to new scenarios, was for some reason still struggling to find solid ground in this shift of circumstances.

'Take it from me—she's definitely *not* the woman who gave birth to the boy. I now have that woman's real name along with a copy of her *death* certificate. She called herself Julie Marshall. Matters are complicated by the fact that from the very beginning of your dealings with Julie, your son's real mother was using Jemima Barber's identity to hide behind.'

'But why? You believe this was a conspiracy from the start?'

'Who can tell? With one of them dead it's doubtful that the full truth will ever be known,' Charles pointed out cynically.

Rage began to shadow Luciano's rational mind as the ramifications for his son began to filter into his thoughts. His son's mother had deceived him and his staff from day one and now she was dead and, as such, untouchable. Luciano was his son's only living relative. He refused to credit that an aunt could possibly have a claim to challenge his own. So, naturally, Jemima had not owned up to the truth. After all, her only way of making a profit through Niccolò was by *pretending* to be his birth mother.

As they climbed into a limousine outside the airport Luciano watched his son nestle trustingly into Jemima's arms and then complain loudly at being placed in the car seat instead. His lean dark features shadowed. He was finally a parent and already he had failed. He had failed to protect his son from hurt. Niccolò had been encouraged to form a bond with his two-faced, duplicitous aunt and would be emotionally bereft when the woman disappeared from his world. Who did Luciano blame for the formation of that deceptive bond? Jemima Barber! She must've known from the outset that her only weapon would be the baby's attachment to her. Niccolò was only a baby but he had already been tricked into bestowing affection where he should not. Luciano, in a rage beyond anything he had ever experienced, ground his even white teeth together while he pretended an interest in the emails on his tablet.

She was a lying, cheating *prostituta* with a stone for a heart! And just like her late sister, the only thing that greased the wheels in Jemima's world was money. There was no other explanation for her behaviour! At any time she could have admitted the truth but she had preferred to lie and stage a scam to ensure that she wielded the greatest power she could and made the biggest possible profit out of her dishonesty. In ignorance Luciano had agreed to settle her debts—her sister's debts?—and had made the mistake of offering her an all-expenses-paid trip to Sicily. And she would have even more cause to celebrate when she saw what awaited her at the castle...

Of course he didn't *want* her now, he told himself fiercely. He wanted nothing more to do with her and out of sight would be out of mind. How long had it been since a woman put one over on him? He suppressed a shudder of all too fresh recollection. What did it say about him that the women who most attracted him were thoroughly immoral and unscrupulous characters? Was that some hangover from his ancestral forebears? Something dark and shady in his blood that slyly influenced his choices?

Although Jemima was trying not to stare at Luciano she was convinced that something unpleasant had happened. She had watched his lean, darkly handsome face freeze into rigidity while he was talking on the phone at the airport. Had he received bad news? Some business setback? Or something of a more personal nature? Jemima acknowledged how very little she actually knew about Luciano Vitale. He was a widower who had lost a wife and a daughter and that was the summit of her information. But whatever was amiss, Luciano's jaw was rock hard with tension and he had barely acknowledged the existence of Jemima and his son since the jet had landed. Ironically, Nicky, who acted up whenever Luciano actively tried to get closer to him, now chose to stretch out an inviting hand towards his father, who might as well have been on another planet for all the interest he was showing in him. Still, there was yet another similarity between the two of them, Jemima reflected helplessly. Neither one of them could *bear* to be ignored...and ten to one that was exactly why Nicky was vying for attention now.

The limousine came to a halt and Jemima looked out of the window, surprised to see various aircraft parked. 'Where are we?' she asked.

'A private airfield. I use a helicopter to fly to my home,' Luciano divulged, his firmly modelled lips compressing.

Jemima's eyes widened in surprise. She had never been on a helicopter before and yet he evidently regularly used them just to travel home. Nothing could have more easily illustrated the vast gulf between their worlds. While they were boarding the helicopter, there was no further conversation, which was probably just as well because Jemima was concentrating on her exciting new experience.

As the helicopter took off Jemima peered out of the window to watch a slice of sea appear at a crazy angle. Her brow pleated in astonishment when the craft then flew out directly over the water. Where on earth were they going? Naturally she had assumed that Luciano's home was either in a city or in the mountainous interior but as the minutes passed on their seabound journey it was clear that their destination could only be another island.

She watched land appear again with keen interest. A bright patchwork of forested slopes, olive groves and a vast brown building on the shoreline of a long beach appeared. The building had towers and turrets like a castle, and as the helicopter dropped down to land in the manicured grounds enclosed by tall boundary walls she realised that it *was* a genuine castle.

'What's this place called?' she asked as she hopped down onto the grass and approached Luciano to take Nicky back off him.

'Castello del Drogo. The island is named for it. I'll keep him,' Luciano told her, hoisting the sleepy baby against his shoulder in a blatantly protective movement, his eyes as dark and cool as the night sky and about as far from melting honey as eyes could get, she thought ruefully.

Refusing to be quieted by his discouraging coldness, Jemima smiled. 'How long have you lived here?'

'A couple of years. It has the privacy I need. Intruders can only approach by sky or sea and both are monitored. I can walk by the sea here without fear of a camera appearing from the bushes,' he spelt out flatly.

They got into the beach buggy waiting to waft them up to the doors of the castle. Jemima was smiling, her earlier concerns forgotten as she rejoiced in the warmth of late afternoon and the beautiful gardens surrounding them. It would be really interesting to stay in a castle, she thought absently, studying the imposing fortress before her. 'How old is it?'

'The oldest section is medieval, the youngest eighteenth century.'

They mounted shallow steps to the giant porticoed entrance where two women awaited their arrival. Both wore black, one of possibly pensioner age and the other around fortyish.

The hall was an imposing oval shape with a marble

floor and black ebonised furniture inlaid with mother-of-pearl. Jemima was silenced by the sheer splendour of the castle, especially when she compared it to her parents' tiny retirement home. How could she ever have denied Nicky the wealthy lifestyle that his father evidently enjoyed?

'Do you own the whole island?' she whispered, unable to contain her curiosity.

'Yes,' he admitted in the sort of tone that implied that it was not a very big deal to own your own island, and in Jemima's mind the gulf between them stretched even wider.

Luciano introduced the older woman as his housekeeper, Agnese, and the younger as her daughter and Nicky's new nanny, Carlotta. He settled the baby into Carlotta's arms and addressed her in Italian. Jemima reminded herself doggedly of her agreement to step back from Nicky as he was borne off screaming, presumably to be fed and put to bed. As Carlotta mounted the stairs Jemima could hear her talking softly and soothingly to the distressed baby and her concern eased a little.

'Agnese will show you to your room,' Luciano announced.

Agnese's small creased face was as frozen as an ice sculpture. Telling herself that that was still preferable to a dirty look, Jemima followed the older woman upstairs and down a tiled passageway with ancient stone walls. Double doors were flung wide and light flooded across the most amazing bedroom Jemima had ever seen. Tall windows cast sunshine over the sumptuously hung four-poster bed. Gorgeous furniture vied with opulent fabric and a glorious floral arrangement to take her attention. Taken aback as she realised that the palatial room was for her use, Jemima hovered by the little table bearing the magnificent flowers and watched wide-eyed as an actual maid in a uniform appeared through one of the several additional doors to smile and stand back as though waiting to usher Jemima into the room she had vacated.

The housekeeper indicated with her hand that Jemima should take the invitation and Jemima obediently walked into a very large dressing room lined with built-in furniture. And that was when the show began. The maid began opening doors and rifling through hangers packed with garments to display them. Racks of shoes, drawers filled with silky lingerie and a dressing-table unit packed with cosmetics below a mirror surrounded by special lighting were duly shown off. Jemima's jaw dropped while she attempted to work out what all these items could possibly have to do with her. The maid passed her a tiny gift envelope and she slid out the card.

With my compliments, Luciano.

Jemima blinked and looked again, fingers tightening round the card as it slowly sank in on her that she had not been measured up for a nanny uniform as she had assumed but for a new wardrobe. She broke out in perspiration, her jeans uncomfortably warm. Luciano had given her a vast new wardrobe and as she flipped with anxious hands through the nearest selection she realised that it was all designer stuff, filled with famous fashion labels that even she, who didn't follow fashion, had heard of. She was gobsmacked, so gobsmacked that when the maid and the housekeeper departed she simply sank down on the boudoir chair by the dresser and stared back at her own unadorned face. Her face looked weird in the fancy lights, oddly bare and shocked, and she breathed in deep and stumbled upright to peel off her jeans before she could expire from heat exhaustion. In the bedroom she opened the suitcase she had travelled with and yanked out a cool cotton skirt to step into it.

But she still couldn't think straight. Indeed all she could think about was the contents of the dressing room. What on earth had she done to give Luciano the impression that such an extravagant gesture would be welcome? Her tummy gave a nauseous flip and she shut her eyes tight, hot colour burning her cheeks. Oh, yes, she knew what she had done. She hadn't said no when she should've. She hadn't said yes either, she reflected numbly. She had simply let him do what he wished. And evidently that had been sufficient to encourage Luciano to go out and spend thousands and thousands and thousands of pounds to enable her to dress like a queen. Hands cool now with shock, she pressed them to her hot cheeks and groaned out loud. My goodness, what was she going to do?

She was supposed to be Julie and Julie would have been ecstatic. Julie had adored clothes and everything her sister wore had carried a logo. Jemima blinked and wandered back into the dressing room. She trailed an uncertain hand across the soft smooth briefs still visible in an open drawer and sighed heavily. The clothing had been tailored to her exact height and size, but how could she wear it? How could she possibly say thank you and just wear it?

Neither a borrower nor a lender be and being wary of unexpected gifts was how Jemima had been raised. She also knew that old adage about being true to oneself. And accepting such largesse when she had done nothing to deserve it ran contrary to her principles. She swallowed back a heartfelt groan while she surveyed the racks of shoes. If Jemima had a weakness, it was for shoes and she swore her toes tingled like a water diviner's when she saw the cross-strapped green high heels studded with tiny twinkly stones. They called out to her feet and, kicking off her serviceable pumps, she slid her yearning toes into those tempting shoes. Yes, this was the way to be gracious, the only way not to throw all of Luciano's generosity back in his teeth; she would accept one small item to show gratitude. Having bolstered herself with that argument, Jemima tottered downstairs in her wholly inappropriate footwear.

Agnese was waiting for her like a little old witch in the hall.

'I'm looking for Luciano,' Jemima announced with a pleasant smile.

Agnese was eying the frivolous shoes with rampant censure. 'Il Capo is in the library.'

Il capo meant 'the boss', Jemima translated, having watched enough Godfather movies to recognise the lingo. Walking with precise but wobbling care in the direction of Agnese's pointing hand, Jemima wondered if the new wardrobe had given Agnese the wrong idea about the precise nature of Jemima's relationship with Luciano, and then she scolded herself for wondering, reckoning she had more to worry about than the suspicion that the staff had disliked her on sight.

Luciano had had four drinks in succession while he waited for Charles to call. His father had been a drinker and it was very rare for Luciano to drink to excess but his impatience to know the finer details of the scam was literally eating him alive. He couldn't wait to confront Jemima but he would not do it until he knew everything there was to know about her. He was *so* angry with her, so bemused by the strange conflict tearing at him. He was in turmoil and he didn't know why, which simply added another layer of hostile frustration to his mood.

Frowning at the sound of the knock on the library door, Luciano strode across the room to drag it open and discover who had dared to disturb him when he had requested peace. When he focused on Jemima's glowing, eagerly smiling face, he found himself taking a step back because he was initially surprised to see that she was happy. *But then she didn't know yet that he knew.* Of course she was happy, he ruminated bitterly, rage arrowing through him afresh. What else would she be but happy when he'd put her in a bedroom next door to his and given her a fortune in designer clothing? She was a gold-digger; naturally she was happy with her rewards. By bringing in Carlotta, he had even released

Jemima from the burden of constant childcare and very probably she was even happier about the prospect of greater freedom as well...

'Luciano...' she said softly and then her eyes flew off him to dart round the book-filled shelves. 'Oh, my, what a wonderful room! You are so lucky to have so much space for books,' she remarked chirpily.

'Is there a reason for your visit?' Luciano enquired forbiddingly, his attention clinging to her when she lurched a little on her path towards his desk at the centre of the room. His gaze skated down over her back view, lingering with pleasure on the ripe, rounded curve of her bottom shaped by the stretchy, clinging texture of the skirt she wore. His attention was then unwillingly caught by the colourful, glittery and ridiculously high-heeled shoes she wore below the skirt. For some reason she had teamed incongruous party shoes with her drab outfit and she could hardly walk in them, he registered in surprise as she clutched the side of his desk to steady herself.

Jemima studied Luciano and any hint of clear thought wilfully evaded her. No male that extraordinarily gorgeous could possibly encourage rational reflection in a woman, she conceded ruefully. He looked so tense and angry. His cheekbones were starkly defined, the line of his strong jaw rock hard. Yes, something had definitely gone wrong in his life. She was knocked sideways by the sudden realisation that just as Nicky's bad moods made her want to fix things for him, Luciano provoked the same need in her, only she didn't for one moment think that a cuddle and a soothing bottle would provide a magic cure for whatever ailed him.

Yet she still could not resist the temptation to offer. 'Can I help with whatever's wrong?'

'Why the hell would you think there's something wrong?' Luciano demanded harshly, hugely disconcerted by the question when in his experience other people couldn't read him at all well.

'Because there so obviously is,' Jemima pointed out, wishing he didn't have such stunning eyes. So dark and lustrous and sexy and absolute killers when fringed by black curling lashes into the bargain.

Unsettled by that assurance, Luciano gritted his teeth.

'You're so cross,' Jemima pointed out gently.

'I am not cross,' Luciano growled.

'I'll just mind my own business, then,' Jemima muttered, caving into the tension sparking like lightning rods through the atmosphere.

'Perhaps that would be best,' Luciano riposted very drily.

Her face flamed and she roamed restively over to the tall windows that overlooked flower beds surrounded by low box hedges and an ancient mossy fountain. 'I came down to speak to you about the new clothes you bought for me.' In emphasis she lifted a foot to show off the shoe she wore and very nearly fell over. All dignity abandoned, she grabbed at the back of an armchair to stay upright and hastily put that foot back on the floor. 'Er…these shoes are gorgeous… In fact it's all gorgeous, but with the possible exception of these shoes I can't possibly accept an entire wardrobe.'

'Why not?' Luciano shot back at her, startling her with that blunt comeback. 'And turn round and face me when you're speaking to me.'

With great reluctance and carefully slow movements, Jemima turned and straight away registered why she preferred talking to him without looking at him. Face on he was too much of a distraction. She lowered her lashes, blocking him out to some extent, her soft mouth unusually taut with nerves. 'Well, I'm very grateful for your generosity but I don't believe in accepting expensive gifts from people—'

'I'm not *people*!' Luciano cut in with ruthless bite. 'And I would hazard a guess that you have often accepted such gifts from men—'

'Yes...er...but that doesn't mean it was right. Having done it before, I don't have to keep on doing it,' Jemima pointed out, gathering steam in her argument. 'Maybe I think it's time for me to change my ways?'

'Maybe there are two blue moons in the sky,' Luciano incised with ringing derision.

'Being with Nicky *has* changed me,' Jemima argued, setting off on another tack. 'It's made me appreciate what's really important in life.'

'Within hours of his birth you had already decided what was really important to you...more money,' Luciano reminded her cruelly.

Jemima lifted her chin. 'But that doesn't mean I can't develop a different outlook. And I have changed. If you must know, I'm trying to turn over a new leaf.'

His dark eyes glittering like polished jet, Luciano vented a laugh of unholy amusement. 'I assume that's your idea of a joke...'

'No, it's not actually,' Jemima told him tightly, thinking sadly of the number of times her late twin had spoken of that same ambition to her. 'Everybody has to start somewhere when they make changes. I mean, why would you give me all those clothes anyway, for goodness' sake?'

'You're not that naïve.'

Her colour heightened. 'So, obviously it was a gift made with certain expectations, and if I'm not prepared to meet those expectations, I can't possibly accept it.'

'Of course you're prepared to meet my expectations.' Luciano surveyed her with galling assurance, smouldering dark golden eyes roaming over her with a potent sexuality that made her tremble. Her nipples prickled below her clothing and a tiny burst of heat ignited in her pelvis, starting up a nagging throb of awareness.

'I'm only here for a few weeks of summer for your son's benefit,' Jemima reminded him stubbornly. 'His benefit, *not* yours.'

Luciano said a rude word in English that made her flinch.

'I'm trying to be reasonable and honest here to avoid misunderstandings,' she told him in growing frustration.

Luciano stalked closer, silent and graceful as a night-time predator, and said an even ruder word in dismissal of that statement. What did such a woman know about honesty? What had she ever known?

He was so close now that Jemima could have reached out and touched him. Her heart was thudding out a staccato beat of apprehension and her breathing had ruptured into winded audible snatches.

She stiffened her spine and tilted her head to one side. 'I don't like your language.'

'I don't like what you're saying. I get very irritated when those around me talk nonsense or tell lies,' Luciano told her grittily, his Italian accent liquefying every vowel sound. 'You're trying to say that you don't want me and that is a *huge* lie!'

Her pale blue eyes widened. 'Are you always this sure of your own attraction?'

Long brown fingers lifted her braid from her shoulder and detached the tie on the end. He began to unlace the long golden strands. 'I want to see your hair loose…'

A new leaf, he was ruminating in disbelief. Could she really believe that he would be impressed by such drivel? How could she look at him with those luminous ice-blue eyes that seemed so candid and continue to lie and lie to his face? She was a completely shameless and stupid liar. Anger, bitter and jagged as a knife edge, cut through Luciano, burning and scarring wherever it touched. He was all too familiar with the cunning cleverness of female lies.

'This is getting too…too intense,' Jemima muttered uncertainly.

Luciano wound long fingers into the golden mane

of her hair to tug her closer. 'You shouldn't lie to me. If you knew how angry it makes me, you wouldn't do it.'

Her nostrils flared on the scent of him that close. Some expensive lemony cologne overlaid with clean, husky male and a faint hint of alcohol was assailing her and her tummy performed a nervous somersault. 'I'm going back home in just a few weeks,' she reminded him shakily. 'I'm only here for Nicky.'

'Liar...my son was not your primary motivation,' Luciano derided in a raw undertone, thoroughly fed up with her foolish pretences. 'You came here to be with me. Of course you did.'

Her brows pleated in dismay. 'Luciano...you're not listening to me—'

'Why would I listen when you're talking nonsense?' he demanded with sudden harshness.

Jemima looked up at him, scanning the dark golden eyes that inexplicably turned her insides to mush and made her knees boneless. As he lowered his head her breath caught in her throat and her pupils dilated. Without warning his arms went round her, possessive hands delving down her spine to splay across the ripe swell of her hips and haul her close. His mouth crashed down on hers with hungry force and in the space of a heartbeat she travelled from consternation to satisfaction. That kiss was what she really wanted, what her body mysteriously craved.

He kissed her and the world swam out of focus and her brain shut down and suppressed all the anxious thoughts that had been tormenting her. It was simultaneously everything she most wanted and everything she most feared. To be shot from ordinary planet earth into the dazzling orbit of passion and need by a single kiss was what she had always dreamt of finding in a man's arms, but Luciano was by no stretch of the imagination the male she had pictured in such a role. After all, Luciano wasn't for real. She might be inexperienced but she wasn't stupid and she knew that sex would only be a game with him and that he would only play with her without any intention of offering anything worthwhile. A woman needed a tough heart to play such games as an equal and she knew she wasn't up to that challenge.

'You want me,' Luciano grated against her red swollen mouth, his breath warming her cheek and bringing the faint scent of alcohol to her awareness.

Jemima shivered violently against the unyielding confines of his lean, muscular body. She loved the strength and hardness of his well-honed frame. Even through their clothes she could feel him hot and ready against her and the tight ache at the heart of her was like a strangling knot that yearned for freedom. The taste of his mouth was still on hers, nerve cells jangling with the longing for a repeat and the erotic plunge of his tongue. With a receptive shudder that signified the strength the gesture demanded, she brought up her hands and pressed against his broad chest to drive some space between them.

'No, not like this,' she mumbled gruffly, fighting herself as much as she was fighting his attraction.

She wanted him. He was right about that. She had never wanted anything or anybody as much as she wanted Luciano at that moment. Pulling free of him, stepping back, physically hurt as unsated cravings set up a drumbeat of angry dissatisfaction throughout her quivering body. Kicking off the silly shoes that limited her mobility was the work of seconds and her sudden loss of height disconcerted him into lifting his arms off her in surprise. Ducking out of reach and barefoot, Jemima darted round him and pelted out of the door as though baying hounds were chasing her.

Black brows pleating, Luciano swept up the abandoned shoes and looked at them incredulously. Did she think she was Cinderella or something? In bewilderment, because a woman had never before treated him to such stop-go tactics, he poured himself another stiff drink. He didn't get it. He really didn't understand why she was running away. Why would she do that? What possible benefit could she hope to attain by infuriating him?

And then the proverbial penny dropped and he wondered why he had not immediately grasped her strategy. After all, it was an exceedingly basic strategy: she wanted *more*. In fact Jemima or Julie or whatever she and her late twin had chosen to call themselves had been born wanting more. And she knew he was rich enough to deliver a *lot* more. Only he wouldn't, Luciano thought angrily, stoking up his resentment and his hostility. He was determined not to further reward a woman who had lied and schemed to make a profit out of his infant son as though he were a product on sale to the highest bidder.

CHAPTER SIX

BREATHLESS, JEMIMA LEANT back against the door she had slammed behind her in her haste to reach her bedroom. Well, so much for turning down the gift of the clothes with charm and diplomacy! Hadn't that gone well? She grimaced and groaned out loud. Why did she make such a mess of everything with Luciano? What happened to her brain? What happened to tact? Why had she kissed him back as though her life depended on it? Resisting him, acting repulsed would have kept him at bay, but instead she had encouraged him.

The trouble was, she thought ruefully, nobody had ever made her feel as Luciano Vitale did. When she was at college before she'd begun seeing Steven, plenty of men had tried to get her into bed. In fact being constantly badgered for sex had put her off dating. Ironically, though, she had not set out to still be virtually untouched at the age of almost twenty-four. Her parents might believe that she should remain a virgin until she married but Jemima had focused on a more attainable goal. She had believed that she would retain her virginity until she met someone she loved and she had believed she loved Steven, but Steven had seemed to prize her virginal state even more than her parents and had insisted that they should respect church teaching and wait until they were man and wife. Yet how quickly he had abandoned that conviction when true temptation had come along in the guise of her much sexier sister, she reflected wryly.

'You can't turn your back on true love,' Steven had told her self-righteously before he had gone off with her twin. 'Julie's the perfect woman for me.'

But Jemima couldn't tell herself the same thing about Luciano, not least because she didn't believe that he was perfect. He was arrogant and domineering and too rich and powerful for his own good. Yet she was madly, wildly and irrationally attracted to him. In addition she respected his sincere affection for Nicky. She also liked Luciano on a level she couldn't quite explain even to herself, for she did not know where that liking had come from or on what she based it. In the same way, when Luciano was angry and exasperated as he had been earlier she automatically wanted to make everything better for him and improve his mood. Why she felt like that she didn't know because common sense warned her that Luciano was wrong for her in every possible way. They were too different as people.

Sex was a pursuit in itself for Luciano, an amusement and not necessarily part of a meaningful relationship. Yet he *had* done commitment in the past. He had been married and a father before she'd even met him and at a relatively young age, Jemima reminded herself, and that suggested that while Luciano might have the reputation of being a womaniser he had always had a deeper and more caring side to his nature.

Across the room, a door opened and she glanced up. Luciano, his jacket and tie discarded, strolled towards her in his shirtsleeves.

'What on earth are you doing in here?' Jemima exclaimed in consternation.

'Finding you. You ran away,' Luciano condemned. 'Have you any idea how irritating that is?'

'You were being too pushy.'

'I'm naturally pushy.'

'That's not an acceptable excuse.'

'You were trying to pretend you don't want me,' Luciano reminded her with a sudden edge of accusation. 'That was an outright lie!'

'It's arrogant to be so full of yourself.'

Luciano shrugged a broad shoulder sheathed in smooth cotton. 'I'm not the modest type and I know when I'm wanted.'

And he would have had plenty of practice in that line, Jemima reckoned, scanning his lean, dark, flawless features and the intoxicating whole of his fallen angel beauty, which knocked her for six every time she looked at him. That was so superficial of her, she scolded herself, but when she was gazing at Luciano her brain could not concentrate on anything else. In any case her body hummed like an engine raring to go in his radius, making it difficult for her to breathe or move, never mind think.

'Perhaps you're waiting for me to offer you a villa or an apartment in Palermo or Rome or Paris...a less temporary and more rewarding position in my life?' Luciano suggested smooth as glass.

'Why would I want you to offer me a villa or an apartment?' Jemima asked him in genuine bewilderment.

'A mistress has some security. A casual lover has none,' Luciano pointed out.

'I really don't know what we're talking about here. I thought mistresses died out with corsets,' she confided jerkily, unnerved by the dialogue because he could not possibly be asking someone like her to be his mistress, his *kept* woman. That idea struck her as so ridiculous that a nervous giggle bubbled in the back of her throat.

'I don't want to talk,' Luciano breathed with sudden lancing impatience as he met her pale aquamarine gaze. He ran his hands through the thick tangle of hair tumbling round her shoulders. 'I like your hair. It's so long. Are you wearing extensions?'

'No, it's all me,' Jemima muttered breathlessly, because he was standing so close now that she could feel the heat of his body striking hers.

And right there, he knew he had her because he knew for a fact that only a few months earlier his son's mother had had short hair. But he had already accepted that she was a lying fake, hadn't he? Charles Bennett didn't make mistakes. Yet, trailing his fingertips through that lustrous skein of golden silk, Luciano couldn't have cared less about who Jemima was or what she was. He only wanted to see that marvellous hair spread across his pillows and without hesitation he bent and lifted her up.

'Put me down, Luciano!' she gasped.

'No,' he said simply. 'I want you.'

'That's not enough!'

Luciano shouldered open the door between their bedrooms. 'It's enough for me, *piccolo mia*.'

And she was on the brink of telling him why it wasn't enough for her when he kissed her, kissed her long and hard and hungrily until the blood drummed in her head and her toes curled and her mind went blank. Her fingers reached up and delved into his black curls, shaping his proud head, roaming down the back of his neck. The need to touch him was so powerful it overwhelmed every other prompting, even the cautious vibes trying to tug her back to sanity.

Luciano settled her down on his bed and studied her with immense satisfaction. He knew what she was. He knew what she was capable of. But he could not be damaged by a known threat. Her greed was a weakness he would use to control her, he reflected with satisfaction while only dimly questioning what had happened to his belief that one night would be sufficient for him. He knew he wasn't fully in control and it made him feel outrageously free of his rigid rules to do as he liked. She would be his for as long as he wanted her and that was all that currently mattered to him. He bent down and crushed her ripe mouth under his again, one hand closing to the rounded curve of her breast and feeling the race of her heartbeat. His own heartbeat was like thunder in his ears. Her mouth was hot and eager and sweet, so sweet that he couldn't get enough of it.

His kisses were like an addictive drug that Jemima

couldn't resist. Time and time again, she told herself, 'Just one more kiss.' And then what? a little voice piped up at the back of her head. Her spine arched as he lifted her and deftly released the catch on her bra. Before she could react he was peeling her top off over her head and tugging the bra down her arms.

'You're glorious,' Luciano husked, tracing her firm, full breasts with an almost reverent hand, pausing to toy with the protruding tips before bowing his head to lash his tongue across the tender crests.

Jemima huffed, lashes fluttering as sweet, seductive sensation snaked down from her nipples to her feminine core and joined the throbbing heat gathering there. Long brown fingers cradled her bare, rose-tipped curves and his mouth grew a little rougher while he teased the engorged buds, licking and suckling and nibbling with an erotic expertise that made her hips writhe against the mattress. She did not have a single thought in her head, only a sense of shock at the raw intensity of what he was making her feel.

With impatient hands he wrenched her out of her skirt and tossed his shirt on the floor to join it. Jemima gazed up at him with wondering appreciation, her attention lingering helplessly on the sleek bronzed torso composed of lean, hard muscle that swooped impressively down to frame a flat stomach and narrow hips. His shoulders were wide and as rounded with rippling muscles as his biceps. Only then as she reluctantly tore her attention from him did she become conscious of her naked breasts, but as she lifted her hands instinctively to cover herself he caught them in one of his and pinned them above her head.

'No interfering,' he told her in a roughened undertone. 'We only do this my way, *piccolo mia.*'

Colour washed her cheeks because she felt literally shameless lying there half-naked. He used his mouth to torment a straining nipple and she gasped, all self-consciousness wrested from her in the space of a moment. 'Let me touch you...' she pleaded.

He released her wrists. 'Some other time,' he mumbled, kissing a haphazard trail down over her ribcage and her tightening stomach to part her thighs.

Jemima froze, incredulous at his position and mortified, at least until he touched her and it was as if wildfire shot through her veins. Just as quickly there was nothing in her mind but a feverish concentration on what he was doing to her and how incredibly good it made her feel. Pushing her thighs back, he started slow with a long swipe of his tongue and when her hips lifted of their own accord he laughed softly.

'I'm really good at this,' he told her shamelessly.

And he didn't lie. He found every sensitive spot of arousal hidden in her tender folds, traced and teased those places with sleek, skilled fingertips, the glide and dip of his tongue and even the edge of his teeth. She could feel herself growing achingly wet in response, her heartbeat thumping inside her chest as if she were running a race. A fullness like a dam began to gather and build low in her pelvis and she turned this way and that to cope with the rise of heat and the throbbing torture of his electric exploration, restricted by his strong hold on her hips. Fire was burning through her as sensation piled on sensation at mesmerising speed. And then her own response started becoming more than she could contain, tiny spasms rippling through her quivering body and finally growing into a convulsive wave that swept her up and flung her high before sending her sobbing to earth again. She felt as though the top of her head were flying off while her body felt detached and heavy.

'I am burning for you, *piccolo mia*,' Luciano growled, sliding up over her to claim her mouth again.

He tasted of her and that shocked her but she was already in a state of shock so a little more didn't seem to matter. She had stepped out of her safe comfortable world into a far more dangerous one and learned weakness. And it wasn't the incredible allure of what he had made her feel that was her weakness, she acknowledged numbly. Her weakness was *him*. It was the heady joy she experienced when she saw the wicked smile in those lustrous golden eyes gazing down at her with satisfaction. It was knowing that his pleasing her had pleased him, made him feel good, lifted him out of the bad mood he had been in. That gave her a high more powerful than anything she had ever felt and incandescent warmth filled her.

'You do something crazy to me,' Luciano groaned as he rolled back from her to deftly take care of protection. 'I almost forgot to use a condom.'

Long fingers gripped her hips as he tilted her back and shifted against her. And she felt him nudge against her most tender flesh for the first time. It relit the fire that he had only recently sated, sending a frisson of reflexive hunger coursing through her again. Below his tousled black curls the arresting planes of his lean dark face were taut; his eyes blazed scorching gold with need. He took her mouth again with his, unexpectedly slow and gentle until his tongue delved between her lips and tangled with her own in a delicious dance. Nothing had ever been as arousing as that kiss and it fired her adrenaline. Her hands lifted to sink her fingers into his luxuriant hair and hold him to her but he pulled away a split second before he pushed into her.

'You're still so tight,' Luciano growled in frustration, stilling in an effort to accustom her to his girth, raw need driving his big powerful body as potently as a gun to his head.

She could feel her body stretching to accommodate him and apprehension gathered. She couldn't tell him that he would be her first because he believed she had birthed his son. He believed she was experienced and would undoubtedly prefer that to the rather pathetic truth. She squeezed her eyes tight shut and arched up to him in determined welcome, keen to get her introduction over with before the little regretful voices inside her head could gain her attention. And she knew what those little voices were about to tell her and she flatly refused to listen. She wanted Luciano and she wanted to know what all the fuss was about. His every tiny movement sent rippling sensation through her outrageously sensitive body.

Luciano pushed her back another few degrees to get a better angle and thrust home.

A searing flash of pain flared through Jemima and she cried out, eyes flying open filled with tears and surprise. 'That hurts!'

Luciano stilled, staring down at her with brooding, dark disbelief. He knew what his brain was telling him. He knew that his body had met with a resistance that he could not credit existed. While he had known she was not the mother of his son, he had certainly assumed she would be almost as practised with men as her sister had been. The awareness that he had got that badly wrong shook him back to full awareness, clearing his shrewd brain of the fog of alcohol and aggression that had clouded it.

'Are you OK?' he asked rawly.

'Yes, of course I am,' Jemima assured him and she shifted under him, washing wild sensation through Luciano's screamingly taut body while need continued to grip him like a hammer blow to the head. He eased out of the wonderfully tight grip of her and sank back into her with a groan of helpless satisfaction.

The pain diminished to a stinging discomfort closely followed by a jolt of exquisite pleasure. As Luciano moved the pleasure kicked in again and again and Jemima clutched at his arms, her knees rising as she arched to meet his next potent thrust. A wild singing impatience shot with primal need held her firmly in its grip and she lifted her hips in time to his fluid movements. He drove deeper and ground down on her and a helpless moan was torn from her lips as he picked up the pace. He slammed into her and her body clenched round him in excitement, her heartbeat thundering.

Glorious sensation shimmied through her pelvis and set up a chain reaction that sent her out of control when she convulsed beneath him. She plunged over the crest into a climax of intolerable excitement that sent spasms of delight rippling through her satiated body.

Weak as a kitten, Jemima wrapped her arms round Luciano only to stiffen as he literally shook her off. In a fluid movement he withdrew from her and sprang off the bed to stride into the bathroom. There was blood on him, Luciano acknowledged incredulously as he stepped into the shower. She had actually been a virgin. Where did that unexpected little attribute fit into the lying and gold-digging and plotting he had ascribed to her? What the hell had he been thinking? What the hell had he done?

Luciano pulled on jeans. Incredibly the mere thought of her lush, shapely body aroused him afresh and he wanted to punch something in frustration. A virgin? He was in deep shock and feeling ridiculously guilty. He had been so convinced that Jemima was a lying, gold-digging cheat like his son's true mother, *like…* No, he refused to go there, believing that the past was better left buried. But that past had made Luciano a cruel, distrustful cynic with women.

Jemima should have warned him. But how could she have without telling him the truth? Hadn't she appreciated that the first time might hurt? He had never had to think of that possibility before because he had never even come close to being any woman's first lover. He had been the first with Jemima, though, and he found himself savouring that knowledge in the weirdest way.

It shouldn't make any difference to his attitude to her... but somehow it did. He could no longer confuse her with Julie the escort or with his late wife, Gigi. Jemima had been considerably more sexually innocent than either.

Hearing Luciano's movements in the bathroom, Jemima emerged from her own reverie and hurriedly yanked the sheet up over her bare breasts even if the gesture did strike her as too little too late. Luciano appeared in the doorway. What did he think of her now? she wondered for a split second before reality finally came crashing back down on her again. In the storm of her personal doubts and insecurities she had miraculously contrived to forget the lies she had told and they were about to catch up with her, she reckoned wretchedly. Luciano knew now, he *had* to know that a virgin couldn't possibly be Nicky's mum.

Where had her wits been when she'd let him sweep her off to bed? How had she managed to overlook the need to protect the one intimate fact that could prove she was a liar? Of course it hadn't once occurred to her that she would have sex with Luciano. Fantasy was one thing, actually *acting* on fantasy something else entirely. Nor had she calculated the very real danger of tempting a male as aggressively dominant as Luciano. He was passionate and oversexed. Knowing she wanted him, he had targeted her and she had been an easy challenge, she reflected shamefacedly.

'So...' Luciano breathed silkily, leaning back against the door frame barefoot and bare-chested, wearing only well-worn jeans. With that much unclad masculine flesh on view she found it impossible not to stare. 'What price do you put on your virginity?'

Jemima blinked. *'Price?'* she parroted in stricken disbelief.

Luciano raised a well-defined black brow. 'Well, obviously there has to be a price for me to pay because you put a price on absolutely everything else. You put a price on my son's worth, didn't you? Giving away something for free isn't your style.'

Her face had flamed hot as a fire. 'I don't know what you're talking about.'

Luciano shifted an impatient hand and studied her fixedly. 'Quit with the lies, Jemima. Lies only make me angry and you don't want me angry,' he warned her.

Lean muscles flexed below bronzed skin as he changed position. The deep chill in his assurance crept through her like the sudden touch of icicles on too-hot skin. He was scaring her but he didn't need to scare her because Jemima was already fully aware of the wrong she had done. 'All right, I won't tell you any more lies,' she muttered heavily. 'You know I'm not Nicky's birth mother now, don't you?'

'Obviously. So what's the going rate for a virgin these days?' Luciano asked with scorching derision. 'Presumably you gave it up for a good reason and with you the reason will always relate to profit.'

'I'm not like that, Luciano!' Jemima exclaimed in consternation.

His beautiful sensual mouth twisted. 'If you can try to sell a baby, I assume you can put a price tag on virginity.'

'I wouldn't ever have tried to sell a baby!' Jemima argued fiercely. 'I know how wrong that would be!'

'But it wasn't wrong to keep his father from him when his mother was already dead?' he shot at her smoothly.

Jemima flinched at that direct question, sudden tears springing to her eyes and stinging like mad. She could not even blame her late twin for her predicament. Indeed she was all too well aware that she had buried herself in the hole she had dug. After all, *she* had lied to Luciano from the moment she'd met him and compounded her errors by having sex with him. She had done worse than blur the boundaries between right and wrong, she had stepped right over those boundaries.

'My first question should be...*who are you*?' Luciano drawled. 'But then that would make me a liar too because I already knew that you weren't who you were pretending to be before we hit the bed.'

Jemima stared at him in dismay. 'You already knew?' she exclaimed, disconcerted yet again. 'And yet you *still*...' Her voice drained away as she glanced involuntarily at the disordered bedding.

Angry tension pulled Luciano's muscles taut. 'I wasn't expecting a virgin...'

Jemima was still struggling to accept his earlier statement. 'You knew I wasn't Nicky's mother and yet you were still willing—'

'Sex is sex, Jemima, and I had had a lot to drink. When the urge controlled me, I didn't really care who you were,' Luciano told her with derision.

Her tightly controlled face washed pink and then ran pale. She knew she was being punished for not being more careful about who she became intimate with. He was telling her that he had just used her to scratch an itch and that the shock of her true identity hadn't been enough to repel him. 'How long have you known?' she whispered sickly.

'Since we landed in Sicily.'

Her pale eyes widened because she was recalling his change of mood at the airport. 'I know what you must think of me—'

'You have no idea what I think of you,' Luciano cut in with icy bite.

'I love Nicky so much—'

'Of course you're going to say that.'

'I was afraid that if I told you I was only his aunt, you'd just take him away immediately.'

'I expected you to say that too,' Luciano incised, lounging back against the door frame, the light behind him glimmering over his powerful pectorals and the hard slab of rippling muscle below.

'I've been with Nicky since he was only a few days old,' Jemima told him in her own defence while struggling not to sound pleading.

'And you knew all along that your twin had acted as a surrogate mother?'

'Yes, but she wouldn't tell me your name or any details. Julie didn't trust anyone…*ever*,' Jemima completed with feeling emphasis. 'She knew that I wasn't comfortable with the decisions she had made and although she left Nicky in my care she didn't give me any information that I could have used to interfere with her plans.'

Luciano wasn't convinced. Consistent liars told more lies with ease, adding complex layers of falsehood to their stories to make them seem more credible. Been there, done that...visited the graves, he conceded with a sudden deep inner chill of recoil from his own experiences. His dark eyes iced over with a diamond glitter.

'You and your sister grew up in separate adoptive homes?'

'Yes...'

'And when did you first meet her?'

'A couple of months before she got involved in the surrogacy agreement with you and she didn't tell me about that until she turned up again with Nicky.' Jemima dragged her attention from him to study her tightly linked hands. Time was flinging her back almost two years and reminding her of her excitement and joy when she had first discovered that she had a twin sister who wanted to meet up with her.

Jemima had not tried to trace her birth parents because she had been fearful of hurting her adoptive family's feelings. It had not, however, occurred to her that she might have a sibling to find and she had been overwhelmed by Julie's first approach. It had hurt to learn that her birth father was unknown and that their birth mother had died from drug addiction, but it had hurt more to hear about her twin's early health problems, her unsuccessful adoption and unhappy childhood.

'I was so much more fortunate than Julie was. My parents loved me from the beginning,' Jemima said tautly. 'It wouldn't have mattered if I'd been a bit slow at school but Julie's family—'

'I'm not interested in Julie's life story,' Luciano cut in smoothly.

'She's Nicky's mother!' Jemima condemned.

'And I'm grateful she's not here to cause my son any more damage,' Luciano told her truthfully.

'That's an appalling thing to say!' Jemima slammed back at him, sliding her legs off the bed and yanking violently at the sheet for cover.

'Is it?' Luciano rebutted grimly, angry dark eyes hard as obsidian. 'She was his mother and that gave her rights over him but she wasn't a decent, caring person fit to exercise those rights!'

With a final forceful jerk, Jemima dislodged the sheet and wrapped it round her naked body to stalk back through the interconnecting door into her own room. Eyes wet with tears, she was trembling. Her first foray into sex had gone badly wrong and made her feel worthless and rejected. Her late sister was being abused and there was very little she could say because Julie *had* done wrong. But very few people were *all* bad. Jemima blinked back the tears as she dug through her case to extract her dressing gown and dropped the sheet to walk into the bathroom.

She needed to shower, wash away the memory of Luciano's touch and the feel of his body on hers. Shivering, she switched on the water. Her mind drifted back inexorably to her sister and powerful regret filled her because she kept on thinking that if she had only had a little more time with Julie she could have got closer to her and somehow changed things for the better. On another, more rational level, though, she was painfully aware that Julie had never listened to her and had neither respected her opinion nor sought her advice, particularly where Nicky had been concerned.

But Nicky had crept into his aunt's heart the moment she'd met him because he had been a most unhappy baby.

'I don't know how to be a mum!' Julie had complained, becoming almost hysterical because her son had been crying and inconsolable. 'You tell me to cuddle him but I don't feel comfortable with that. He's making *me* feel bad!'

Nicky had suffered from colic and Julie had not been able to cope with him or the sleepless nights. Jemima had tried to help and had ended up taking over. She had blamed herself when Julie had gone back to London to work, leaving her baby in Jemima's care. She had blamed herself too when her twin had failed to bond with her child but she had also been aware of Julie's chequered past history. In truth Julie had had many troubled relationships in her life and rarely settled anywhere for any length of time. Running away from difficult situations had been the norm for Julie.

Luciano had no compassion, Jemima thought wretchedly. Julie had done bad things but her sister had not set out to be a bad person. Tightening the tie on her dressing gown, Jemima walked back to the door that still lay open between the two bedrooms.

'I loved my sister…and I won't say sorry for that!'

Jemima told Luciano defiantly. 'But I *am* sorry I lied to you. That was wrong. I got too attached to Nicky and I was frightened of losing him but I do appreciate that that doesn't excuse my not immediately telling you that his mother had passed away.'

Luciano's full sensual mouth twisted. 'It was a power play, wasn't it?'

Jemima gazed back at him without comprehension. 'Power didn't come into it...'

Somewhere in the distance she heard a thin high-pitched wail and stiffened. 'Nicky's crying,' she muttered, walking to the door.

'Carlotta will take care of him,' Luciano countered.

Wrenching open the door, Jemima listened to the wails drifting down from the floor above and started down the corridor. 'I can't leave him upset,' she called apologetically over her shoulder, sensing Luciano's disapproval and refusing to look back at him.

She would be gone from his fancy island castle soon enough, she reflected wretchedly. He was hardly likely to allow her to stay now that he knew she had lied to him and had no real claim to Nicky. Yet it still stunned her that he had gone to bed with her in spite of that knowledge. He had admitted that he had been drinking. Inwardly she cringed. Had alcohol made her seem more attractive than she was? Why was she even thinking in such a way? What did it matter now? They had had sex and there was no going back from that. It had been a casual thing for him and he had been quick to vacate the bed afterwards. He had actually asked her what price she put on her virginity, she recalled painfully. She felt ashamed and humiliated and blamed him for it.

Why, oh, why had he had to make her feel so bad about their ill-starred intimacy?

CHAPTER SEVEN

CARLOTTA WAS ANXIOUSLY rocking Nicky in her arms. His little face was scarlet with tears and he was sobbing noisily.

'He doesn't like being rocked when he's upset,' Jemima told the brunette in an apologetic tone, thinking that it would have made more sense if she had been given the opportunity to consult with the nanny *before* the other woman started taking care of Nicky.

A voice spoke up in Italian from the doorway and Carlotta gave Jemima a frowning look of surprise before turning rather abruptly to hand Nicky over to her. Although conscious that Luciano was present and had acted as an interpreter, Jemima ignored him and concentrated on his son. Nicky went rigid as he was passed over and then sagged against her, shoving his face into the curve of her neck and whimpering.

'He has nightmares. He's frightened when he wakes up. He only needs to be soothed,' Jemima declared, walking the floor of the elaborately decorated room with Nicky cradled in her arms. She was still alarmingly conscious of the ache at the heart of her body and hot pink flushed her cheeks as she buried her face in Nicky's tumbled curls, revelling in the clean baby scent of innocence. With a heavy sigh she sank down into the rocking chair beside the cot.

Luciano had paused long enough to grab up a shirt and don it on his way to the nursery, but nobody seeing his bare feet and rumpled damp hair could doubt that he had recently undressed only to get dressed again in a hurry. Naked below her sensible dressing gown, Jemima could feel her face burning as if she were on fire. Their mutual state of undress was noticeable and embarrassing. She didn't want anyone to know or guess that she had slept with Luciano. That was her private disgrace and not for public sharing. Carlotta, however, simply smiled at Jemima, clearly relieved that the baby had calmed down.

His son's sobs had subsided almost immediately, Luciano registered without surprise while he watched. The baby's fingers clutched convulsively at Jemima for reassurance. Niccolò had missed her. Obviously he had missed her. How much of the little boy's misery had been caused by the sudden change in his routine and surroundings and the equally sudden absence of the one person he trusted? Luciano paled beneath his dark skin, shaken by the reality that he had set down rules that could well have hurt his son and caused him unnecessary suffering. He had instructed Carlotta to deal with the baby alone and to involve Jemima as little as possible in his care.

But how could he love his son and yet deny the child the one person whom he so clearly loved and wanted?

Shame writhed inside Luciano, a reaction he had not experienced in more years than he cared to count. He watched her smooth the baby's head with a tender hand and read the softness in her eyes.

'He knows his mother,' Carlotta said quietly in Italian to her employer.

It seemed a terrible irony to Luciano at that moment that Jemima was *not* his son's mother because the boy was deeply attached to her and she was equally attached to him. He realised he needed to talk to his lawyer to find out exactly what kind of woman Jemima Barber was. How could he trust his own instincts now? Nor could he have any faith in what Jemima's version of the truth might be. Anyone determined to speak up in defence of Julie Marshall would have failed to inspire Luciano with confidence.

As he stepped unconsciously closer to the woman in the rocking chair Nicky lifted his head off Jemima's shoulder and stared at Luciano with wide dark eyes. And then he smiled with sudden brilliance, freezing his father to the spot in shock for it was the very first positive response Luciano had received from his son. It was significant too that the child had smiled only when he was secure in Jemima's presence, he acknowledged ruefully.

Resting his head back down drowsily again, Nicky fell asleep. Getting to her feet, Jemima lowered him with care into the cot, straightened his sleep suit and covered him up gently. 'He should sleep the rest of the night now,' she whispered.

Luciano stared down at his slumbering son, then

glanced up again and noticed that Jemima was deliberately avoiding looking at him. Annoyance skimmed along the edges of his sensitised awareness as they left the room. She tried to step past him out in the corridor but he rested a staying hand on her arm.

'Jemima...we—'

'I'm really hungry,' Jemima proclaimed in a rush, jerking her arm back out of reach and addressing his shirt-clad chest. 'Would it be too much trouble for me to have something to eat in my room? Even a sandwich and a cup of tea would do.'

'Put on something in your new wardrobe and come downstairs to join me for dinner instead,' Luciano suggested, falling into step beside her as she walked down the corridor.

Her facial muscles clenched tight. 'Thanks but no, thanks... I'm not in a very sociable mood.'

As she descended the stairs she saw a huge portrait of an exquisite brunette on the landing and, already regretting her tart reply to his invitation, she said in an effort to break the pounding silence, 'My goodness, who's that?'

'My mother, Ambra. It was painted shortly before she married my father. She probably never smiled like that again,' Luciano breathed harshly.

His intonation made Jemima wince. 'When did she die?'

'When I was three years old,' Luciano admitted between gritted teeth, fighting off his terrible memories with all his might.

'Did your father remarry?'

'No.'

Jemima was already scolding herself for surrendering to her low mood and turning down the dinner invite. She had allowed Luciano to believe that she was the surrogate mother of his son and had used that pretence as a means of staying in Nicky's life. Was it any wonder that he despised her? Or that he had assumed that she was like her sister and after his money? Julie had worshipped rich men and money. Yet no matter how much money Julie had had it had never been enough and money had trickled through her fingers like water.

'We'll talk over breakfast in the morning,' Luciano breathed in a driven undertone as he came to a halt outside his bedroom door, which was mere feet from hers.

'I shouldn't have lied to you,' Jemima began, and then an unfamiliar stab of angry bitterness powered through her regret and she added, 'But you had no right to insult me by suggesting that I would use sex as a means of making money!'

Luciano ground his teeth together and watched her long, unbound mane of golden hair slide off her shoulders and fall almost to her waist as she moved her head. He wanted to run his fingers through that glossy golden hair so badly that he clenched his hand into a fist to restrain himself. So, he liked the long hair? OK, he really, *really* liked the long hair, particularly now that he suspected it was one hundred per cent natural. He also liked her body…and her eyes…and… With a huge effort he focused on what she had said and murmured grimly, 'I've met a lot of women who sell sex like a product.'

Jemima was so shocked by that blunt admission that she turned up her head to stare at him, ice-blue eyes visibly dismayed. 'Seriously?'

Teeth gritted more than ever at such naivety, Luciano nodded and wished he'd kept his mouth shut. Now she was probably thinking that he consorted with hookers and he didn't want her thinking that. *What the hell does it matter what she thinks?* he snarled at himself, thoroughly disconcerted by his loss of concentration and self-discipline. What was wrong with him? Had the few drinks he had imbibed in his bad mood completely addled his brain? Telling Agnese to hold dinner, he strode downstairs to call his lawyer.

Charles did a great deal of groaning and apologising during the lengthy exchange that followed. Nothing about the situation was quite as anyone had assumed or as clear. Charles still couldn't answer all his employer's questions and reluctantly gave Luciano the phone number of his own chief informant. Breathing in deep, Luciano telephoned Jemima's adoptive father, Benjamin Barber. And not one thing that Luciano learned in the subsequent conversation made him feel happier. Instead he came off that call marvelling at the older man's optimistic and forgiving outlook while feeling a great deal worse about his own opinions, suspicions and activities. Knowing that the least he owed Jemima was a polite warning about what he had done, he mounted the stairs again and knocked on her bedroom door.

Half asleep after her delicious meal, Jemima rolled off the bed and lifted her tray, assuming someone was calling back to collect it. Instead she was faced with Luciano, infuriatingly immaculate again in tailored chinos and a black tee shirt. 'Yes?' she said discouragingly, clutching the tray and feeling horribly irritated that she had not known it would be him at her door.

He leant down and took the tray, setting it down on the table to the side of the door. 'I have something to tell you—'

'Can't it wait until breakfast time?'

'I'm afraid not.' Soft pink mouth compressed, Jemima grudgingly stood back to allow him into her room. Since she had no idea what he had to say to her, keeping him out in the corridor where their conversation could be overheard struck her as risky.

'I spoke to your father an hour ago and we talked for quite some time.'

Transfixed by that staggering announcement, Jemima stared back at him in horror. 'I beg your pardon?'

'I phoned your father and he's now aware that you were pretending to be your sister for my benefit,' Luciano divulged.

'Oh, my goodness...how could you *do* that?' Jemima was aghast at the news. 'I just can't believe you told him!'

'The investigators my lawyer employed had already contacted him and it made sense for me to address my questions to your father direct. He was troubled that you hadn't told him what you were doing but he understands why you did what you did and he wants you to know that he forgives you. I had to warn you in case you were planning to phone home.'

Knees weakening, Jemima sank down on the foot of the bed and bowed her head into her raised hands. 'I can't believe you approached Dad... I've tried so hard to keep my parents out of all this!' she exclaimed reproachfully.

'I wanted a clearer picture of what happened and you're too emotionally involved,' Luciano drawled in self-defence. 'It was...enlightening to hear the facts from your father's point of view.'

'I hate you!' Jemima flung at him furiously. 'You had no right to go snooping and interfering!'

'I'm as trapped in the mess your sister left behind her as you are,' Luciano contradicted coolly. 'The legal ramifications of her having stolen your identity will take a long time to unravel. She gave birth to a child using your name. She contracted debts in your name and she broke the law using your name—'

Jemima flew upright in one tempestuous movement. 'Do you think I don't know all that?'

'She took advantage of you and your parents,' Luciano delivered grimly.

'There's no way my father said that!' Jemima accused furiously.

'Your father is a rather unworldly man and I imagine he has had little contact with the criminal element. I'm rather less innocent and much more accustomed to dealing with life's users and abusers.'

'Bully for you!' Jemima snapped back childishly, marching back to her bedroom door and dragging it open in invitation. 'Right now all I want to do is go to bed and forget you ever existed!'

Luciano lifted his hand and a forefinger flicked the full tense line of her lower lip in reproof. 'What a little liar you can be. Without me there would be no Niccolò...and somehow I don't think you'd give him up so easily.'

The touch of his hand against her lip made her entire skin surface tingle. Her breathing quickened and she pressed her thighs together to suppress the tiny clenching liquid sensation low in her pelvis. Her lashes swept up fully to collide with stunning dark golden eyes welded to her every move and change of expression. Her cheeks coloured, her lashes swept down and she backed away from him, furious that without even trying he could still get a physical reaction out of her.

'Goodnight,' she said flatly.

Luciano wanted to scoop her up and carry her back to his bed. It was pure lust, he told himself furiously, the sort of irrational, ungovernable lust that sent a man into cold showers and the depths of neurotic desire. And unlike his late and unlamented father, who had once become obsessed with a woman, Luciano was not the obsessive type. He stayed up late working and by the time he finally fell into bed he was too exhausted to do anything but sleep.

The next morning, Jemima felt more like herself and less traumatised. The truth had come out and she couldn't hide from it. Lying had gone against her nature and weighted her conscience and she was relieved not to be pretending any more. Her parents knew. She chewed her lower lip and decided to phone home that evening, although she dreaded dealing with her father's disappointment in her behaviour. Luciano and Nicky, however, were an even bigger challenge.

Presumably over breakfast Luciano would tell her what he wanted to do next and when she would be flying home. She had lied to him. She might have convinced herself that she had lied for her nephew's sake but in her heart she knew she was lying to herself. In reality, she had not been able to face parting with Nicky and that had been selfish when Nicky's father was available to take charge of his son. While she thought unhappily about her mistakes, she rooted through her suitcase, grimacing at the reality that there was really nothing in her case suitable for a hot day. At least nothing presentable, she affixed ruefully, choosing not to examine why what she wore had to be *more* presentable than usual when Luciano was around. After a few moments, she stalked into the dressing room and skimmed through the hanging dresses. What would he do with them after she had gone? Chuck them out? Pass them on to staff or recycling? She lifted down a fitted blue cotton sundress, plainer in style and less revealing than most of the other garments, and began to get ready.

Seated on the floor in the nursery, Nicky was happily playing with his new toys. Carlotta was friendly, addressing Jemima in broken English to let her know that he had slept well and eaten. A maid met Jemima at the foot of the stairs to show her where she was to go to join Luciano. They trekked across the vast building, mounting stairs and crossing hallways before walking down a long picture gallery that opened to an outdoor area that overlooked the sea and the shore.

The panoramic view and the sunlight blinded her and she had a split-second sizzling snapshot of Luciano, rising with fluid grace from his seat, his lean, powerful body sheathed in an exquisitely cut pale grey suit teamed with a black shirt. *'Buon giorno,'* he murmured smoothly. 'You look amazing.'

Jemima flushed. 'Let's not get carried away,' she told him reprovingly. 'I'm wearing this because it's so hot and I have nothing suitable *and*—'

'Rest assured I will not assume that you are wearing it either to please or attract me, *piccolo mia*,' Luciano incised as drily as though he could read her mind.

Her flushed cheeks turned a solid mortified red and she averted her eyes as she dropped down hurriedly into a seat. Dishes were proffered by one manservant, beverages by another. Her attention briefly falling on the bodyguards standing several yards away, it occurred to her that Luciano lived rather like a king in a medieval court with an army of staff and everyone bowing and scraping and doing their utmost to ensure his protection and his comfort. It was an isolated lifestyle, divorced from normality, and she wondered how it would affect Nicky to grow up like a crown prince in the lap of such indescribable luxury.

From below her lashes she stole a helpless glance at Luciano. He was looking out to sea, his flawless classic profile turned to her. Her heart thumped very loudly in her ears because she was remembering his mouth, that wide, sensually skilled mouth, roaming over her and making her writhe with raw need and then the dynamic flex and flow of his lithe body over hers, driving her to the apex of excitement. Perspiration broke out on her skin and she quickly looked away from him again. No, try as she might to be sensible, she could not forget the intimacy, the first she had ever known and, much like Luciano, utterly unforgettable.

'So, what next?' she muttered in the pulsing silence.

Lustrous dark golden eyes ensnared hers and her breath tripped in her throat. 'That's what we have to decide.'

Jemima tore her eyes free and bit into her fresh fruit. He was using the royal 'we'; she didn't think she would have much actual input into what happened next.

'Tell me how your sister got hold of your passport,' he invited, startling her with that request.

'It happened by accident. The first time we met she showed me her passport because she had worn her hair long then too, and I got out mine and we were laughing and somehow our passports got mixed up.'

'And?' Luciano prompted.

'Julie only realised she had my passport when she was flying out to Italy and she travelled on it because she didn't want to miss her flight.'

'She lied,' Luciano murmured without any expression at all. 'She had already used *your* passport in her application to be the surrogate I hired. And the reason she lied was that she had several criminal convictions in her own name. She probably tracked you down quite deliberately. She set you up to steal your identity, Jemima. Accept that.'

Jemima paled. She was remembering laughing with her sister as they compared unflattering passport photos. 'It was months before I found out about the...er... exchange and when I contacted her about it, she said she'd give it back when she returned from Italy.'

'Only she never did,' Luciano completed.

'Obviously you think I'm very stupid,' Jemima said tartly, burning her mouth on an unwary sip of coffee and swallowing hard, burning her throat into the bargain, tears starting into her eyes at the discomfort.

'No, I think you were scammed. She was a practised, confident trickster and she was your sister and you didn't want to accept the truth,' Luciano said in a surprisingly uncritical tone. 'I can understand ignoring the evidence and wanting to believe the best of someone close to you. It happened to me once.'

'Oh...' Jemima was taken aback by that admission. 'I loved her—I felt an immediate sense of connection with her.'

'Scammers have to be attractive to pull people in.'

Jemima concentrated her attention warily on eating.

'Why didn't you go to the police about your passport when she refused to give it back?'

'I didn't need my passport because I couldn't afford to travel at the time...and I didn't want to get her into trouble. For a long time she made excuses about why she wasn't returning it and I believed her,' she admitted with a rueful roll of her eyes.

A manservant topped up Luciano's black coffee. He rose lithely from his seat and lounged back against the stone balustrade girding the terrace. He surveyed her with satisfaction. She was elegant as a swan in the tailored blue sundress, her hair restrained in its usual braid, only stray little golden hairs catching the slight breeze round her troubled face. She had loved and cared for her sister, contriving to mourn Julie Marshall's passing in spite of all the damage her sibling had done. Jemima had a lot of heart and a generosity of spirit that he admired even though he couldn't emulate it. And he wanted what she had to offer for his son. He sensed that she could be the greatest gift he would ever give him.

For once he wasn't going to be selfish and he wasn't going to remind himself how often he had sworn never to surrender his freedom again. In any case he owed Jemima a debt. In the grip of ignorance and lacerating bitterness at her betrayal of trust he had seduced her and she hadn't deserved that. Virginity had to matter to a woman who had reached almost twenty-four years of age without experimenting and he had taken it from her. Carelessly, thoughtlessly, cruelly.

'I took advantage of you last night,' Luciano breathed in a driven undertone. 'I was angry. I was drunk.'

Her pale blue eyes widened and she set down her cup with a sharp little snap. 'No, nobody took advantage of anyone last night. I'm an adult and I made a choice.'

'You weren't in any fit state to make a choice.'

Anger flared in her mutinous gaze. 'I chose you because I've never been so attracted to anyone before. I'm not proud that I was that shallow but it *was* my decision!'

Silence lay thick and heavy between them in the

heat and she shifted uneasily in her seat, embarrassed by her own vehemence. Had she really had to admit that she had never wanted any man the way she had wanted him? Didn't that sound a bit pathetic?

'The odd thing about decisions is that when you make major ones you're always convinced that you'll never change your mind. After my wife died in the crash I decided that I would *never* marry again,' Luciano confessed tautly, unsettling her with that admission. 'I did not want to share my life with another woman but I was grieving for the child I had lost and I did still want to be a parent. That is why I came up with the idea of a surrogacy agreement. I thought it would be a simple business contract and problem free, but I didn't count on dealing with a woman like your sister.'

Jemima heaved a sigh but said nothing. By running away with Nicky after the birth, Julie had changed everyone's lives and there was no getting away from that. She was, however, far more interested in wondering why Luciano had decided never to remarry. Had that been a tribute to the wife he loved? Gigi Nocella had been a gorgeous and very famous movie star. What woman could possibly follow in such gilded footsteps?

'You have had complete responsibility for my son since he was only a few days old,' Luciano pointed out.

'Yes.' Jemima snapped back to the present and shook irritably free of her futile speculation about Luciano's past. 'Julie went back to London to work. She told me that she earned good money working in PR and I had no reason to doubt her. I continued my teaching job and placed Nicky in a nursery nearby. Julie didn't help with the expense and it was a challenge to afford it on my salary and my savings were soon gone. My parents were struggling too, so it made sense for me to give up my apartment and move home again.'

'You've made sacrifices to look after my son,' Luciano acknowledged grimly. 'And you have looked after him well. I believe that you love him and that he loves you.'

'I couldn't help loving him.' Jemima sighed.

'But he's not your child.'

Jemima grimaced at that unnecessary reminder. 'That didn't come into it for me.'

Luciano continued to study her with brooding intensity. 'My son may not be your child now but he *could* be…'

Jemima stared back at him in bewilderment. 'What on earth are you saying?' she framed uncertainly.

'I'm asking you to marry me to become my son's mother and my wife,' Luciano clarified with silken sibilance, his dark eyes glimmering golden as a lion's in the sunlight. 'It makes sense—in this situation it makes the very best sense. Think about it and you'll see that.'

CHAPTER EIGHT

Jemima was in shock.

Luciano Vitale was asking her to marry him. How was that possible? She had joined him at breakfast expecting to be told when she would be flying home and instead he had proposed marriage. Her lashes fluttered down to screen her eyes.

'Nicky's mother?'

'And the mother of any other children that we might have together,' Luciano slotted in smoothly, catching her startled upward glance and looking steadily back at her. 'I'm talking about a normal marriage and a family. Be assured of that.'

Jemima felt rather like a mouse cornered by a cat. His brilliant dark eyes sought out hers, level and direct and forceful, as if seeking assurance that she was listening properly. A normal marriage, a *family*. Shock was piling on shock. Her taut lips parted and she blurted out, 'But you're not in love with me!'

Luciano inclined his arrogant head to one side and compressed his sensual mouth. 'Is that kind of romantic love so necessary to you?'

Jemima went pink. 'I always assumed that I would only marry for love.'

'But love doesn't always last,' Luciano parried wryly. 'It can also encourage unrealistic expectations in the relationship. I can't offer you love but I can offer you respect and consideration and fidelity. I believe there is a very good chance that a marriage created on such practical foundations would succeed.'

She thought he was quite probably the most beautiful man in the world as he leant back against that balustrade, black curls ruffling in the breeze above his darkly handsome features. He was offering her respect, consideration and fidelity. Didn't he believe in love? Or did he still think he was in love with his first wife? She wanted to ask but it felt like the wrong moment. Luciano had proposed marriage. Wasn't that supposed to be special? It was obvious he had thought in depth about marrying her.

'Why me?' she asked baldly.

'Primarily you love my son and he loves you. I grew up without a mother and I want more for him.'

'You could marry anyone,' she cut in helplessly.

'But to any other woman Niccolò would always be second best once she had a child of her own. I don't believe you will react like that but many women would,' Luciano fielded quietly.

'Yet you planned his birth knowing you intended to raise your child without a mother,' she reminded him.

'That was before I saw the strength of the bond between you and him and the happiness that gave him.'

Having heard enough, Jemima forced a smile and

rose from her seat. 'I'm afraid the man I marry would have to want me for more than my child-rearing abilities,' she told him stiffly, struggling to keep the little amused smile in place and mask the deep hollow of hurt opening up inside her.

Luciano dealt her a seething look of frustration and strode after her. 'Jemima!'

Jemima didn't turn her head, she just kept on walking away fast, unable to face any further dialogue. She was so hurt and she didn't really understand why. Surely it was always a sort of a compliment if a man asked you to marry him? Even if you didn't want to say yes. And at that point, she realised what was wrong. She wanted *more*. She wanted him to want her personally and that was downright silly as well as unlikely. So many more beautiful and sophisticated women would have snatched at Luciano's offer with two greedy hands. Who did she think she was to be so finicky?

'Jemima…!' Luciano exclaimed, closing a powerful hand round her shoulder to spin her round in the picture gallery. 'You know very well that I want you for more than that!'

Jemima sucked in a gulp of oxygen and almost lost it again as she clashed with blazing dark golden eyes. 'Do I?' she slashed back in challenge.

'You *do* know,' Luciano told her, crowding her back against the wall behind her.

'How *would* I know?' Jemima flamed back at him. 'Nicky loves me and you think I'm good for him. That's why you're asking me to marry you.'

His white teeth flashed against his bronzed skin. 'Last night, we—'

'No, don't try to drag last night into it,' Jemima warned angrily. 'Your proposal made it clear that providing your son with a mother was your main motivation!'

'*Accidenti*... I was taking a conservative approach. I assumed you would prefer that!'

'Why would a woman want a conservative proposal?' Jemima countered impatiently.

'You would've preferred me to take you to bed again before I proposed?'

Jemima recognised the difference between her outlook and his and almost screamed in vexation. She thought of love and romance while he thought of sex, and wild, raunchy sex at that. Well, he had been upfront about not being able to offer love, so what more could she reasonably expect from him? And did she really *want* to say no? No to being Nicky's mum? No to being Luciano's wife and the potential mother of his children?

Luciano planted his hands squarely on the wall either side of her head, his lean, powerful body effectively imprisoning hers. Her ice-blue eyes widened as she felt his erection push against her belly, his hard readiness formidable even through the barrier of their clothes. Heat coiled at the heart of her rose up and clear thought process broke down. Hunger settled in a tight, hard knot inside her, constricting her breathing.

'No. On bended knee and dinner by candlelight would have been more your style,' Luciano derided.

'I'm not that old-fashioned,' she told him in exasperation.

Lowering his head, he brushed his lips almost teasingly against hers and then lingered to capture and suckle her lower lip, one hand sliding down the wall to close on her hip and jerk her into closer contact. His tongue eased between her readily parted lips and delved in an unashamedly sexual sortie. Her breathing fractured as she came off the wall to wrap her arms round his neck, fingertips sliding into his luxuriant hair.

'So, is this a yes, *piccolo mia*?' Luciano husked sexily against her swollen mouth.

'Are you *always* calculating the odds?' Jemima complained, jerking her head back out of reach.

Luciano gave her a wicked grin that loosed a flock of butterflies in her tummy and left her feeling dizzy. 'I don't switch off my brain very often,' he admitted.

She could have him if she wanted him, Jemima reflected on a heady high. And she wanted him—oh, my goodness, yes, she wanted him. But it would be crazy to make an impulsive decision based on the feelings of the moment. And her feelings just then were overwhelmingly physical and dangerously unreliable. Close to Luciano, her body vibrated like a tuning fork. He made her want to drag him off to the nearest secluded corner. That awareness cooled her heated blood and made her take a mental step back to take stock.

'I have to think about this,' Jemima declared, ignoring the frowning slant of his black brows above his stunning eyes. 'I need to be on my own for a while. I'm going for a walk on the beach.'

Recalling the flight of winding stone steps that led down to the shore from the terrace, she walked back into the sunlight. Round and round and round she went, moving faster and faster in her need to escape until her heels finally sank into the blissfully soft sand at the bottom. With a sigh she slipped off her shoes, closed her fingers through the straps and walked barefoot down to the shore.

The surf dampened her feet as she moved away from the castle. Little white houses straggled up the hillside on the other side of the horseshoe-shaped bay and boats bobbed in the harbour. A church with a bell tower made the village look even more picturesque in the sunshine.

So, how did she really feel about Luciano? Did she want him for the right reasons? Shouldn't Nicky be her driving motivation? Did it matter that she was thinking less about Nicky and more about becoming Luciano's wife? Why couldn't she think about anything but Luciano? Was she infatuated with him? No doubt that would wear off with continued exposure to him and prevent her from behaving like an embarrassing teenager with a crush, she thought with an inner wince. After all, it was obvious that if such a marriage of convenience was to work she would have to be more practical in her outlook.

Could she happily settle for respect and consideration and fidelity? Well, she thought wryly, maybe not *happily*, but, if the alternative was not to have Luciano at all, her choice was being made for her. If the chance was there, she definitely wanted to take it and give it a go. And what about her family, her friends and the teaching career that she loved? Living abroad in Sicily? Could she adjust to that change? Friends and family would be able to visit as she would be able to visit them, she told herself, and, while she would miss her job, raising Nicky and having more children would certainly fill her time.

Registering that she was walking straight for the natural rock formation that cut off the beach at one point, Jemima changed direction in favour of the path running between the shore and the single-track road. She put her shoes back on, relieved she had worn low heels, and only as she straightened did she appreciate that she was not walking alone. Three of Luciano's bodyguards hovered several yards away and she made a shooing motion of dismissal with her hands before turning defiantly on her heel and picking up her pace towards the village. Why on earth were they following her? Were such precautions really necessary for her safety?

Tired and hot, she paused at a café above the beach and walked in to sit down. It was busy. A large group of elderly men sat playing a board game in one corner and several other tables were occupied. As soon as Jemima sat down a bodyguard approached her to ask her what she wanted, acting as a liaison between her and the proprietor, who was viewing them nervously. Freshly squeezed orange juice was brought and she sipped, cooling off from the early-morning heat while watching a handful of children play ball on the beach below.

Nicky would have a whole beach to himself at the castle, she thought heavily. Would he even be allowed to play with other children? Had Luciano the smallest idea of what an ordinary childhood was like? What had his own been like? He had shared so little with her. All she knew about his background and his first marriage had been gleaned from the Internet. Luciano was not a male who willingly opened up about his past.

A sports car purred to a halt outside and Luciano sprang out of it. The proprietor bowed almost double and the waiter copied him. The old men stopped their game, suddenly rigid, their chatter silenced. As he strode in Luciano addressed the owner and then settled down lithely opposite her, seemingly impervious to the apprehensive silence that had greeted his arrival and that of his protection team.

'Why did you have me followed?'

'My father died when his yacht was blown up in the harbour out there,' Luciano volunteered. 'I have lived a very different life but there are still those who hate and fear me because of the blood in my veins. I can't take the risk of ignoring that.'

Jemima had gone very pale. She brushed his hand soothingly with her fingers. 'I'm sorry...'

His lush lashes lifted and dark golden eyes scanned her as a glass of water was brought to the table for him. 'For what? For old history? Nobody grieved for my father, least of all me,' he admitted bluntly.

'Was your childhood unhappy?' she murmured tautly, her eyes on his lean, dark face and the strong tension etched there.

'Is knowing such things about me important to you?'

Amazed that he should have to ask that, Jemima nodded confirmation.

Luciano drank his water. 'It was a nightmare,' he admitted gruffly. 'That's why I want a normal family life for Niccolò.'

Jemima wondered what a nightmare entailed and wasn't sure she could live with further clarification. The haunting darkness in his eyes sent a chill racing down her spine. The old men in the corner were still staring and she glanced away, wondering what it had been like for Luciano to grow up as the son of a man who was loathed and feared and whose reputation for corruption had stretched beyond death to shadow his son's. Frustrated tenderness laced with intense compassion twisted through Jemima. A normal family life. It was not so much to ask. It was not an impossible dream, was it? In fact it was a modest aspiration for so wealthy and powerful a male and that knowledge touched her heart more deeply than anything else could have done.

Luciano wondered why Jemima appeared to be on the brink of tears. He could see moisture glimmering in her ice-blue eyes. He didn't want to talk about his dirty past; he didn't even want to think about such things. It had soiled him for ever—how could it not soil her? Furthermore, he was still reeling from his own behaviour the night before: he had lost control of his temper and acted with dishonour. Even his father had waited to marry his mother before sharing a bed with her. He repressed his troubled thoughts, knowing the futility of regretting what was past.

'I want to marry you,' he told her very quietly.

'I know,' she whispered, her heart beating so fast it felt as though it were in her throat. 'But I'm not sure what that means to you.'

'I wanted you the first moment I saw you,' Luciano ground out in a driven undertone. 'Is that what you want to hear? I thought you were your sister then and I couldn't believe that I could want such a woman, so I fought it. You're a very loving woman, Jemima, and my son needs that. I don't think I'm capable of giving that kind of love, but you are.'

Yes, that was what Jemima had needed to hear. A blinding smile curved her lips and lit up her face. 'OK...you've won me over,' she told him shakily.

Luciano snapped his fingers and the proprietor came running. He spoke in Italian. The waiter scurried around serving everyone in the bar, even Luciano's protection team. The café owner reappeared with a dusty bottle, which he proffered with pride. The wine was poured and toasts were made.

'I bought everyone a drink to celebrate our wedding plans with us,' Luciano explained as her eyes widened.

'We're talking weddings now?' Jemima parroted as he nudged her nerveless fingers with a wine glass. 'You want me to have a drink? But it's only ten o'clock in the morning!'

He groaned out loud and raked impatient fingers through his black curls. '*Santa Madonna!* I forgot to give you the ring!'

In a daze, Jemima moistened her dry mouth with the wine. 'There's a ring?'

'*Certamente*…of course there's a ring!' Luciano withdrew a tiny box from his pocket and flipped it open to a spectacular sapphire ring surrounded by diamonds. Removing it from the box, he lifted her hand and slid it onto her engagement finger. 'If you don't like it, we can choose something else.'

'No…it's beautiful,' Jemima whispered dizzily. 'Where did you get it from? I mean, we only arrived…'

'It belonged to my mother's family…and no, before you ask, it never belonged to Gigi,' he assured her.

Smiles had broken out all around them. Several solemn toasts were made. Luciano seemed taken aback by the warmth of the good wishes offered. Jemima drank her wine and watched the sunlight glitter off her amazing ring while wondering with a little frisson of excitement if Luciano would be sharing a bed with her again that night.

'Why did Gigi never wear this ring?' she asked baldly.

'It wasn't flashy enough for her. She only wore diamonds.'

It was the first time he had voluntarily mentioned his first wife. Jemima supposed that in time she would learn more but she could tell by his tension that, although he was trying hard to be more open with her, it was a tender subject and he was struggling. So much had already changed between them but the biggest alteration in Luciano's attitude had occurred as soon as he'd realised that she wasn't her twin sister, Julie. The awareness that he had fought any attraction to her before he'd known her true identity soothed Jemima's concerns. Luciano was willing to overlook her lies because he respected her attachment to Nicky and her principles. In other words, what was important to her was equally important to him.

'So, when will we be getting married?' she asked as Luciano tucked her into the elegant sports car outside.

'As soon as possible. Draw up a guest list of friends and family.' Curling black lashes shaded Luciano's gaze, his wide sensual mouth relaxed. 'My staff will take care of all the arrangements. We'll have the wedding here.'

Her eyes widened. '*Here* in Sicily?'

'I don't think it would be a good idea to trail Niccolò back to the UK again,' Luciano commented with a frown. 'You would have to stay somewhere where my security people could look after you both because when word of our relationship breaks in the media you will both be a paparazzi target. It will be easier if you remain here on the island, where your privacy can be assured.'

Jemima tried to absorb the realities of her new life and slowly shook her head in bemusement because she could not even begin to imagine being a target for the paparazzi. But, more importantly, a further change of climate and yet another selection of strange faces would not benefit Nicky either, she conceded ruefully. If Castello del Drogo was to be the little boy's permanent home, he should be allowed to settle into his new surroundings without the stress of having to adapt to any additional challenges.

'I have a tour of Asia scheduled and, as I'll be away

for a couple of weeks, I suggest that you invite your family out to keep you company until the wedding,' Luciano remarked, disconcerting her.

He was leaving her. Jemima refused to betray any reaction. Obviously he would travel on business and such temporary separations would be part of their lives. She had never been the clingy type. She was independent and self-sufficient, she reminded herself doggedly. Wanting to climb into his suitcase with Nicky was just plain stupid.

'I'm surprised you're prepared to leave Nicky so soon,' she admitted.

'When the tour of my holdings was organised, actually finding my son still seemed like a fantasy,' he confided ruefully. 'Now that I have found him I have no intention of being an absent parent. Once I'm home again I'll be spending a lot of time with him.'

They returned to the *castello*. 'What made you buy this place?' Jemima asked curiously. 'Was it purely for the private setting?'

'I didn't buy it. I inherited it. It belonged to my mother's family. She grew up here.' His lean bronzed face shadowed.

'Did you stay here when you were a child?'

'No. My mother never returned after she married my father. He first saw her playing on the beach down there as a teenager,' Luciano told her, tight-mouthed. 'When I was older he called it love at first sight. I would call it lust...'

Like what Luciano had felt on first seeing Jemima? Jemima wondered ruefully. An instant attraction, similar to what she herself had felt, so how could she look down on that?

'How did they get together?' she prompted.

'In a decent world they would never have got together. He was a murderer, a thief, a gangster,' Luciano declared without any expression. 'She was the adored only child of a titled, educated man. But that man gambled and got into debt and my father bought his debt and soon my father owned him. My father wrote off the debt in return for my mother's hand in marriage...'

'My goodness,' Jemima said sickly. 'What did she have to say about it?'

'She loved her father and she did what she had to do to save him from the shame of bankruptcy,' Luciano revealed. 'I can't imagine she was happy about the price she had to pay. She married a brutal man.'

Jemima heard the chill in his dark-timbred voice and decided it was definitely time to change the subject. He didn't want to talk about his parents' marriage and in the circumstances that was hardly surprising. As she recalled, his mother had died when he was only three years old and it was unlikely that he remembered much about the beautiful brunette in the portrait on the stairs. It was something they had in common and she commented on the fact.

Luciano turned frowning eyes on her.

'Have you forgotten that I was adopted? I don't remember anything about my birth parents but what I do know now, thanks to Julie's research, is that there's nothing there to be proud of. Our birth mum was a drug addict and I'll never know who our father was.'

The grim edge stamped round his beautiful mouth eased. 'Ignorance could be bliss.'

'Leave it in the past where it belongs,' she urged, closing her hand round his. 'We're not responsible for what our parents did, nor do we have to resemble them.'

Luciano smiled at her simplistic advice and her unsubtle attempt to offer him comfort. He didn't need comfort. He knew who he was and where he had come from and what he had to avoid to achieve a reasonably happy and successful life. Caring too much about anything, be that women, work or money, was what he had surrendered to embrace peace of mind.

Nicky was surfacing from a nap when they entered the nursery and he held out his arms to Jemima with a huge smile. She hauled him up and turned to Luciano with a grin, wanting to include him, wanting to encourage father and son to get to know each other properly. 'Let's take him down to the beach. He's never seen the sea.'

She changed into her serviceable and rather faded blue racer-back swimsuit, unable to face the challenge of modelling one of the daring 'barely there' bikini sets in her new wardrobe. Luciano joined her in swim shorts, lifting a delighted Nicky high and smiling with satisfaction when the little boy laughed. She watched the long, lithe line of his muscled back flex as he tucked Nicky securely below one arm and strode downstairs. Not an ounce of fat clung to his well-built physique and it showed in his narrow waist and lean hips.

A picnic lunch was delivered and food for Nicky. The baby loved getting his toes wet in the surf. He loved even more being held up in the air and looking down at his father. Jemima watched father and son, relieved at how naturally they could interact in a more relaxed setting. Clearly no longer uneasy in Luciano's presence, Nicky dug his hands into his father's hair and touched his face with growing familiarity.

'That was a good suggestion,' Luciano told her appreciatively as they headed back to the *castello*.

A blonde waved and smiled at them from the terrace as they climbed the steps up from the beach. She surged forward to greet Luciano and kiss him Continental-style on both cheeks. She was a beauty, a tall, slender blonde with dark eyes and great dress sense.

'Jemima, meet Sancia Abate...' Luciano made the introduction casually. 'Sancia, my wife-to-be, Jemima, and my son, Niccolò.'

Sancia barely glanced in Jemima's direction but fussed in a very feminine way over Nicky.

'Who is she? Does she work for you?' Jemima asked as they walked away.

'No. She's Gigi's kid sister,' he confided, startling her. 'I still let her use the guest house here when she needs a break. Nicky gets tired quickly, doesn't he?'

Jemima watched the baby stick his thumb in his mouth and close his eyes against her shoulder and she smiled in spite of her surprise at that revelation concerning the svelte blonde. 'You exhausted him. He's not used to that kind of play. My father's past that stage.'

'But he's very fond of him,' Luciano cut in.

'Yes, he is. Did you have grandparents?'

'No, my grandfather died soon after my parents

married.' His strong jaw clenched, his mouth flattening. 'Agnese was my nurse when I was a child. She was the closest thing I had to a grandparent.'

'I didn't have any either. Mum and Dad met and married later in life,' Jemima told him as she passed Nicky over to Carlotta in the hall and joined Luciano on the stairs. 'You lost your mother young.'

'Yes.'

'How did it happen?'

Luciano strode across the landing without answering her.

'Was she ill?' Jemima persisted, following him down the stone passageway and into his room.

'No,' Luciano gritted impatiently, slamming the door closed behind him with a frustrated hand. 'Don't you take hints? I don't want to talk about this…'

Jemima reddened uncomfortably, feeling like a rude nosy parker for having continued to ask questions even after he walked away. 'I'm sorry…'

His lustrous dark golden eyes glittered. 'No, I don't want to lie but I don't want to tell you the truth either.'

She turned round and smoothed her hands up over his cheekbones in what was meant to be a comforting and apologetic gesture. 'I'm a horribly nosy person,' she confessed guiltily. 'Give me an inch and I'll take a mile. Don't even *hint* at a secret…it turns me into a bloodhound that won't quit!'

Reluctant laughter escaped Luciano. He stared down at her anxious face and a deep hunger for the warmth of her engulfed him in a tidal wave of need. He pulled her into his arms and claimed her mouth with devastating urgency.

Taken by surprise, Jemima laughed and then gasped beneath the savage onslaught of his mouth. Her body caught flame like hay, a burning ache stirring between her legs, a hot, prickling awareness stiffening her nipples.

'*Madonna!* I think I'll die if I don't have you now,' Luciano growled, long fingers closing into the shoulders of her swimsuit to wrench it down and release her breasts.

He tumbled her down on his bed and skimmed off his shorts in an impatient motion, coming up on the mattress to join her unashamedly naked and eager. He knelt at her feet and yanked her swimsuit down her hips to toss it aside while his smouldering gaze wandered at will over her splayed body.

'I love these...so pretty, so lush,' he husked, his fingers cupping the curves of her high, full breasts before rising to stroke the pouting crests. 'And these.' A lean hand travelled up a slender thigh and nudged her legs apart to display a tantalising ribbon of soft, glistening pink. 'And *this* perfect place, *piccolo mia*. I am enslaved...'

He found that feminine perfection with the erotic expertise of his mouth and it was magical and then terrifying to lose control so fast. She clutched at his hair. She sobbed. She gasped. Ultimately she cried his name in an ecstasy of quivering, wanton pleasure, her body weak and heavy with satisfaction as she lay beneath him, too stunned by his passion and the explosive response he had roused from her to move again.

'What was it about me…er…being nosy that set you off?' she whispered helplessly.

Luciano's brow furrowed. He honestly didn't know. He had looked at her and an uncontrollable urge to take her to bed had overpowered him. He couldn't explain it. Her wild response to him had soothed the savage turmoil inside him in a manner beyond his comprehension. He touched her with gentle fingers, put his mouth to a rose-pink nipple, toying with her for a few moments, smiling against her flushed skin as she muttered his name as though she were saying a prayer. He turned her over onto her stomach. She complained about being moved and he ignored it, lifting her up, aligning their bodies and then plunging into the damp, silken heat of her with a raw groan of enthusiasm, swiftly echoed by her boneless cry of encouragement.

Delicious sensation ricocheted up through Jemima's body, building from the hot, aching heart of her into a blaze that consumed as Luciano slammed into her with compelling strength. Her excitement climbed with the sweet, earthy delight of his penetration. And just when she believed that powerful excitement couldn't reach any greater height he sent her flying into an orgasm that snapped taut her every muscle and blew her apart in a sublime surge of drowning, melting pleasure.

'Oh…wow…' Jemima mumbled, flopping down against the pillows.

Luciano flipped her over and gathered her damp, trembling body close. 'Oh…wow…' he teased. 'Well, you have no choice but to marry me now.'

'How's that?' she framed, barely able to think straight.

'I didn't use a condom—'

Her brows pleated in dismay. 'Luciano—'

'Having unprotected sex is a sign of commitment, which I have never risked before with a woman,' he announced above her head.

'You want a brass trophy or something?' Jemima looked up at him with wry amusement.

'No, I want a repeat...' Luciano growled, treating her full lower lip to a tiny carnal nip swiftly followed by a soothing stroke of his tongue. 'That was the best sex I ever had, *piccolo mia*.'

'Good, because you won't have got me pregnant,' Jemima told him with assurance. 'It's the wrong time of the month for that.'

Luciano stared down at her with brooding intensity, his lean, darkly handsome features set in unsettlingly serious lines. 'Don't be too curious with me.'

Jemima had become very still and her eyes were troubled. 'Why not?'

'Unlike you, I'm not the sharing type. I have too much stuff to hide.'

'Red rag to a bull, Luciano,' Jemima warned. 'And if we're getting married there's nothing you should need to hide from me.'

Luciano sat up, his dark eyes veiled, his lean, strong body taut with tension. 'My father killed my mother when I was three,' he breathed in a constrained undertone. 'She was trying to take me and leave him... He threw her down the stairs and she broke her neck. I saw it happen.'

Jemima froze and then consciously unfroze again to

close her arms protectively round him. 'How horrible for you to be forced to live with a memory like that.'

Luciano was rigid in the circle of her arms. 'It's my past.'

'Yes...*past*,' Jemima stressed, stringing a line of haphazard kisses along the clenched line of his strong jaw until some of his tension eased.

He frowned down at her. 'Doesn't it bother you, knowing what I just told you?'

'Not as much as it bothered you telling me.'

'I've never told anyone before,' he breathed into her hair. 'I used to have nightmares about it.'

'And who comforted you then?' she whispered.

'Agnese...she was always there for me. She saw it happen too.'

'And nobody went to the police?'

'My father had too many friends in high places and corrupt connections within the police. My mother's death was written off as a tragic accident and he got away with it. By the time I was old enough to do any different he was dead. But he would have killed anyone who stood as a witness against him, even if I had been the witness,' he explained heavily. 'That was his life. That is the kind of environment that I grew up with and it is exactly those experiences that made me swear that I would never ever be like my father in any way.'

'And you've lived up to that promise,' Jemima reminded him quietly. 'Haven't you?'

'Yes, *piccolo mia*.'

'So, you should be proud of what you have achieved and celebrating your success,' Jemima told him, shifting her hips in the hope of giving his thoughts a different direction.

Being highly suggestible, Luciano lifted his tousled head with a sudden smile and kissed her again with all the pent-up fire of his hot temperament. She smiled up at him, satisfied that she had finally got behind his barriers, broken through the hard shell to the real man within. He didn't have to love her to confide in her. Somehow at that instant it seemed more than sufficient compensation.

CHAPTER NINE

'COME FOR TEA, said the spider to the fly,' Ellie mocked with a grimace. 'I don't like Sancia.'

Jemima wrinkled her nose. Her best friend, Ellie, was very quick in her judgements but Jemima tried to give everyone a fair hearing. And that included Sancia Abate, the gorgeous blonde who had stepped unannounced and unforeseen out of Luciano's past. After all, Jemima would have been the first to admit that the main source of her unease about Sancia was the other woman's close blood tie to Luciano's celebrated first wife. Luciano, however, had been so casual about the continuing friendship that only an extremely jealous and possessive woman could have been suspicious of the relationship. Sancia was evidently still accepted as family and Jemima was happy to respect that.

In any case, she had to admit that Sancia had proved to be an almost invisible guest over the past two weeks while Luciano had been abroad. For the past three days, Jemima had been entertaining Ellie and her parents' friends and relatives, all of whom Luciano had had flown out for the wedding that was scheduled to take place in forty-eight hours' time. Her parents and their closest friends had already settled into a comfortable routine of strolls on the beach and visits to the village café, while Jemima had whiled away many a happy hour trying on wedding dresses and relaxing with Ellie.

'I mean, what's a blonde that looks like that doing hanging round here on a very quiet island without even a boyfriend in tow?' Ellie remarked suspiciously.

Jemima had learned that Sancia was not only gorgeous to look at but also multitalented. Sancia had written a bestselling biography on her much-loved sister's life and currently seemed to drift between stints as a well-known fashion model and a less-well-known actress. The guest house was situated beyond the castle gardens above the beach, a former boathouse that had been renovated to offer extra accommodation. Bearing in mind the sheer size of the castle, the cottage was virtually never used.

Jemima was wryly amused that she had found it necessary to dress up to visit Sancia. More and more she was making use of the wardrobe Luciano had bought for her, recognising that the garments might be more fashionable and form-fitting than she was accustomed to wearing but were also more flattering in style and shape. To enjoy tea with the glamorous Sancia, she was wearing a lilac skirt and top with an unmistakeable designer edge.

'Oh, you haven't brought Nicky.' Sancia sighed in disappointment as soon as she opened the door. 'Come in.'

'He always has a nap straight after lunch.'

'*Porca miseria!* You sound like one of those rigid English nannies people joke about!' the blonde commented with a teasing smile.

'I hope not...' Jemima stilled on the threshold of a spacious reception room that was dominated by photos and portraits of Gigi Nocella.

'Oh, didn't you know that the guest house is where Luciano keeps his stash of memorabilia?' Sancia remarked in apparent surprise. 'I thought you would have guessed. I mean, there's nothing at all to be seen up at the castle.'

'No, nothing,' Jemima agreed, having naturally noticed that, surprisingly, Luciano had not a single photograph on display anywhere of his late first wife or their little daughter.

'I know. He had the place stripped...the poor guy.' Sancia sighed. 'Once Gigi was gone, he just couldn't live with even the *smallest* reminder of her. It was too painful for him. Haven't you noticed that he never ever mentions her?'

Jemima was not very practised at female games of one-upmanship but she knew enough to know when she was being targeted and she murmured quietly, 'Are we having tea?'

'I'm not very domesticated but I do have the tray ready for us.' Sancia gave her a wide grin, unperturbed by Jemima's cool intonation, and stepped out into the room that Jemima assumed held a kitchen.

Jemima hovered by the window overlooking the fabulous view of the beach before succumbing to a curiosity that she simply couldn't suppress. The room she stood in was ironically both her worst nightmare and her most precious discovery. All around her sat the means to satisfy her curiosity about Luciano's first wife. Giving way to temptation, Jemima wandered around peering at the photos and the paintings.

There was no denying that Gigi Nocella had been superbly photogenic and immensely gifted in the genes department. The brown-eyed blonde, of whom Sancia was but a pale, more youthful copy, was exquisite to a degree very few women were and had reputedly been mesmerising on-screen. And here she was represented in all her earthly glory in various attitudes that ran from young and naïve to sexy and smouldering to pensive and mysterious. But the photos that Jemima paid most heed to were the ones that also contained Luciano.

The first she noted was their wedding photograph, in which he looked ridiculously youthful, reminding her that he had been very young when he married and that Gigi had been several years older.

'He worshipped the ground she walked on,' Sancia murmured from behind Jemima, making her flinch.

'Oh, my goodness, you gave me a fright!' Jemima spun and fanned the air, refusing to react to the blonde's provocative statement.

In any case, she didn't need the verbal commentary when she could see the adoration etched in Luciano's lean dark face as he looked intently at the mother of his daughter. It hurt Jemima to see that light in his eyes. She knew that he would never look at her with that depth of caring and concern. She would never be that important to him or that perfect in looks and figure that every head would turn to watch her walk by. No, she conceded sadly, she was in a totally different category from Gigi and, whether she liked it or not, Luciano would probably not have looked twice at her had his son not looked at Jemima with love first.

But she would have to learn to live with that reality, wouldn't she?

'After the crash, Luciano said he would never ever love a woman again,' Sancia delivered.

'Ah, well, life moves on and now he's getting married and he's starting another family,' Jemima responded with deliberate insensitivity before adding, 'It's different for you, though, as her sister. You'll never be able to replace her and you must miss her terribly.'

Red coins of colour accentuated the blonde's cheekbones. 'You have no idea.'

'I do actually. I didn't know my sister for very long before I lost her but there was a special bond there... at least on my side,' Jemima confided.

With hindsight she had begun to accept that her twin had not had the capacity to care for others in the same way as she did. She could not argue with the evidence and it was surely better for her to remember her sibling as she had been rather than idealise her memory.

'Gigi was irreplaceable,' Sancia told her a tad sharply.

'But I'm not trying to replace her,' Jemima responded quietly. 'How could I? And why would I even want to? Luciano and I have a completely different relationship.'

As Jemima walked back from the beach through

the castle gardens her pale blue eyes were overbright with tears. She didn't want to let the tears fall, not with her usual bodyguards bare yards from her, silent and watchful of her every move. Furthermore she had not the slightest doubt that anything unusual she did would be reported straight back to Luciano, who seemed to worry a great deal about her while he was away from her. He phoned her several times a day and questioned her right down to asking what she ate at mealtimes. And when she had asked him why he bothered when she had so little news to relate, he had told her teasingly that he liked the sound of her voice and could listen to her reciting an old phone book just as happily. The minutiae of Nicky's day were of equal interest to him and it was obvious to Jemima that Luciano really did miss seeing his son. His conversations with her, however, were just polite and sort of flirty, she reasoned ruefully. He wasn't a teenager, after all, he was a man of almost thirty-one with sufficient experience to know exactly how to charm a woman.

Especially if that woman wasn't Gigi Nocella, Jemima thought, her throat closing over convulsively on a sob. He wouldn't have had to make a special effort to say the right thing to a woman as perfect as Gigi had been. So, how often did he go down to visit that personal shrine in the guest house? If Jemima hadn't existed and Luciano hadn't been away on business, would he have been with Sancia right now happily reminiscing about the old days when his first wife and child had still been alive? It was hardly any wonder that Sancia resented Jemima and clearly felt threatened by her appearance on scene. Nothing could put Gigi more effectively back into the past than her once-besotted widower having another child and taking a second wife to put in Gigi's place.

Well, it wasn't Gigi's place any longer, Jemima told herself urgently. In less than two days Jemima would be Luciano's wife and she could hardly wait! She wasn't so silly as to allow Sancia's mean outlook to affect her personally, was she?

As her mobile phone rang she dug it out, grateful for an interruption that would hopefully give her thoughts a new and more positive direction. When she heard Steven's familiar badgering tones she almost groaned, however, for she had thought she had heard the last from her ex-boyfriend when he had phoned her to say he wouldn't be attending the wedding—he hadn't been invited!—because he knew she was making a dreadful mistake.

'Luciano has turned your head with his wealth,' Steven told her, merely starting a new angle of attack.

'His wealth doesn't matter to me. His kindness does,' Jemima parried, thinking of the generosity of Luciano's invitation to her parents and their friends, who were all enjoying a wonderful holiday in the run-up to their wedding. And by bringing her family and Ellie out to join her, he had ensured that she wasn't lonely and without support.

'You may not see it but I see very clearly that you are paying me back for what happened with Julie.' Steven sighed. 'You weren't able to forgive me.'

'I *did* forgive you, Steven. I simply didn't want to

take back up again where we'd left off and I think that's fair enough,' Jemima fielded. 'I saw you in a different light when you were with my sister.'

'I made a dreadful mistake, Jemima,' Steven groaned. 'But I *do* love you.'

'Not the way you loved her,' Jemima told him without heat.

'That wasn't genuine love and you don't love Luciano either. You're marrying him to keep Nicky,' Steven protested.

Jemima sat down on a stone bench surrounded by glorious rose beds and stared out blindly at the magnificent view of the bay. 'That's not true.'

'Marriage is a sacrament and it shouldn't be used.'

'But I *do* love him,' Jemima heard herself say and her whole mental view of the world lurched as she made that belated discovery. She was thinking about the male who had chilled her at first meeting and travelling at supersonic speed through the whole history of their relationship, ranging from his laughter in bed with her to the brutal background that he had triumphed over.

And there at the very heart of all her turmoil was the love she had neither acknowledged nor understood. She loved Luciano with all her being and easily zeroed in on every kind and caring thing he did for her from his hesitant tendering of his mother's ring for their engagement to his patient, undemanding love for Nicky in which he was willing to wait and earn his son's trust and affection. In the same moment she recognised why her encounter with Sancia and Gigi's shrine in the guest house had distressed her so much. It had hurt to see Luciano's love for her predecessor. It had hurt even more to frankly admit that she could never emulate such a woman to win that level of appreciation. With Luciano, she would always be Nicky's loving stepmother first and his wife second. Second best, second best for all time...

Could she truly live with that?

'Sorry, Steven. I have to go,' she said, cutting the call on Steven's expostulations with relief.

Her face was wet with tears. She had been crying without knowing it and she mopped her face, praying her mascara hadn't run. There could be no pleasure in appreciating that she would always be inferior in her future husband's eyes and heart to his first wife, but she was a practical, realistic woman and there really wasn't much she could do about that hurt. Was there?

She wouldn't even consider abandoning Nicky, for he felt as much her child as if he had been born to her rather than her sister. She saw no advantage to refusing to marry Luciano either. What would that achieve? She didn't want to be Nicky's nanny for the rest of her days or merely Luciano's lover. And if she didn't choose to marry him and give him more children, some other woman eventually would.

Not on my watch, Jemima conceded fierily.

CHAPTER TEN

SOMETHING VERY LIKE panic sent chilling tentacles travelling deep to pierce Luciano's usually rock-solid sense of security. He completed the phone call to his future relative, which had been preceded by one from Agnese. He had made a mistake, a *serious* mistake, he acknowledged with a sinking heart, and now he had to pray that he had sufficient time and the opportunity to put it right. And if he didn't?

Santa Madonna, that option could not even be considered!

Why the hell had he valued his pride above every other thing in his life for so many years? How on earth had he allowed a past bad experience to cast such a dangerous shadow over the present and potentially destroy his future?

And you thought you were so cool, so clever, he reasoned in a daze of growing shock at the mess he had created. But the creed of silence as a form of protection had been bred into his very bones at his father's knee. Never tell, never explain, never apologise. And before he had experienced that one weak moment with

Jemima he had *never* broken that rule. He had kept his secrets. He had kept them from the media too. Indeed he had buried those sleazy secrets deep and had refused even to think about them, for that was the safest, wisest way to hold on to sanity.

He had never dwelt on his mistakes because he was a rational man and it came naturally to him to move on past and not look back at car wrecks. Even so, those mistakes had seriously influenced the choices he had made, he conceded belatedly. Furthermore, Jemima didn't have his conditioning or his inhibitions and she would not understand…

The helicopter came in over the bay while Jemima was having breakfast with everyone in the shaded loggia on the ground floor. Nicky dropped his toast as he waved his hands with excitement, straining in his high chair to get a better view of the craft as it dropped down out of sight to land in the castle grounds.

'Is that Luciano coming back?' Ellie asked uncertainly.

'I doubt it. He's not due until tomorrow,' Jemima said a little tiredly because she had not slept well. 'And he's a stickler for his schedules.'

'I suspect,' her father murmured warmly as he stared over her shoulder, 'that your bridegroom missed you more than you know because here he is now…'

Jemima twisted her head round so fast she risked a whiplash injury and she thrust her chair back and stood up to stare in surprise at the male striding through the gardens towards them. It was, without a doubt, Luciano.

Sheathed in a dark business suit teamed with a white shirt and silvery tie, he looked both formal and formidable. His lean, darkly handsome face was taut, the line of his beautiful mouth forbidding. A jolt of dismay ran through Jemima and quite instinctively she found herself wondering if she had done something wrong.

His stunning dark golden eyes immediately sought hers as though he was looking for something and then he quickly turned his attention on to their guests and his first physical meeting with her parents. To a backdrop of Nicky's squeals of excitement and loud vocal appeals to be noticed, Luciano responded smoothly and pleasantly to the tide of introductions before stooping to detach Nicky from his harness and lift him into his arms.

'Hush,' he said softly to his son while ruffling his hair. 'You can't always be the centre of attention.'

'Well, when he isn't he likes to let us know he doesn't like it!' her father quipped cheerfully. 'He's a terrific little scene stealer.'

'Let me take him,' Jemima's mother urged, holding out her arms. 'You and Jemima should have some time together in peace.'

Nicky complained loudly at the transfer, demanded Jemima with pleading arms and then sobbed. Carlotta came out of the house to help while Jemima hovered, her attention anxiously pinned to Luciano, for all her nervous antennae were still telling her that something was badly wrong. His long, lean, powerful body was incredibly tense, his movements less fluid than usual and his lean, strong face taut with self-discipline.

Oh, my goodness, she thought in sudden consternation. Maybe he had returned early because he had changed his mind about marrying her! It was a nightmare scenario with the wedding guests and her family already staying at the castle, but it was perfectly possible that he had got cold feet and come back early to tell her. Jemima was quite convinced that such disasters had occurred to better women than her and it was surely more likely to happen when a man wasn't in love with the woman he had asked to marry him.

Luciano shot another veiled glance at Jemima. She was pale and there were shadows below her beautiful pale eyes and he could see that she looked nothing like a happy bride on the brink of her wedding. Inwardly he cursed himself again and he reached for her hand.

'Will you come for a walk with me?' he intoned in a roughened undertone. 'We have a visit to make.'

Her brow furrowed as he deftly walked her away from the breakfast table. 'A visit?'

'I believe you had tea with Sancia yesterday—'

'My goodness, the grapevine around here is positively supersonic!' Jemima countered while she thought fast.

'I like to keep an eye on events when I'm unable to be present in person,' Luciano assured her with a perfectly straight face.

Controlling...*much*? But Jemima said nothing because she knew that he was upset and she couldn't bear that. Glancing up at him, she could see the haunted look she had seen before was back in his eyes and she could see that, for all that he looked spectacular, he must have been travelling all night and lines of strain were etched between his classic nose and even more perfect mouth. Of course, if he wanted to cancel the wedding, he would be feeling awfully guilty about it, she thought painfully.

'What did you think of Sancia?'

'We don't have much in common,' Jemima replied mildly.

'She was a bitch to you, wasn't she?' Luciano growled within sight of the guest cottage above the beach.

Taken aback, Jemima came to a halt and stared up at him. 'I—'

'I can be selfish but I'm not stupid...most of the time,' Luciano tacked on, compressing his hard mouth. 'I've been foolish—'

'It's all right...whatever you decide to do, it's all right. Just don't be upset about it,' Jemima mumbled helplessly, resisting the urge to wrap both arms around him and offer him comfort. Even in the overly emotional mood she was in, she knew that was not the normal way to behave when a man dumped you and that the very last thing she should be worrying about was how *he* felt. And yet that urge was engrained in her when he was around, she thought painfully as he closed his hand firmly round hers and urged her on towards the cottage.

'Why are we going to see Sancia?' she prompted uncomprehendingly. 'I admit she wasn't the kindest hostess but I have nothing more to say to her.'

'But I have plenty to say,' Luciano incised, banging on the door with his fist.

Sancia opened the door little more than three seconds later. It was barely nine in the morning but she was wearing a pristine white sundress and had a full face of make-up on, so she had evidently been expecting visitors. 'Luciano...' she said, wreathed with welcoming smiles.

'Sancia...' he grated, moving past her to stare in shock at the array of photographs and paintings decorating the cottage living room. 'What is all this?' he breathed.

'Well, you should know,' the blonde said archly. 'You insisted on giving it to me.'

'You asked me for it—you wanted it for your book,' Luciano reminded her.

Only moments into their visit and Jemima was already feeling better, for she could already see that Luciano had had no part in creating the shrine in the room to his late wife. That, it seemed, had been solely Sancia's doing.

'It's been like this ever since the year she died,' the blonde fielded, playing it for all she was worth.

'You're the only person who has ever used this place.' Luciano released Jemima's hand and swept up a book from the coffee table. 'Wasn't the book enough for you?'

'I don't know what you mean?'

'Sancia, I was married to Gigi for five years. This isn't a biography, it's a work of fiction. You gave her fans what they wanted to read, not the truth. The truth would have been too ugly,' he breathed, his deep, dark drawl roughening along the edges.

Sancia switched to Italian and spoke at length.

'No, we will discuss this in English so that Jemima understands,' Luciano decreed grimly. 'I want to know what Sancia told you yesterday.'

'Nothing that was untrue,' Sancia trilled, sweetly saccharine. 'That you don't like to talk about Gigi and that you *said* you'd never love a woman again.'

Luciano grimaced. 'Sancia! Where is your compassion? Your sister almost destroyed me!'

'There is no need for you to tell—' Sancia began urgently.

'A couple who are about to marry should have no secrets from each other,' Luciano declared, and as Jemima stiffened in surprise he smiled ruefully. 'A very wise woman once told me that but I wasn't listening.'

'But you have never wanted the truth to come out!' Sancia was still arguing. 'You were happy for me to write a whitewash!'

'I've matured.' Luciano tossed the book back down on the table and looked at Jemima. 'Gigi was not the glowing star and wonderful woman described in this book. I married her because she told me I was the father of the child she carried. She was repeatedly unfaithful to me with the leading men in her movies, and the day she died she was leaving me for another man.'

'Oh, no...' Jemima mumbled, pained by the look in his eyes.

'That man, Alessio di Campo, is a famous producer and he was the love of Gigi's life—well, as much as she could love anyone, she loved him,' Luciano revealed doggedly. 'He was a married man with a wife and only when his wife died were the two of them willing to go public about their relationship. Their affair had, however, apparently continued throughout our marriage. I told her that she was welcome to leave but that I would not let her take our daughter, Melita, with her.'

'How can you trust her? She could go to the press with all this!' Sancia screeched accusingly.

'Jemima won't and even if the story was to get out, so what?' Luciano shrugged a broad shoulder with fluid fatalism. 'It's all done and dusted now. To finish the story, Gigi told me that Melita was *not* my daughter but Alessio's,' he revealed heavily. 'I had stayed in a bad marriage for years for my daughter's sake and suddenly she wasn't my child any more. That truth was more devastating than Gigi's departure with Melita that day.'

'It was a cruel lie,' Sancia swore, desperate to be heard again. 'I never believed that!'

'Testing was carried out after the crash,' Luciano cut in flatly, his lean, masculine face unrelentingly grim. 'Melita was *not* my child but I loved her as though she was and had she survived I would have kept her with me had I had the choice. As it was, both mother and child died instantly when the helicopter Alessio had sent to pick them up crashed on the flight to Monaco.'

Jemima's eyes were stinging. Only Sancia's sullen, resentful presence prevented her from saying what she really felt because her heart was bleeding for him. He had been hiding the truth from her all along and she was deeply shaken by the true version of what his marriage had entailed. It had not occurred to her that Gigi could have been anything less than perfect. In reality, though, Gigi had been a horribly disloyal and dishonest partner and Jemima was no longer surprised that Luciano had required DNA testing before he had been prepared to accept Nicky as his son.

'Let's go...' Luciano breathed, curving a protective arm to Jemima's spine.

'I could sell Gigi's *true* story for a fortune,' Sancia remarked quietly.

'Go ahead. I no longer care,' Luciano responded almost cheerfully. 'But if you go naming names you will probably make a lot of dangerous enemies amongst the very people whom you still want to employ you. But that's your business now that I will no longer be settling your bills. My pilot's waiting for you at the helipad. I'm sure I don't need to add that you're no longer welcome here.'

And with that final withering speech they were both back out in the fresh air and sunshine again. Shell-shocked, Jemima leant against Luciano for a few seconds, revelling in the strength of his tall, powerful body and the gloriously familiar scent of him. All she could think about was that Gigi had been a dreadful liar and then Julie had lied to him and cheated him and then Jemima had lied to him as well! How could he ever fully forgive her for having lied to him after what he had had to endure in his first, unhappy marriage?

'You know... I thought you'd got cold feet about the wedding,' she told him dizzily. 'I believed you were back early to dump me—'

'No, I was too scared I was losing you. I didn't know

what Sancia had done but I always suspected she could be poisonous.'

'But how could you even find out that I was seeing her yesterday? The bodyguards?'

'No, Agnese. She's like a bloodhound. She phoned me to tell me that Sancia had invited you and informed me that that was suspicious because Sancia is not friendly towards other women.'

'Why were you paying Sancia's bills?'

'At first I felt sorry for her because she was always overshadowed by Gigi. Of course, she knew all her sister's dark secrets because she worked as Gigi's assistant on the Palermo estate we lived on in those days.' He hesitated. 'With the timing involved, nobody guessed that Gigi had been in the act of leaving me when she died and I told myself that it was my private business. But, more honestly, I chose to save face rather than tell the truth. The paparazzi had dogged us obsessively throughout our marriage because, of course, there were always rumours about Gigi's behaviour but she was never caught out.'

'I can understand you not wanting people to know that she had affairs,' Jemima murmured ruefully. 'It hurt your pride and Sancia played along with that because it suited her to do so.'

'She made a killing on the book because she wrote what Gigi's fans wanted to read. They didn't want to hear about the man-eater with the monstrous ego who seduced me when I was twenty-two and too rich and naïve to smell a rat. Of course, she was already pregnant when she first slept with me.'

'And you didn't even suspect?'

'I was infatuated with her. It was probably a little like the way you reacted to your unknown twin when she first turned up. I only saw what I wanted to see in Gigi and I was flattered by her interest.'

'But the marriage only lasted because of Melita?'

Luciano could not hide his sadness. 'The marriage died within months of Melita's birth. I loved that little girl and she loved me. Gigi had no interest in her daughter but she wouldn't have given up custody of her because she said that would damage her reputation as a mother.'

'And *did* you say that you would never love a woman again after her?'

'Yes,' Luciano admitted freely. 'Because loving Gigi was a horrendous experience and I couldn't forgive myself for being such a fool. I sincerely believed that it would only be safe to love a child, which is why I planned the surrogacy arrangement.'

'You do think in some seriously screwy ways sometimes,' Jemima told him gently.

His nostrils flared as he thrust open a side door into the castle. 'It seemed perfectly logical to me at the time. Gigi did a lot of damage and I didn't want to be burned again.'

'It was still a little over the top,' Jemima criticised. 'You may have decided to live without love but most children want two parents.'

Luciano shot her an impatient look. 'All right, I'm selfish...and maybe I didn't think it all through the way

I should have done. But look how it turned out,' he said with a sudden grin. 'I got you... Have I still got you?'

'It would take more than Sancia to scare me off.'

'Yet you actually thought I could be about to dump you?' An ebony brow quirked in wonderment. 'What makes you so modest? I cut my trip short a day and travelled all night to get to you because I heard that you were upset.'

Jemima stiffened. 'Who *said* I was upset?'

'I promised not to name names,' Luciano revealed.

'I wasn't upset yesterday,' Jemima insisted out of pride. 'I was just working through some stuff and thinking a lot. Getting married is a big challenge.'

'Especially when the groom is someone like me,' Luciano slotted in without hesitation. 'Someone too proud and private to admit that his first marriage was a disaster and that his first child wasn't his child.'

Jemima wrinkled her nose as he walked her up the rear staircase she had never used before. 'But I sort of understand you keeping quiet about that, although that doesn't mean I approve of you being that secretive.'

'And the prospect of marriage must become even more challenging for a woman when the bridegroom refuses to admit that he loves you,' Luciano told her in a rush shorn of the smallest eloquence. 'That wasn't just secretive, that was stupid, because if you'd known how much I love you yesterday you would have laughed in Sancia's face and I wouldn't have been panicked into rushing halfway across the world to assure myself that you weren't going to desert me.'

'I wouldn't desert you...or Nicky,' Jemima added,

still working very slowly through what he had said. 'You love me?'

'Insanely.' A flood of dark colour accentuated his high cheekbones. 'The thought of life without you downright terrifies me. A couple of weeks being without you has proved a chastening experience. I've never missed anyone or anything so much in my life...'

Jemima suddenly realised that they were having a very private conversation in the corridor and she walked on a few steps and thrust open his bedroom door. 'Never missed anyone...'

Luciano leant back against the door to close it fast behind him. 'Jemima, does it take a hammer to knock an idea into your head?' He groaned. 'I phone you every hour on the hour and you think that's normal? I invite your whole family here to keep you company so that you can't even look at another man while I'm away. Don't you ever get suspicious, *piccolo mia*? You think I don't realise that wet blanket, Steven, is sitting out there waiting for you, hoping like hell that I'll screw up and lose you?'

'But I don't fancy Steven...and even when you upset me or I get annoyed with you, I still fancy you,' Jemima confided a little desperately, because he was smiling that wicked smile of his that made her heart beat crazily fast.

'Is that a fact?' Luciano teased, shifting off the door to shed his jacket and jerk loose his tie. 'I had this unrealistic fantasy where I came home and everything would be all right and we would go straight to bed... Don't know what I thought we'd do with all our guests.'

'Everything *is* all right. Our guests are also remarkably good at entertaining themselves,' she opined. 'Oh, by the way, I love you…loads and loads…and it's got nothing to do with your money like Steven thinks.'

'Honestly…you love me?' Luciano growled. 'But why?'

'That's the weird bit… I truly don't know. One minute I was fancying you like mad and the next I was wanting to make your life perfect for you,' Jemima confided with an embarrassed wince.

'Equally weird for me from the very first moment. Took me a long time to realise that not wanting to love again was basically a fear of being hurt again, which is cowardly,' he declared with disdain. 'And then you were there and I liked just about everything about you and it wasn't only sex. I should've told you the truth about Gigi sooner but I suppose I didn't want you to think less of me.'

'How could I think less of you for her bad behaviour?'

Luciano shrugged. 'I love the way you are with Nicky because she was so cold with Melita. Comparisons are tasteless but…'

'So, don't make them.' Jemima unzipped her dress and shimmied out of it while he watched.

'Your parents…' Luciano began, slightly shocked.

'I think everyone will mind their own business rather than ours,' Jemima whispered sagely. 'But you do realise that you still haven't told me who told you that I was upset?'

Luciano expelled his breath on a slow hiss. 'Your father.'

Taken aback, Jemima blinked. 'Say that again?'

'He thinks I make you happy and he likes the fact that I'm honest with him,' Luciano told her guiltily, as if he had been consorting with the enemy. 'I was grateful that he called me.'

Jemima was secretly pleased that the father she loved so much clearly liked and trusted the man she was about to marry. 'I've got no complaints either. We love each other and that's special.'

'Simply finding you was special, *piccolo mia*,' Luciano told her as she unbuttoned his shirt, undid his waistband, sent her fingers roaming over the prominent bulge at his groin with a daring new to both of them and even more thrilling. '*Dio mio*, I love you...'

'Me too...*so much*,' she managed to say just before his mouth came crashing down on hers with all the passion she adored.

Jemima walked down the aisle of the little village church in her lace wedding dress and with her hand on her father's arm. Off the shoulder and styled with tight sleeves and a fitted bodice, her wedding gown made the most of her hourglass figure and the exquisite lace fell to the floor, showing only the toes of the extravagant shoes she wore.

Luciano was so entranced by the sight of her that he couldn't look away and play it cool. His son, Nicky, sat on his grandmother's lap near the front of the church and began to bounce and hold out his arms when he laid eyes on Jemima, the closest thing to a mother he would ever know. Luciano smiled, the happiest he had ever been in his chequered life and far happier than he had ever even hoped to be.

Jemima focused on the man she loved and her heart jumped behind her breastbone. All hers at last, officially, finally, permanently hers. As if a wedding ring were the equivalent of a padlock, she scolded herself. It was the love she saw in his beautiful dark eyes that would hold him and she rejoiced in the thought of the future that awaited them and their son.

EPILOGUE

'IL CAPO!' AGNESE SIGNALLED Jemima from the door of the castle with a beatific smile that said that all was now right with the housekeeper's world because Luciano was finally home again after a week away on business.

Jemima thought back four years to the days when the elderly Agnese, Luciano's fiercest admirer, had still been unsure of her former charge's second wife. She and Agnese had started out being excruciatingly polite to each other while Jemima had become friendlier with the housekeeper's daughter, Carlotta, whose English had come on as quickly as Jemima's Italian during the first year of her marriage. And then Concetta, their first child, had been born and Agnese had crumbled like a meringue at first sight of Il Capo's daughter to reveal the kindly, loving woman she hid behind her tough little image.

After Concetta, the nursery had got even busier and had had to expand because two children had been born to swell the family. Jemima's second pregnancy had produced twin boys, Marco and Matteo, and she had decided to take a break from the production line for a year or two at least. Three little boys ranging from Nicky, who was almost five, and the twins, who were two years old, had proved quite a handful. Concetta was three, clever and well behaved, certainly easier to control than three rumbustious little boys. Jemima's daughter was very fond of raising her brows in the boys' direction and mimicking her father with an air of female superiority.

Jemima's life had changed so rapidly from the moment she had become a mother for the first time after Nicky that she sometimes could hardly recall the period before she had met Luciano. Real life and fulfilling happiness had begun for her in Sicily at the *castello*. Occasionally she had thought sadly about the job she had left behind, but caring for Nicky had kept her very busy and Concetta's arrival had persuaded Jemima that she was perfectly happy shaping her routine round her husband and children. Such an existence might not be perfect for everyone, but it was perfect for her.

She adored Luciano and she adored her kids and her home and the staff who looked after them so well. She never ever forgot either to be grateful for her good fortune. Luciano had bought a comfortable house for her parents back in the UK, but they remained regular visitors to the island, most often staying in the cottage by the beach. Her husband had become almost as fond of his in-laws as his wife. He appreciated the retired couple's loving interest in their grandchildren and rarely went to the UK without taking them out to dinner. Jemima's friend, Ellie, was a regular visitor as well, but there had been no further contact from Steven, who had married a couple of years back.

Now awaiting Luciano's arrival, Jemima smoothed her hands down over the elegant blue dress she wore with the most ridiculously high heels in her wardrobe. He bought her shoes everywhere he went without her because he knew that, even though she preferred to spend most of her time at home rather than shopping or partying as she could have done, she got a kick out of wearing that kind of footwear. It was the type of thoughtfulness and all the little caring touches that accompanied it that made Jemima such an adoring wife.

The shouts of three little boys backed by the far more muted tones of her little daughter warned Jemima that Luciano was in the hall. She grinned as he raised his voice to be heard above the hubbub and then there was silence, the sound of quick steps across the tiles as he made his escape and the door opened.

And there he stood, her beautiful Luciano, who still thrilled her as much at first glance as he had five years earlier. 'You look very beautiful, Signora Vitale,' he told her teasingly.

She encountered his stunning dark golden eyes and her heart sang as she surged across the room to throw herself into his arms. 'I missed you.'

Luciano gazed down at her with smouldering appreciation. 'The kids are waiting in the hall.'

'They want to see you too.'

'Can't be in two places at once, *amata mia*,' he husked, claiming a passionate kiss with raw, hungry enthusiasm.

'Carlotta will distract them,' Jemima mumbled.

'We're being selfish,' he groaned, lean brown hands worshipping her generous curves. 'But I can't… Bedtime's hours away,' he muttered defensively.

'So it is… I love you,' Jemima confided, enchanted by the level of passionate appreciation in his smouldering scrutiny, for it was wonderful to feel that desirable to the man she loved.

'Not one half as much as I love and need you,' Luciano countered. 'It isn't possible, *amata mia*.'

'What have I told you about that negative outlook of yours?' Jemima censured, backing down on the sofa in what was a decidedly inviting way with happiness and amusement and passion all bubbling up together inside her and making her feel distinctly intoxicated on love.

* * * * *

COMING SOON!

We really hope you enjoyed reading this book. If you're looking for more romance be sure to head to the shops when new books are available on

Thursday 23rd April

To see which titles are coming soon, please visit
millsandboon.co.uk/nextmonth

MILLS & BOON

TWO BRAND NEW BOOKS FROM
Love Always

Be prepared to be swept away to incredible worldwide destinations along with our strong, relatable heroines and intensely desirable heroes.

OUT NOW

Four Love Always stories published every month, find them all at:

millsandboon.co.uk

FOUR BRAND NEW BOOKS FROM
MILLS & BOON MODERN

Indulge in desire, drama, and breathtaking romance – where passion knows no bounds!

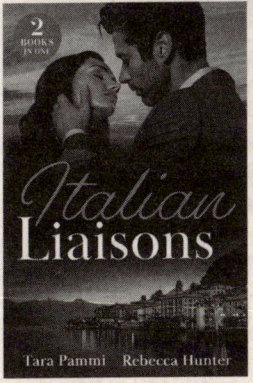

OUT NOW

Eight Modern stories published every month, find them all at:
millsandboon.co.uk

OUT NOW!

Available at
millsandboon.co.uk

MILLS & BOON

LET'S TALK
Romance

For exclusive extracts, competitions and special offers, find us online:

- **f** MillsandBoon
- **X** @MillsandBoon
- **◉** @MillsandBoonUK
- **♪** @MillsandBoonUK

Get in touch on 01413 063 232

For all the latest titles coming soon, visit
millsandboon.co.uk/nextmonth

MILLS & BOON

THE HEART OF ROMANCE

A ROMANCE FOR EVERY READER

MODERN — Prepare to be swept off your feet by sophisticated, sexy and seductive heroes, in some of the world's most glamourous and romantic locations, where power and passion collide.

HISTORICAL — Escape with historical heroes from time gone by. Whether your passion is for wicked Regency Rakes, muscled Vikings or rugged Highlanders, awaken the romance of the past.

MEDICAL — Set your pulse racing with dedicated, delectable doctors in the high-pressure world of medicine, where emotions run high and passion, comfort and love are the best medicine.

Love Always — Celebrate true love with tender stories of heartfelt romance, from the rush of falling in love to the joy a new baby can bring, and a focus on the emotional heart of a relationship.

HEROES — The excitement of a gripping thriller, with intense romance at its heart. Resourceful, true-to-life women and strong, fearless men face danger and desire – a killer combination!

 — From showing up to glowing up, these characters are on the path to leading their best lives and finding romance along the way – with plenty of sizzling spice!

To see all our latest titles, please visit

millsandboon.co.uk/NewReleases